Lincolns

Th

THE PIMLICO MURDER

By Mike Hollow

The Blitz Detective
The Canning Town Murder
The Custom House Murder
The Stratford Murder
The Dockland Murder
The Pimlico Murder

THE PIMLICO
MURDER

MɪᴋE HᴏʟʟᴏW

Allison & Busby Limited
11 Wardour Mews
London W1F 8AN
allisonandbusby.com

First published in Great Britain by Allison & Busby in 2021.

A CIP catalogue record for this book is available from
the British Library.

First Edition

ISBN 978-0-7490-2684-4

Typeset in 11/16 pt Sabon LT Pro by
Allison & Busby Ltd.

FSC
www.fsc.org
MIX
Paper from
responsible sources
FSC® C020471

The paper used for this Allison & Busby publication
has been produced from trees that have been legally sourced
from well-managed and credibly certified forests.

Printed and bound by
CPI Group (UK) Ltd, Croydon, CR0 4YY

For Grace,
love's precious gift

CHAPTER ONE

He was tired – it had been a busy night – but he was doing his best to concentrate. There was still noise outside, but not as much as there had been, and it sounded as though the anti-aircraft guns had at last packed in their deafening racket. What a mug's game that must be, he thought. Out in the cold all night, firing a gun in the dark at planes ten thousand feet up in the air and hoping to hit one. Fat chance, he reckoned, even if they did have searchlights. No wonder people talked about a shot in the dark; it must be pure luck if they actually brought one down.

Whichever way you looked at it, war was a stupid business run by stupid people, and the only solution was to make the best of it you could. For a start, that meant keeping as far away from any fighting as possible, and preferably not getting dragged into the army, the navy or the RAF in the first place. As for volunteering, well, that was a form of madness he just couldn't understand.

He worked the screwdriver carefully, lost in his thoughts. In the distance he faintly heard a vehicle roaring past: probably some other mug on their way to do their duty. The only duty he believed in was his duty to himself, and that was self-preservation. This war wasn't going to last for ever, and he wanted to be alive when it ended, preferably with his own nice little house to live in and plenty of cash under the mattress.

The important thing was to have a plan. He'd got one, and so far it was working. He reckoned he'd fixed things all right so he wouldn't be called up, and if he was, he'd make damn sure he landed some job that didn't involve going anywhere near the front, or got himself posted to somewhere cushy like Singapore – nice weather and thousands of miles away from the war. He'd had enough of being told what to do and when to do it, and he wasn't going to settle for that. No: life was like a game. You had to play hard and take your chances when they came – and not worry too much about the rules.

The only thing he wanted to do in this war was get through it in one piece, and the key to success was simple: if you want to survive, you've got to be strong. That was one thing he'd learnt in the camp. Look after number one, and not just physically, but mentally too: that was another thing he'd learnt. You had to train your mind. It didn't matter whether the whole world wrote you off as a good-for-nothing: you just need to know you're a winner and think like a winner, even when things are really bad.

All things considered, he could see it was beginning to pay off, and it looked like his situation was about to become significantly better. The icing on the cake, he thought, and smiled to himself.

He'd been listening, of course – that's what you were supposed to do, to be polite – but only with half an ear. He had a habit of tuning everything else out when he was concentrating, especially when he was making a plan. Sometimes it annoyed people, but that was their lookout, wasn't it? Now, though, something changed, and the space he was in was so cramped he couldn't ignore it. What had been just a quiet background to his thoughts turned within seconds into an angry clamour battering his ears.

What was going on? He dropped the screwdriver and spun round, only to feel a sharp pain in his left arm. His body flinched, and he stumbled back, fighting to keep his balance. There was another pain, and another. He could see the way out only feet away and fought to reach it but couldn't. This was supposed to be a safe place, but now it felt like a trap. Survive, he thought, survive.

He felt his foot strike something and heard a crash of glass breaking as the lamp fell to the floor. Its light flickered and went out: there was nothing to see by except for the pale moonlight that seeped in through the entrance. He lurched towards it but his way was blocked. An icy panic began to grip his mind.

Somewhere in the distance he heard the mournful clang of a fire engine's bell as his boot crunched on the broken glass. He looked up, his eyes straining to adjust to the gloom. Still struggling to understand this sudden and violent interruption to his plans, he glimpsed something flashing down towards him and felt a stab of crippling pain at the side of his head. The bell rang again, but this time he heard nothing.

CHAPTER TWO

Anniversaries didn't figure large in Detective Inspector John Jago's life. With no wedding anniversary to forget at his peril, no children's arrival in the world engraved on his memory, even his own birthday more often than not marked merely by a quiet whisky at home on his own, the familiar milestones of passing time were largely absent. Only one date had a firm hold in his mental calendar: the eleventh of November, the day the Great War had ended twenty-two years ago, and that was today. Armistice Day.

Most people commemorated it by wearing a poppy, and for Jago, like millions up and down the country, it was a time to remember the dead of that war – the sons, brothers and fathers who hadn't come home. For him, today would be a normal working day, but he knew the lost friends and comrades in arms who would be on his mind.

The weekend had brought news of Neville Chamberlain's death, and with it the memory of that Sunday morning just over a year ago when, as prime minister, he'd declared on the wireless that the country was now at war with Germany. What Jago most clearly recalled of that broadcast was the air of fateful resignation in Chamberlain's voice, as if he was already mourning the passing of peace, his hopes cast down by the brutal reality of the Nazi threat.

So different, Jago thought, to the jingoistic crowds that had celebrated the outbreak of war in 1914. How little conception they'd had of what the next four years would bring, and how swiftly the men who marched so bravely to the front would have their illusions and their bodies torn to shreds. Perhaps that was why similar scenes had been unthinkable in September 1939: the memory of those years was still too raw in people's minds.

There'd been precious little good news since, he reflected, with Hitler's conquest of the Netherlands, Belgium and Norway followed by the fall of France, and now Britain subjected to the nightly terrors of the Blitz.

As Jago drove to West Ham police station, with the sun beginning to peep above the houses behind him, he could see the evidence of the previous night's air raid. Sunday had mercifully passed without a daylight raid, but nightfall had brought the fiercest attack for weeks. He scanned the street. A parade of small shops on the left now had a gap like a missing tooth, the space filled by a heap of rubble and splintered timbers, while on the right, three firemen were dousing the last flickers of fire in a pair of wrecked houses. It was like a lottery, he thought: a business wiped out in a moment, families losing everything overnight while their neighbours were spared. Images of shell-blasted villages he'd seen in France during the Great War stirred uneasily in his mind. There was something so grievous about the sight of a home burnt down: it wasn't just a building destroyed, it was someone's memories, their past.

He could see no poppy sellers. Perhaps it was too early in the day for them to be out, or perhaps worse: they were no more immune to the ravages of the Blitz than anyone else. He arrived at the station, still without a poppy. He would have to get one later.

He parked his car, and as he swung his legs out and made for the entrance he caught himself yawning. Despite yesterday being the first Sunday off he'd had in weeks and a welcome respite from the job, any chance of a decent night's sleep had gone out of the window when the enemy planes growled overhead and unleashed their bombs onto the streets below. But at least no one had hauled him out of bed to attend to a case, and that, he supposed, was one of those small mercies you were supposed to be grateful for. Perhaps he'd be granted the small mercy of a quiet day in the office too.

This happy thought lasted until the station door closed behind him.

'Morning, sir,' said the sergeant on the front desk. 'Mr Soper wants to see you immediately.'

Divisional Detective Inspector Soper was the head of all CID operations on K Division of the Metropolitan Police, and that meant he was Jago's immediate superior. In Jago's experience, if a summons was immediate, it usually meant the DDI had some work he wished to deposit on his shoulders. He knocked on his boss's door, wondering in which particular way his quiet day was about to be dismantled.

12

'Come in,' said the familiar voice within.

There was something about its flat tone that made Chamberlain's broadcast flash through Jago's mind again. He opened the door and stepped into the office.

'Ah, good morning, John,' said Soper from behind his desk. 'Sit down.' He looked troubled.

Jago sat, as instructed.

'Look, John, this is going to be a busy day, so I'll get straight to the point.'

'Sir?'

'I've had a phone call this morning from Detective Superintendent Ford, that pal of yours at Scotland Yard.'

Jago had tried to explain to Soper many times that just because he'd worked for Ford during his six-month secondment to Special Branch in 1936, it didn't mean they were 'pals'. He sensed, however, that his boss might not take even mild correction kindly today, so kept his mouth shut as Soper pressed on.

'The thing is, he's not Detective Superintendent Ford any more. He's been promoted – he's Chief Constable Ford now. Chief Constable CID, in charge of the entire detective force in the Metropolitan Police, and that makes him my guv'nor's guv'nor, so I don't have any choice in the matter.'

'In what matter, sir?'

'The matter of why you're sitting here now. He says he's got a manpower crisis on his hands – as if I haven't got one of my own. He's got a case and no one to handle it, so he says he wants to "borrow" you. Poaching, more like, if you ask me. But whatever you call it, the fact is he's seconding you to Scotland Yard, and there's nothing I can do about it.'

13

Jago said nothing as he took this in. No wonder Soper had looked troubled: the DDI had never struck him as a man who embraced challenge warmly. Questions were already tumbling into his mind, but it would be prudent not to fire too many of them at his harassed boss at once.

'May I ask where the case is, sir?'

'It's over in the West End, in the borough of Westminster. Pimlico, to be precise – on B Division. Do you know the place?'

'Pimlico? I know it's down past parliament where the river bends round towards Chelsea, and I know it's by Victoria station, but that's about it, I'm afraid.'

'Well, you'll be getting to know it better pretty soon.'

'So, when's this happening, sir?'

'With immediate effect.'

More questions added themselves to Jago's unspoken list. 'And what about Detective Constable Cradock, sir? What happens to him?'

'The chief constable said you're to bring your sergeant with you, and I explained you've only got a detective constable, because your sergeant's been recalled to the army, but he said if that's the man you work with, bring him too.'

'I assume Cradock doesn't know about this yet?'

'No. I've just told him to wait for you in the CID office and not go wandering off. You can explain to him on the way. Any more questions?' His tone of voice suggested that Jago should stick to the essentials.

'Just one, sir, if you don't mind. What's the case about?'

'I don't know – all he said was it's a suspected murder and it's in Pimlico, so you and Cradock are to get yourselves over there in double-quick time. I'm to phone ahead when you set off.'

'Who do I report to?'

'Detective Superintendent Hardacre – head of Central Branch. He's based at the Yard, of course, but he's going over to the local Pimlico nick at Gerald Road to brief you, so that's where you'll find him. Have you met the detective superintendent?'

'No, sir, but his reputation precedes him.'

Soper's expression suggested he wasn't sure whether he detected a trace of irony in Jago's response. 'Yes,' he said, 'a man with a considerable reputation. He likes original thinkers – I expect you'll get on like a house on fire.'

Given what Jago had seen on his drive to the station, this wasn't the most encouraging prediction of how his imminent meeting with the detective superintendent would go, but for the time being he'd hope for the best.

'And,' Soper added, 'the chief constable said I was to tell you Mr Hardacre isn't a man who likes to be kept waiting – so get cracking.'

'Thank you, sir,' he said, rising from his seat. 'Will that be all?'

'Yes, be on your way, and I'll start thinking about how I can plug the gaps here.'

The last thing Jago heard as he closed the door behind him was a heavy sigh. In other circumstances, thought Jago, Soper might have taken the popular view that a change was as good as a rest. But not today.

CHAPTER THREE

Jago found Cradock in the CID office, reading a newspaper. The young constable hastily folded it shut and jumped to his feet.

'Morning, guv'nor,' he said.

'Morning, Peter,' Jago replied. 'Been educating yourself?'

'Of course, sir.'

'I'm glad to see it. You'll have to finish that later, though – we're going out for a little excursion.'

'Really, sir? Is that what DDI Soper told me to wait here for? Where are we going?'

'The other side of London – Pimlico. We're going to pay a little visit to our friends and colleagues on B Division, and we may be there for a few days.'

'B Division? Should I go back to the section house and pack a bag then, sir?'

'No, our orders are to go immediately to Gerald Road nick and report to Detective Superintendent Hardacre, so we'd better get our skates on. We can come back and pick up whatever we may need later. Grab your coat and hat and come with me – and don't forget your gas mask.'

Jago hurried to the car, with Cradock struggling into his overcoat as he followed. The Riley's engine started first time, and they headed off in the direction of central London with Jago driving as fast as his vehicle and the state of the roads after a night's bombing allowed.

'What's going on in Pimlico that needs us then, sir?' said Cradock, bracing himself while trying to get comfortable in his seat.

'A suspected murder. That's about all I know at the moment, but no doubt Mr Hardacre will tell us more when we get there.'

'But why us? We're K Division – we don't do cases over there.'

'I know, but it seems there's a manpower shortage on B Division and they've got no one available to take it on locally, so we've been pulled in to help. Now, I know my way from here to Victoria but I'll need a bit of help finding Gerald Road, so have a look in that little cubbyhole in the dashboard in front of you and fish out my *A to Z* map book.'

Cradock took the book out, pleased at the thought of being useful. He looked up their destination. 'I've found Gerald Road, sir. It's just a couple of streets away from Victoria Coach Station.'

'That should be all right, then,' Jago replied. 'Keep the map handy, though – you can direct me if we run into any hold-ups on the way.'

'Righto, sir.'

Cradock found the page that showed Stratford and did his best to keep up with the route Jago was taking through the East End of London.

'So how's Mr Soper going to manage without you, sir?'

'I'm sure he'll cope, Peter. Sometimes when you've got no choice it's easier to cope.'

'No choice? He's the DDI.'

'Yes, but this was an order, and it came from the top.'

'The top?'

'Yes – he told me we've been seconded to Scotland Yard.'

The brief silence that followed suggested that Cradock needed time to take this in.

'Blimey, guv'nor,' he said. 'Who'd have thought? Scotland Yard.' He sounded suitably awed by the last two words.

'Don't get too excited, Peter,' Jago replied. 'I doubt whether it'll mean a pay rise.'

'But even so, sir. Scotland Yard. Wait till I tell my mum.' He smiled to himself: she'd feel proud of him. 'So who's this Detective Superintendent Hardacre we're reporting to at Gerald Road?'

'He's the head of Central Branch – that's the Yard's own squad of detectives that get deployed wherever they're needed. I believe that also makes him in charge of the Flying Squad.'

'The Flying Squad? Wow – does that mean we might get one of those Railton cars? They can do a hundred miles an hour, can't they?'

'Ah, yes, the Railton Straight Eight – beautiful cars. Since we're not going to be in the Flying Squad, though, I doubt very much whether Mr Hardacre will have a spare

18

one in his back pocket for us. I shall assume we're sticking with this faithful old Riley Lynx until and unless advised otherwise.'

'So what's he like, then? Do you know him?'

'No, I've never met the man – I only know him by reputation.'

'And?'

'It's only hearsay, so it's not admissible as evidence, as you know. I don't want to prejudice you, so I think I'd better leave you to form your own impression.'

Jago drove on, passing through familiar scenes of overnight destruction and of the usual morning recovery efforts in Mile End and Stepney. At Aldgate he turned down towards the Thames, skirting the north side of the Tower of London. Speeding along Tower Hill beside the moat that surrounded the fortress, he glimpsed through leafless trees on his left more evidence of the power of German bombing. What had once been the squat, round bastion at the midpoint of the outer wall was now a ruin, its shattered insides exposed as nakedly as those of the humblest working family's dwellings in West Ham's dockland.

There was something shocking about the sight. For Jago, the Tower was like Buckingham Palace, St Paul's Cathedral and Tower Bridge: an indelible symbol of London. For so many centuries the capital city's protector, now it was as vulnerable to attack as anywhere.

He drove on in silence until a blazing warehouse on a wharf near Blackfriars Bridge forced him to seek his colleague's map-reading assistance. Cradock, anxious not to be the one to blame for any delays, managed to direct his boss on a hasty detour away from the river and back again to join the Victoria Embankment. The road ahead was clear, and Jago increased his speed. He noticed a poppy seller across the road but was loath to risk incurring the wrath of Detective Superintendent Hardacre by being late for their first meeting. His poppy would still have to wait.

They continued west along the river, neither man speaking. On the opposite side of the Thames, a jumble of barges were loading and unloading at the haphazard succession of ancient wharves and jetties that lined the south bank, while overhead the silver-grey barrage balloons rode gently at anchor against a sky of similar colour. It seemed to him there were more of them than he was used to seeing in West Ham. Perhaps that was because the width of the river made him feel he could see more of the sky, or maybe the powers that be reckoned there were more things important enough to protect from enemy aircraft in central London than on his own home turf. Not that it made much difference: as Stanley Baldwin had told the House of Commons eight years ago, if it came to war, the bomber would always get through, and now it seemed the Germans were proving him right.

The road took them under Waterloo Bridge, and as they emerged on the other side Jago couldn't help glancing to his right to where the Savoy hotel stood. He wondered whether Dorothy was in her room, typing out some article about Britain at war, unaware that he was passing. Or perhaps she had a suite? He realised he'd never asked. He wouldn't be surprised, though, if it turned out an American newspaper like the *Boston Post* thought nothing of providing such accommodation for one of its reporters. He was meant to be taking her out for a meal this evening, and he hoped today's sudden redeployment wouldn't prevent him keeping their appointment. If it was in his power to keep it, nothing would stop him.

For now, though, he had to try to take his mind off her.

'Right,' he said to Cradock, 'I'll stick to the Embankment now, if I can – it should give us a clear run all the way round to Westminster, give or take the odd bomb crater or traffic lights, and then it's not far to Pimlico. I'll need your help to get through the place, though. Do you know it?'

'What, Pimlico, sir? I do a bit, of course, from my basic training – you know, Peel House.'

'Ah, yes.'

'I remember it well, sir – me and the other new recruits. We all turned up in civvies with a suitcase, and ten weeks later we came out the other end policemen, with a uniform and a warrant card.'

'Yes – a frightening thought.'

Cradock carried on regardless. 'They didn't let us out much, but I did get to see a bit of the area. I remember there was a nice little shop just down the road that used to sell everything you needed. There was this lovely couple who ran it – they were very kind to me. Do you reckon I might be able to pop in while we're there?'

'I don't suppose we'll be working twenty-four hours a day, so I dare say that'll be possible.'

'Oh, thanks, sir – if they're still there, of course.'

'Of course. For a man of your advanced age it must've been a long time ago. When were you at Peel House?'

'In 1932, sir – a bit after your time, I suppose. When were you there?'

'I wasn't. I joined just after the war, and there were so many new recruits that they couldn't fit us all in at Peel

House, so some of us ended up at a place called Eagle Hut, down at the Aldwych, where India House and Bush House are nowadays. Very different. It was some kind of club for American and Canadian servicemen in the war, and it really was just a load of wooden huts – you could see right over it to the church in the middle of the Strand, which you certainly can't now. And facing it on the opposite side of the street was the Waldorf Hotel, just to remind us of our station in life.'

'So what was it like back in those days, sir? The training, I mean.'

Jago smiled to himself: to a man of Cradock's youth, the world of twenty years ago was probably not far short of the Dark Ages.

'Oh, enough to scrape by on, I suppose. We only had eight weeks, of course, so I imagine it wasn't as advanced as yours. We covered the basics, though – even how to fire a pistol, although I doubt there were many men of my age on the course who needed to be taught that. The thing I remember most clearly was the superintendent in charge – he told us when we started that by the end of the training if we were any good we'd be allowed on the street, but we'd still know practically nothing. Good advice, I think, looking back – but by then I suppose he'd probably seen a lot of raw young constables who knew nothing.'

He gave Cradock a knowing glance as he said this. The young constable's face suggested he wasn't sure whether Jago had spoken in jest, but wasn't going to pursue the point in case he hadn't.

Jago took pity on him and allowed himself a brief reassuring smile. 'But you're a detective now, aren't you?

And if nothing else, you can be thankful you don't have to get up at half past four in the morning to polish your boots and buttons in time for parade, can't you?'

Cradock was tempted to correct the word 'detective' to 'Scotland Yard detective' but decided to think it rather than say it.

'Oh, yes, sir,' he replied. 'Definitely.'

CHAPTER FOUR

Vauxhall Bridge lay ahead of them, spanning the Thames in five shallow arches. Each of its piers was decorated with a conspicuously large statue, but Jago didn't know who or what they were supposed to represent, and now was certainly not the time to stop and admire them. He pressed on. The classical portico of the Tate Gallery flashed by on their right, and as the road swung away from the riverside towards Vauxhall Bridge Road, Cradock checked the map again and began to direct them towards their destination, Gerald Road police station.

Jago's initial impression of Pimlico was that it must once have been a rather genteel place, but it seemed to have fallen on hard times. He saw roads flanked by Regency terraces of narrow, stucco-fronted houses four or even five storeys high, many with columned porticos and even cast-iron railings that had somehow escaped the ravages of the government's scrap metal salvage campaign. Grand residences of wealthy people a century ago, today they presented a scene of at best faded elegance and at worst the shabby decay of poverty. Clusters of bell pushes by front doors indicated that comfortable Victorian family homes with servants had now been carved up into flats.

The style was a far cry from what he was used to in West Ham, where homes were plain, cramped and cheaply built: here the streets looked as though they'd been designed to impress. But however superior their origins, the years had taken their toll. Many of the properties were patched and dishevelled, grimy with generations of soot from London's chimneys, and now had fallen prey to a greater devastation. He passed a terrace that might once have been an architect's proud achievement. Now it was fractured by a bomb-blasted gap marking a lost home, little of which remained except smashed joists and rafters, twisted metal pipes, and fragments of peeling stucco facade mingled with the nondescript London brick it had concealed for a century or more. To Jago it seemed like a desecration.

He thought of the humbler but no less cherished dwelling he'd seen burnt out on his way to work this morning. Here in Pimlico he felt a long way from home, but it was clear that West Ham wasn't the only place to have received close attention from the Luftwaffe in recent weeks. When Cradock's map-reading brought them to a bridge spanning the tight ranks of railway tracks squeezing into Victoria station, he could think of one reason why. This major rail terminus would be an important target for the raiders, and the fact that Pimlico, like West Ham, was on the river would no doubt offer the enemy bombers a priceless navigational aid.

'Almost there now, sir,' said Cradock, snapping him out of his thoughts.

The bridge brought them to Buckingham Palace Road, where Jago recognised on the opposite corner the sleek art deco lines of Victoria Coach Station.

'Straight up there, sir,' said Cradock, pointing across the road, 'then it's second on the left.'

When they arrived at Gerald Road it proved to be a sleepy residential side street that had so far been spared the random levelling of the air raids. It struck Jago as a secluded, even refined, setting for a police station, but he thought whoever built the station had made it fit in well with the smaller houses that made up the rest of the street. It looked almost homely beside them.

He parked the car and went in through the front door with Cradock. They were taken straight to a small office that Detective Superintendent Hardacre had commandeered for their meeting and where he was now waiting for them. He looked older than Jago, with thinning grey hair and the beginnings of a double chin, and was wearing a black suit that had seen better days, with a poppy in its lapel buttonhole. He was also a little shorter than Jago, who thought he must barely have met the height requirement for joining the Metropolitan Police. Perhaps it was due to many years of looking up to taller colleagues, or perhaps it was just in hope of concealing the excess flesh developing on his neck, but he stood with his chin jutting out, looking Jago up and down through round, wire-rimmed spectacles with a sceptical curl of his lip, as if inspecting a guardsman on parade.

'Right,' he said. 'So you're Jago?'

'Yes, sir.'

'And this is?'

'Detective Constable Cradock, sir.'

'Step outside for a minute, Constable,' said Hardacre with a cursory glance in Cradock's direction. 'I want a word with your guv'nor.'

Cradock turned away, as instructed.

'And close the door behind you,' Hardacre added.

Cradock did so, taking up a position on the opposite side of the corridor until bidden to re-enter. He felt suddenly glum. In the car he'd been daydreaming about the exciting prospect of becoming a Scotland Yard insider, but now, within seconds of meeting the big man from the Yard for the first time, he was a deflated outsider.

Alone now with Jago, Hardacre sat down behind a desk and motioned his visitor to take the wooden chair in front of it.

'So,' he said, 'you're the new chief constable's blue-eyed boy, eh? Well, I've never met you before and I don't know anything about you, but he seems to think you're going to be the solution to all my problems, so let's hope he's right. I'm a busy man, so let's get one or two things straight before we start. The fact that you've got friends in high places cuts no ice with me, Detective Inspector. I judge a man by results, so you'd better get some, otherwise trust me, Mr Ford'll be the first to know, and your new career as a Scotland Yard man will be over before you know it.'

'Yes, sir,' Jago replied. It already looked like the sort of conversation in which this was the only reply he'd be required to provide.

'I don't know what you're used to over on K Division,

but I learnt what effort and discipline are in the British Army, and I run a tight ship.'

Jago wondered briefly which branch of the army involved naval command, but knew better than to open his mouth. He'd met men before who claimed to run a tight ship, and it usually meant they were either self-important or bullies, but he gave Hardacre the benefit of the doubt and waited for him to continue.

'I'm told you were in the army yourself, Jago,' said Hardacre. 'Is that right?'

'Yes, sir.'

'A captain, I gather, with an MC to boot.' He gave a sort of derogatory sniff.

'Only a second lieutenant, actually, sir, and it was just a temporary commission when they were desperate for officers and promoted men like me from the ranks.'

'You came out of it with a nice Military Cross, though, didn't you? That can't have done your career any harm.'

'I don't think I did anything that warranted an MC, sir.'

'I dare say you didn't. They gave those things out like sweeties to the young officers, didn't they? See this?' He ran his finger along a scar in front of his right ear. 'Retreat from Mons, September 1914. I was there, with the West Kents. An Old Contemptible, that's what I am, and proud of it. That was the Kaiser's first big mistake, calling us a contemptible little army – a lot of men joined up because of that, and we showed him we weren't so contemptible after all. He thought he was insulting us, but for us it was like a badge of honour. You don't look old enough to have been there at the beginning, though. Were you?'

'No, sir, not till it was halfway through.'

'Conscript, or volunteer?'

'Conscript, sir, 1916.'

'Well, I may not've been an officer, but I was a volunteer – regular army, before the war. I made it to sergeant, and I don't need to tell you it was the sergeants who ran the army in the field, nursemaiding the officers and leading the men.'

Jago would have agreed with this if asked, but Hardacre was telling, not asking.

'I haven't got time to nursemaid you, though, so you'd better make sure you're on your toes and keep your nose clean. Is that understood?'

'Yes, sir.'

A detective superintendent whose main instruction was to 'keep his nose clean' didn't quite seem to match DDI Soper's description of Hardacre as a man who liked original thinkers. Jago wondered whether Soper might have a previously unrevealed sense of intentional irony, but soon dismissed the idea. More likely it was just Soper's way of getting Jago off on the wrong foot with his new boss.

'Right,' Hardacre continued. 'If you're working for me, you'll need one of these.' He reached down below the desk and produced a brown leather attaché case. 'I've got nine of these in my office at the Yard, and the rule is that no officer of mine investigating a suspected murder goes out to the scene without one. So this is your little box of tricks – take it with you.'

He passed the case to Jago, who supported it carefully with both hands and set it flat on his knees.

'It's what we call a murder bag,' said Hardacre.

'I know, sir. I've heard of them but I've never had the use of one. May I take a look inside?'

'Go ahead.'

Jago lifted the lid and scanned the contents. It was like stepping into Aladdin's cave.

'Those are for the use of my department because I'm required to send men out at short notice to anywhere in the country they're needed,' said Hardacre, 'and given that some of those little provincial forces have got hardly any CID at all, they have to go fully equipped. You'll find everything you need in there for the crime scene – rubber gloves, test tubes, envelopes, measuring tape, fingerprint kit, the lot. Your man's trained, is he?'

'Cradock, sir? Yes, he's done the course.'

'Good. He should enjoy playing with this too. Even got a pair of handcuffs, see?'

Jago could see them, and much more.

'There's thirty quid's worth of stuff in there,' Hardacre continued, 'so make sure you don't lose it.'

'I won't do that, sir. This is going to be very useful.'

'Tell your constable he'll be docked a couple of months' pay if he does – that should keep him on his toes.'

Jago half-thought Hardacre might laugh after saying this, but he didn't.

'Right,' the superintendent continued, we'll get him back in now, and you can meet Wilks too.'

'Wilks, sir?' said Jago, not having heard the name before.

'Detective Sergeant Wilks – he'll be your point of contact here at Gerald Road. Based here, very experienced, been on the force for years, but he was over at Savile Row in September when West End Central got hit. You heard about that, I suppose?'

'The bomb, sir? Yes, we all heard about that. It was a land mine, wasn't it?'

'Yes, nasty business. I suppose Goering reckons we've got used to those screamer bombs making that horrible noise that's supposed to frighten us, so now someone's had the bright idea of sticking a bomb on the end of a parachute so we can't hear it coming. Only it's not a bomb. Turns out it's a blinking navy mine big enough to sink a battleship – you can imagine what that can do to a police station. Only been open since July too, that West End Central nick – one almighty bang and it's gone. Two good detectives and a PC killed, and I don't know how many injured.'

'Including Wilks?'

'He had to be dug out. No major wounds, but he's still a bit shell-shocked. He'll be fine, though – just needs to pull himself together.'

'Will he be working with us, sir?'

'Not if you can manage without him. He's got more than enough on his plate already, so leave him alone if you can, right? It's looting mainly, all over the West End – they've got four and a half thousand cases to deal with up on C Division, and they're up to their eyes in it here on B as well.'

'Yes, sir – we've had a lot on K Division too.'

'Right, well, when you get to know me a bit better you'll find out it's not just murderers I don't like – I hate thieving too, and I hate thieves. This looting's getting out of hand, and it's a fight we can't be seen to be losing.'

'Like the war itself, sir?'

'Be serious, man. If people see looters getting away with it, they'll all start doing it – and where'll we be then, eh? The law says they can be shot, but there's still too many magistrates letting them off with ten-bob fines. Sometimes I wonder what side those people are on.'

'On the side of justice, presumably, sir.'

'On the side of law and order, that's what I'm talking about – it's either that or anarchy, and if we don't crack down on it, that's where we're heading. You've got bigger fish to fry, of course – but if you see a looter anywhere, you make sure you nick him, right?'

'Yes, of course, sir. Is there anything else I need to know about the murder?'

'No. The new chief constable's decided in his wisdom to bring you in, and I'm sure that can only be because he thinks the local men can't handle it. Whether he's right or not is none of my business. Either way, you're here now, so as far as I'm concerned you just need to get on with it. Understood?'

'Yes, sir,' said Jago.

Hardacre jumped up, bustled out of the door and shouted an order in the corridor. Moments later he was back with Cradock, followed by a thin, middle-aged man in a crumpled suit who was puffing on a cigarette with what seemed to Jago to be more compulsion than pleasure.

Hardacre motioned for the two men to pull up a chair each and resumed his position behind the desk. The thin man took the cigarette from his mouth as he sat down, a tremble in his hand causing a quarter-inch of ash to fall onto his trouser leg.

'Sorry, sir,' he said, brushing it off. 'All right if I smoke, sir?'

'Yes, yes, carry on,' said Hardacre, pushing an ashtray across the desk towards him. 'Right,' he continued, now directing his comments to Jago, 'this is Detective Sergeant Wilks. As I said, he'll help you if he can, but—' His eyes switched to Cradock. 'The only reason you're here is because he's too busy, so don't go wasting his time.'

'Yes, sir,' Cradock mumbled.

'What's that?'

'I said "Yes, sir", sir,' Cradock replied, feeling as disconcerted as he sounded.

'What's your name again?'

'Cradock, sir.'

'Right, Cradock, I've just entrusted one of our murder bags to your guv'nor.' He jerked a finger in Jago's direction. 'Take it off him, lad.'

Cradock's eyes widened slightly at the mention of a murder bag, and he picked it up with what seemed like something approaching reverence.

'Now then, Cradock, it's your job to carry that, not his, and you make sure you look after it. Got it?'

'Yes, sir.'

'Good. Now then, Detective Sergeant Wilks will take you two gentlemen over to Tachbrook Street. Some woman found a body in an Anderson shelter there this morning – it's over on the far side of Pimlico, and not quite as salubrious as here. Built over a sewer, I believe – is that right, Wilks?'

'Yes, sir.'

'Pimlico's the poor end of Westminster, you see – not like Gerald Road. People who live round here prefer to think they're in Belgravia, much fancier – all very spick and span. None of your hoi polloi round these parts. Here, Wilks, tell them about your famous neighbour.'

'Yes, sir. I, er, I think what the superintendent's referring to is Mr Coward – Noel Coward, that is. He lives just a few doors down the street from here – number 17.'

'Quite a swanky place, from what I've heard on the grapevine,' said Hardacre. 'Three places knocked into one, apparently, that he's had tarted up for parties or whatever with his theatrical pals. Lord knows what goes on at those little capers – not circles I move in, that's for sure. You neither, I should think, Wilks.'

'Er, no, sir.'

'Good job too, on police wages, eh?' Hardacre turned to Jago. 'And speaking of the high and mighty, that reminds me – our new chief constable wants to see you in his office at the Yard tomorrow morning. That's just you, not your man.'

'Very good, sir. What time?'

'Eight o'clock, sharp.'

'Yes, sir.'

'Right. Now, any questions before you go?'

'Just one small thing, sir,' said Jago. 'Will we be billeted somewhere nearby?'

'What, you're thinking maybe Mr Coward'll put you up in a spare bedroom? I don't think so. We've got something much more homely organised for you. You can't stay here – it's too small to take guests in, unless you fancy sharing a cell – so it'll be Rochester Row nick for you, for the time being. I know it's on A Division, but it's closer to Scotland Yard than this place, and closer to where the body was found, for that matter. We've got a little married-quarters flat above the stables there that's empty, so you can have that. A bit pokey, but more than enough room for one.'

Cradock looked as though he was about to say something, but Hardacre continued, 'And we're putting your constable in the section house at Ambrosden Avenue, just up the road from there.'

Jago could see the hint of disappointment in Cradock's face – hearing the word 'flat' must have raised his hopes of being spared yet another tiny cubicle in a police section house – but Hardacre seemed not to have noticed.

'So that's all sorted,' he continued. 'Now, Sergeant Wilks here will go with you over to Tachbrook Street to where the body was found, and then he can make his own way back. We've got a man guarding the scene until you get there. Not a proper PC – we're too short to spare one for that – just one of those War Reserve men. As far as I'm concerned they're a bunch of untrained amateurs, but they're all right for standing about stopping anyone getting into a house, so I suppose we should be grateful.'

'And a pathologist, sir?'

'Yes, yes, don't worry, I've got one standing by. He's called Dr Gibson, and he's at St George's Hospital, just up the road at Hyde Park Corner. Knows his onions and does a lot of work for the Yard. I'll give him a call and tell him you're on your way over – he'll join you at the scene. I've got a photographer on his way down from the Yard too.'

His instructions seemingly completed, Hardacre stopped and looked Jago and Cradock over again with a questioning air.

'One last thing before you go, you two,' he said. 'It may've escaped your attention, but the regulations changed last year – police officers in uniform are allowed to wear a poppy for Armistice Day now.'

'Yes, sir, I know,' said Jago.

'Well, if uniform can wear it, I see no excuse for a plain-clothes man like yourself not to. I believe in respect for the fallen, Detective Inspector – and I expect men under my command to show it, so don't let me see you or your constable again without one. Understood?'

'Understood, sir.'

'Off you go then – get cracking.'

'Yes, sir.'

They left the office, with Wilks in tow, and returned to where the car was parked. On the way, Jago reflected silently on the meeting he'd just had. How his relationship with Hardacre would develop remained to be seen, but he'd already formed the conclusion that if it came to conflict, explanation might not be a reliable form of defence.

CHAPTER FIVE

They set off in the Riley with Wilks installed in the front seat as navigator and Cradock relegated to the back, examining the contents of the attaché case.

'Superintendent Hardacre was right, guv'nor,' he said. 'They've got everything in here. Even some little tweezers for picking things up, and a rubber blower for blowing the fingerprint powder off.'

'Good,' said Jago. 'You can get to work with it as soon as we arrive, then – we don't want to keep the pathologist waiting.'

'Yes, sir.' Cradock pictured himself strolling onto the scene, murder bag in hand, asking bystanders to stand back while he started the vital work of dusting for fingerprints. 'They know how to do things properly at Scotland Yard, don't they, sir?' he said.

'I hope you're not suggesting we don't, Peter,' Jago replied. 'Scotland Yard has probably got more money to spend than we do, but I'd like to think we manage very well in West Ham CID under wartime constraints and with very limited resources.'

'Of course, sir, yes. I'll, er, continue familiarising myself with this stuff.'

Within a few minutes they were in Tachbrook Street, where Wilks directed them to pull up outside a tired-looking house of the age and style that now seemed to Jago typical of the area. It was narrow, three storeys high with a basement, and wedged into a long, curving terrace – perhaps, he thought, reflecting the course of the sewer that Hardacre had said it was built on. The locals might prefer to keep that unsavoury part of the street's history to themselves, but now, unbeknown to most of them, one house in this bland row held another unsavoury secret: a dead body.

They got out of the car, and Jago was about to go and knock on the door but noticed Wilks was hanging back, lighting a cigarette. His hand was trembling as before, causing the match to flicker.

'Are you all right, Sergeant?' he said.

'I'm sorry, sir,' Wilks replied. 'It's just – well, the detective superintendent said the body's in an Anderson shelter, and I'm not too good at confined spaces at the moment, especially underground. I know it sounds silly, but I had a spot of trouble a few weeks back. I thought I'd be OK, but now we're here, I don't think . . .' He stopped mid-sentence and drew deeply on his cigarette.

'Was that the West End Central business?' Jago asked. 'Superintendent Hardacre mentioned you'd been there.'

'That's right, sir, so if you don't mind . . . would it be

all right if I got back to Gerald Road? Only I've quite a lot to do.'

'Of course, don't worry – you get along there as soon as you like. I'll let you know if we need you.'

'Thank you, sir. Much obliged.'

It seemed to Jago there was a note of genuine gratitude in the detective sergeant's voice, not to mention relief, as he trod out the butt of his cigarette under his foot and set off slowly back down the street.

'Poor fellow,' said Jago to himself.

Cradock came to his side. 'Bit twitchy, isn't he, guv'nor?' he said.

'Twitchy? You'd be twitchy if you'd been blown up by a land mine and had to be dug out. You should be thankful you're not, Peter.'

'Ah, yes, sir,' said Cradock meekly. 'And I am thankful, sir.'

Jago knocked on the front door. It was opened by a young War Reserve constable who identified himself as Bennett.

'Good morning, sir,' he said, admitting them to the house. 'The body's out the back, sir, in the Anderson shelter, and the photographer's already taking his pictures.'

'Thank you, Constable.'

Bennett pointed to a door at the side of the hallway. 'The landlady's in there, sir,' he added in a hushed, reverential tone, which Jago guessed was more out of respect for her than for him. 'She's Mrs Baker, sir, Mrs Nancy Baker. She's quite upset, but I've made her a cup of tea and told her to have a sit down until you're ready to talk to her. She's the one who found the body – she says it's her lodger.'

'And the lodger's name?'

'She says he's called Terry Watson.'

'Right, let's just say hello to her, then we'll take a look at him.'

Bennett knocked on the door and opened it. 'Excuse me, Mrs Baker,' he said, 'only I've got the detective inspector here now, and he's going to have a look round out in the back yard.'

Over Bennett's shoulder Jago saw a modestly furnished living room and a woman sitting in an armchair, dabbing at her eyes with a handkerchief.

'That's all right, Constable,' she said in a weak voice. 'Do you need me?'

'Sir?' said Bennett, turning round to Jago for the answer.

'No, we'll be OK, Mrs Baker,' said Jago. 'We'll just go and have a look at the Anderson shelter and then we'll come back and have a word with you, if that's all right.'

'Help yourselves,' she replied. 'I don't think I want to see all that again.'

Jago and Cradock went to the back of the house and out into a narrow strip of garden. A path made from old bricks led down towards the corrugated-iron Anderson shelter sunk into the earth at the far end, and the rest of the meagre space was given over to a vegetable patch. The photographer was setting up his camera on a tripod near the shelter. He stopped when he saw them approaching and introduced himself as Nisbet.

'I've done my photos of the body and the inside of the shelter,' he said, 'so I'll keep out of your way until you want me to do pictures of fingerprints or anything else.'

Jago thanked him and peered down into the shelter

through the rectangular hole in the front wall that formed its entrance. He saw the body of a fair-haired young man sprawled face up on the concrete floor. So this was where Mr Terry Watson had ended his days. He felt an involuntary shiver in his back and shoulders: it was a cold and ugly place to die. He became conscious of the chill penetrating his overcoat, and a memory flashed into his mind – a dugout in France in 1917, its occupants slain by a pitiless shell burst in the trench. But that was on the battlefield. Here in southwest London, amidst the domestic ordinariness of a Pimlico street, there was something offensively inappropriate about the sight of a man slaughtered in his place of refuge, lying dead in what was supposed to be a safe haven.

He climbed down into the shelter, followed by Cradock.

It was the standard Anderson shelter that had become a familiar feature in back gardens across London, albeit with one slight variation from the norm. If it had been fitted out according to the official instructions, with bunks for four adults and two children, there would barely have been room for the body, but this one was different: it had bunks on only one side. On the other side was a maroon-coloured sports bicycle, upside down on its saddle and handlebars.

'Mending it, do you think, sir?' said Cradock, squeezing in beside Jago.

'Possibly,' Jago replied. 'Watch where you put your feet, now, Peter. And first things first – get your rubber gloves on, and give me some too.'

Cradock produced two pairs of gloves from the case and gave one pair to Jago, feeling like a magician's assistant.

Jago crouched down beside the body. The dead man was dressed in a worn-looking blue plaid overcoat, a brown scarf and gloves, black boots and grey flannels with an oil stain near the turn-up on the right leg. A cap lay on the floor behind him. Everything about the man looked ordinary, with one exception – there was no missing the ugly wound on the left side of his head. The hair around it was matted with blood, and more blood had seeped down onto his collar and soaked his shirt. There was no other obvious sign of injury, but to Jago's eye that one wound looked enough to have snuffed out a young man's life. He would wait to hear what the pathologist had to say.

He stood up and glanced at the bunks to his right. A threadbare blanket hung down from the upper one, and another lay in an untidy heap on top of it. At the end of the lower bunk stood a half-empty bottle of whisky with its cork in and two tin mugs. Close to the man's feet lay an upturned Tilley lamp, its glass globe smashed, and on the floor by the bicycle's handlebars were an oily rag and a screwdriver.

'Adjusting his gears, perhaps?' said Jago, shifting to one side so that Cradock could see the screwdriver. 'The bike's got derailleur ones.'

'Yes,' said Cradock, 'and they're not cheap, are they? Drop handlebars too – serious cycling.'

'It's been a long time since I did any cycling,' said Jago, 'and I've certainly never had derailleur gears. Have a look under that bunk and see if you can find anything – your knees are younger than mine.'

Cradock craned his neck under the lower bunk. 'Aha,' he said, 'this might be what we're looking for.' He knelt down on the floor and reached a hand under the bunk. 'Here we are, guv'nor,' he said, getting back to his feet.

'What do you make of that? Murder weapon, perhaps?'

He held out his hand for Jago to inspect his finding. It was a rat-tailed spanner, about nine inches long, its open end bearing traces of what looked like blood.

'Perhaps,' said Jago. 'We'll see what the pathologist says when he's had a look at it. In the meantime, you get started on checking for prints, starting with that spanner. And don't forget that whisky bottle and those mugs – it looks as though this fellow might've had a drinking companion. I'm not sure we're going to fit that photographer in here with us, so I'll send him in and he can take pictures of any prints you find as you go along. I'll stay outside – shout if you need me.'

'Will do, sir.'

Jago left the shelter as Cradock began dusting the spanner with fingerprint powder. He remained just outside the shelter's entrance, however, keeping a close eye on Cradock's fingerprint work until he had finished. The photographer came out of the shelter first.

'That's me all done, sir,' he said, handing Jago a piece of paper. 'There's the number to call at the Yard if you want me to do any more pictures. In the meantime I'll get this lot developed double-quick.'

'Thank you,' said Jago.

When Nisbet had departed, Jago climbed back down into the shelter.

'What did you find, then, Peter?' he said.

'Nothing much, sir.' Cradock sounded disappointed. 'But then if Watson was wearing gloves all the time he was in here, he wouldn't have left any fresh prints of his own and could've spoilt anyone else's.'

'Yes, and if he was wearing them because of the cold, it's quite likely whoever hit him was too. Did you find anything on the spanner?'

'No. I've put it in that envelope on the bunk for safe keeping, but there were no prints on it. Same thing with the screwdriver, and the whisky bottle and mugs too, although they had some greasy smears on them, so they might've been wiped with something. I did find a few on the Tilley lamp and the bike, but they could be Watson's.'

'Yes. We'd better not take Watson's gloves off till the pathologist's finished with him – you can take his prints at the mortuary. Now, let's have a look round before Dr Gibson arrives.'

'OK, sir. By the way – that broken lamp on the floor. Do you think that could be a sign of a struggle?'

'It could be, although if there was more than one person in a space as small as this a lamp could plausibly get broken with or without a struggle.'

'Yes, I suppose so. Shall I check his pockets, guv'nor?'

'Yes, let's see what we can find out before we talk to his landlady.'

Cradock began to search through the dead man's pockets. 'Here we are,' he said, producing the contents of the left-hand coat pocket. 'Identity card, name of Terry Watson and this address, plus a comb, and about ten bob in assorted coins. Nothing too exciting there, then.'

He reached into the right-hand pocket. 'Just a couple of keys. One looks like a front door key, and there's a little one too – don't know what that'd be for.' He checked the trouser pockets. 'Only a handkerchief and a few more coins in the trousers, sir. That's all there is.'

'Does the coat have an inside pocket, Peter?'

'Oh, yes – sorry, sir.' Cradock unbuttoned the man's overcoat, revealing a green woollen pullover, and found the pocket. 'Yes, there is one,' he said, feeling inside it, then extended his hand with palm open towards Jago. 'Just these, sir. It's a bit odd, though – looks like a couple of Armistice Day poppies, but they're supposed to be red, aren't they? These ones are white – what's that supposed to mean?'

'I think it's something to do with peace – you know, people who're against the war. I imagine it could be a bit risky to wear one in the current climate, though, if that's what they stand for.'

'He's not wearing them, though, is he, sir? He's just got them in his pocket. What do you reckon he'd got them for?'

'It's an interesting question, Peter. They might tell us something about him, but on the other hand we don't know for sure that he'd put them there himself.'

'You mean someone else could've put them in his pocket to make us think he was whatever it was they wanted to make us think he was?'

'You could've put it more concisely, Peter, but theoretically that's possible, isn't it?'

'Yes, sir. Shall I have a look in the saddlebag on that bike too, sir?'

'Yes, do that.'

Cradock crouched down by the bicycle and undid the buckles on the linen bag hanging by leather straps from the back of the saddle. A puncture repair outfit, tyre levers and two small spanners spilled out onto the floor, together with a padlock and chain. Jago quickly tried the small key in the padlock and found that it worked.

Cradock, meanwhile, hadn't taken his hands off the bag. 'That's funny, sir,' he said. 'It still feels heavy.' He lifted the upside-down bag higher and removed the remainder of its contents. 'Would you believe it?' he said. 'Look, sir, see what else he had in it – a pair of house bricks.'

'Yes, I can see that,' Jago replied. 'Now you tell me – what do you make of them?'

'Well, sir . . .' Cradock began, still thinking. 'Do you reckon he could've been going to drown himself? That's what they do, isn't it – weigh themselves down if they're going to chuck themselves in the river. And the Thames is only just down the road from here, isn't it? And that big bridge we came past – maybe he was planning to do himself in, only someone else got here first with the same idea.'

'That's good, Peter, although it may not be as dramatic as that. I've heard that racing cyclists sometimes put weights like bricks in their saddlebag to build up their strength so they can cycle faster and longer – a bit like when we make soldiers run with a pack on their back to get them fitter.'

'Yes, I didn't think of that, sir. So he could've just been a keen cyclist.'

'Yes, although from what I've heard, there are men who've taken to going out after dark in the blackout with a couple of bricks with a view to putting them through a jeweller's window while there's no one around. Maybe Mr Watson here was partial to a spot of larceny.'

'Yes. Done in by another crook – arguing over the loot, perhaps.'

'I can't see any loot in here, though. Can you?'

'No, sir. Maybe in the house, though?'

'Don't worry – we'll take a look before we go. Now, let me see those poppies again.'

Cradock handed them to him.

'That's a bit curious,' said Jago, turning them over. 'It might mean nothing, but look, one of them's clean, but the other one's dirty. I can imagine someone having two clean ones at this time of year, but you wouldn't want to wear a dirty one, would you? Especially if the whole point about them is that they're white. Still, that's another question we can't answer, isn't it?'

CHAPTER SIX

There was a polite tap on the corrugated-iron wall of the shelter, and PC Bennett stuck his head in at the entrance.

'Excuse me, sir, but the pathologist's arrived – Dr Gibson. Shall I bring him down?'

'Yes, please do,' said Jago.

Bennett went back to the house and returned a few moments later with a man of about Jago's height and age, perhaps a little older, carrying a leather bag. Jago climbed out of the shelter as they arrived.

'This is Dr Gibson, sir,' said Bennett. 'Will that be all, sir?'

'Yes, thank you,' said Jago. 'You can go back to the station now, unless you've got other instructions. We'll manage here.'

'Very good, sir – I'll just say goodbye to Mrs Baker and then I'll be off.'

Gibson thanked Bennett as he departed, then turned to

Jago and Cradock with a smile. 'Good morning,' he said, extending a hand in greeting. 'Detective Inspector Jago, I presume.'

'That's right,' Jago replied, taking his hand and shaking it. 'Good morning to you, too – very nice to meet you. This is Detective Constable Cradock.'

Cradock responded with a polite nod to their visitor, judging it better not to speak until spoken to. Jago was silent too for a moment, distracted by Gibson's overcoat and trousers: close up, he could see they were rather more battered than he'd expected.

'Please excuse my appearance,' said Gibson, as if reading his mind. 'Most people expect physicians and surgeons to turn out in a morning coat when they're doing their rounds, but I'm a forensic pathologist, so my rounds include things like grubbing around on the floor in an air-raid shelter. I prefer to wear more expendable clothing. Besides, my patients are all dead, so they don't mind what I'm wearing.' He chuckled at his own joke and climbed down into the shelter. 'Right,' he said, 'Let's see what we've got here.'

Jago considered the state of his own dress as he followed him. He too had taken to wearing old clothes to work now that being caught out in air raids meant having to fling oneself onto the ground at the sound of a whistling bomb, so Gibson's approach seemed encouragingly sensible.

He turned to face Cradock.

'I don't think you'd better try to squeeze in here too, Peter. Best if you stay outside, so that Dr Gibson has room to move – you can watch and listen from there.'

'Very good, sir,' Cradock replied, crouching by the entrance.

Gibson knelt beside the body and began to examine the wound on Watson's head. 'Hmm, this will certainly have given him something to think about – but not for very long, I fear. It may well be what did for him, but I'll need to make a more detailed examination at the hospital before I can give you chapter and verse. Any sign of a possible weapon?'

'Yes,' said Jago. 'We found this.' He took the spanner from the buff envelope on the bunk and passed it to Gibson.

'Yes,' said the pathologist, examining it, 'this looks like a possible candidate. I'll be able to tell you more when I've done some tests in my laboratory. All right if I take it back with me?'

'Yes, of course. Do you recognise it?'

'No – apart from the fact that it's a spanner, of course.'

'You don't have an Anderson shelter, do you?'

'No, I don't – where I live we've got a big basement and we shelter in that. But how did you know? You sound like Sherlock Holmes.'

'Nothing as clever as that, I'm afraid. If you'd had an Anderson, you'd have known this was the spanner they supplied with it. The instructions say you should keep it handy inside the shelter, so that if a bomb blocks the front entrance you can undo the clip-bolts on that panel in the back wall over there and get out that way – like an emergency escape hatch.'

'I deduce, then, that unlike me, you do have an Anderson shelter.'

'Correct.'

'Elementary, my dear inspector. I also deduce that these spanners must be quite common – two a penny, in fact, and therefore of limited value as evidence.'

'Yes. There must be a couple of million or more of these up and down the country, and they'll all look exactly the same, so we won't be able to tell whether this one came from this shelter or from any other place you'd care to name.'

'And the fact that there isn't one hanging on the wall in here doesn't prove ours is the one that belongs here, nor that the killer brought it with him.'

'Exactly. The only hope we had was that there might be some fingerprints on it, but there aren't any, so we haven't a clue.'

'Excuse me, sir,' said Cradock from the shelter's entrance. 'I've just been thinking.'

'I'm always pleased to hear that, Peter,' Jago replied. 'About what?'

'Well, sir, assuming that spanner's the murder weapon, it's strange that whoever killed him didn't take it away and get rid of it somewhere. I mean, that might've made us think this was an accident, mightn't it? You know, bloke's down here in his shelter, he's had a few drinks, climbs up to the top bunk to try and get some sleep, slips and falls off, smashes his head on the concrete, and that's the end of him.'

'Doctor?' said Jago.

'Yes, I imagine you might well have thought it was an accident, but it's actually rare for a head injury like this to be caused by a fall onto a flat surface, so even if you hadn't found that spanner you might still have had grounds for suspicion. However, as for the question of why an assailant might leave the weapon at the scene of the attack, that's something I must leave in your hands. I think common sense would suggest, though, that it has to be a possibility. I mean, if you've just hit someone on the head with a spanner and you think you may have killed him, you've got to make a lot of decisions very quickly – you don't necessarily have time to think it all through. Do you run or do you stay? If you run, do you take the weapon with you? If you take it you may be able to get rid of it, but what if you run straight into a policeman or an air-raid warden, or anyone else for that matter? Then you're incriminated. We can stand here now and speculate on how someone might have reasoned, but when you're in the situation and under pressure you don't always make the right decision.'

'Yes, of course,' said Jago. 'Common sense, as you say, Dr Gibson.'

'I was thinking about that whisky and the mugs, too, sir,' said Cradock tentatively, as if wary of being caught out in his reasoning abilities by the doctor again. 'It makes it look like he was drinking with someone, as you said, but we can't be sure of that, can we? And even if there was someone else drinking with him, that wouldn't necessarily mean they were here when he was killed, would it? The other person could've left before whoever attacked him arrived.'

'Correct,' said Jago.

Cradock looked relieved to have got something right.

'Regarding this business of the whisky, Doctor,' said Jago to Gibson, 'we're only assuming that Mr Watson was drinking it – we've no evidence. Can you let us know if you find any alcohol in his blood?'

'Yes, of course.'

'And if he was, will you be able to give us some idea of

how long it was between him drinking and when he died?'

'Yes, I'll see what I can do.'

'Thank you. And what about time of death?' Jago asked.

'I was just about to take his temperature,' said Gibson, 'so if you'll bear with me . . .'

Jago averted his gaze while Gibson took a thermometer from his bag and carried out the procedure: it was an undignified business, and for Jago, respect for the dead required him not to gawp.

'Right,' said Gibson, 'all done. Now, I'm sure you know, Inspector, that this sort of calculation can only be approximate, because so many things can affect the body's temperature. That kerosene lamp on the floor, for example, would have put out quite a lot of heat, not just light, but if it was smashed and went out at about the time he was killed – which is only an assumption, mark you – it would quickly have got pretty chilly in here. So . . .' He paused to write in his notebook. 'My best estimate would be that he died sometime between ten o'clock last night and two o'clock this morning.'

'Thank you, Doctor, that's very helpful. Anything else you can say at this stage?'

'No – you'll have to wait until I've opened him up. I'll have the body taken to the mortuary, and if you'd like to drop by later I'll let you know what I've found. Do you know St George's Hospital?'

'I know it's at Hyde Park Corner, but I've never had occasion to visit it.'

'Well, you can't miss the place – it's a very grand white building with columns and a pediment opposite the Royal Artillery Memorial. I know there are buildings like that round every corner in that part of London, but we're easy to spot – if you look up at the pediment on the front you'll see "St George's Hospital" in big letters across the frieze. That's where the front entrance is, but if you're coming by car, I suggest you park at the back of the hospital, in Grosvenor Crescent Mews – that's where the back entrance is, and it's closer to the mortuary. Just ring the bell at the door and ask for me, and the porter will bring you through. I like to think of it as the tradesmen's entrance – the front one's where the consultants who are rather more handsomely rewarded than I am get dropped off by their chauffeurs, so given the state of my clothes, the back way seems altogether more appropriate.'

CHAPTER SEVEN

Jago and Cradock walked up the garden path to the house and peered in at the back window. Seeing Nancy Baker sitting inside but facing away from them, Jago rapped on the glass to attract her attention and she came to the door. She was still holding a handkerchief in her left hand, but her eyes were now dry.

'I'm sorry we've had to keep you waiting, Mrs Baker,' said Jago. 'Thank you for your patience. I don't know whether PC Bennett gave you our names, but I'm Detective Inspector Jago and this is Detective Constable Cradock. May we come in?'

'Yes, of course,' she replied.

Standing, she seemed stronger and more sturdily built than when he'd first seen her on their arrival at the house, but her voice still sounded fragile. She showed them in, offered them a wooden kitchen chair each, and sat down in a worn, high-backed easy chair beside the range.

'I'm afraid we'll have to ask you a few questions about what's happened here today,' Jago began, 'but we won't be any longer than necessary. I realise this must be very upsetting for you.'

'Yes, yes. I'll be all right, though – it's just the shock. I wasn't expecting to find Terry like – like that. I know it must sound silly. Obviously I wouldn't have been expecting it, but even so, Terry was so full of life, and now he's – well, he's gone, hasn't he?'

Jago nodded in respectful silence and waited for her to continue.

'Still,' she said, 'what can you do? Life must go on – that's what they say, isn't it? So, what is it you want to ask me?'

'Well, first of all, am I right in understanding this is your house?'

'Yes, that's right.'

'Does anyone else live with you here?'

'Yes. Apart from poor Terry, of course, there's my daughter, Jenny – she's out at work. My husband died at the beginning of the year, so now it's just the two of us.'

'I'm sorry.'

'That's all right. Jenny and I are getting by OK. Like I say, life has to go on.'

Jago nodded his agreement. 'Can you tell me where your daughter works? We'll need to talk to her.'

'Yes. She's got a nice little job at the Victoria telephone exchange.'

'And where's that?'

'In Greencoat Place, just the other side of Vauxhall Bridge Road. It's very handy for her – only about ten minutes' walk.'

'And I understand it was you who found Mr Watson's body.'

'Yes,' she whispered, wincing.

'And can you tell me what time that was?'

'It would've been about a quarter past eight, I think. I usually make a bit of breakfast for me and Terry when I get home in the morning – he was very fond of a proper fried breakfast, was Terry, although there's not much chance of that these days on the rations. Anyway, a bit of breakfast and then I go to bed for a sleep later on.'

'You work night shifts then, I assume.'

'Yes. Not every week, mind – sometimes it's nights, sometimes it's evenings. I've got a job in a clothing factory down by Pimlico Wharf. The last couple of weeks I've been on nights – we're making corduroy breeches for those Land Army girls at the moment. They've got their offices in Tothill Street, only about a mile up the road, so I suppose we're local suppliers for them.'

'So what time did you get home this morning?'

'About ten past eight. Some days Terry's already up and about when I get in, but if he's not I go out and see if he's awake. If he is, I see what I can rustle up for us to eat.'

'Out? You mean to the shelter?'

'Yes. That's where Terry sleeps. Nasty, damp thing it is.'

'Do you use it too?'

'No, I don't like it. I tried one where we lived before, when we had that first air-raid alert the day war broke out, but I couldn't get on with it. Too cold and cramped for my liking – and that first time was a false alarm anyway, so it was a waste of time. Then when the real bombing started, I decided I'd rather sleep in my own bed and take my chances – I mean, who's to say where a bomb's going to land? My sister-in-law – she lives over in Peckham – she told me about a family round the corner from her. They all went out to the Anderson shelter, ten feet from the back of the house, and the bomb hit the shelter. All killed.'

'But Mr Watson preferred to use the Anderson shelter?'

'Every night, yes. A lot of people do, though, don't they? Mind you, the way I look at it, if that bomb's got your name on it, there's nothing you can do.'

'And you said, "where we lived before" – was that including Mr Watson?'

'No, I took him on after I moved into this place. It was on account of my husband dying, you see. Percy, he was, by the way. We used to run a pub – the George, up the other end of Lupus Street – but the tenancy was in his name, so when he died, the brewery turfed me out. Luckily I got myself a job at the clothing factory, like I said, and I moved over here. It's a good job, so I'm just hoping the factory doesn't get blown up – it breaks your heart to see all these places burning.'

Jago nodded in agreement, reluctant to interrupt her.

'They'll regret it, though, that Hitler and his mob,' she continued. 'An eye for an eye, that's what I say. We need to give them a taste of their own medicine.'

'Getting back to Mr Watson, would you say you knew him well?'

'Not especially. I didn't see all that much of him really – he was always going out, and he was only the lodger, after all.'

'How long have you known him?'

She paused to count on the fingers of both hands

before replying. 'About ten months, I reckon. I came here in January, and he took the room quite soon after that. There'd been a fire at his previous digs, so he was looking for somewhere he could move in straight away. And I needed the money, see, what with losing the pub so suddenly.'

'When did you last see him?'

'Yesterday teatime. Sometimes he eats with us in the evening, if I'm at home and he's not out somewhere. Yesterday Jenny and I were both in, so we all had a bite together.'

'And then?'

'Well, we chatted a bit and listened to the wireless, then Jenny and Terry offered to wash the dishes, bless them, and I went off to do my duty.'

'To work, you mean?'

'No, no – didn't I say? I do six nights a week at the clothing factory but I'm off on Sunday nights, so then I do a spot of voluntary helping out at the rest centre instead, looking after the people who've been bombed out or had to move out because there's an unexploded bomb near where they live – that sort of thing. I reckoned I might as well do something useful on my free night, and it means I don't have to break my sleep pattern.'

'Do you know how old Mr Watson was?'

'I'm not sure. I remember him saying once that he was four when the war started – the last war, I mean – so that would make him about thirty, wouldn't it.'

'Old enough to be called up, then. Had he received his papers?'

'He never mentioned it, so I suppose they hadn't got

round to him yet. Mind you, I don't think he was too keen on the idea of being in the army.'

'What makes you say that?'

'Oh, nothing really, but he hadn't volunteered, had he? He could've done if he'd wanted to, and he never mentioned being in a reserved occupation.'

'I see. What sort of work did Mr Watson do?'

'I'm not sure. It seemed to be a bit of this, a bit of that, but he never told me, and I didn't like to ask. You know how it is with some men – you just don't, do you?'

'You mean you think he was involved in something shady?'

'No, I'm not saying that – he just kept that sort of thing to himself. Some people are like that, aren't they? A bit private – and why shouldn't they be? As long as he paid the rent I didn't mind – a bit of extra cash comes in very handy when you're a widow, I can tell you.'

'Did Mr Watson have any family you know of?'

'I don't think so – he never mentioned anyone, at any rate.'

'Friends?'

'Yes, he had one or two mates who used to come round here for him sometimes. I think they were all in the same cycling club. Very keen on his cycling, he was.'

'So the bicycle we saw in the shelter was his?'

'That reddy-brown one? Yes, his pride and joy, that bike was. I suppose he was worried about losing it if the house was hit while he was out in the shelter, so he used to keep it in there with him. He took the bunks out on one side to make room for it. I wasn't keen on him bringing it into the house, especially when the wheels were muddy, but that

60

was the only way he could get it through to the back yard, and bless him, he always carried it through so as to keep my floor clean.'

'Do you have names for any of his friends?'

'Not really, no. The only one I can give you a name for is Dennis Bateman. He knew me from the old pub – one of our regulars, he was. He looks after that vegetable patch of mine in the garden – you'll have seen it when you went down to the shelter. Got proper green fingers, he has. Anyway, he sent Terry round to me when he heard I was looking for a lodger.'

'No one else you can remember?'

'No. There was one other bloke who came to see Terry once or twice, but he never said what his name was, and I didn't like to ask. Apart from that I can't help you.'

'Do you know what Mr Watson's connection was with this other man?'

'How he knew him, you mean? No, but the only thing I know Terry was part of was the cycling club. I know Dennis was, so maybe this other bloke was too.'

'What did he look like, this other man?'

'He was a small sort of fellow, not much meat on him, and he was getting on a bit, going thin on top. Nothing else about him to catch your eye, as I recall.'

'And do you happen to know where I can find the first man you mentioned – Mr Bateman?'

'Yes, he lives in one of the Peabody Avenue flats, over near the railway line, but I don't know what number it is. If you want to find him in the daytime, though, you'd best pop across to Battersea Park, just the other side of Vauxhall Bridge – he works there, as a gardener.'

'Thank you. And what about lady friends?'

'Girls, you mean? Well, if there were, he never brought them home, as you might say. But what he got up to when he wasn't here I've no idea. Sorry I can't be of more help.'

'You've been very helpful, Mrs Baker. Now, I'd like to have a look at Mr Watson's room, please.'

'His room? Oh, right, OK then.'

'You sound a little hesitant, Mrs Baker.'

'No, I'm all right. It's just that, well, you know, he was a private sort of person, like I said. And now you want to go poking around in his room when he's only just died – it doesn't seem quite right, somehow.'

'I'm afraid we have to.'

'Yes, I know – you're only doing your job. But I'll come with you, if you don't mind. I feel like he needs someone there to protect him.'

CHAPTER EIGHT

Jago and Cradock followed Nancy Baker up the narrow staircase to the bedroom at the back of the house. It had little furniture to speak of: a single bed, a sagging green armchair and a walnut combination wardrobe. A rusty-brown patterned carpet covered part of the floor, and a lone spindle-back kitchen chair stood by a table near the window.

While Cradock began to search through the drawers in the wardrobe, Jago crossed the room to the window, which overlooked the back garden and provided a good view of the Anderson shelter. The table, a simple oak affair, was home to the previous Saturday's newspaper, a cheap glass tumbler, an almost-empty whisky bottle, and a two-month-old issue of a magazine called the CTC *Gazette*, the front page of which was mostly taken up by an advert for BSA bicycles. He turned to Nancy, who was keeping a close eye on their examination of the room from the doorway, and gestured towards the bottle.

'Was Mr Watson fond of whisky?' he asked.

'No more than any other man, I imagine,' she replied.

'Do you drink, Mrs Baker?'

'I've spent most of my life running a pub,' she laughed. 'Of course I drink. What's it to you?'

'It's just that there was half a bottle of whisky in the shelter, and it looks like Mr Watson may've been sharing it with someone.'

'Well, I like a drop now and then, but if you think I was down in that shelter knocking back Scotch with Terry, you're mistaken – I've already told you I was out all night.'

'Yes, you did, thank you. But I was wondering if you might know who else could've been with him.'

'Sorry, no – can't help you there.'

Jago glanced across to the bed. The paint on the cast-iron frame was chipped, and one of the brass knobs on the foot end was dented. The linen bedspread looked undisturbed.

'Is the bed always as tidy as that?'

'Yes,' said Nancy. 'Not that Terry would've been bothered about making it up if it wasn't, but like I said, he preferred to sleep in the shelter.'

Jago moved to the bed and picked up the only object that lay on it: an old leather strap, about four inches long, with a small piece of grey cloth attached to one end. Beside it was what looked like a scrap torn from a brown paper bag, with the word 'Thanks' scrawled on it.

'Any idea what this is doing here, Mrs Baker?' he said.

She came over and took a closer look. 'Oh, yes, Terry said he'd leave that out for me. He asked me if I could sew it back on, and I said I'd give it a go, but it's not easy sewing

64

leather onto canvas if you haven't got the right needle. It's off a rucksack of his – filthy old thing it is, but I suppose it's handy for carrying things when you're on a bike. Anyway, he said that strap had got torn off one of the pouches – I expect he was trying to stuff too much into it.'

She looked round the room. 'Come to think of it, he said he'd leave the rucksack out for me too, but it's not here. He always used to hang it there, on the end of the bed. He must've taken it with him to the shelter. Did you see it down there, Inspector?'

'No – there was no rucksack.'

'Well, that is funny. He always seemed quite attached to it.' She seemed lost in thought for a moment. 'I was meaning to mend it for him but I hadn't got round to it. I suppose I never will now.'

Jago put the strap into his pocket and returned to the table. 'We'll need to check this bottle and glass for prints, Peter,' he said. 'Give that photographer a ring and see if you can do it first thing tomorrow when I'm at that meeting.'

'Yes, guv'nor,' Cradock replied, closing a drawer and rummaging in the bottom of the wardrobe's hanging section.

'Will that be all right with you, Mrs Baker?' Jago added. 'OK if they turn up about a quarter past eight, if you expect to be home by then?'

'Yes, that's no problem.'

Jago checked the pockets of a black jacket with frayed cuffs that was draped over the spindle-back chair, finding a pencil, a bus ticket, a grubby handkerchief and a comb.

'Nothing much here,' he said, showing the items to Cradock.

'No,' said Cradock. 'Two combs, though – one in his

coat and one in his jacket.'

'Is that unusual? How many combs have you got?'

'One, of course, sir.'

'I see. So we've got a man with frayed cuffs and two combs – what would Sherlock Holmes say about that?'

Cradock couldn't tell whether the question was serious, but he thought it best to treat it as if it was. 'A man who cares about how he looks and likes to make a good impression but can't afford the smart clothes to go with it?'

'Yes, quite possibly. Or why not a man who's so forgetful he buys a comb without realising he's already got one? Or a man who's stolen someone else's jacket and found a comb in it? That's the trouble with Sherlock Holmes, isn't it? When he deduces something from a little scrap of evidence like that, he somehow always turns out to be right, but I've never found it's like that in real life. Pity, eh?'

'Yes, sir.' Cradock sounded glum.

'Have you found anything yourself, Peter?' said Jago.

'Just a few clothes and a pair of old boots with a hole in one sole,' Cradock replied. 'But I did find this,' he added, his voice brightening. He held up a small card. 'Looks like a membership card for a cycling club. It says "Pimlico Wheelers" and it's got a name on it – Cecil Trubshaw, Chairman – and it gives the address as Trubshaw Cycles, 69 Lupus Street, Pimlico SW1.'

'Well done, Peter.'

'Thank you, sir.'

'I think we'll have a word with him. Do you know this man, Cecil Trubshaw, Mrs Baker?'

'No, can't say as I do,' Nancy replied, shaking her head.

'Could he be the other person you mentioned who

used to visit Mr Watson?'

'I wouldn't know, would I? He never gave his name, like I said, and Terry never introduced us. It could've been anyone under the sun, couldn't it?'

'Indeed. Was the Pimlico Wheelers the name of the cycling club he belonged to?'

'Sorry, I don't know that either.'

'Is there anywhere else on the premises where Mr Watson kept things, Mrs Baker?'

'No – apart from the Anderson shelter, where I let him keep his bike. He just rents the room, so that doesn't entitle him to fill the rest of my house with his clutter – not that he had much in the way of clutter, as you can see.'

'Yes – he seems to have been a man of few possessions.'

'That's right. As I recall, when he moved in he just had his bike and a suitcase, and that old rucksack I told you about on his back. But I suppose when you're a lodger moving around from place to place you can't keep a lot of stuff, can you? Anyway, at least it meant he kept the place pretty tidy, which is something to be thankful for. I clean in here from time to time, and it's a lot quicker if you don't have to move a ton of rubbish to get to the dust.'

'Have you ever come across anything unusual in here?'

'Depends what you mean by unusual, doesn't it? I wouldn't say so – just the normal kind of stuff. And I may clean a bit, but I don't go poking round in his pockets like you do. Now, Inspector, is that all you need to know? Only I need my sleep, otherwise I'll be no good for work tonight.'

'Yes, Mrs Baker, that'll be all for now. I'd like to come back and talk to you a little more, though. Would sometime tomorrow suit you?'

'Don't see why not. Soon as you can after I get home from work, if you don't mind, so I can get a bit of sleep.'

'I've got a meeting at eight o'clock, so I won't be able to get here as early as Detective Constable Cradock and the photographer.'

'How about nine o'clock?'

'I'll do my best.'

'Good – I'm off, then. You can let yourselves out.'

She turned on her heel, and seconds later they heard the slam of a bedroom door closing across the landing.

CHAPTER NINE

The Victoria telephone exchange sprawled along one side of Greencoat Place, occupying the block between Willow Place and Stillington Street. Four storeys high and built in red brick, it bore a superficial resemblance to the houses opposite, but even before its name came into view above the door, there was something about the look of the place that marked it out as official.

Jago and Cradock went to the main entrance and identified themselves. They had to wait only a few minutes before Jenny Baker appeared.

She was a slim brunette in her early twenties, smartly but modestly dressed. She looked concerned, glancing around the entrance lobby as she approached them.

'They said you're the police.' Her quiet, well-modulated voice struck Jago as a marked contrast to her mother's more workaday diction. 'Has something happened?'

'We'd like a word with you, Miss Baker. Is there

somewhere we can talk?'

'Yes, of course – we can sit in that corner over there.' She pointed to some chairs on the far side of the room and hurried towards them. Jago and Cradock followed.

'I'm Detective Inspector Jago, and this is Detective Constable Cradock,' Jago began as they took their seats.

'Detectives? What on earth do you want with me?'

'It's to do with your mother's lodger – Mr Watson.'

'Terry? Is he in some kind of trouble?'

'I'm very sorry to have to tell you this, Miss Baker, but Mr Watson was found dead this morning.'

'Dead? Oh my goodness – that's awful.' She sat in silence, eyes wide and mouth half open, as if unaware of their presence. Then she blinked, shook her head and stared intently at Jago. 'What happened?'

'I'm afraid we believe Mr Watson was murdered.'

'Murdered? But who would want to do that?'

'We're hoping you might be able to help us with that, Miss Baker. That's why we're here.'

'Well, yes, if there's any way I can, but I really don't think . . . I mean, this is a shock – I had no idea.'

'We'd just like to ask you a few questions.'

'Of course, yes, please do.'

'Thank you. First of all, can you tell us when you last saw Mr Watson?'

'Yes. That would have been yesterday afternoon. He had tea with me and my mother.'

'Ah, yes – your mother mentioned that.'

'Right, well, then she went off to do her volunteering at the rest centre.'

'What time was that?'

'I didn't really notice what time it was, but she starts at eight, and the rest centre's only a few minutes' walk away, so she probably left about ten to eight.'

'And what did you do?'

'Terry and I washed the dishes, and when we'd finished he went out.'

'Did he say where he was going?'

'No, I don't recall he did.'

'And what did you do after he went out?'

'I listened to the wireless and read for a bit, then I went to bed.'

'What time was that?'

'Well, you know that new thing they've started doing on the BBC?'

'I'm not sure. What new thing is that?'

'They have Big Ben chiming at nine in the evening, then a minute's silence before the news so you can think about your dear ones or pray or whatever. Last night was the first time. So I did that and listened to the news, and then I turned in for the night. The news finished at a quarter past, so I must've gone to bed about half past nine or so.'

'I see. And do you sleep in the house, with your mother? She told us she prefers to sleep there rather than in the shelter.'

'No, definitely not – I don't like either of them. I prefer the coal cellar. I think most of us do round here, don't we?'

'The coal cellar?'

'Yes – you know.' She looked at him quizzically. 'Are you not the local police, then?'

'No, we've been brought in for this case.'

Jago had almost said 'We're from Scotland Yard,' but

the words had stuck in his throat. It seemed like showing off.

'Well,' Jenny continued, 'you may have noticed we've got a lot of old houses in Pimlico. No front gardens, and not much at the back either, but they do have basements and that thing at the front where you can go down steps from the street and there's a little space between the house and the pavement.'

'Ah, yes. I've seen that. What's it called?'

'It's called the "area", although a lot of people round here call it the "airey". I think whoever built the houses did it that way so they could put a window or two in the outside wall of the basement and get a bit of light and fresh air in for the servants. But the thing is, a house like that usually has little vaults on the opposite side of the area that run out underneath the pavement, and that's where you keep your coal and stuff. When the war kicked off, people started clearing them out and using them as air-raid shelters. We've got one at home, and we've cleaned it all up and put a bed in, and that's where I sleep.'

'And it's as safe as an Anderson shelter?'

'Oh, yes – even a little bit safer, perhaps, because it's made of bricks and it's got the paving stones above it. I've got a friend who works for the council, and she told me there's only about a couple of hundred houses in the whole of Pimlico with gardens big enough for an Anderson shelter, but we've got eight thousand coal-cellar ones. They still wouldn't stop a bomb if it landed right on top of you, of course, but that's the same with an Anderson, and it doesn't look like the government's going to build those deep shelters everyone's been asking for. I'm told they think if we had places like that to go to, we'd stay there and never come up again, and none of the work would get done – that's what Terry used to say, anyway.'

'But you have an Anderson shelter too.'

'Yes, the previous owner had it put in, apparently.'

'But you never use it yourself.'

'Of course not. Wouldn't be proper, would it? Being in the shelter on my own all night with Terry? What would my mum say?'

'Of course.'

'Anyway, it worked out well, having the Anderson – for Terry, I mean. I think he liked having a little world of his own out there. He'd snuggle down in that shelter every night with that precious bike of his – I reckon he loved that bike more than anything in the world.'

'So you were in the coal cellar alone all of last night while your mother was out?

'Yes, that's right.'

'I was about to ask you whether you'd seen or heard anything unusual – anything that might shed some light on the circumstances of Mr Watson's death – but I suppose that's not very likely in a coal cellar.'

'Not a chance, unless I'd gone into the house and right to the back for any reason. I might've been in earshot or sight of the back yard if I had, but I didn't. And even if I'd gone up to my bedroom to fetch an extra blanket or something I wouldn't have seen, because it's at the front, same as Mum's. The one at the back's for the lodger, because it's a bit bigger than mine – that was Terry's room.'

'So you didn't see or hear anything.'

'No, not a thing. I wasn't asleep all night, of course,

because of the air raid and the guns firing. My mum said I ought to get some of those free ear plugs the local council was supposed to be giving us, but I can't see the point – it just means we won't hear the bombs coming, so what's the use of that? Giving us something bomb-proof to sleep in would be better. But anyway, I didn't hear anything suspicious, and once all the noise had stopped I had quite a good sleep.'

'You said Mr Watson left the house when you'd finished washing the dishes. Do you know what time he came home?'

'No. Sometimes I hear the front door closing if it bangs, because it's just above the area, but I didn't last night, so he must've come in quietly.'

'And what time did you leave the house this morning?'

'Twenty to eight – that's my usual time for going to work.'

'Did you see your mother before you left?'

'No – she doesn't get home till after eight o'clock when she's on nights or at the rest centre, so I'm long gone by the time she's in. Listen, have you got many more questions? My supervisor's going to start docking my pay if I'm not back soon.'

'I won't be much longer. Do you happen to know what Mr Watson did for a living?'

'Well, now you come to mention it, I don't think he ever said. He was always out and about, though, so he must've been doing something. And I don't think Mum's ever had any trouble with him over the rent. But no, I don't know what he did.'

'By the way, Miss Baker – do you drink?'

'Drink? Alcohol, you mean?'

'That's right.'

'I can't see what that's got to do with anything, but no, I don't, and I never have done. Did my mum tell you we used to have a pub?'

'Yes, she did mention that.'

'Well, you might think growing up in a pub would've given me the habit, but I can assure you that's not how it works with everyone. When you've seen what drink can do to people the way I have, it can just as easily have the opposite effect. I never liked living there when I was a kid. It was a rough place, with too many rough people, and you know what it's like with some of them – when they've had a few drinks they lose control, and someone gets hurt.'

'Yes, policemen get to see quite a lot of that, sadly.'

'I saw more than enough. When I grew up, I wanted to be somewhere that was quiet and orderly, and that's why I love my job here. It's changing, of course, like everything else – the Post Office started converting us to the new automatic system last year, so now some of our subscribers can dial direct to some of the other exchanges without needing the operator. Although we do still have to handle a huge number of manual calls, including that new 999 number for emergencies. But what I like about working here is that everything's under control – we're trained not to get flustered, we have to speak calmly and clearly, and we have to be formal. We have to say the same things every time, like reading a script – you know, "What number do you require?" "Press button A, caller," "I'm sorry, the line's engaged." And we have to pronounce everything properly too. If you drop your aitches or speak with a local accent they don't take you on. It's a bit like being a machine, and I like that. I never want to end up like some of those old soaks I used to see in the pub, so when it comes to alcohol, I don't touch the stuff, Inspector. Why do you ask?'

'It's just that we found evidence suggesting Mr Watson might've been having a drop of whisky with someone in the Anderson shelter, so we're wondering who that might've been and seeing who we can eliminate.'

'Well, you can cross me off your list, especially if it was whisky – I wouldn't drink that if you paid me to.'

'Right, thank you. Now, after Mr Watson went out yesterday evening, did you see him again?'

'No.' She paused and wiped a finger across her eye. 'I'm sorry, Inspector, it just doesn't seem real – to think I'll never see him again. It's so sad.'

Jago waited for her to compose herself. 'Just one last question, and then I'll let you get back to work. What was your relationship with Mr Watson?'

'My relationship? I don't know what you mean – he was my mum's lodger, that's all.'

'Nothing closer than that?'

'No. Look, Inspector, I should explain – the boy I was walking out with was killed.'

'I'm very sorry. Was it to do with the war?'

'Yes. He was from round here, like me, and we went to school together. He was called Ron. He couldn't get a job, so he joined the navy in 1938. I used to see him whenever he had a spot of leave, and the rest of the time we used to write to each other. But then the war started, and that was that. It only lasted a few weeks for him – he was on that battleship that got sunk by a U-boat in Scapa Flow, the *Royal Oak*. Eight hundred men lost, and he was one of them.'

'I see.'

'It was Ron and all the other men who went down with that ship that I was thinking of yesterday evening when they had that minute's silence on the wireless. That was sad too. But it's not as though we were married or anything. I liked him, yes, but it obviously wasn't to be. Life has to go on, doesn't it? That's what my mum always says, and I think she's right – we can't live in the past. I suppose you could say now I'm waiting for the right man to come along – waiting and hoping.'

CHAPTER TEN

Jago drove past the ranks of double-decker buses drawn up at the bus terminal outside Victoria station and headed north towards Hyde Park Corner. It felt strange to be going about his day's work here instead of in West Ham, but at least there were fresh sights to see. An Anderson shelter in a tiny back yard was the same wherever you were, but there was something invigorating about the bustle in a place like this.

'Do you know what that is?' he said to Cradock, gesturing towards the long brick wall they were passing on their right.

Cradock peered across the road. 'A brick wall, sir?'

'Yes, well done – but who does it belong to?'

'I don't know, sir.'

'Well, you should. It belongs to the man you did solemnly and truly swear to serve when you became a police constable – our Sovereign Lord the King. The other side of that wall's his back garden at Buckingham Palace – a bit bigger than that back yard we were crawling about in this morning, that's for sure.'

'Oh, right.' Cradock tried to sound impressed. 'So he might be in there having a stroll around to stretch his legs even as we speak, I suppose. I expect he's had his lunch too.'

'Ah, Peter, do I detect a subtle hint that you need feeding again?'

'Well, sir, since you mention it, I am feeling a bit peckish. It's been a long time since breakfast.'

'You'll just have to control yourself. I want to know what Dr Gibson's found out about our Mr Watson first.'

At Hyde Park Corner the hospital came into view, as readily identifiable as Gibson had said. Jago parked the car behind it, in Grosvenor Crescent Mews. A narrow passageway led him and Cradock to a door, where a ring of the bell duly summoned a porter to admit them. The man, clearly briefed to expect these police visitors, took them straight to the mortuary.

At first sight the post-mortem room struck Jago as grimly familiar. Despite the grandeur of the hospital's front elevation, it was just like any other repository of the dead he'd been in: a cold dungeon of a place, with the same white-tiled walls, the same array of ugly tools, the same pungent smell of formalin hanging on the air.

Gibson, now dressed in a white coat, looked more like a doctor than he had at the shelter. 'Welcome to my workplace,' he said. 'Although I don't think I can claim it's a particularly welcoming environment in here.'

Jago took in the fittings: the post-mortem slabs with their

ominous drain holes, each with a hosepipe hanging down from the ceiling ready for sluicing it out, a few shelves and cupboards and a stark electric light, and that was about it. Not that the provision of a couple of comfortable chairs for visitors would have made it any more attractive: the very idea was grotesque.

'Thank you, Dr Gibson,' he said. 'I must confess that attending post-mortems isn't high on my list of pleasures. In fact, I usually try to avoid them. It's not that I don't have great respect for your work, but do you think you could excuse me if I don't want to look over your shoulder and follow each incision?'

'Of course, my dear chap. No need to worry, though – I've finished my cutting, so I'll let you know what I found, shall I? It won't take long.'

A second man, also wearing a white coat, entered the room and began to run water into a Belfast sink in the far corner.

'Ah,' said Gibson, 'let me introduce you to my colleague, Mr Spindle.'

The man stepped forward. He had the face of a pallbearer but greeted them with the merest hint of a smile.

'Spindle is our lab technician,' Gibson continued, 'but don't let that title mislead you. He actually assists me in just about everything that needs doing, including keeping me cheerful when the going gets a bit sticky.'

Looking at the technician, Jago couldn't help wondering what state Gibson must get into if this was the man who kept him cheerful.

'He's been working here since he was a boy,' said Gibson. 'Well before my time. How many years is it now, Spindle?'

'Must be getting on for forty, sir,' Spindle replied in a voice that matched his face. 'I was fourteen when I started here, Inspector – straight from school. I knew nothing, of course, but I took to it, and the doctors were kind enough to teach me. It might seem strange, but I've always enjoyed it. The people we get in here have such interesting stories to tell.'

'Even though they're dead?' Jago couldn't help asking.

'Yes – but then Dr Gibson has such a skilful way of, er, drawing it out of them, as you might say.'

Spindle allowed himself a slightly wider smile at his own wit and seemed suddenly more human. He returned to the sink and began putting glass jars into the water.

'So,' said Gibson, 'Spindle's been busy with various tests on the deceased, and I've had a good poke around too, so we should be able to answer some of your questions. I should mention that I've measured him, and he was five feet nine inches tall. Fair hair, blue eyes, average build, as you can see. As for the cause of death, his skull was fractured by a blow on the side of the head with a blunt instrument, causing injury to the cranial contents. I don't suppose you'd like to see the cranial contents?'

'No, I wouldn't, thank you very much. Even if I did, I'm not competent to deduce anything from them, so I think I'll leave that to you.'

'I quite understand. To put it simply, the fracture caused laceration of the brain and intracranial haemorrhage.'

'What people call bleeding in the brain?'

'That's right, and death occurred as a consequence.'

'And the blunt instrument was that spanner?'

'That's not something I can be categorical about – all

I can say is this man has a blunt instrument wound, and the spanner is the kind of blunt instrument that could have caused it. There's a few other points worth noting, too. If you hit someone on the head with a blunt instrument, you're more than likely to have removed it before they start bleeding, so in such cases we often find no blood on the weapon. The fact that there was blood on the spanner could suggest that Mr Watson was struck more than once.'

'Which would mean it was intentional?'

'That's for you to establish, not me, I fancy.'

'Yes, of course. What else?'

'I should just mention what we found concerning the blood. I expect you know there are four blood groups.'

'Yes, I do, although I've heard it's getting more complicated than that nowadays.'

'Yes, that's right – there are some extra distinctions that have been identified in recent years, such as the Rhesus factor, but they haven't come into accepted forensic use yet, so I needn't trouble you with them.'

'I see. So what did you find?'

'We tested the blood on the spanner and found it to be Group A, which is the same as the victim's, but that's of little help – forty-two per cent of people in England have that blood group, so it doesn't positively prove it's his blood. We did find a hair stuck to the spanner by the blood, though. I identified it as head hair, and it was identical with a sample we took from the dead man's head. But that doesn't mean it was necessarily one of *his* hairs, because all we can tell by looking at it is the colour, the texture, and so on. That's not conclusive proof that it was a hair from Mr Watson's head.'

'Not much to go on, then, it would seem.'

'Not a lot, no.'

'Going back to the wound – would the fact that the blow killed him suggest it was more likely to be a man who struck him than a woman?'

'Well, that's where there's a rather more interesting finding. This man's injury was severe, and one might think it would take a heavy blow and therefore greater strength to kill him with something like a spanner. Under normal circumstances, that might lead you to take the view that a man did it, but my examination showed that Mr Watson had an abnormally thin skull.'

'Making him more susceptible to serious injury?'

'Precisely. The human skull is typically between a quarter of an inch and a third of an inch thick, but I found Mr Watson's was only between a quarter and an eighth of an inch, and even thinner in parts – thin enough to mean it wouldn't necessarily need a heavy blow to cause a severe injury to the brain.'

'So it could be either a man or a woman who did it?'

'That would be my conclusion, yes.'

'Thank you. And did you find any alcohol in the deceased's blood?'

'I did, yes, although whether it came from the particular bottle you found in the shelter or from any other I can't say.'

'Of course. And were you able to tell how long after drinking he died?'

'Well, we usually do that by comparing the alcohol content in the blood and in the bladder – it gradually decreases over time in the blood, but in the bladder it doesn't change significantly. That means if we measure the difference in the ratio between the two we can estimate how much time elapsed between the last drink and death. But in this case the result I got suggests that Mr Watson's last ingestion of alcohol was very shortly before his death.'

'So does that mean he could've been having a drink with someone just before he was killed?' asked Cradock.

'It's a possibility, and the result we obtained wouldn't be inconsistent with that, but, of course, it doesn't prove anything. All I'm saying is that my examination indicates he had a drink very shortly before he died. There may have been someone else with him, who may have been drinking, and perhaps from that second mug, but I don't have any way of confirming any of that. You'd need something like a fingerprint other than Watson's on the second mug if you want to suggest that, I suspect. Do you have one?'

'No. I tried, but I think the mug might've been wiped.'

'In that case I'm afraid you'll have to rely on your own professional skills to find out.'

Cradock sighed. 'Yes, I suppose you're right.'

The brief silence that followed was punctuated by an unfortunately conspicuous rumbling from Cradock's stomach.

'I say, Inspector,' said Gibson, 'I suspect your colleague needs fortifying. May I prescribe some treatment? You'd both be very welcome to join me for a restorative bite of lunch in the refectory.'

'That's very kind, Doctor,' Jago replied before Cradock could speak, 'but we have to be going. We'll grab a sandwich on the way.'

'Well, look, why don't I ask Spindle to take Detective

Constable Cradock to the refectory and he can choose some for you both to take with you. They do some very good sandwiches up there.'

'Thank you, Doctor,' said Cradock, his face brightening.

'You see, Inspector – the patient's recovering just at the thought of the treatment.'

'Very well.' Jago slipped Cradock some money. 'Off you go, Peter.'

Cradock departed briskly with Spindle before any minds might be changed.

'Thank you, Doctor,' said Jago when they were out of the door. 'You've been most helpful, and it's been nice getting to know you.'

'You, too,' said Gibson, 'and if you find there's anything else you want to know, don't hesitate to get in touch.' He produced a card from his wallet and handed it to Jago. 'In fact, since you're new to these parts, why don't you come round for a drink one evening? Wednesday would suit me, if you're free – I have a little flat in Knightsbridge, just round the corner from here.'

Jago took the card, wondering whether he should apologise for not having one to give in exchange. 'Thank you,' he said. 'Wednesday evening should be fine.'

CHAPTER ELEVEN

'Right,' said Jago as he started the car, 'you can eat your sandwiches now. What did you get for me?'

'Cheese and pickle, sir. Mr Spindle recommended them.'

'Good. Hand them over, then.'

Cradock crammed one end of a sandwich into his mouth and passed a brown paper bag to Jago, who balanced it on his lap as they set off.

'I want to see if we can find that man Bateman that Mrs Baker mentioned, before he finishes his labours in Battersea Park for the day,' said Jago. 'If he was a pal of Terry Watson, he ought to be able to tell us something useful about the man. I don't propose to ask him whether he knew Watson had a thin skull, though, nor anyone else for that matter – it could be valuable evidence later.'

'Don't worry, sir – I'll keep it under my hat.'

Jago gave Cradock a sideways glance, but his colleague's face was straight.

'Still, it's interesting, isn't it, sir,' Cradock carried on, oblivious. 'What the doctor said, I mean, about Watson's skull. If no one knew, that would mean the person who hit him wasn't to know it'd kill him, so would that mean it wasn't murder?'

'That would be for the judge and the jury to decide, but I believe the law usually takes the view that if you hit someone on the head and they die, it's no defence to say you didn't know they had a thin skull. The fact that they were more vulnerable doesn't make any difference – it'll still be murder or manslaughter or whatever the charge may be. As far as we're concerned, we just need to find out who did it and decide whether there was malice aforethought.'

Jago headed back down towards Victoria and onto Vauxhall Bridge Road. They were a few hundred yards away from the bridge itself when Cradock jumped in his seat and pointed ahead to their left.

'There's one, sir,' he said. 'Shall we stop?'

'One what?' said Jago, braking.

'A poppy seller, sir – I was thinking of what Superintendent Hardacre said.'

'Ah, yes, of course – well done, Peter.'

He brought the car to a halt and got out to see what Cradock had been pointing at. A short way back down the road a middle-aged woman in a smart bottle-green coat and beret was balancing on a pile of debris from a bombed building behind her, only a couple of yards from the cleared pavement. The collecting tin in her left hand and the cardboard tray suspended from a string round her neck, with the words 'Remembrance Day' printed across its front, identified her immediately as a poppy seller. As he set off towards her with Cradock in his wake, he saw a man in a trench coat extend a hand to help her down, scribble something in a notebook, doff his hat and hurry away. The woman brushed a patch of dust off her coat and glanced around, as if hoping no one had witnessed the scene, but in so doing caught sight of the two approaching men. Her face suggested she was embarrassed to have been seen, so Jago raised his own hat and gave her a reassuring smile.

'Good morning, madam,' he said. 'I've been looking for a poppy seller. Could I buy one, please, and one for my colleague here?'

'Of course,' she replied, returning his smile as she picked two penny poppies from her tray.

Jago took a ten-shilling note from his wallet and slipped it into her tin.

'Thank you,' she said. 'That's very generous.'

'Not at all. I'm just thankful I've got my health.'

'You served?'

'Yes, two years in France. No one needs to convince me what we owe to those men.'

'It's a comfort to hear that – I'm a war widow. My husband was in Mesopotamia.'

'I'm sorry.'

'Thank you. At least you'll understand, and that means something to women in my position. I've been on my own since he died, so doing this every November is my own little act of remembrance – and a way of justifying my existence too, I suppose. I seem to have become one of those women they call "full of good works" – if only to fill my time.'

'It can't be easy.'

'One just has to keep busy. So I sell these poppies for

the British Legion once a year, I'm active in the women's section, and I'm on the local branch committee – I'm the treasurer. I do some part-time voluntary administration at the head office too – Haig House is only about ten minutes' walk from here, in Eccleston Square. All rather typical fare, I suppose, but I can't bear the thought of wasting my life when so many have had theirs snatched away or ruined. It's not just men's sufferings I care about, either. I'm on the board of the Pimlico Emergency Home in Gloucester Street too. It does wonderful work – for girls, you know.'

'Is that for girls who've, er, got themselves into, er . . .' said Cradock, his voice trailing off into what seemed to Jago an embarrassed uncertainty.

'Trouble?' she replied.

'Er, yes,' said Cradock.

'That's what some people like to say, but to me they're just women who've found themselves in difficult circumstances, usually through no fault of their own, and we're offering them a refuge.'

Jago sensed it was time to rescue Cradock, and he didn't want to miss Bateman. He glanced at his watch.

'It's been very nice to meet you, Mrs . . .'

'Edgworth.'

'Mrs Edgworth, but my colleague and I had better be on our way. There is something I'd like to ask you before we go, though. We're police officers, you see – I'm Detective Inspector Jago and this is Detective Constable Cradock.'

He produced his warrant card for her inspection, and Cradock followed suit.

'Really?' she replied, perusing the cards briefly. 'Well, of course, I'd be only too pleased to help you. What is it?'

'It's to do with white poppies. I wondered if you might be able to tell me anything about them, particularly with regard to their use here in Pimlico.'

'Well, it wouldn't take long to tell you all I know, but I'm having a cup of tea with a friend this afternoon, and she knows all about them. Would you like to meet her?'

'Yes, please, that would be helpful.'

'In that case, if you're free at four o'clock you'd both be very welcome to join us. Come to my house – it's in Ponsonby Place, where it meets Causton Street. I've lived there for nearly thirty years. Do you know it?'

'No, we're new to this area.'

'I see – well it's a turning off Millbank, near the Tate Gallery and Millbank Barracks, just by the river.'

'Actually, I know it,' said Cradock. 'Causton Street's where Peel House is, isn't it? I did my training there.'

'That's right – you should have no trouble finding us, then.'

'Excuse me for asking, Mrs Edgworth,' he continued, 'but I used to know a Mr and Mrs Silver, who had a shop in Causton Street. Are they still around?'

'Oh, yes. I know them – a lovely couple. But I think things got a bit tight for them and they had to move – they've got a smaller shop now, in Rampayne Street. It's on the right-hand side as you go down from Vauxhall Bridge Road, just opposite the timber yard and Lomath's furniture depository.'

'Thanks. I'd love to see them again.'

'I'm sure they'll be pleased to see you too – as shall we. My house is number 44 – I look forward to seeing you, Inspector. There'll be home-made cake too.'

'That's most kind of you,' said Jago. 'We'll see you at four, then. In the meantime, I hope your sales go well. Goodbye.'

'Goodbye.'

He gave her a final sympathetic smile, then walked back to the car with Cradock.

'She seemed a nice lady,' said Cradock.

'Yes,' said Jago. 'I couldn't help feeling sorry for her.'

'Me too. Still, we've got our red poppies now, so that should keep Superintendent Hardacre off our backs, and we might find out everything we want to know about the white ones over a nice cup of tea later.'

'Not to mention the home-made cake, Peter – that might go some way towards keeping you alive and kicking for another day, I hope.'

'Oh, undoubtedly, sir – undoubtedly.'

CHAPTER TWELVE

Jago started up the car and resumed their journey to Battersea Park, taking Grosvenor Road to skirt the southern edge of Pimlico. To their left was the Thames, grey and sluggish, where crewmen on a passing flat-iron collier were raising the ship's funnel and mast back into their vertical positions after passing under Vauxhall Bridge. A pair of similar vessels could be seen moored at a jetty a little farther upstream, where the southern shoreline was dominated by the new Battersea power station, an art deco brick cathedral that loomed above the river, its two chimneys reaching still higher like twin spires towards the heavens.

Four large cranes were lifting coal from the moored ships' holds and dropping it onto conveyor belts to feed the furnaces. They reminded Jago of the cranes he'd seen on his own side of London, unloading richer assortments of cargo in the Royal Docks. He turned left onto the recently completed Chelsea suspension bridge, and glancing up the river to his right he spotted a distinctively less elegant newcomer: a temporary steel box girder bridge that he guessed was a hastily assembled wartime reserve thrown up in case the German bombers damaged or destroyed the one he was on. Straight ahead, however, he could see a more attractive sight: the gentle greenery of Battersea Park nestling by the waterside.

The impression of gentleness was short-lived. Once Jago and Cradock had left the car and entered the park, they headed to the park superintendent in his lodge and obtained both Bateman's cap number and directions to where they might find him. They set off along the path and were soon greeted by the incongruous sight of a bank of fierce-looking anti-aircraft guns embedded on concrete in the middle of what looked like a running track. They walked on farther and came to an area which looked as though it too had been upended by the war. Here, instead of being concreted, the grass had been dug up and the bare earth ridged into row upon row of vegetables, like a neat market garden.

Bateman was standing alone, smoking a cigarette, with his foot resting on a spade. Unlike the uniformed park keepers, he was dressed anonymously in a heavy jacket, trousers and mud-caked boots, but identifiable by the number on his round, felt London County Council cap.

'Mr Bateman?' said Jago, as they approached him.

'That's me,' he replied, taking his foot off the spade and facing them squarely. 'Who wants to know?'

'I'm Detective Inspector Jago and this is Detective Constable Cradock.'

Bateman took the cigarette from his mouth and looked

them up and down with a wary expression. 'And?'

'We're here with some bad news, I'm afraid. I understand you're a friend of Mr Terry Watson.'

'That's right. What's happened?'

'I'm sorry to have to tell you that Mr Watson was found dead this morning.'

Bateman was silent for a moment, then slowly shook his head from side to side. 'No,' he whispered, 'that can't be . . . I'm sorry – it's a bit of a shock. I . . . How did he die?'

'I'm afraid we're treating it as a case of suspected murder.'

'But . . . who'd do that to Terry? I can't believe it.'

'We don't know yet, but we'd like to talk to you in case there's anything you know that might help us in our enquiries.'

'Of course – whatever I can do to help.'

'Thank you. Were you and Mr Watson close friends?'

'I wouldn't say we were specially close – I don't see him all that often. But we do go back a few years. Who told you we were friends, anyway?'

'It was Mr Watson's landlady, Mrs Baker.'

'Ah, Nancy. Aye, I've known her a while too. When I moved down here from Derbyshire her pub was my local – she told you she used to run a pub, did she?'

'Yes – the George, she said.'

'That's the one. She was behind the bar the first time I went in there and she was friendly to me – helped me settle in and get my first job. That was hod carrying – I may not've had much schooling, but I'm fit and a good worker, and it suited me fine. They were just starting work on the second stage of the power station then, and Nancy put me in touch with someone she knew who took me on. It'll be twice as big as it is now when it's finished, apparently, although I don't know when that'll be now there's a war on.'

'Can you tell me when you last saw Mr Watson?'

Bateman took a final drag on his cigarette and ground the butt into the soil with his boot. 'Let me see, now. That would've been last Thursday – that's my day off. I was round at Nancy's and I saw him there – I was mainly doing a bit of work on the garden for her, but she needed an old wardrobe shifting and he gave me a hand. I like to do odd little favours for her if I can, by way of a thank you – I owe her everything, really.'

'Yes, she told us you look after her vegetable patch for her.'

'Well, at least that's one thing I do know about, being a gardener by trade nowadays. It's all changed since I started, though – normally I'd be planting tulip bulbs here now, ready for the spring, but you can see the park's all been dug up. Thirty acres of allotments we've got now, where it used to be just grass. A ten-rod plot can produce enough vegetables to last a family most of the year, so now we've got loads of enthusiastic local folk trying to grow as much as they can – you know, "Dig for Victory." Keen as mustard, they are, but half of them haven't a clue what they're doing, so I end up having to teach them what's what, like taking the yellow leaves off those sprouts over there so they don't go mouldy. That's why I'm off on Thursdays – I have to work the weekends, because that's when most people can get here to look after their plots. But anyway, what else do you want to know?'

'Did Mr Watson ever say anything that might make

you think he had enemies?'

'What, Terry? No, never.'

'Do you know of anyone who might've wanted to do him harm?'

'No.'

'Do you know of any other friends he had, apart from you?'

Bateman paused, his lips pursed in thought. 'Not particularly, no, now you come to mention it. He could be a bit private when he wanted to – kept himself to himself.'

'Mrs Baker mentioned that you and Mr Watson were members of the same cycling club.'

'Aye, that's right.'

'She said there was another man who visited Mr Watson at her house, and she thought he might be a member too.'

'What's his name?'

'She didn't know, but she said he was an older man, on the short side, and going thin on top. Do you know who that might be?'

'It sounds like Fred Cook.'

'Can you tell me where I might find him?'

'I can. He lives in Hugh Street, over by the railway lines, where that pilot landed the other week.'

Jago's blank look must have betrayed his ignorance of the incident.

'He was an RAF lad – Hurricane pilot. There was a daylight raid – a bunch of Dornier bombers trying to hit Buckingham Palace, or so they say. This lad shot one of them down, but his own plane was damaged and went down too. He bailed out and landed in Hugh Street, right as rain. Had a spot of trouble, though, by all accounts –

some of the locals thought he was a German at first, but he managed to convince them he was one of ours.'

'I see. And what number is Mr Cook's house?'

'It's number 76, just opposite Alderney Street – him and his wife have got the bottom flat. But if you're looking for him during opening hours it might be worth calling in at the pub first. The Duke of Clarence, at the top end of Sutherland Street – that's his local. If he's there you can't miss him – he's always in the saloon bar at his own special table over in the back corner, with a couple of big potted ferns next to it, like it was his private office.'

'Thank you. And the cycling club – would that be the Pimlico Wheelers?'

'Aye, that's the local club – it's part of the CTC.'

'I saw that on a magazine cover this morning. What does it stand for?'

'Cyclists' Touring Club. Some people say it stands for Collar and Tie Club, because it's all solicitors and accountants and the like, and I don't think Terry would've joined if there'd been any choice, but the Wheelers are the only club in Pimlico. Mind you, they didn't turn their noses up at having me and Terry as members, nor Fred Cook for that matter, so maybe they're not as bad as people make out. Terry was more a Clarion man at heart, I think.'

'Clarion?'

'The Clarion's another national cycling club, and a big rival to the CTC – very socialist. Terry loved his cycling, though, and I think what he liked about being in a local club was the competition, the racing and such like, so he'd probably have joined anything as long as it could give him that. Besides, he introduced me to the Wheelers, so he can't have thought they were that bad.'

'And I gather it was you who introduced him to Mrs Baker – she said you sent him round to her when there was a fire at his previous lodgings, because you knew she needed a lodger.'

Bateman looked puzzled. 'Well, I certainly sent him round, but he never said anything to me about a fire. He just said he didn't like it where he was and wanted a change.'

'That's curious. Is there any reason why he might say one thing to her and another to you?'

'Not that I can think of. But anyway, I don't even know if he did – I mean, I wasn't there when he was talking to Nancy, was I? She might've got mixed up. Can't help you there, I'm afraid.'

'Never mind, Mr Bateman. Just one last question – can you tell me where you live, in case we need to speak to you again outside working hours?'

'Aye, I'm in the Peabody buildings – those long blocks of flats over by the railway. Some rich American put them up in Queen Victoria's time, apparently, for the working poor, which is what I am, I suppose. I'm in Y Block, flat number 3.'

'And what time do you normally finish work?'

'At this time of year about five o'clock, sometimes earlier. The council always cut our hours down from now till February – not so much for us to do in the winter, you see, although that's not true now with this war on. Not that I mind – I'm glad to have a council job. There's plenty of gardeners in this country who find themselves unemployed for most of the winter, and if they've got a family they can all end up starving. Thankful for small mercies, that's what I am.'

A uniformed park keeper in a peaked cap strolled by, eyeing them officiously.

Jago glanced at his watch. 'Well, thank you, Mr Bateman, you've been very helpful. We'd better not keep you from your duties. I expect you have a lot to do.'

'You can say that again – we've got a ton of horse manure over there that's not going to dig itself in, so if you'll excuse me, gentlemen, I'll bid you good day.'

CHAPTER THIRTEEN

Sally Edgworth's home in Ponsonby Place was a neat little terraced house that reminded Jago of the ones they'd seen that morning in Gerald Road. Her own appearance when she opened the front door was equally neat – in a smart turquoise dress and impeccably made up, she looked like a woman who took pains from the moment she rose to ensure she was fit to welcome whatever visitors the day might bring.

She invited the two detectives in with a smile, hung their coats on a stand and showed them into a small front room that was conventionally furnished but bedecked with a surprising number of garish paintings. They struck Jago as very modern in style, and he hoped he wouldn't be asked to express an opinion on them.

'It's so nice that you're able to join us this afternoon, gentlemen,' she said.

'Very kind of you to invite us, Mrs Edgworth,' Jago replied.

'Oh, do call me Sally.'

Jago gave only a polite smile in reply. It was indeed kind of her to entertain them for tea, but the purpose of their visit required that he maintain the formality of his duty.

'A charming house,' he said.

'Thank you – though you might not think so if you visited when the Thames was running high. We've had water halfway up the street before now.'

'Really?'

'Yes, but I think we're safe today.'

'I'm glad to hear it. And I see you still have your railings.'

'Yes, they're the original ones from about a century ago, so they may have been excused on grounds of historic value, but I think it's probably because if they were taken away we'd get people falling ten feet down into the areas every night in the blackout and breaking their necks. Imagine the casualty rate.'

'Not a happy thought, I grant you. By the way, is your friend joining us?'

'Oh, yes – she'll be here in a moment. I'll just go and put the kettle on. Do take a seat at the table.'

She left the room, and they could faintly hear the sounds of activity in the kitchen. When she returned, she found Jago staring at the wall.

'Ah, the paintings,' she said, joining them at the table. 'I should explain – my husband was an artist. He saw some of Kandinsky's work at an exhibition at the Albert Hall about thirty years ago and they inspired him – he completely changed the way he painted, and these are some of the works he created before he was taken away by the war. There's so much vibrant colour in them, isn't there? So much energy. He was very talented.'

'Yes, er, the colours are certainly very strong,' said Jago. Sensing he was already at the limit of his ability to voice an intelligent appreciation of abstract art, he didn't attempt to elaborate.

'Not your cup of tea, perhaps, Inspector?'

'It's more a case of ignorance, I'm afraid – I've never been taught how to understand painting.'

'I'll have to teach you then – when you're not so busy, perhaps. And you, Detective Constable – do you enjoy modern art?'

She might just as well have pulled a gun from her pocket and aimed it at him. Cradock opened his mouth, but no words came out.

'Not your cup of tea either, perhaps,' she said. 'Well, I think I can hear Alice coming down the stairs, so we'll all have a proper cup of tea, shall we?'

Jago had assumed that Mrs Edgworth's friend would be arriving at the front door rather than from upstairs, but it was not the sort of thing a man should ask about.

Sally left the room again and returned a couple of minutes later, followed by a shy-looking young woman in a plain, high-buttoned dress carrying a tray laden with a tea set and a round cake, which she deposited on the table. To Jago's eye she looked more like a live-in maid than a fellow guest for afternoon tea, but jumping to conclusions was a practice he discouraged. He got to his feet to acknowledge the arrival of the second woman and caught Cradock's eye with a faint twitch of his head to ensure his young colleague observed the social niceties of the occasion and stood too.

'Alice,' said Sally, 'this is Detective Inspector Jago, and

this is Detective Constable Cradock. They're the policemen I told you about. And this, gentlemen, is my friend Alice Mason. Now, let's all sit down and have some tea.'

They sat, and she poured four cups of tea from a china teapot. Jago could see Cradock was eyeing the cake and hoped their hosts could not.

'Here's that cake I promised you,' said Sally, apparently reading his thoughts. 'Home-made sponge. I must apologise if it's not quite as light as I usually manage, but unfortunately my grocer didn't have any eggs and he'd sold out of egg powder too, so I've had to make it without one. They seem to be in rather short supply at the moment, don't they? Eggs, I mean. More expensive too, when you can find them. I do hope the government doesn't start rationing them – although I suppose that might mean I'd get one instead of none.'

She cut portions of sponge and passed them round on small china plates, together with cake forks and cups of tea. Jago was prepared for a stodgy disappointment, but when he took his first bite of the sponge he was pleasantly surprised. It was a little drier than some he'd had, but it tasted very good.

'No need to apologise, Mrs Edgworth,' he said. 'It's delicious.'

Cradock nodded his head in enthusiastic agreement but appeared to have too much cake in his mouth to speak.

'You're too kind,' said Sally. 'And how do you find it, Alice?'

'Oh, yes, very nice, thanks. Your baking's much better than mine.'

'Not at all, dear – yours is excellent. Now, Alice,

I must tell you how I met these policemen. It was most extraordinary. I was out on Vauxhall Bridge Road when a man came up to me quite out of the blue and said he wanted to take a photograph of me – because I was selling poppies, you see. It was all a bit embarrassing, really.'

She turned to Jago. 'You must have thought it a very strange scene, Inspector.'

'No, not at all,' Jago replied. 'Just a little unusual. Was that the man in the trench coat?'

'Yes – he said he was a newspaper photographer, and he wanted a picture for his paper. I'm always one to be helpful if I can, so I agreed, but I soon wished I hadn't. He made me stand on a pile of rubble that some Pioneer Corps soldiers were clearing up on a bomb site, then just grabbed the nearest one and told him to stand next to me while I gave him a poppy, so he could take a few pictures. I know newspaper people have to be confident, but really . . .'

Jago smiled to himself. He was thinking of a particular newspaper person who was certainly nothing if not confident. When he'd first met Dorothy Appleton, London war correspondent for the *Boston Post*, he'd been annoyed to find himself, a detective inspector in the Metropolitan Police, ordered to nursemaid her round the blitzed areas of East London while she did her reporting. But he'd soon discovered she didn't need protecting. Yes, a very confident woman, but then perhaps all American women were – he wasn't in a position to judge.

'You wouldn't catch me talking to the press,' said Alice. 'They're all scoundrels – at least, that's what my dad used to say. And anyway, how did you know he was a newspaper man? He might've been just a common thief trying to get his hands on your collecting tin.'

'I'm not that naive, Alice. I demanded some confirmation of his identity, and he gave me his card. I'm sure that's what you would have said I should do, isn't it, Inspector?'

'Oh, yes,' said Jago. 'And make sure it looks genuine, of course.'

'Yes, and it did. I asked him why on earth he wanted a picture of me, and he said he wanted to show me climbing over the wreckage to give the soldier a poppy, then the paper could use it with a caption saying something like the air raids on Armistice Day didn't stop the poppy sellers doing their job. I felt a fraud, to be honest, because for one thing there were no air raids while I was on duty, and in any case I don't normally climb over wreckage to sell them, and I certainly didn't have the right shoes on for it. I thought my fellow poppy sellers would think I was showing off or would just laugh at it, but he said a picture like that would be a good morale-booster.'

'Perhaps he was right,' said Jago. 'You know – plucky British people carry on undaunted, that sort of thing.'

'Yes, I can understand that, but I found it a little confusing. What I mean is, that's exactly what we are doing, isn't it? We're all trying to do our bit to keep normal life going and not to let the bombs get us down, and people are being terribly brave about it all. But photos like that always look specially posed – because that's what they are – so they're clearly not real. Do the newspapers think we can be fooled that easily?'

'I don't know. Perhaps they think pictures of people keeping their spirits up help everyone to do the same, in which case maybe it's excusable. We certainly need all the help we can get. Maybe they thought it'd be good publicity for the Haig Fund too – I mean, if it reminds people and prompts a few more to buy a poppy, it can only be a good thing, can't it?'

'Yes, I suppose you're right. But I don't sell poppies so I can get my picture in the papers. I do it for the same reason as all the other women – for those poor men who came home from the war maimed and crippled and ended up selling matches and shoelaces on the streets. When I think what they did for us, I feel ashamed. We broke faith with them – we should have treated them better. There can hardly be a family in the country that wasn't touched by that war.'

She fell silent and turned her head away towards the windows and the street beyond.

'Sally lost her husband in the war,' said Alice quietly.

'Yes, I know,' Jago replied.

Sally turned back to face him. 'That's why I sell those poppies too,' she replied. 'For my husband – to keep him alive in my heart. People seem to have no idea how awful that Mesopotamia campaign was. Mention the siege of Kut to young people today and their faces are blank, yet it was one of the worst disasters of the war. It must have been unbearable for the men, fighting for their lives against overwhelming odds and with disease everywhere. I met a man a few years ago who'd been a stretcher-bearer there, and he told me nearly all our troops had malaria – in fact, he reckoned that killed more of our men than the Turks did. Charles was one of them.'

She picked up the teapot and silently topped up their cups.

'And now here we are again, with all our young men going off to fight. Do you have any sons, Inspector?'

'No, I don't.'

'Neither do I. I would have liked to have children, but now . . . I sometimes think what if I'd had a son twenty years ago? He might be in the army now, and I'd be worried about him being killed. When I'm selling those poppies I'm thinking about the past, but I can't help wondering how many of today's young lads will end up joining the men we're raising money for.'

'I suppose we should be thankful they're not stuck out in Flanders fighting and dying in trenches this time.'

'Yes, but what comes next? And even if we're not invaded this winter, how will we ever get the Germans out of France and everywhere else? France was so strong in the last war, but now she's beaten – and last time we had the Americans with us towards the end at least, but now we're on our own. It seems a wicked thing to say, but I find myself glad I didn't have any children, and doubly glad I had no sons.' She took a deep breath, as if to steady herself, and forced a smile. 'More cake, anyone?'

Cradock responded eagerly, but Jago, still hoping to keep his appointment this evening and eat with Dorothy, politely declined, as did Alice.

'There you are, Detective Constable,' Sally continued, handing Cradock a generous second portion. 'I'm glad you're enjoying it. Now, Mr Jago, you must forgive me for digressing – you wanted to ask Alice about the white poppies. Is that all right, Alice?'

'I suppose so,' said Alice. 'But I'm a bit suspicious when policemen come round asking questions.'

'Why would that be?' said Jago.

'Because policemen take their orders from the bigwigs, the high and mighty, and they're the people who start all these wars in the first place. They seem to think it's a great idea to send all our men off to fight other countries – they say it's for God, the King and the Empire, but some of us aren't so sure.'

'I can understand that. Is that why you sell the white poppies?'

'Yes. We don't agree with what the red poppies represent, so we sell white ones instead.'

'And what do you think the red poppies represent?'

'All those things I just said – celebrating war, making it sound like something wonderful, going out and attacking other countries to make them part of our empire, glorifying death – all that, and more. Do you wear one?'

'A red one? Yes, I do, but I can assure you I'm not celebrating things like that when I do.'

'In that case, perhaps you should be wearing a white one.'

'I think I might be in trouble with some of those bigwigs you mentioned if I did.'

This didn't bring a smile to her lips, but she seemed to relax a little.

'Do you sell them every year?' Jago asked.

'If you mean me personally, this was my first time, but other people've been doing it for six or seven years, I think. Have you heard of the Co-operative Women's Guild?'

'Yes, it's part of the co-operative movement, isn't it?'

'That's right, and it doesn't mean they're co-operative. You'd probably think they're a bolshy lot – they want to change things. Anyway, some of them started it – they wanted it to be a symbol of peace. The British Legion hated it.' She glanced at Sally. 'Sorry, Sally, you know I don't mean that personally. I don't know how you can sit through all those meetings with that Mr Trubshaw, though.'

'Trubshaw?' said Cradock. 'Is that the cycling club man? We came across his name somewhere else this morning.'

'Yes,' said Sally. 'Mr Trubshaw and I are both on the local British Legion branch committee, and he has some rather strong views on the subject of white poppies, shopkeepers, wars and foreigners in general. I don't believe he speaks for the rest of the committee on such matters, let alone for the Legion as a whole, and I for one find his opinions very distasteful. And since I work for the British Legion, I should mention that in the last few years running up to the war it tried very hard to prevent one starting. The national chairman made official visits all over Europe – he even had a meeting with Hitler. I think most people in the Legion are too well acquainted with the misery of war to want another one.'

'Thank you for explaining that,' said Jago. 'So, Miss Mason – it is Miss, isn't it?'

'Yes, it is.'

'Thank you. So, could you tell me when you were selling your white poppies?'

'Just this last weekend – yesterday and Saturday.'

'And where was that?'

'In Battersea Park.'

'Oh, really? Why there?'

'It's just a place I like. I grew up in Battersea and I still go to the park whenever I can. If you're going to stand around for hours trying to sell poppies you might as well have some nice trees to look at.'

'Do you sell many?'

'Not really, but it always takes time to change how people think, doesn't it? People over there seem to be too keen on the war, as far as I can tell. Look at what happened to that bloke who stood in the by-election in North Battersea back in April – said he was the anti-war candidate, and hardly anyone voted for him. I suppose people are just angry about the bombing. Still, I sold a few, so it was worth going.'

'I'd be interested to know whether you sold a couple of poppies to a particular young man.'

'Well, if you can give me a bit of a clue – what did he look like?'

'Of course. He would've been about five foot nine, average build, fair hair, blue eyes. And he may have had a bicycle with him, but not necessarily.'

'And young, you said? How young?'

'About thirty.'

She screwed up her face in thought. 'No, I don't think I recall anyone like that buying one. It's mostly women that want them, and they're a bit older. War widows, I suppose, but you never know, do you?'

'I suppose you don't.'

She got to her feet and gave a faint smile. 'Anyway, I'm afraid I have to pop out now. If I remember your young man I'll be sure to let you know. Will that be all?'

'Yes – thank you,' Jago replied. 'But before you go, could you just tell me where I can find you if I need to know more?'

She glanced at Sally, who broke into the conversation.

'Alice is staying with me at the moment, Inspector. I have a telephone, so if it would be more convenient you can call in advance to check that she's in or to arrange a time to drop by. The number's Victoria 3157.'

By the time Jago had written the number in his notebook, Alice was closing the door behind her.

'I'm sorry about that,' said Sally. 'She can be a little abrupt at times, but she's a rather shy girl, and I think talking to the police may have been a daunting experience for her. She's only twenty-one, but she's already had some bad experiences in her short life.'

'With the police?'

'No, no. I don't want you to get the wrong impression of Alice. She's a sweet girl, but it's just . . .'

'Yes?'

'Well, the thing is, that's why she's staying with me. I'm trying to help her and support her. I told you I'm on the board of the Pimlico Emergency Home, didn't I?'

'Ah, yes. I think I begin to see. She was one of the girls there?'

'Yes, that's right. I think you'll understand if I say she's not very confident with men, especially strong men. She may have found being questioned by two policemen intimidating.'

'I'm sorry.'

'It's not your fault. I didn't think you were intimidating at all, but she's easily frightened.'

'Not too scared to stand in a park trying to sell white poppies to people who all support the war, though?'

'It was I who encouraged her to do it when she

mentioned the possibility. I thought it might help to build her confidence – she's got to learn to believe in herself or she'll always be a victim. I've been trying to teach her to stand up for herself and not let men bully her.'

CHAPTER FOURTEEN

'A penny for your thoughts?' said Dorothy, leaning forward to catch Jago's attention.

'Oh, I'm sorry,' he said with a jump, like a man caught napping in front of guests. 'My mind was elsewhere.'

The restaurant, tucked away in a side street near Drury Lane, was quiet, a perfect place for relaxed conversation, but he realised he'd neither spoken nor touched his food. For how long, he couldn't tell, but it was clearly long enough for her to notice.

'Where was it?' she asked. 'Back on your latest case, whatever that may be?'

'Not this time, no. I was just looking at the clock over there and thinking about what I was doing at this time twenty-two years ago.'

'In 1918?'

'Yes, on the eleventh of November.'

'Ah, of course. Armistice Day. So, what were you doing?'

'I was still at the front when the war ended, and I think by this time of the evening I was just trying to take in the idea that it was really all over, and I'd drunk rather more than I should have. Probably celebrating because we'd won – it was like we'd come to the end of history. Everything would be simple and peaceful from now on.'

'The innocence of youth, eh?' she laughed.

'Too true. Best not to think about that, though.'

He took a mouthful of food, grateful to her for snapping him out of his memories. She was the one he wanted to focus on, and having managed to keep their appointment, he didn't want to waste a moment. Three-quarters of an hour had passed since the blackout began, but so far the sirens had not been called into action. How long that would remain the case was anyone's guess.

'So,' he said, 'how's your day been?'

'I've been busy. I was in Whitehall this morning, at the Cenotaph.'

'You were there? I thought the Armistice Day service had been cancelled.'

'It was. So I went down there at eleven o'clock to see what happened, or rather what didn't happen. I wrote a piece about it for the paper this afternoon. You weren't there yourself, were you?'

'No. I was otherwise engaged with a body in an Anderson shelter, unfortunately, but I knew there wasn't going to be one this year. It's not surprising, really – the government was bound to be worried there might be an air raid while the King and the prime minister and the rest of the great and the good were all out there on the street laying wreaths. It was the same last year. Was anyone there today? Normally there'd be people standing twenty deep near the Cenotaph.'

'I saw a few officials laying wreaths on behalf of the King and so on, and some members of the public too, but there was no formal service or marching or anything like that.'

'I heard they cancelled the two minutes' silence as well.'

'Yes. I thought that was sad. I was told it was because your government reckoned there was a risk of confusion with the air-raid warning signals, which I didn't understand, but they said it's because you used to use sirens to mark the two minutes. Anyway, the ordinary people who were there still did it, all standing in the bitter cold.'

'Good. I'd have liked to be there myself, but duty called. I did go to a Remembrance Day service yesterday, though.'

'Really? You surprise me. I didn't think you went to church.'

'I don't, but I was thinking of something I read in the paper the other day about the Archbishop of Canterbury. Apparently he said we should remember our recent dead as well as the less recent, and I thought that was good – we've had so many losses this year. I also liked what he said about the war – he said we must win it, but when we get victory we've got to make sure we make proper use of it. I don't think we made proper use of it last time, and if we had done, Germany might not've needed a Hitler.'

'Where did you go?'

'St Paul's.'

'The cathedral?'

'Yes. I thought tongues might wag if I was sighted in a local church. Besides, I reckoned the choir would be better there, not to mention the acoustics – but when I arrived I discovered the service was being held down in the crypt, because last month a bomb went through the roof and smashed up the altar.'

'And was the service good?'

'Yes – the choir lived up to my expectations. Did you go to one somewhere?'

'No – I had to work, unfortunately.'

'On a Sunday?'

'If you're a journalist you work whenever your paper tells you to.'

'So what was the story that chained you to your typewriter?'

'Neville Chamberlain, of course. As soon as they announced his death yesterday lunchtime I knew I'd have my editor wanting something double-quick, so I got straight down to it.'

'And what did you say about him?'

'I decided to quote what Churchill said when Chamberlain resigned from the War Cabinet last month – "You did all you could for peace, you did all you could for victory." I thought that summed it up nicely. I guess his whole life's overshadowed now by that word "appeasement" – people only think of him as the weak guy with the wing collar and umbrella who tried to appease Hitler and kept giving in to him. But what else could he do? Your country wasn't in a position to stop Hitler, but Chamberlain bought you some time to build up your armed forces. I doubt whether you'd have all those Spitfires fighting off the Luftwaffe today if he hadn't. I think he was a decent and sincere man who tried to do the best for his country and had the misfortune to be leading it when he did.'

'And now he'll never know how it all ended. But we don't choose when we die, do we?'

'No, we don't.'

Dorothy's voice caught, and she fell silent. She looked down at the table as if not wanting to meet Jago's gaze, then took a small lace handkerchief from her handbag and dabbed at her eyes.

'Is something the matter?' he asked gently.

'I'm OK,' she replied. 'It's just that I've had some bad news – about another war a long way away.'

'I'm sorry – what's happened?'

She looked up at him. 'It's a friend of mine, Judith. She's a foreign reporter on the *Boston Post*, like me, and she's been out in China covering the war with Japan. She was in Chungking. Most people have never heard of the place – it's right in the middle of the country, and the government moved the capital there when Nanking fell in thirty-seven. The Japanese air force has been bombing it for more than a year now, and it seems like she just got caught in one of the attacks. She was killed – the paper cabled me yesterday to let me know. When you said we don't choose when we die it made me think of her, and what a waste it is.'

Jago could see the sadness in her eyes. He wanted to take her hands and comfort her. He wanted to be the one she felt safe to release her grief with, but he couldn't bring himself to invade her privacy. Instead he waited for the moment it took her to compose herself.

'I'm sorry,' he said. 'I really am – it must've been an awful shock for you.'

She put the handkerchief back in her bag and smiled. 'Thank you, John. It was. I wanted to tell you because you know what it's like to lose dear friends in a war. I knew you'd understand and wouldn't just come out with some trite platitudes.'

He said nothing in reply but gave a self-effacing shrug of his shoulders.

'No, really, John. You're like a rock, an anchor, and I need someone like that.'

Inside, he felt a momentary joy that she might perhaps need him, but his face gave nothing away. 'I'm not one for clever words,' he said, 'and I don't think you need them. War is cruel, and there's no way round it.'

They sat in silence for some time. Dorothy was the first to speak.

'OK, I can't sit here feeling sorry for myself – that's not going to help anyone. When you go to a war zone as a journalist you have to accept it – you always know it's the price you may have to pay. A bit like being a policeman, I guess – you're the one who has to face the danger when other people are getting out as fast as they can. My job's a duty, the same as yours. Now, let's talk about something else.'

There was something else Jago wanted to talk about, something important that had been nagging at his mind, but he didn't know how to start. There was an awkward silence, relieved only by the arrival of the waitress with their desserts. When she had gone they began to eat, but without speaking. Jago was still struggling with what to say when Dorothy put her spoon down and gave him an attentive look.

'So, what have you been doing today, John?'

'Well,' he replied, thankful that she hadn't asked anything more demanding, 'I actually drove past your hotel this morning.'

'And you didn't drop by?'

'I imagined you'd be working, and it sounds like I was right. I was driving along the Embankment, heading for Pimlico. When I got to work today I discovered I'd been poached by the new chief constable of the CID – that's the man in charge of all the detective work for the Metropolitan Police. He had a suspicious death over in Pimlico and no one there to deal with it, so he pulled me in, which means now I'm attached to Scotland Yard.'

'And Peter?'

'Him too. It was a bit of a surprise, I can tell you.'

'This is the body you mentioned, in the Anderson shelter, right?'

'Yes.'

'So is it a murder case?'

'Looks like it.'

'And you're both Scotland Yard detectives now? That sounds exciting.'

'Not to me. I'm happy just keeping things as straight as I can in my little corner of south-west Essex. I've never been desperate to do the same job anywhere else, but now life and the Metropolitan Police Service seem to have decided differently. I suppose I'll just have to put up with it.'

'I can't imagine you just putting up with it, John. I think you'll do the best you possibly can, and that'll be a lot better than what most other men do. And believe me, if my experience is anything to go by, if you can do a job half decently in one place, you can do it anywhere.'

Jago pictured in his mind what little he knew of her previous reporting assignments. 'I suppose you're right,' he said. 'And being sent to help out on the other side of London isn't exactly going to live in Poland or Czechoslovakia, is it? I dare say I'll cope.'

'Cope? You won't just cope, John, you'll love it. But hey, does that mean no more good times at Rita's cafe? I'll miss her – she's a good source for how people are getting on with the Blitz.'

'You've no need to worry on that score. I'm certainly not forsaking Rita, and as far as I know young Peter isn't giving up on her Emily. It's not even ten miles from there to Pimlico, and I've got to pop back to pick up a few odds and ends, so why don't we try to meet up for lunch at her place?'

'I'd like that. I can be free tomorrow – would that be OK?'

'It depends what's happening on the case, but let's say yes, subject to operational requirements.'

'It's a date, then. Twelve-thirty? And you'll bring Peter?'

'Of course. Shall I pick you up somewhere? I'll be driving across London.'

'Thanks for the offer, but I'm not sure yet where I'll be tomorrow morning. I'll just take the train from Liverpool Street and see you at Rita's.'

'OK.' Jago glanced up at the clock again. 'Look,' he said, 'I don't want you to think I'm fussing over you, but I think you should be getting back to your hotel. We could be in for a raid soon, and I'd feel happier knowing you were within easy reach of that basement shelter you've got there.'

'But what about you?'

'Oh, I'll be all right. I'm an old soldier, aren't I? I'll get the Tube back over to Pimlico in no time at all.'

He paid the bill and fetched her coat for her. They walked back down Drury Lane to the Aldwych and then round to the Savoy in the cold evening air. When they arrived at the hotel's front entrance Dorothy reached out her hand towards the door.

'Wait a moment,' said Jago, steeling himself. 'There's something I have to ask you.'

'Yes?'

'Let's move over here.'

He took a few steps towards the corner of Savoy Court, and she followed him.

'What is it?' she said.

'It's rather delicate. Do you mind?'

'Of course not,' she replied. 'You can ask me anything.'

'It's about the last time I saw you – it's been nagging at me all the time, and I can't get it out of my mind.'

'Get what out of your mind?'

'What happened that evening when I was walking you back here. We came along the river and stopped to sit on that bench in the Victoria Embankment Gardens, and I told you about that German soldier in the shell hole. Do you remember?'

'When you said you wanted to be known and understood by someone, and you thought that person was me? Of course I remember. I felt honoured that you should say that.'

'That's why I wanted you to know the truth about me – to know the worst of me, the worst thing I'd ever done.

That's why I told you about that soldier – the fact that I could've chosen to let him go but I killed him. I took a man's life, just like that, and I've never forgotten it. I needed to know whether you'd reject me when you knew that.'

He tried to search out the expression in her eyes, but everything around them was blacked out and there was too little moonlight to tell.

'I didn't, John,' she said. 'I think I understand what you felt then and what you feel now.'

'But when I told you what I'd done, I saw a tear in your eye, and that picture's printed on my mind. I didn't dare ask you what it meant, but ever since then I've been desperate to know. So what was it? I didn't mean to upset you. Should I not have told you? Can you ever think of me as a friend again now you know I'm capable of such a thing?'

'I accept that you were, because you've told me you were, but I don't believe you're capable of such a thing now. We can't change the past, but we can learn from it and change the future. That tear didn't mean I was upset – your story made me cry because I could feel just a little of how awful that moment must have been in your life. It's an experience I wouldn't want anyone to have to go through. And you needn't worry that I'd reject you because of that – I felt doubly honoured because you'd chosen to tell me the worst thing I might ever find out about you. Really, John, I mean it – I'm honoured.'

'Thank you. That means a lot to me – more than I could say.'

'Well, I'm glad you've asked me. And now I think I'd better go in, don't you?'

'Yes, yes, of course.'

They took the few paces back to the Savoy's entrance together.

'Well, goodnight, John,' she said. 'And thank you.'

'Goodnight,' he replied, and stood aside as she stepped through the door into the warmth of the hotel.

When she was lost to his sight he turned away and walked back towards the Strand, his heart lighter.

CHAPTER FIFTEEN

At eight o'clock sharp the next morning Jago was in New Scotland Yard, stepping into the office of Arthur Ford, newly promoted Chief Constable of the Metropolitan Police CID. He was not surprised to find it was a little more spacious than the one in which they'd last met, when Ford was a detective superintendent in Special Branch, and that it also commanded an agreeable view over the Thames. Now, as then, he received a warm welcome.

'It's good to see you, John,' said Ford, clasping his hand. 'Take a seat.'

Jago did so and faced Ford across the desk.

'I'm sorry if I've dragged you here against your will,' Ford continued. 'I seem to remember not so very long ago telling you I'd be glad to have you in Special Branch on a permanent transfer after you did that secondment to us, but you didn't exactly leap at the chance, did you?'

'You're right, sir, I didn't. I hope you know I really

enjoyed working for you, but I think my heart was more in what I'd call ordinary policing. Liaising with the French police over that arms smuggling into Spain was interesting, but I realised I get more satisfaction from taking a murderer off the streets here.'

'I can understand that, and it's because you're good at it that I've got you here. I've brought you in because we're running short of good men – seventy-eight Metropolitan Police officers killed by enemy action in the last couple of months since the Blitz began, and more than four hundred injured. It's something I've been thinking of doing for a while, but now I've got a detective inspector smashed up in hospital with injuries from an air raid, so this new case was the straw that threatened to break the camel's back. I've poached you to make sure that doesn't happen.'

'I see, yes. I'll do my best.'

'You probably think over in West Ham that the West End's got it easy, and you're probably right, but there's been a lot of bombs falling round Pimlico way. There was a nasty one three or four weeks ago – a land mine in Alderney Street. Two dozen people killed, a hundred and fifty houses wrecked, three hundred people made homeless in the blink of an eye. So what with the bombing and the crime, we're stretched pretty thin – I'm going to be depending on you.'

'Any idea how long this secondment will last, sir?'

'It's definitely temporary, as things stand. Technically, you'll remain on the strength of K Division – you'll be on loan here. But it won't just be for this one case, so you should assume months, not weeks, and quite frankly, the way things are going right now, who knows what might happen? You could find yourself sitting in that chair someday soon reporting to a Gestapo officer. But let's not think about that – it's not going to happen. And there's no promotion in it for you, I'm afraid, or for your man Cradock – money's short at the moment, as I'm sure you'll understand.'

'Yes, sir.'

'I gather we're putting you up in Rochester Row for the time being.'

'Yes, sir – and DC Cradock in the Ambrosden Avenue section house.'

'Right, well, I hope it's not too unbearable. We'll see if we can sort something better out for you, but being in Central Branch means you'll be deployed anywhere in the Metropolitan Police District and beyond – wherever we need you – so you'll probably find yourselves moving around a bit. I believe you've sampled the exotic delights of Gerald Road already.'

'Very briefly, sir, yes – yesterday morning.'

'Nice little nick, isn't it? Mind you, it's a bit poky inside – hardly enough space to move.'

'Yes, very cosy, sir, from what I could tell. Classy sort of area for a police station, though.'

'You've met the neighbours, then, have you? Some of them are a bit classy too.'

'They did say Noel Coward lives down the road a bit, if that's what you mean, sir, but I don't suppose he'll be inviting the likes of me round for a drink.'

'You never know. But according to the papers he's on his way from America to Australia at the moment, so you won't be bumping into him when he's putting the milk bottles out.'

'Yes. It's got a few backs up, hasn't it – him swanning off round the world while the rest of us have to stay here and face the bombs.'

'You're right, but don't be too quick to judge – there may be more to it than meets the eye. He was in Paris at the beginning of the war, but I heard he was doing some official work for the Admiralty that he didn't talk about in public. Then he went to America on a business trip to do with his theatrical ventures, but the press said he was on some kind of secret mission for the government too. He's a personal friend of President Roosevelt, so I wouldn't be surprised if he actually went there to wave the flag and boost the cause in high places, if you know what I mean.'

To Jago this sounded like the man he'd known when Ford was still Detective Superintendent Ford of Special Branch and his information came from the intelligence services. He noticed that the newly appointed chief constable was still careful not to mention any official sources, but he clearly had his finger on the pulse.

'So let's not be too harsh on our Mr Coward,' Ford continued. 'People may think he's just an entertainer with a cut-glass accent who sings frivolous songs in a silk dressing gown, but he may be providing a valuable propaganda service to his country, and possibly more. Who can say? Perhaps we should just give him the benefit of the doubt.'

'Indeed, sir. And if I run into any of his servants on my way down Gerald Road I'll be careful not to grill them too much on their master's movements and motivations.'

'Exactly,' Ford laughed. 'And now, to go from one extreme to the other, I understand you've had your first meeting with Detective Superintendent Hardacre. What did you make of him?'

'He reminded me of some of the old sweats I used to know in my army days – an Old Contemptible and all that.'

'Ah, yes, he's very proud of his war record. I believe he did seven years in the regular army before he joined the police, and that was well before the last war. He told me he was in the Army Reserve then, so he was mobilised the day after war was declared. Invalided out in 1915, though – that seems to be a bit of a mystery, so I don't know how or why. He was fit enough to come back into the police, though, and he's worked his way up ever since. Did you find out about anything else apart from his soldiering days?'

'Not much, sir, but he appeared to have a bit of a bee in his bonnet about looters.'

'That's probably because they're stealing other people's property – I believe he has some strong views on property, and no doubt on other matters too. I expect you'll learn more about what gets his goat in due course.'

'No doubt, sir. I'm only going by first impressions, of course, but to be honest, the main thing that struck me is he seems to have a big chip on his shoulder about something – he didn't exactly welcome me with open arms.'

'Is that a problem?'

'No, sir – I've seen a lot worse. All part of life's rich pageant, as they say.'

'Good man. I think Superintendent Hardacre's the sort of man who'd say you have to take him as you find him. A bit set in his ways, perhaps, between you and me, and we both know that's not always an advantage in times of war, but he's got a lot on his plate. He was put into that job not long before I got mine, and only on a temporary basis at that – his predecessor's been shunted off onto some hush-hush committee that was set up after France fell.'

Jago was intrigued, but knew it would be inappropriate to enquire further, so he kept his mouth shut.

'Anyway,' said Ford, 'we all have more than enough to put up with at the moment, don't we? Hardacre's where he is because he's got a reputation as a first-class thief-taker, and that's no bad thing for a copper, is it? He's got a job to do and so have you. I've brought you in here because I know your qualities, and because you're the sort of man I need. You'll be reporting to him for day-to-day matters, and he'll be deploying you, but I've told him I'll have a hand in that too, because I want to use you to plug the gaps wherever they occur. I've also told him you'll have direct access to me whenever you need it. Clear?'

'Yes, sir. Forgive me for asking, sir, but is Mr Hardacre happy with that arrangement?'

'Happy? I didn't ask. It's my job to run the CID, not to make people happy.'

'I see, sir. Thank you.'

CHAPTER SIXTEEN

When Jago pulled up outside Nancy Baker's house, he found Cradock standing in the open doorway, saying goodbye to the police photographer. Jago added his own brief word of thanks and the man left.

'Morning, Peter,' he said. 'How was Ambrosden Avenue? Up to the usual high standards of Metropolitan Police accommodation?'

'What can I say, sir?' Cradock replied. 'Dark, smelly, and tiny cubicles with no room to swing a mouse, never mind a cat. Just a typical old Victorian section house, really. You'd think maybe up here in the West End things might be a bit more comfy, but not a bit of it. They don't spoil us, do they?'

'Good for the character, though, Peter. They don't want you going soft on them.'

'No, sir. Not much chance of that.'

'Not to worry, though – I'm going to treat you to

something nice to eat today.'

'Really? Thanks, sir.'

'My pleasure. I thought we should pop back to West Ham and pick up anything we need for our camping trip here – like clothes, for example. And I thought we might have a bite to eat at Rita's while we're there. That'll be nice, won't it?'

'Very nice, sir. And, er, will anyone else be there?'

'You mean Emily? I shouldn't think so – she'll be at work. If you want to see her you'll have to make your own arrangements.'

'No, I wasn't thinking of Emily. I was wondering whether someone else might be there – like, er, Miss Appleton, for example?'

'Oh, it's possible she might join us,' Jago replied airily. 'We'll have to wait and see.'

'Very good, sir.' Cradock suppressed the urge to grin, putting on the most serious expression he could manage.

'But we've got things to do before that,' said Jago. 'So, I assume if the door's open that Mrs Baker's home from work?'

'Yes, sir, she's in here waiting for you.'

'Good. Let's get started, then.'

They knocked on the living room door and found Nancy Baker in the same spot as they had the previous morning, sitting in an armchair, only now she was reading the morning newspaper and looked relaxed. She rose when they entered.

'Good morning, gentlemen,' she said, putting the paper down. Her voice was firm and confident. 'Do take a seat. Can I get you a cup of tea?'

'No, thank you, Mrs Baker,' said Jago before Cradock could speak. 'I don't want to keep you up any longer than we have to, so we'll just have a chat and then go, if you don't mind.'

'That's fine with me – like I said yesterday, it's nearly my bedtime.' She smiled at her own remark and resumed her seat. 'So what was it you wanted to talk to me about?'

'Just a few things you might be able to help us with.'

'Assisting you in your enquiries, eh? That's what you policemen like to say, isn't it? Or maybe you don't say that nowadays. By the way, you're new round here, aren't you?'

Like mother, like daughter. Jago remembered that Jenny had asked the same question. He was still feeling disoriented after being plucked out of the place he knew like the back of his hand and dispatched to this unfamiliar corner on the other side of London. He didn't like the idea of being a stranger, but perhaps it would be good for him.

'Yes, we are,' he replied. 'Now, I'd like to know a bit more about Mr Watson, Mrs Baker. What kind of man was he, in your opinion?'

She thought for a while before answering. 'It's difficult to say, really. I mean, he didn't give much away. I got the impression he'd had a raw deal in life, though. It's all right if you're born into a bit of money, but if you're not it can be really tough. Dog eat dog, that's what they say, isn't it? I had the idea maybe it'd been like that for him, but he didn't talk about it. He was always a bit wary, as if people had let him down or cheated him. I wouldn't want a child of mine to have a life like that.'

'Anything else?'

'Overall, I think I'd say he was a plain man. Not one to

put on airs and graces – you know. But there was something about him – I suppose you might call it a natural charm.'

'Not many friends, though.'

'Well, like I said yesterday, I never saw much evidence of friends, except for Dennis and that other fellow, but that's not to say he didn't have any.'

'By the way, we saw Mr Bateman yesterday. You said that Terry Watson moved into your house because there'd been a fire at his previous lodgings, but when we mentioned that to Mr Bateman, he said Mr Watson had told him it was just because he fancied a change. Are you sure he said there'd been a fire?'

'I'm pretty sure he did, yes. I remember the look on his face – he had that way of making you feel like you had to look after him, like a lost puppy. Maybe he thought I'd feel sorry for him and drop the rent a bit.'

'And did you?'

'No,' she laughed. 'I've been round the block too many times to fall for that.'

'We also met your daughter Jenny yesterday,' Jago continued. 'We went to see her at the telephone exchange.'

'Yes, she told me when she got home from work yesterday. She's done very well, hasn't she? I mean, they're very choosy at the GPO about who they take on as operators. You've got to be able to speak really nice – you get all sorts of important people making calls, and most people who've got phones at home are posh, so they don't want to hear some rough old Cockney when they dial the exchange. I'm proud of her, you know. I never wanted her to end up with a life like mine, chucking drunks out of a pub every night, and I don't think she did either. Now she's got a proper job, a respectable one, and she'll be able to meet some nice professional man and get married and settle down in a nice little house and have a family. Yes, I'm very proud of her.'

'I'm sure you are, Mrs Baker.'

'I worry about her, though. Did she tell you she's been sleeping in that coal cellar of ours since the air raids have been on?'

'She did mention it, yes. She said she preferred it.'

'Yes, well, that's as may be, but I remember those floods we had in 1928, when the Thames burst its banks in the middle of the night. That was terrible. A friend of mine was living in Grosvenor Road, down by the river, and she had her two kids sleeping in the basement, because that was all they had – they were both drowned. Pimlico's low-lying, you see – before the houses were built it was all marsh country, so if the river gets over the wall it's a disaster. I've never forgotten that, so I really wasn't keen on the idea of Jenny sleeping in the vault.'

Talk of drowning was stirring uncomfortable memories in Jago. He decided to change the subject. 'Something else your daughter mentioned was that Mr Watson left the house not long after you did on Sunday evening. Did he tell you where he was going?'

'No, he didn't. Why?'

'We're just trying to piece together his movements. Do you know what he generally used to do on his Sunday evenings?'

'No, I don't – not Sundays or any other day. If he was going out in the evenings, I'd be out at work as often as not, so I wouldn't know. Besides, he was a grown man, wasn't he? It was none of my business what he chose to get up to after dark. Mind you, I must say sometimes I felt more like his mum than his landlady.'

'Doing his sewing, you mean?'

'Yes, well, the only men I know of who can do that properly are tailors, and he wasn't one of them. Terry sometimes used to ask me to mend this and that, and I never had the heart to say no.'

Jago smiled. 'I got the impression when you were talking yesterday about mending his rucksack that you're handy with a needle and thread.'

'I reckon I am, yes – I used to work at the Army Clothing Depot in my younger days. It was good there. Huge place it was, down by the river – they had hundreds of women working there in the old days, and they only took first-rate seamstresses. By the way, I noticed yesterday you put that strap in your pocket, the one I was going to sew back onto Terry's rucksack for him. Don't suppose there's any point in that now, but why are you interested in it?'

'In an enquiry of this sort I'm interested in everything, Mrs Baker. So when did you stop working at the depot?'

'Oh, that was back in the last war – I got married and went to work in a pub. The depot's not there now – it got closed down seven or eight years ago. The whole place was demolished then – shame to see it go. They built that Dolphin Square on the site – have you seen it?'

'No, I haven't.'

'Well, if you go down towards the river, the other side of Lupus Street, you can't miss it. It's all big blocks of flats. But not cheap, oh no. It's for people with money – politicians and suchlike. Even that Oswald Mosley lived there until the government locked him up in May. It's all very fancy, but even so, that hasn't stopped it getting bombed.'

'I see. And you said now you're working in a clothing factory again?'

'Yes, I've gone back into the needle-and-thread business, as you might say. I don't know what'll happen to the job when the war's over, but it's no use worrying about that – the way things are with these bombs, tomorrow might never come. I hear some terrible stories at the rest centre, you know.'

'You mentioned that you do some voluntary work there. Could you tell us where it is?'

'Why do you want to know?'

'It's so that we know where you were on Sunday night. It's just a formality.'

'Like an alibi, you mean?'

'A formality, as I said.'

'Well, if you must know, it's in Thorndike Street. I don't do anything special – just make people cups of tea, and corned beef sandwiches if they're hungry. You see all sorts there. Some of the old dears who've been bombed out, their nerves are shot to pieces, you know – they're broken, can't stop crying, just helpless. But a lot of the young ones just seem to take it in their stride. They remind me of Jenny – so convinced she'll be safe in that coal cellar.'

Nancy's voice faltered. She placed both hands on the arms of the chair and abruptly pushed herself up, facing Jago and Cradock.

'And before you tell me I'm a hypocrite because I don't go to any shelter and I sleep upstairs in the bedroom, let me tell you that's not because I think I'm indestructible, it's because I've had my life and I don't care if I get killed. At least I'll be tucked up in my own bed if it happens. Sometimes I don't understand the kids, though – these young people, they think they're invincible, nothing can harm them, but when we get older we know better, don't we? Life has a way of putting you in your place.'

CHAPTER SEVENTEEN

'She seems to have recovered from finding a dead body in her back garden, doesn't she?' said Cradock as they left the house and got into the car. 'Almost chirpy at times, I thought.'

'You can probably put that down to age, Peter,' Jago replied, putting his key in the ignition. 'Like she said, she's been round the block a few times. She's lost her husband, and I dare say she's had a few other knocks along the way. That sort of experience tends to put things in perspective for you.'

'Where next, then, sir?'

'I want to have another little chat with Alice Mason, preferably on her own. I got hold of her before I left Scotland Yard, on that number Mrs Edgworth gave me – she said she was expecting to be in all morning.'

'Right. How did it go, sir – your meeting with Mr Ford?'

'Oh, fairly painless. I asked him how long this

secondment of ours is for, and he said we should expect months rather than weeks.'

'Did he say anything about accommodation?'

'He said he'd try and sort out something better, but I wouldn't get your hopes up – he said we'll probably be moving around a bit. Oh, and he said something about promotion.'

'Really?'

'Yes. That there won't be any, for either of us – they can't afford it.'

'Oh.'

'Never mind, Peter. You can console yourself with the thought that the longer you stay a constable, the safer the streets of London will be.'

Cradock fell silent, wondering whether this was a compliment but suspecting it wasn't.

'Off we go, then,' said Jago. 'Next stop, Ponsonby Place.'

He pressed the starter button and pulled away from the kerb.

'Actually, guv'nor,' said Cradock, 'I've just thought.'

'Yes?'

'If we're going down Vauxhall Bridge Road we'll probably go past Rampayne Street on the way – you know, where that shop is, Mr and Mrs Silver's, the people I used to know. Do you think we could pop in and say hello on the way? I'd love to see them again.'

'Does their shop sell things you can eat?'

'I expect so – they used to sell a few sweets. Why?'

'Just checking whether you've got more than one motive for visiting, that's all. I'm sure we can stop off briefly, but don't let them start getting the family photos out.'

'Thank you, sir.'

The Silvers' shop proved easy to find. It was just a matter of yards down Rampayne Street, at its junction with Dean's Place, and the sign on the front identified it as a newsagent, tobacconist and confectioner. Jago let Cradock enter first, then followed him into a small space that seemed to be crammed with everything that could conceivably come under those three headings. A thin man with black-framed glasses was squeezed in behind a counter on one side. He looked about the same age as Jago, but possibly a little older: his dark hair was streaked with grey.

'Hello, Benny,' said Cradock. 'Remember me?'

The man looked wary, but then peered over the top of his glasses. 'Peter?' he said.

'That's right – Peter Cradock. How are you?'

The man's face broke into a broad smile, and he held out his hands in welcome. 'I'm fine, thank you, and very pleased to see you.'

'Allow me to introduce you – this is my boss, Detective Inspector Jago. And this, sir, is Benny Silver, the proprietor.'

'Pleased to meet you, sir,' said Jago.

'You're very welcome here, Detective Inspector,' said Silver. 'My wife and I are very fond of Peter, and you know what they say – any friend of his . . .' Cradock looked a little flustered, but Silver gave a gentle laugh. 'Sorry, Peter – I'm only teasing. I realise your superior officer is not necessarily your friend.' Silver gave Jago a wink which suggested this wasn't the first time he'd teased Cradock. 'So, Peter,' he continued, 'what brings you here?'

'The detective inspector and I are working round here for a while and I heard you'd moved your shop here, so he kindly said we could drop in and say hello as we were passing.'

'Let me call Miriam. Would you like something to drink?'

'I think we'd better not – we're on our way to see someone.'

'Never mind, that's OK, but wait while I fetch her.'

Silver wriggled out from behind the counter and hurried to a door at the back of the shop. He opened it and shouted: there was the sound of shoes on a staircase and a woman appeared. She was short and plump, and had her hair tied back in a bun.

'Look who's here,' said Silver. 'It's Peter.'

Her reaction was as warm as his: she went straight to Cradock and gave him a hug as he tried to introduce Jago.

'Peter and Mr Jago are working in the area, my dear,' said Silver. He turned to Cradock. 'How long will you be here?'

'We don't know at the moment,' Cradock replied, extricating himself from Miriam's arms. 'It depends.'

'You must come and visit us properly when you have more time,' Silver continued. 'Come and eat with us, both of you. Daniel will be very sorry he missed you – he's out doing a delivery.'

'How is Daniel? Last time I saw him he was only a boy.'

'He still is a boy, Peter, but he's becoming a grown-up boy – he's seventeen now. He works with us here in the shop, but I expect he'll be in the forces before long, and then who knows? When he was born I had such hopes that he'd never see war the way I had, but I was a fool, I suppose. It's hard for his mother too – and now she has two children to worry about.'

'Really? I had no idea. Congratulations!'

'No, it's not what you think,' Silver laughed. 'Eliza's fourteen, so if she was ours you'd have known her when you were here doing that training of yours. No – she's only been with us for a couple of years, although sadly she's ours now.'

'What do you mean?'

'She's actually my cousin's daughter – one of my Austrian cousins.' He turned to Jago. 'I should explain, Detective Inspector. As Peter knows, I'm British, born and bred in London. I fought for my country in the last war, as you did, perhaps, but my grandfather came here from Austria and I still have relatives there. My cousin Otto fought for the Austro-Hungarian Empire in that war, so we were on opposite sides, but fortunately we never had to face each other in battle, because his regiment was fighting the Italians, who of course unlike now were our allies. Mercifully we both survived. He got his medals and I got mine, but now that Hitler has Austria under his heel, if you're Jewish, the fact that you have medals for serving your country in war counts for nothing.'

'So you mean Eliza's here because she's Jewish?'

'It runs in the family, Mr Jago,' Silver replied with an ironic smile of resignation. 'That is our blessing and our misfortune. The poor child's real name is Liesel, but we call her Eliza now – we think it might make life a little easier for her.'

'Sounding more English, you mean?'

'Exactly.'

'So what happened?'

142

'It was that terrible Kristallnacht business in Germany and Austria two years ago almost to the day, when the Nazis smashed all the Jewish businesses' windows in Vienna and set fire to the synagogues. Jews were dragged from their homes and taken away. My cousin and his wife could see it was too dangerous to stay, so they decided to send Liesel to us. Once she'd arrived here safely, they were planning to go to the British consulate in Vienna and say they had a young daughter alone in England, so could they have a visa to come here and join her, but the officials at the consulate kept putting the date back. Then word reached us that my cousin and his wife had been arrested. I fear that's the end of the story.'

'But at least Liesel escaped – Eliza, I mean.'

'Yes, we're thankful for that. It's a pity she's not here for you to meet her – when all the school-age children were evacuated last year, we thought it might bring back terrifying memories to her if she were suddenly put on a train and taken away from her new family to a strange place, so we kept her here and got her into one of the emergency schools. That's where she is now, and she loves it. Things have still been very hard for her, though. When the war started she was suddenly not a Jewish refugee any more – she was an enemy alien. I just thank God we didn't lose her in May.'

'You mean when the government rounded up all the Germans and Austrians and interned them?'

'Yes. If she'd been a sixteen-year-old boy instead of a fourteen-year-old girl she'd have been taken with the rest. At least it means she's still here, safe at home with us, but even so, some people have been very unpleasant.'

'In what way?'

'Just the usual ways. Some people don't like people like us.'

'I'm sorry to hear that, Mr Silver. Is there anything you'd like me to do? In my official capacity, I mean – I can have a word.'

'No, there's no need for that, Mr Jago – but thank you for offering.'

'Very well – but do let me know if you have any trouble.'

'I will.'

'I'm afraid we'll have to be on our way now, but perhaps we'll be able to take you up on your kind offer of hospitality – home cooking's probably as rare a treat for Peter as it is for me.'

'We'd be delighted.'

Jago realised too late that his mention of home cooking would no doubt have brought on hunger pangs in Cradock, so he pulled some change from his pocket. 'I'd like to buy something before we go, please.'

He studied the confectionery on display and asked Silver for a Mars bar, then scanned the front pages of the newspapers. A small report caught his eye: more than six thousand people had been killed in the previous month's air raids, including six hundred and forty-three children. He thought of the child Liesel, seeking refuge in a place where her life was now once again in danger, but he said nothing: they didn't need him to remind them of that. He took the newspaper and put it on the counter next to the Mars bar, then added a silver threepenny bit.

'Please take them,' the shopkeeper smiled. 'No charge.'

'No – I insist, please.'

144

Silver acquiesced. He rang the money up on his cash register, dropped the coin into the till and pushed the drawer shut.

'There you are, Peter,' said Jago, handing the Mars bar to Cradock. 'That's to keep you going till lunchtime – I wouldn't like your friends to think I don't look after you.'

'Perish the thought, sir. Thanks very much.'

The Silvers accompanied them to the door.

'Goodbye, Mr Silver,' said Jago, 'and you too, Mrs Silver. It's been nice to meet you.'

'It's been a pleasure to meet you too, Mr Jago,' Silver replied. 'I hope we see you again soon and that you enjoy your time in Pimlico. But take care – there are some nasty people out there.'

CHAPTER EIGHTEEN

This time it was Alice Mason who came to the door when Jago rang the bell at the house in Ponsonby Place. She was wearing an overall and had a duster in her hand, but hid it behind her back as she welcomed them into the hall.

'Thank you for giving us a little more of your time, Miss Mason,' said Jago. 'I just wanted to ask your help with a few more questions, if you don't mind.'

'Yes, that's fine.'

'Shall we go and sit in the living room, then?'

'Oh, yes, of course, sorry.'

She darted to the door and opened it for them, then stepped back so that they could go in first.

'Thank you,' said Jago, taking a seat. 'Now, we won't be long – you look rather busy yourself.'

'What, this, you mean?' She put the duster down on the floor beside her chair. 'Don't worry – I can finish that later. It's one of my days off today.'

'Days off?'

'Yes, I've got a little job. I work in the laundry at the Westminster Hospital – the, er, the home helped me get it. It's a nice place to work – the hospital's all brand new, much better than the old one. The job's only part time so far, but it's a start, and I'm hoping I'll get more hours soon, so I can earn enough to rent a room somewhere for myself. Sally's very kind to me – isn't charging me anything to stay with her – so I do a bit of housework for her when I'm off. She told you about the home, I suppose.'

'Yes, she did mention it.'

'She wants me to stand on my own two feet, you see, and she's helping me to do that. But what is it you wanted to ask me about?'

'I'd just like to know a little more about those white poppies. Mrs Edgworth told us it was she who encouraged you to sell them – is that correct?'

'Yes, she thought it'd help make me more confident, and that's what I want.'

'I'm glad to see you get on so well, considering you're selling white poppies and she's selling red ones, although I gathered from what she said over tea that she doesn't share the views of everyone she works with.'

'Oh, yes, definitely. Sally isn't pro-war. She sells red poppies because she cares about the men who came back wounded from the Great War or didn't come back at all. Remember – she lost a husband, and I didn't.' She was silent for a moment, as if distracted. 'Anyway,' she resumed, in what seemed to Jago a half-hearted attempt at breezy cheerfulness, 'I didn't offer you anything to drink. Can I get you a cup of tea?'

'No thank you,' said Jago. 'We need to be getting along. Before we go, though, could you tell me how you got involved with those white poppies? Was that Mrs Edgworth's idea?'

'No, it was my own idea – I think she was pleased that I'd had one. It was a lady from that Co-operative Women's Guild thing I mentioned. She came to the home to give us a talk about . . . things. You know, about men. She said it's powerful men that start wars, and she talked about how they're responsible for most of the bad things that happen in the world, and how we mustn't let them push us around – I suppose she knew we'd all agree with that. She said the men who went off to be soldiers in the Great War were tricked – all those songs in the music halls about joining up and going off to the front to fight the foe, all the posters, the bands, the appeals, the patriotism. They paid for it with their lives, but the powerful men who started the whole thing off did very well out of it, thank you very much – they stayed at home in their big houses and soft feather beds and got fat on the proceeds. There's no justice in that, is there?'

'And the poppies?'

'Oh, yes – well, she said she knew the people who'd come up with the idea of having white poppies instead of red ones. The white ones were to say we don't ever want it to be like that again – we want peace. We're standing up for what we believe and we're never going to let men like that bully us again.'

'Are there other people that you know of who sell white poppies in Pimlico, or perhaps in some of the neighbouring areas?'

'I think there are some, but I don't know who they are.'

'I'd be interested in speaking to them. How would I get in touch with them?'

'I'm not sure, really – I'm a bit new to it all. But I can ask Sally if she knows how to get hold of that lady from the Guild, then you can talk to her, and maybe she could tell you who the others are and where they live. Would that help?'

'Yes, thank you. That would be very helpful.'

'OK. In that case, I'll let you know.'

CHAPTER NINETEEN

Lupus Street was a busy thoroughfare running from east to west in the southern part of Pimlico and was home to more shops than the other streets Jago and Cradock had seen so far. Trubshaw Cycles stood on the south side of the road at number 69, next to the White Horse pub. It seemed a good location, but the front windows were grubby and the sign above them looked in need of some attention from a competent signwriter. The brass bell over the door jangled discordantly on its spring as Jago and Cradock entered.

On the inside, the shop resembled something of a cross between a showroom and a workshop. To their left was a display of new bicycles, while to their right was a motley collection of older machines, some partly dismantled for repair, and a jumbled assortment of tyres, saddles and other accessories. The whole place smelt of bicycle lubricating oil.

A woman was standing among the new models, slowly

wiping a cloth along the handlebars of a men's racing bike. She was smartly dressed with neatly permed hair and looked perhaps in her late thirties. She glanced up at them as they came in, but didn't speak. Instead she smiled and struck a pose that suggested she might have seen too many Mae West films.

A male figure clad in a brown dustcoat emerged from the rear of the shop. Older than the woman, with a round bespectacled face and hair that was suspiciously black for his years, he advanced towards them with chin up and back straight. To Jago he looked like a man straining to affect the bearing of a guardsman whilst denied by nature the height.

'Good morning, gentlemen,' he said. 'How may I assist you?' His manner was as stiff as the crease in his trousers.

'Good morning,' said Jago. 'Are you Mr Trubshaw?'

'I am.'

'We're police officers. I'm Detective Inspector Jago, and this is Detective Constable Cradock.'

'Really?' said Trubshaw, raising his eyebrows. He sounded sceptical, so Jago produced his warrant card, and Cradock followed suit. The shopkeeper examined the cards carefully.

Out of the corner of his eye Jago saw the woman stop her wiping. He couldn't be sure, but he thought she might possibly have directed a wink at him.

'Very well,' Trubshaw continued. 'And what brings you here?'

'We understand that you're the chairman of the local cycling club.'

'Correct.'

'And we believe a gentleman by the name of Terry Watson was one of your members.'

'Was, Inspector? He still is, as far as I'm aware.'

'Well, that's why we're here, Mr Trubshaw. I'm afraid Mr Watson has been killed.'

'Oh, dear. Poor chap. What happened?'

'We're treating his death as suspicious – we believe he was murdered.'

'My goodness. Did you hear that, Deirdre? These policemen say Terry Watson's been murdered.'

The woman hurried over to them, still clutching her cloth, her air of composure dispelled. 'That's terrible,' she said. 'Who could possibly want to do that?'

'I'm sure I don't know,' Trubshaw replied. 'Perhaps these gentlemen do.' He turned to Jago. 'By the way, Inspector, this is my wife.'

'Good morning, Mrs Trubshaw,' said Jago.

'Good morning, Inspector,' she replied. 'Do you know who did it? Such dreadful news. I didn't know him as well as my husband, of course, but he seemed a nice young man.'

'We don't know who was responsible for Mr Watson's death yet, Mrs Trubshaw, but having learnt he was a member of the cycling club, we came here to see what we could find out about him. Are you involved in the club?'

'Me?' she replied. 'Goodness, no – you wouldn't catch me on a bike.'

'I think I should take care of this, my dear,' said Trubshaw. 'I did know him better, as you say. What would you like to know, Inspector?'

'Tell me what kind of man he was, please, from what you knew of him.'

'Well, he wasn't a very easy man to know. I always found him rather secretive, to be perfectly frank. By the way, how did you discover he was a member of the club?'

'We found a membership card at his lodgings, and we also met Mr Bateman – I gather he's a member too.'

'Ah, yes, Dennis – a solid working man, salt of the earth. I believe he rides a bike because he likes to keep fit, and I must say that's always been my own motivation in cycling – you know, *mens sana in corpore sano* and all that.'

A bemused look appeared on Cradock's face.

'It's Latin, Constable,' Trubshaw added. 'It means "a healthy mind in a healthy body" – an aspiration that I'm sure you must share.'

'Oh, yes,' said Cradock uncertainly.

'I'm not sure I could say the same of Watson, though – being a solid working man, I mean.'

'Do you know what he did for a living?' said Jago.

'I haven't a clue – that's something he never let slip in my hearing. But as I said, he could be somewhat secretive. He had some wild ideas too.'

'Wild ideas?'

'Yes. A man of the left, I should say. I wouldn't have been surprised if he'd turned out to be some sort of communist dreaming of the socialist paradise where nobody has to work more than two days a week. I don't have any evidence to prove that, of course – I've no idea what company he kept outside the club. He just always gave the impression that he might be up to something but you'd probably never know what.'

'How did he get on with people in the club?'

'All right, I think – I'm not aware of him ever having

153

caused any trouble. As far as cycling's concerned, he was definitely an asset to the club. He was a very competitive rider and always did well in races and time trials. It was never just a social activity for him, nor even an excellent way to keep fit – he really wanted to win, couldn't stand coming second. A laudable attitude, in my view, and one we're going to need if this country's to maintain its rightful place in the world. We need men who are willing to live for Britain and put Britain first in order to build a Greater Britain, before it's trampled down into the dust by foreigners.'

'The Germans, you mean?'

'Well, we must defend ourselves, of course, but they're not here, are they? No, I'm talking about the real threat – the foreigners in our midst. We were betrayed by our own government twenty-six years ago. You go out there and ask the man on the street about the British Nationality and Status of Aliens Act and he's probably never heard of it, but he jolly well ought to – it swept away centuries of laws protecting us. It gave those alien international financiers a free hand to exploit us, and now they're the ones who control the chain stores all over the country. Some would say they control everything, but it's those big chains that are hitting traders like me the most. They're killing off the small shopkeeper, you know. They move in and open a cut-price store, then they run it at a loss until they've strangled us – we can't compete. And the war's only made it worse. Thousands of shops in London have gone out of business. Wherever you go now you'll see empty shops, and they're all small shops – men like me have our backs to the wall, and it's the alien financiers who've pushed us there while the government does nothing to protect us. It's about time they realised sometimes you have to fight fire with fire.'

'Did you ever discuss this sort of thing with Mr Watson?'

'No, certainly not. I don't think he would have understood.'

Deirdre Trubshaw gave a sigh, followed by a somewhat theatrical yawn, and edged away to wipe another nearby bicycle with her cloth. She was still listening, however, as far as Jago could tell.

'I see – thank you, Mr Trubshaw,' he said. 'There's one more thing I must ask you as a matter of routine before we go.'

'By all means.'

'Where were you overnight from Sunday to Monday?'

'I was at home, of course – in bed. I'm always here in the shop before eight in the morning, so I don't stay up late at night. On Sunday I went to bed early, as usual, and slept like a log. I've been particularly busy over the last few days because of the poppy appeal. So much to organise, you understand – I do a lot of work with the British Legion.'

'Yes, I've heard you're on the local branch committee.'

'My, you detectives certainly do keep your ears to the ground. What else do you know about me?'

'Someone just happened to mention it, Mr Trubshaw.'

'Well, there's no shame in being a member of the British Legion, I trust. I just happen to think Armistice Day is a very important event. I'm proud to have served my country in the last war as a patriotic Englishman and I believe we owe an eternal debt of respect and gratitude to all men who did the same. They sacrificed their lives to save their country from defeat and destruction, in the hope that a new and greater Britain would arise from the flames of war. And what have we done for them in return? We've let them down. We've betrayed that belief in the future that inspired their heroism, and we've failed to create that land fit for heroes that they deserved. The very least we can do is to remember them once a year by wearing a poppy – a red one.'

Jago felt that if he'd read these words about sacrifice and a debt of respect and gratitude in a book he'd have wholeheartedly agreed with them, but there was something about the pompous tone in which Trubshaw delivered them that grated on him.

'I believe there are also white poppies on sale,' he replied. 'What do you make of them?'

'Is this of any relevance to Watson's death?'

'I'd just like to know, Mr Trubshaw.'

'Well, if you want my opinion, it's short and sweet – the whole idea's outrageous. It's an insult to the fallen and an offence to the widows and orphans those brave men left behind. The blood our men shed was red, and the poppies that grow on their graves in Flanders are red. White is the colour of cowardice, and white poppies are anti-patriotic. I think the government should put a stop to it.'

'I see.' Jago turned to the shopkeeper's wife. 'And you, Mrs Trubshaw? Where were you from Sunday night to Monday morning?'

'Me?' she said, as if surprised to be included in the conversation. 'I was in bed too, and dead to the world – I take a sleeping draught nowadays, because of the dreadful din, and it knocks me out for the night. Fortunately I'm

156

not quite as enthusiastic as my husband about bicycles – I'm more of what you might call an accessory here in the shop – so I don't have to start work as early as he does.'

'Thank you.'

As Jago spoke, the doorbell jangled again, and a man in a well-cut suit entered the shop.

'Will that be all, Inspector?' said Trubshaw. 'If you'll excuse me, I must attend to the customer.'

'Yes, thank you. You've been most helpful.'

'You're very welcome,' said Trubshaw over his shoulder as he bustled away across the shop.

'And thank you for your help too, Mrs Trubshaw,' Jago continued.

'Think nothing of it, Inspector. And as my husband said, please excuse him – he suffers from what I believe is known as the profit motive.'

'It's all right – I think we've finished anyway. We may want to talk to you again, though, so may I have your home address? Or do you live over the shop?'

'No, we rent the shop, but we do have a little house nearby. It's number 10, Cornwall Street – out of the door here and turn right down Lupus Street, and it's the fourth turning on the right.' She lowered her voice. 'If you need to see me for what one might call an unsupervised discussion, I'd suggest you drop by at about ten o'clock tomorrow morning. I have things to do and I'm not planning to report for duty here until later, so I should be at home then.'

'I see. Thank you.'

'And by the way,' she added, 'I hope you weren't offended by my husband's views on foreigners – he sometimes speaks a little more forcefully than perhaps he should. Cecil says he's always believed in *mens sana in corpore sano*, but when it comes to that particular category of people of foreign extraction, or "aliens" as he prefers to call them, I'm afraid he's always been a bit short on the healthy mind side of it. I can only apologise. I blame his father – he was a member of the British Brothers League, you know. They were particularly unwelcoming to the Russian and Polish Jews who'd moved into the East End. That was all before I was born, of course, so I really don't know much about it, but I do know he used to take Cecil to meetings. I've been married to Cecil for twelve years now, and in that time I've come to understand that what people are exposed to in their youth can have a lasting influence on the type of person they grow up to be later, for better or for worse. In Cecil's case I'm afraid the result has not been entirely edifying.'

CHAPTER TWENTY

'Right, Peter,' said Jago, checking his watch as they made for the car, 'if we get a move on we should just about get to Rita's in time for a bite of lunch. And a change of air might be good for us too – help us make sense of what's been going on here.'

He waited until Cradock was safely ensconced in the seat beside him, then turned the car towards the Thames and their route across London to West Ham.

The roads were clearer than they'd been on their last journey across London, and it was a comparatively easy drive. Jago was surprised by how pleased he felt to be returning to West Ham after such a brief absence, but then it was home, after all, and Rita's cafe was the homeliest place he knew. He'd promised to treat Cradock to some good food today, but this lunch would be a treat for himself, too. Icing on cakes was a forgotten luxury these days, now that sugar was rationed, but the fact that Dorothy would be there was undoubtedly the icing on this particular cake.

By midday they were collecting a few essential belongings from Jago's home and the West Ham section house, and at just before twelve-thirty they drew up outside Rita's cafe. Jago's only disappointment as they went in was to see that Dorothy was already there: he hoped she hadn't been waiting long.

Rita came from her post at the counter to welcome them. 'Hello, Mr Jago – lovely to see you. Your friend Miss Appleton's here, but she's only beaten you by a few minutes. You go and sit down, and I'll come and take your orders in a moment.'

Jago and Cradock joined Dorothy at the table. They had barely exchanged greetings before Rita appeared at their side.

'Now,' she said, addressing Jago, 'before you start thinking about your lunch, I want to know what's been going on. My Emily told me you'd both gone away somewhere – she said your young lad here phoned her to say he wouldn't be around for a bit. You didn't tell me, though. I might've been worried about you.'

'Sorry, Rita, it was all a bit sudden. We've been to work on a case over in Pimlico.'

'Pimlico? That's a bit posh, isn't it?'

'Well, it's London SW1, which is definitely posher than Stratford E15, and I suppose it's not very far from Buckingham Palace.'

'There you are, then – you can't get much posher than that.'

'Yes, but it's closer to Victoria station and the railway line, so it's not as posh as all that. I think it used to be in the old days, but it's gone downhill – you know how it is.'

'I'm not sure I do – I think West Ham's always been downhill and never gone uphill.' She laughed at her own joke. 'So what's happening over there that's so bad they need to bring you in?'

'Oh, just a shortage of detectives and one murder too many – so I'm camping out in Rochester Row police station, and they've found a corner for Peter in the local section house. Not ideal, but it won't be for long. We've just come back to pick up a few clothes and things – and to see you, of course.'

'I should think so, too. We can't have you disappearing off to foreign parts like that. And what about your washing? You bring your laundry over here and I'll do it for you – you've only got to ask.'

'I'm sure I'll be able to make some local arrangement if I start running out of clothes, but it's very kind of you to offer.'

'Actually . . .' Cradock began.

'Not so fast,' said Rita, twitching her apron at him. 'I wasn't offering to do yours, you cheeky boy. If you don't fancy doing your own washing you'd better try and find yourself a wife who'll take pity on you.'

He closed his mouth and fell into an immediate silence, which Jago assumed was the best and perhaps only defence Peter had to hand.

Dorothy came to his aid. 'Rita,' she said, 'has John told you who he's working for?'

'What do you mean? He's still in the police, isn't he? He wouldn't be investigating over in Pimlico if he wasn't.'

'Yes, but has he told you he's now working for the chief constable of the whole Metropolitan Police CID?'

161

'No. Is that good?'

'It is if you think being a Scotland Yard detective is.'

'Scotland Yard? Ooh, I say – are we still allowed to speak to you, then, Mr Jago?'

'Rita, there will never be a time when you can't speak to me. And who could stop you anyway? All it means is that Peter and I have been temporarily seconded to Scotland Yard to plug a few gaps.'

'All the same – Scotland Yard. Oo-er. I suppose we're honoured to have you here, then – but no free lunches, even so.'

'I'm not allowed to have free lunches, Rita – my new boss might think you've been trying to corrupt me. Now, we'd better get on with some food – Peter and I have to get back to work.'

'What a pity – but it's lovely to see you. It's just a shame my Emily couldn't get time off work to join us, isn't it?'

She looked pointedly towards Cradock, whose eyes widened in alarm at the mere thought of eating lunch with Emily under the scrutiny of her mother, his boss and the American journalist. He had the sense that his every word, look and gesture would go into their respective notebooks for possible use as evidence against him.

Rita gave him a pitying smile. 'So what are you having to eat?'

'I'd like sausage, egg and chips,' said Jago. 'And you, Dorothy?'

'I'll have the same, thanks.'

'And you, Peter?'

'Yes, that'll be fine for me too, sir – but could I possibly have a bit of toast as well, and maybe an extra sausage?'

'Of course, Peter – you need to keep your strength up.'

'All right,' said Rita, writing their orders on her notepad. 'And cups of tea all round?'

'Yes – three mugs of your finest Ty-phoo please, Rita – "the tea that doctors recommend".'

Rita tucked her pencil behind her ear and swept away in the direction of the kitchen.

Jago focused his eyes and his attention on Dorothy. 'So,' he said, 'are you still writing about Neville Chamberlain, or has America lost interest in him now?'

'Not quite, but you know how it is – the news moves on. I think people are going to be arguing about him for years to come, though. He was an interesting man. Right now the verdict among my American press colleagues seems to be that he was a failure but it wasn't his fault – he just inherited the situation from the men who'd gone before him. And they reckon the big problem was he just didn't realise what kind of people he was up against – he was an honest English gentleman trying to negotiate with a bunch of violent, arrogant thugs. The experts are saying it would never have worked, but it's not so long ago that a lot of ordinary people thought he was a hero who'd saved the world from war. I'd be interested to know what Rita made of him.'

'Indeed. I'm not sure Rita's a very close student of international politics, but she's had the vote since 1928 like everyone else, so she may well have a view.'

'Do you have a view, Peter?' she said to Cradock.

'Me?' he replied. 'I don't think I do, really. I mean, Chamberlain tried, he hoped it'd work, but it didn't. Now we've got Churchill instead, so I suppose he'll try a few things, and if it works he'll be a hero, and if it doesn't, well, who knows what he'll be then? Up the creek without a paddle, along with the rest of us, I reckon.'

'You can quote that in your next article if you like,' said Jago, 'but please don't mention that he works for the Metropolitan Police.'

'OK, I'll just say "according to a Scotland Yard detective with connections in high places", shall I?'

'Those people in high places being?'

'Why, you, of course,' she laughed.

Rita arrived with a large tray onto which she'd squeezed their three lunches and cutlery, which she now arranged neatly on the table.

'There we are,' she said. 'Phyllis is bringing your drinks.'

Rita's waitress appeared at her elbow and deposited three mugs of tea on the table with a vacant expression and without a word, then lingered until Rita shooed her away with her cloth.

'Honestly,' said Rita, shaking her head as Phyllis drifted away, 'that girl would lose her own head if it wasn't screwed on.' She ran her eye over the table to check that everything was in order as they began to eat.

'Hmm, this is delicious,' said Dorothy, engaging for the first time with one of Rita's best sausages.

Jago found himself wondering whether this appreciation came from the heart or sprang simply from Dorothy's kindness.

'Now, Rita,' she continued, patting the empty chair beside her, 'would you like to join us for a moment? It'd be nice to catch up with you.'

'Certainly,' Rita replied, sitting down, 'I'll be glad to

take the weight off my feet.'

'Good. We were just talking about Mr Chamberlain, and what people thought about him. What's your view?'

Rita looked surprised. 'Well now, I'm not so sure I've got one. I mean, I liked him – he was a bit on the lanky side, but a real gent, always very well turned out. Not like that Anthony Eden – he's a bit too flashy for my liking, but then I dare say he's a very nice man too.'

'What did you think about Mr Churchill replacing Chamberlain? Did you approve?'

'Approve? Ooh, that's not for me to say, is it. That's for the toffs to sort out. As long as they get this war over and done with I don't mind who the prime minister is.'

'But you vote, don't you?'

'Oh yes, but the last time we had an election was five years ago, and that was Stanley Baldwin. I don't think we ever voted for Chamberlain or Churchill – as I recall it was their lordships and suchlike who decided who was going to be in charge then. Still, if anyone doesn't like what the prime minister's doing, at least that means it's not my fault.'

'And what do you think about appeasement?'

'Well, to tell you the truth, I don't think I'd ever heard that word till people started talking about old Umbrella Man, and I still don't know whether it's right or wrong. I mean, if you manage to talk your way out of a war with a bit of give and take, that's got to be a good thing, hasn't it? But then if the bloke you're trying to do a deal with turns out to be a bit shifty and tries to cheat you, you're going to end up with a bigger war. It's like that business of turning the other cheek, isn't it? I know it was Jesus what said it, and I'm sure he meant well, but if you're up against a bully, isn't it better just to punch him on the nose instead? I know that's what my old dad always used to say when I went to school.'

'Thanks, Rita,' said Dorothy. 'That's very interesting.'

'Is it? You can put it in your paper if you like. The voice of the British public. If you ask me, though, I think we should all just be nice and get along with each other – even with foreigners. Then we wouldn't have all these wars and things.'

'You're right,' said Jago. 'That would be wonderful.'

'Anyway, I must be off now. Will you be wanting anything for pudding?'

'Not for me, thanks,' said Dorothy. 'I'm full.'

'Me too,' said Jago.

Cradock looked disappointed but shook his head as politely as he could.

Rita left them, and Dorothy turned her attention to Cradock.

'Now, then, Peter,' she said, 'let me catch up with you.'

Cradock began to feel nervous but tried to comfort himself with the fact that at least Rita had gone. 'Yes?'

'How are things going with Emily?'

Jago smiled to himself. He'd learnt that Americans could be direct and he imagined Cradock might be wishing some traditional British reserve had rubbed off on Dorothy during her time in London – but it looked as though any such hopes would be in vain.

'Things?' said Cradock, as though he had no idea what she was talking about.

'Yes, things.' She leaned conspiratorially across the table towards him. 'You're still going out together, aren't you?'

'Er, yes.'

'So how's your relationship developing?'

'Well, I don't know, really – I mean, I don't know how it's supposed to develop.'

'Let me help you, then. It's simple – are you getting on well together?'

'I suppose so, but I'm not sure. It's just that, well, sometimes she does little things that irritate me, and I don't know whether that means we're not suited to each other.' He glanced over his shoulder in case Rita was returning. 'Do you think it does?'

'Not necessarily. I think maybe it just means she's got one or two little imperfections. But maybe you have some too – I know I do.'

She cast a glance at Jago, as if inviting him to bare his heart too, but he wasn't going to drop his guard in front of Cradock. Instead he affected an air of mild surprise that she should think he'd been listening to them, but he knew she'd see through it and was secretly pleased at the thought.

Cradock assented to her assumption with a shrug.

'We all do, Peter,' she said. 'The important thing is do you want her to like you in spite of yours and accept you the way you are?'

He nodded meekly.

'Or do you think she doesn't have to make any allowances because you're so easy to get on with?'

He shook his head.

'Good. Then I think you can put your mind at rest. Neither of you is perfect, and as long as you both know that, you should get along fine. You just have to like her enough, imperfections and all – and she has to like you enough the same.'

Dorothy looked again at Jago, but he avoided her eyes and checked his watch instead.

'I think it's time we got going,' he said. 'Peter and I have a lot to do this afternoon.'

'Me too,' said Dorothy. 'But I must have a quick word with you before we go. A private word, that is.'

'Yes, of course.' Jago pulled the car keys out of his pocket. 'Here, Peter, you take these and wait for me in the car while I pay the bill.'

Cradock took the keys and made a quick exit.

Jago paid Rita for their meals and said goodbye, then moved away with Dorothy from the counter to the corner where they'd left their coats.

'What is it?' he said. 'Is everything OK?'

'Yes and no, I guess. Look, we're both in a hurry so I'll get to the point. I didn't want to mention it in front of the others, but the thing is . . . well, I've just had some news – I've been offered a job.'

'Another reporting job?'

'Yes.'

'Congratulations. Is it a cause for celebration?'

'I don't know – I only found out this morning. It's more what you might call a new challenge. My paper's asked me if I'd consider becoming their new Chungking correspondent – basically, it means I'd be replacing my friend Judith.'

'Don't they just send you where they like?'

'Not for a job like that – it would be for a couple of years, in a dangerous location. They're good like that – very considerate. It's up to me whether I take it or not.'

Jago hesitated before expressing the question that was

darting through his mind. 'Have you, er, made your decision?'

'I've told them I need some time to think about it.'

'And they said?'

'They said that's fine, it's up to me, but they don't want me to take too long.'

'I see. So you have to jump one way or the other pretty quickly.'

'That's about the long and the short of it.'

Jago nodded calmly, fighting to maintain a dispassionate air. 'You'll let me know what you decide, then, will you?'

'I will.'

There was a brief silence: their conversation seemed to have run out of steam. Jago felt uncomfortable, uncertain how to respond. He knew with all his heart what he wanted her to do, but she was a free agent, and he had no right to try to influence her.

CHAPTER TWENTY-ONE

Cradock was staring out of the Riley's side window at the passing streets as they drove back towards Pimlico. A bag of his belongings was stowed on the back seat, along with one that Jago had brought. He hoped he'd got enough things to last for the rest of their stay in south-west London, but how long that would be was anyone's guess.

Jago had been unusually quiet for most of the journey so far, leaving Cradock wondering whether he'd said or done something wrong. He decided to test the water by breaking the silence.

'So, then, guv'nor,' he said, turning to face the front, 'do you think that change of air helped? Are we any closer to working out what happened to Terry Watson?'

'I hope so,' said Jago, keeping his eyes on the road, 'but to be honest, I don't feel I'm any further forward than I was before we went.'

'Perhaps we were a bit optimistic thinking the air might

be fresher in West Ham.'

'Yes, I think perhaps we were, Peter.'

Jago fell to thinking again about the conversation he'd had with Dorothy as they left Rita's cafe, but he knew he couldn't let it dominate his thoughts for the rest of the day.

'Anyway,' he said, 'we've got work to do. I want to see if we can find Fred Cook at that pub of his before closing time, so we'll go straight there.'

When they arrived in Pimlico they drove the whole length of Sutherland Street in search of the Duke of Clarence but couldn't see any drinking place with this name. It was only when they turned round and checked again that they spotted it, nestled down a narrow side street. Jago parked the car close to the kerb and they got out. It looked like a homely, traditional pub, untouched as yet by the bombing.

'Let's see how reliable Mr Bateman was with his directions for finding Fred Cook,' said Jago as he opened the door to the saloon bar. 'See any potted ferns?'

The bar was busy, but in the far corner they could indeed see a balding man sitting at a glass-topped wicker table that was partly shielded from the rest of the room by a pair of expansive ferns in large brass pots, as predicted by Bateman.

'He must definitely be a regular here if he gets his own table,' said Cradock. 'Pal of the landlord?'

'Probably,' said Jago. 'Especially considering what I can see under that table of his. I don't think Bateman was joking – this is his office.'

Cradock glanced across to the table. On the floor beneath it he saw a stout canvas bag with a metal plate fixed across its top.

'Oh, yes,' he said. 'A clock bag. I remember that was one of the first things they showed us at Peel House, when they were telling us how street betting works – explaining bookies to rookies, that's what they called it. So if he's a bookie's runner, he won't be too pleased to see us turn up.'

'We'll see,' said Jago. 'Let's go and introduce ourselves.'

The man was getting up from his chair and beginning to reach under the table for the bag when he noticed them approaching. He froze, his weaselly face fixed and unsmiling. Only his eyes moved, flitting from side to side like those of a cornered animal.

'Excuse me, sir,' said Jago. 'Can you spare a moment?'

'No, I can't. I've got to go.'

'It'll only take a second or two.'

'All right, then, but be quick about it.' Outnumbered, he slumped back onto his chair.

Jago slid into the empty chair by the table, and Cradock pulled over another and joined him.

'Mr Fred Cook?' said Jago quietly.

'Who are you?' said the man.

'We're police officers.'

'No, you're not. I know every copper round here and I don't know you.'

'We're visiting. Do you want me to show you my warrant card?'

The man glanced round again anxiously. 'Don't wave it about in here. Just open it and slide it onto the table nice and discreet, like, so I can see.'

Jago did as he was asked. 'Is that all right?'

'Yes, that'll do. So what do you want?'

'There's no need to worry – we're not here to nick

172

you for street betting offences.'

'What?'

'If you're in such a hurry to be off, Mr Cook, stop wasting my time. I've seen your clock bag under the table.'

'Oh.'

'We just want to know if you can help us. You are Mr Cook, aren't you?'

'Yes. What do you mean by help?'

'We're investigating a suspected murder.'

'Murder? I don't know anything about a murder. What poor soul's copped it?'

'Someone we understand you know, Mr Cook – Mr Terry Watson.'

'Terry? He's been murdered?' Cook bit his lip and looked down at the table top as if searching for what he should say next. He raised his eyes to Jago. 'That's terrible, but I don't see how I can help. I mean, I know Terry, but I've got no idea why anyone would want to murder him.'

'Were you and Mr Watson friends?'

'Well, I knew him well enough, I suppose, and we got on all right. He was quite a bit younger than me, though.'

'I believe you were both members of the same cycling club.'

'The Wheelers? Yes, that's right, but it's quite big. I didn't really get to know Terry until a few weeks ago.'

'How did you get to know him?'

'Oh, it was just a mate of mine thought I could help him and introduced us.'

'Was that mate of yours Mr Bateman?'

'Yes – how did you know that?'

'Just a guess – I know Mr Bateman helped him with

his lodgings too. How did he think you could help Mr Watson?'

'He said Terry was looking for work.'

'Work in your line? As a bookie's runner?'

'I'm a turf commission agent's assistant, Inspector.'

'Yes, like I said, a bookie's runner. Let's see – I'm guessing you work for a bookmaker, you collect cash bets on the street for him from punters who fancy a flutter on the 2.30 at Haydock Park. You put the money and the betting slips in your clock bag, you set the clock so it'll lock the bag shut just as the first race starts and your boss'll know there's no dodgy bets in it, and then you run the bag over to him. Is that what you do?'

'Well, yes.'

'In that case you're a bookie's runner, aren't you? And the reason why you're in such a hurry now is because you've got to get moving and pick up your next lot of bets somewhere else. Correct?'

'Yes, all right.' He hesitated. 'Can I go now?'

'Not yet. Look, I told you we're not here to nick you. Just answer my questions and you can go. I asked you whether you got Terry Watson work as a bookie's runner.'

'Yes, I did.'

'Thank you.'

'The thing is, working as a runner's the obvious thing to do if you need to earn a bob or two and you've got a bike. The faster you can get to the bookie, the more bets you can collect – and Terry was very fast. You've got to be careful these days, what with all the bombs and the blackout and the holes in the road, but he was a devil-may-care sort of bloke – he'd ride through anything.'

'And who's the bookie he was working for?'

'Mr Ashdon – Bill Ashdon.'

'Is he the one you work for?'

'Yes, he is – he's my cousin, see. He's very good to me. It's not just about how many bets you can collect, it's about what rate your commission is. You know we get paid a commission on the bets?'

'Yes, I do.'

'Well, most runners get one-and-six in the pound, but he pays me six bob a day plus two bob in the pound commission.'

'Is that what Terry Watson was being paid?'

'I wouldn't know that – none of my business. I shouldn't think so, though. I mean, I'm family, aren't I? Bill's always looked after me.'

'Just one last question, Mr Cook.'

'Yes?'

'You're saying Terry Watson was a bookie's runner, but when we had a look round his lodgings after his death, there was no sign of a clock bag. Any idea why that might be?'

'No, I haven't, Inspector – I wouldn't know. You'll have to ask Bill about that.'

'Right. Can you tell me where I can find him?'

'Yes. He's got a nice little house in Caroline Terrace, number 37 – that's over in Belgravia, the other side of the railway tracks. Very posh. But for work he uses a flat in Wilton Road, next to Victoria station – it's over the grocer's shop, just down by the Biograph cinema.'

'Thank you, Mr Cook. We appreciate your help.'

'You're welcome. You'd know all that anyway if you

were stationed round here – all the local coppers know where to find Bill Ashdon. But if there's anything else I can do to help, just say.'

'One small thing – is he likely to be there now?'

'More likely than not, I'd say. All right if I go now?'

'Yes, that's fine.'

Cook picked up his bag, tucked it under his arm and scuttled out of the pub without a backward glance.

CHAPTER TWENTY-TWO

Cook's prediction was accurate: Jago and Cradock quickly located the grocer's shop by the cinema in Wilton Road. They parked on the street and went in through the door to one side of the shop that led up to the first floor. There was just one door at the top of the stairs, a heavy wooden one with a small window at which a man's head appeared when Jago knocked.

'Who are you?' said the man.

'Police,' said Jago, holding up his warrant card. 'May we come in?'

'Hang on a minute,' the man replied. There was the sound of a key turning in the lock, and the door opened. 'Come in, then,' he said.

He stepped back so that they could get in, then locked the door after them. They followed him down a narrow corridor to a gloomy, nondescript room with a faded patch of carpet on cracking linoleum, some drab bits of office furniture, and similarly faded curtains. Jago imagined that the nice little house in Belgravia that Cook had mentioned was probably where Ashdon spent his money. This flat would just be a place to make that money.

'I'm sorry to interrupt you, Mr Ashdon,' said Jago once they had introduced themselves, 'but I need to ask you a few questions.'

'That's all right, Detective Inspector,' Ashdon replied. 'The police are always welcome visitors here, and I do my best to be of assistance. Take a seat.' He nudged a cigarette case across the desk and opened the lid. 'Cigarette?'

'No, thank you,' said Jago, pulling across a cane chair and sitting on it. Cradock did the same.

'Apologies for all the rigmarole with the door – it's just that I usually have quite a bit of cash in here and I'm not keen on giving it away to passers-by who fancy helping themselves to it, so I keep the office locked whether I'm in or out.' He took a cigarette for himself and lit it. 'So, how did you find me?'

'Fred Cook gave us the address – is that a problem? I understand he's your cousin.'

'Yes, that's right – he's my only family, actually. And no, it's not a problem – I just wondered, that's all. Anyway, how can I help you?'

'It's to do with Mr Terry Watson.'

'Ah, yes, I know – shocking news. I gather you're treating it as murder.'

'You know, then?'

'Yes, I had a phone call just before you got here.'

'Would that be from your cousin?'

'It was, actually. Fred's very thoughtful like that – he

178

knew I'd want to know.'

'Yes, I imagined he might be in touch with you.'

'Well, I like to know what's going on, and something like this, well, it sounds like a terrible business. So fire away with your questions, and I'll help you if I can.'

'Thank you, Mr Ashdon. First of all, I understand you're a bookmaker. Is that right?'

'Yes, that's how I earn my humble crust. All strictly above board, though, no shady business. Some people out there are very critical of my profession, but it's unfair. As far as I'm concerned, if I can help ordinary working people to bet a few pennies on a horse it's a service to the community.'

'How's that, exactly?'

'Because it gives them hope, Inspector, the most precious commodity of all. They might only be able to spare sixpence, but they could win enough to buy themselves a gramophone. On their income, the only other way they'd get something like that would be to steal it, and I'm sure you wouldn't approve of that. No – we bring hope.'

'And it enables you to earn a good living too, I expect.'

'Of course, but only if I'm fair – if people think a bookie's cheating them, they don't use his services, and he's finished. It's not for me to say, but I like to think I'm well respected in this community and my clients regard me as an honest man. I do earn a good living, as it happens, but if you want to know the secret of my success, I put it down to hard work and good service.'

'Eloquently put, Mr Ashdon. Now, to get back down to earth, can you please confirm that you employed Mr Watson as a runner?'

'He used to do a bit of work for me, yes.'

'Which would've involved him using a clock bag?'

'Well, yes, as it happens. There's nothing unusual about that, though, is there?'

'No, but if he was working as a runner I'd have expected to find at least one at his lodgings, but we didn't. Can you explain that?'

Ashdon hesitated before replying.

'Well, let me see now . . . Ah, yes, I remember. Terry asked for a bit of time off, so I said yes and I kept the bag.'

'When was this?'

'It was the Saturday before last, and I can tell you the time, too – it was about a quarter past three in the afternoon.'

'That's very precise.'

'Well, it was the New Cambridgeshire Stakes up at Nottingham at five past three that day, and he'd just brought his bag in with the bets. The reason why I remember is because of the winner. Do you follow the horses?'

'No, I don't.'

'It was an outsider called Caxton – started at a hundred to seven but won by half a length. Unfortunately, Terry had picked up a couple of bets on it – probably printers hoping for a spot of luck, with a name like that. That horse was so unlikely to get anywhere, even the trainer hadn't bothered to come and watch – and I mean that, seriously. That was an expensive day for me, I can tell you. Bookies lose too, you know.'

'Was that the last time you saw him?'

'Yes.'

'And why did he want some time off?'

'He didn't say, actually.'

'Didn't you ask him?'

'No. The thing is, I could manage without him – the war's affected racing as much as everything else, so business has been quieter than it used to be, and the flat season ends a week next Saturday, so it'll be even quieter soon. Besides, I was only employing him on trial, commission only, so if he's off it doesn't cost me anything – I just get someone else to do the job and pay the commission to them. It was none of my business why he wanted a break, so I didn't ask him.'

'I see. Thank you. So businesses like yours are feeling the pinch, are they?'

'A lot are, but some of us aren't doing too badly – it's the survival of the fittest, isn't it? You've got to adapt to the times, diversify your business interests.'

'So that's what you're doing?'

'Of course. The smart men are moving into property these days – you know, houses, shops and whatever. It's surprising what you can pick up cheap in a war if you've got the cash to spare, and whoever wins this one, people are still going to need somewhere to live and buy their groceries. It's what you might call a safety net. Not that I'm giving up on the racing – that's still the main interest for me. The thing is, there's a lot of people who depend on me for a living, so it's my duty to run a good business and look after my employees.'

'Like paying your runners' fines, I suppose?'

'Please don't start on that subject, Inspector – everyone knows we do. We can't help it if one of your boys decides to charge a runner with loitering, but a man like me feels a sense of social responsibility, so we help them out. Having said that, I must say the police round here are very obliging and hardly ever bother us, if you know what I mean.'

Jago did know what he meant, but now was not the time to discuss which local bobbies turned a blind eye to street betting in exchange for a small consideration, let alone which of their senior officers might come to similar arrangements.

'Besides,' Ashdon continued, 'the government doesn't seem to mind us doing it.'

'What do you mean?'

'Well, last year the income tax people said if you're a bookie and your runner's found guilty and fined, you can deduct the fine from your tax assessment as expenses – but only if it's wholly and exclusively for the purposes of your business, of course. So there you are. If you can claim it as expenses it must be legal – and you coppers know all about claiming expenses, don't you?'

He concluded with a wink and a knowing grin, which Jago ignored.

'That's as may be, Mr Ashdon. It's not my job to enforce the Inland Revenue's income tax regulations, so I say good luck to you, but as far as I'm aware the law on loitering hasn't changed.'

'Yes, but my runners don't loiter in the streets, so they're not breaking the law.'

'Which is why your cousin was in the pub when we met him, I suppose.'

'Exactly – you can't be done for loitering in the street if you're in a pub, can you? Not even if you're there for the purpose of receiving or paying out bets, as the law puts it – and yes, I do know the Street Betting Act inside out and back to front, in case you're wondering. I learnt my lesson years ago – one of my runners was fined for loitering in the street for that purpose, and then your pals decided to charge me too.'

'You have a conviction?'

'No, of course I haven't – I'm an honest businessman, like I said. But that's just the point – some people try to persecute us.'

'So you got off?'

'Yes – it was ridiculous. That was the day I realised the law really is an ass. I used to have a few runners working for me on the street, and one of them got fined a couple of quid. Fair and square, I suppose, but then the police hauled me up in court too, on a charge of aiding and abetting him. My lawyer gave them a hard time, I can tell you. He stood up in front of that magistrate and said you can fine a bookie's runner if he loiters on the street for the purpose of receiving bets, but how can his employer aid and abet him to loiter? He said the charge was nonsense, that a man can't be held criminally responsible for the criminal acts of his servants, and he was right. The case was dismissed. That taught me two things. One, to take my runners off the street and put them in places like pubs instead, and two, not to expect the police to be too bright – present company excluded, of course, I'm sure.'

'I appreciate you making that distinction, Mr Ashdon. You'll understand that I'm investigating a much more serious matter – a murder. Who do you think might've wanted to kill your employee?'

'My goodness – sounds a bit stark when you put it like that, doesn't it? To be honest, I can't begin to imagine.'

'What kind of man was Mr Watson?'

'Pretty reliable, as far as I could tell. He got the job done, did what I told him, and never gave me any grief. That's about all I can say.'

'And how long have you known him?'

'Since he started working for me – that was a few weeks ago. But look, I've got two dozen like him, so I don't have time to sit down for a cup of tea and a heart-to-heart with them. As far as I'm concerned, as long as young Terry turned up on time with his bag and didn't lose any of the money or slips on the way, his job was done. I couldn't care less what he did in his own time, or who he did it with.'

'I see. Well, thank you for your assistance, Mr Ashdon,' said Jago, getting up from his chair. 'We'll be in touch if we need to speak to you again.'

'You're welcome – come back any time and ask me whatever you like. You never know, I may be able to help you – but then again,' he paused, 'I wouldn't bet on it.'

CHAPTER TWENTY-THREE

'Interesting bloke, that,' said Cradock as they crossed the pavement to the car. 'I didn't know quite what to make of him, though. He says he looks after his employees, but then when Watson asks him for a bit of time off he doesn't even ask why – it could've been some family crisis or something, couldn't it?'

'If Watson had a family,' said Jago.

'Well, yes, but it could've been something else really important. You'd think he'd at least ask. And then he says he couldn't care less what our Terry was doing in his own time. That doesn't sound very caring.'

'You're right, Peter. He had a smooth tongue, but he left me thinking I should maybe keep a pinch of salt handy when he's wagging it. I'd still like to find out why Watson should suddenly need some time off just days before he's murdered. He was working for Ashdon because he needed the money, after all, and so far he doesn't seem to have had any other job. I think we need a quick word with his pal Bateman to see if he can shed some light – if we go now we should be able to catch him before he knocks off for the day.'

They drove to Battersea Park and found Bateman by the allotments, as before.

'Good afternoon, Mr Bateman,' said Jago. 'I wonder if we could take just a few minutes of your time. I don't want to stop you if you're busy.'

'No, that's all right,' said Bateman, leaning on a rake. 'It's been a long day – I've just been trying to explain to some novices attempting to grow cauliflowers for the first time in their lives that with tender plants like that you've got to do something now to protect them against the frost with a bit of old carpet or something, otherwise they'll be ruined. Some of them still seem to think you just plant things and water them and they'll be fine.'

'I'm sure they must appreciate your advice.'

'Maybe – sometimes I feel more like a schoolmaster than a gardener. Still, I'll be knocking off soon and putting my feet up for the evening, Hitler permitting. I'm still not used to all this messing about with the time that's been going on, though – by rights it ought to be getting dark by now, but it's still light. I don't know whether I'm coming or going. It always used to be put the clocks back first weekend in October, then last year they changed it to third weekend in November because of the war or something, and now this year they've said don't put them back at all. I can't keep up with it – it's supposed to be good for us to have more light in the evenings, but all that means is you can't see what you're doing in the mornings. Doesn't make sense to me, but then I'm just a gardener. By the way, do you want to get the weight off your feet? I could certainly do with a sit down.'

'By all means.'

'We've got a shed behind that hedge.' He pointed vaguely to his left. 'Follow me.'

He led them across some residual grass that bordered the allotments and into the shed, where he offered them folding wooden chairs and took one himself.

'That's better,' he said. 'I suppose this is about Terry again, is it?'

'Yes, I'm afraid it is.'

'I still can't believe he's dead, you know. He was so fit and strong – a proper athlete, like, and such a good cyclist, better than me. He could be a bit quiet, bit of a loner, you might say, but put him on a bike and he was a changed man. You can forget what they say about sport being all about the taking part. For someone like Terry, it's not – it's about winning, beating the other man, and that's all there is to it. The chance of a bike race always just brought him to life – oh, I'm sorry, that's not really the right thing to say, is it? But he was like that ever since I first knew him.'

'How did you get to know him? You said you went back a few years.'

'Aye, to 1935, actually. We met in the labour camp.'

'The what?' Jago's mind had flashed to the Soviet Union's forced labour camps that he'd read about in the press.

'The labour camp – that's what we called it, anyway. Well, I say we – Terry used to call it a slave camp, but I never knew whether he was joking or not. He was a bit more left-wing in his politics than me, I think. Anyway, the camp wasn't like that – plenty of good food, you got paid an allowance on top of your unemployment assistance, and you could leave any time you wanted to. The government called them instructional centres.'

'Ah, yes, I've heard of them. For training unemployed men, weren't they?'

'That's right. Ours was in Norfolk. The idea was if you were young and out of work for too long you'd go soft, so you'd get sent to one of these places for three months and do some manual labour to toughen you up, as well as things like spelling and arithmetic, and that'd make you physically and mentally fit enough to get a job. The government said it was so that men from what they called the "distressed" areas could get jobs in other parts of the country. I think distressed areas meant places with no jobs, but to me it was just home. I told you I'd come down from Derbyshire, didn't I?'

'You did mention Derbyshire, yes.'

'Well, that was pretty distressed at the time. I was a lead miner, but it was already a dying industry, and the Depression was the final nail in the coffin. The mine closed down, and I was out of a job and couldn't find another one. I suppose that's why I like what I'm doing now – when you've spent years working three hundred feet under the earth in a lead mine it's wonderful to be out in the open air all day.'

'Sounds like you didn't need much toughening up, though.'

'No, I think with me it was about building up my confidence, and the camp was good for that. It was where I learnt about gardening, too – well, they called it horticulture, but it was about growing things, and I loved it. I'm still not afraid of putting in a hard day's labouring and I'll be out there doing my fair share of double digging this winter, but what I really love is the smell of that freshly turned earth and the feeling you get when you've a tender young plant in your hands. It doesn't matter whether it's a cauliflower, like I said, or a chrysanthemum, all tiny and frail – it's just wonderful to think you're the one who's going to help it survive and grow into something beautiful for everyone to see. That's better than hacking at rock at the bottom of a mineshaft all day, I can tell you. I was hoping I'd find some work like that when Terry and I finished the camp, but it didn't work out. He had contacts round here, so he moved down pretty soon after that, but I went back to Derbyshire. I still couldn't find a job there, though, so I moved down here too in the end – it was Terry's idea.'

'And Mrs Baker helped you find work.'

'That's right – she's very kind, that woman.'

'How did Mr Watson get on with being in that camp?'

'He was fine with the physical work. They got him doing forestry – felling trees, logging and suchlike. I think he liked working with the axe, and it got him fit. That's why he took up serious cycling when we came out – it kept him in condition. He didn't get on so well with all the rules in the camp, though – it was a bit too regimented for his liking.'

'You mentioned Mr Watson's politics – can you tell me more?'

'Not a lot – I'm not one for having political arguments with people, and it doesn't interest me much. He was a

Labour man – I think he'd been a member of the party, but when they stopped being anti-war and switched to backing rearmament he resigned. That was a couple of years ago, I think.'

'Do you know if he ever wore a white poppy?'

'I've never seen him with any kind of flower in his buttonhole – I don't think he had the money for that kind of thing.'

'No, I mean an artificial one, for Armistice Day.'

'But they're red.'

'Some people wear a white one – it means they're against war.'

'Oh, I see. No, I've never noticed him wearing one.'

'Was he against war?'

'Judging by what he said about Attlee and the Labour Party, aye, I think he was.'

'Had he received his call-up papers yet?'

'I don't think so – he never mentioned it, anyway. I haven't had mine yet, but gardening's a reserved occupation, so I'm not expecting to be called up. You still have to register, of course, even if your job's on the reserved list, and I'm thirty-five, so my date for registering was last week. I'm a bit older than Terry was, so he must've had to register a while back. But in any case, he seemed to think he wasn't going to get through the medical. He said something about diabetes, but I'm sure he wasn't diabetic, so maybe he was just worrying. He was never a great one for going to the doctors, though – he used to say he couldn't afford to and he reckoned his cycling kept him fit and healthy anyway, so he didn't bother.'

'Thank you. Now, there's just a small point we'd like to clear up, Mr Bateman. We've been told that Terry Watson asked his boss for some time off work recently but didn't say why he wanted it. I'd be interested to know why he asked, so I'm wondering whether he happened to mention it to you.'

'When would this have been?'

'The Saturday before last.'

Bateman pursed his mouth and shook his head. 'No, doesn't ring any bells with me. Mind you, when we were moving that wardrobe of Nancy's that I told you about he did say he'd had a spot of trouble at work, so maybe it was something to do with that.'

'Remind me when you were moving that wardrobe, please.'

'Last Thursday.'

'And when you say he'd had trouble "at work", do you mean the job you helped Mr Watson to get?'

'Who told you that?'

'You mentioned that Fred Cook was a member of the cycling club, and we've been told that you introduced Mr Watson to him because he was looking for a job. Is that correct?'

'Aye, I suppose it is.'

'You suppose?'

'No – I mean, I did.'

'And the work you helped to get him was as a bookie's runner?'

'Aye, it was. What of it?'

'You didn't mention this when we spoke to you yesterday.'

'So? You didn't ask. And anyway, I told you where to find Fred, so I assumed if you wanted to know anything more about that job you'd find out from him.'

'Right. So presumably Mr Watson didn't know Mr Cook well enough to ask for help on his own behalf?'

'No – I knew Fred Cook better, so I put in a word for Terry. They became more pally later.'

'Because then they were both in the same line of work?'

'Aye, I suppose so.'

'As bookie's runners. Have you ever been in that line of business yourself, Mr Bateman?'

'Certainly not.'

'You find the suggestion offensive?'

'No, it's just that it's a bit illegal, isn't it? And besides, I don't like bookies – my dad bet on horses, and the bookies took everything he had. I don't approve of betting, but this was about getting a job for a friend.'

'Quite. So what was this spot of trouble that you say Mr Watson had at work?'

'I don't really know much about it – Terry just said that he was in trouble because he'd been robbed, and some bag he'd been carrying for his boss was stolen.'

'And presumably this boss of his was a bookmaker?'

'Aye.'

'Did he say what this bookmaker's name was?'

'He did, but I don't remember – something like Aston, I think.'

'Could it have been Ashdon?'

'Aye, maybe, something like that.'

'Did he report this robbery to the police?'

'He didn't say he had, but I don't know – maybe if you're

working for a bookie you don't get the police involved.'

'Did he report it to his boss?'

'I think so.'

'And did he say how Mr Ashdon reacted to the news?'

'Aye. He said he didn't believe him.'

'That sounds strange. Did he say why?'

'No. I thought Terry was going to tell me he'd got the sack. I mean, you're responsible for the man's property and you lose it, and he doesn't believe your explanation – I'd expect to be fired. But he wasn't. The funny thing was he just said this Mr Ashdon or whatever his name was had told him to lie low for a bit, keep his head down and steer clear of trouble.'

'Do you know why Mr Ashdon said that?'

'No idea, no. Strikes me as odd, though.'

'Did Mr Watson know who'd robbed him?'

'I asked him that myself, obviously. He said no. He was pretty shaken up – I think he was afraid. He also said I wasn't to tell anyone what he'd just told me, but I suppose now he's dead it makes no difference.'

'Well, sorry though I am to have to say it, Mr Watson's beyond the reach of anyone he might've had cause to fear now. I want to find out who killed him, so I'd like you to tell me everything you can remember him saying about this robbery.'

'OK. It won't be much, though. He didn't go into detail – he just said he'd been working as usual, collecting bets and taking them to the bookie and all that, but three men had jumped him, roughed him up and stolen his bag.'

'And is that all?'

'That's pretty much it. There was just one other thing –

he said they told him to give a message to this Mr Ashdon.'

'Yes? What was it?'

'They said, "Tell Ashdon we're waiting to hear from him, and we're not waiting much longer." That's all.'

CHAPTER TWENTY-FOUR

'What do you make of that, then, Peter?' said Jago as they left Bateman in his shed and tramped back across the grass towards the park gates.

'Well, they can't all be telling the truth, can they, sir? About that clock bag, I mean. Fred Cook says he doesn't know why it wasn't with Watson's things, you'd better ask Ashdon. Ashdon says he kept it because Watson wanted some time off but didn't say why. Then Bateman says he doesn't know anything about Watson asking for time off but he does know he said he'd been jumped by three men who stole the bag and he told Ashdon. Now, I know most of that's just hearsay and Watson's not here to speak for himself, but on the face of it, he told Ashdon one thing and Bateman something quite different.'

'And if we're to believe Cook, Watson told him nothing.'

'Yes. You think that might not be the whole story?'

'I'm thinking Cook might have reasons not to tell us the

whole story. Maybe we should have another word with him – see if he can improve his recollection.' Jago glanced at his watch. 'It's not opening time yet, so we might catch him at home. Let's go.'

Hugh Street, where the Cooks lived, looked like a small-scale afterthought shoehorned in between the grander houses of Belgrave Road and the railway line without an inch to spare. Number 76 was towards the end of the terrace. Jago rang the bell for the bottom flat, and a woman came to the door.

'Mrs Cook?' said Jago.

'Yes,' she replied, eyeing them up and down warily. 'And who are you?'

Jago produced his warrant card. 'We're police officers – Detective Inspector Jago and Detective Constable Cradock.'

'Oh, that's all right, then. I thought you might be selling insurance. Is this to do with poor Terry Watson? Fred told me when he got back from the pub – what a terrible business.'

'It is, I'm afraid. Is your husband still at home?'

'No, he had to go out again, but I'm expecting him – he must've got delayed.'

'Could we wait for him?'

'Of course. Come on in. You'll have to take us as you find us, though.'

She let them in and marched down the narrow hall ahead of them. A smell of baking wafted from the back of the house, and with it came the familiar sound of Sandy Macpherson at his theatre organ, performing one of his regular selections of popular melodies on the BBC.

She opened a door and led them into the kitchen. It was

a small room with a couple of easy chairs by the fireplace, a table with a gingham tablecloth and three wooden chairs by the back wall, and an old dresser in the alcove next to the chimney breast. A crumpled shirt with a needle and thread stuck into it was draped over the arm of one of the easy chairs, with a dirty cup and saucer on the floor beside it. In the corner of the room was the source of the music: a wireless set perched on a small cabinet. She crossed straight to it and turned it off.

'I don't suppose you want to listen to that, do you? I only had it on for company. Can I get you a cup of tea or something? I've got the kettle on ready for when Fred comes home.'

'Thank you, but no,' said Jago.

'Sit yourselves down, then.' She took the cup and saucer away to the scullery, then returned and put the shirt into a sewing basket. 'Just doing a bit of mending for Fred while I was waiting,' she said. 'There you are – you two take these chairs and I'll bring one over from the table.'

Jago and Cradock did as she instructed.

'Fred told me you're new to the area, Detective Inspector,' she continued.

'That's right, Mrs Cook.'

'Oh, no need to be formal – all the coppers round here call me Dolly.'

'I see,' Jago replied. 'So you're acquainted with all the local police officers, are you?'

'I suppose so, yes.'

'And what's the nature of your acquaintance, if you don't mind me asking?'

'I suppose you could say we're just supportive local

residents. My Fred's always tried to be helpful to the police, if you know what I mean – keeps his ear to the ground, like. There was this old copper years ago who was very kind to us, you see, and ever since then Fred's tried to help out when he can – passing on bits of gossip and all that. I'm not saying he's a saint, mind – he has been a bit naughty once or twice, but I suppose now the local coppers know he can be helpful, they don't give him a hard time.'

'Really? That is interesting.'

'Oh, yes. If you need to know anything, I'm sure Fred'll be pleased to help out if he can. And me too, of course.'

'Thank you, that's most kind of you.'

'So do you know who killed poor Terry?'

'Not yet. Did you know him well?'

'Can't say I knew him well, no – not as well as Fred did, anyway – but he used to come round from time to time. I thought he was a nice lad. I liked him, and I wasn't the only one – I got the impression he was popular with the girls.'

'His landlady's described him as charming. Would you agree with that?'

'Yes, I think I would – he was always very polite to me when he came visiting. But I think I'd call him more of a loveable rogue,' she chuckled. 'Not that I really knew him well enough to be a judge of that, but he had a bit of spirit about him, and I like that in a man. He only had one room to live in and he never seemed to have much cash to spare, but I got the impression he never let it get him down – he wasn't afraid of working, and he was always coming up with new ideas, like his scavenging.'

'Scavenging?'

'Yes, you know, like those people they call mudlarks –

the ones that muck about on the foreshore down by the river looking for things that get left behind in the mud when the tide goes out. He called it treasure hunting, but I don't think he ever found anything you might call treasure.'

'This wouldn't be the kind of scavenging that involves going out and looking for interesting things in the blackout that belong to other people, would it?'

'I don't know – he didn't say.'

'Do you know what he did with the things he found?'

'No, sorry. I don't mean he was doing anything criminal. It's just, well, he was a bit of a rogue, like I said. Sometimes Terry had that sort of twinkle in his eye – you know, a cheeky look. I remember him mentioning that girl once. The landlady's daughter – I don't recall her name. I said, "Just you watch out, Terry my lad. Don't get on the wrong side of her mum – you're only the lodger, and you don't want her to chuck you out on the street, do you?"'

'We've also been told Mr Watson was quiet and kept himself to himself, but that doesn't sound entirely consistent with the idea of a man with a cheeky twinkle in his eye who was popular with the girls.'

'I suppose it depends who you're talking to, doesn't it? Like I said, I met him a few times, so maybe I just saw a different side to him. Mind you, I'm no spring chicken myself, am I? So maybe I'm not the best person to tell you what the girls thought of him.'

The noise of the front door opening came from the hall, followed by what sounded like something being hauled in.

'Ah,' said Dolly, 'that'll be Fred bringing his bike in. There's a few light fingers round here, so you have to be a bit careful.'

She got up from her chair and moved towards the door. 'We're in here, Fred. We've got visitors.'

The door from the hall into the kitchen opened.

Dolly stopped in her tracks. 'Blimey, Fred, what's happened to you?'

Cook limped into the room. His clothes and hair were dishevelled, and there was a red swelling below his left eye, which was half-closed.

'What are they doing here?' he said, squinting at Jago and Cradock with his good eye.

'We've just dropped by to ask you something, Mr Cook, but I think you'd better let your wife see to that first. What happened?'

'Never mind that, Inspector,' said Dolly. 'You come over here, Fred, and let me get something on that eye.'

She steered him towards one of the chairs by the table. He winced and gasped as he sat down.

'You get your shirt off, love, so I can see what you've done.'

She fetched a bowl of water and a cloth as Cook slowly and cautiously removed his jacket and shirt, revealing more red bruises on his arms and shoulder. Pausing only to soak the cloth in water, wring it out with her hands and tell her husband to hold it on his eye, she moved behind him and gently lifted his vest. Jago stepped across the room to stand behind her and saw, like her, similar marks on Cook's back.

'Off with your vest too, Fred,' she ordered, and held the cloth while he eased the vest off, wincing again as he bent his arm. She went to get another cloth as he put the first back on his eye.

'So, Mr Cook, what happened?' Jago repeated.

200

'I walked into a lamp-post.'

'Really? And it's still half an hour to blackout time. It's surprising how many people walk into lamp-posts, isn't it? You'd think now they've got those white bands painted on them to help us see them in the dark, we ought to be able to spot them in broad daylight.' He moved round from behind Cook to face him. 'And bruises round the kidneys too – you don't get them from walking into a lamp-post. How do you explain that?'

'Just a little accident, Inspector, that's all.'

'Come along, now. You'd have to walk into the lamp-post forwards and then turn round and walk into it backwards to get damage like that. This was a fight, wasn't it? Are you in some sort of trouble?'

'Nothing I can't handle, Inspector.'

Dolly snorted.

Cook gave his wife a cautionary look and a curt shake of his head that intimated he didn't want to hear anything more on the subject.

'Something you'd rather a policeman didn't know about, is it?' said Jago. 'Something not particularly legal?'

'Now, come on, Inspector,' said Dolly, 'there's no need for you to go on at him like that. He's a good man, not a criminal – I told you he likes to be helpful to the police, didn't I?'

'You did, yes. Now, tell me, Mr Cook, who was it who gave you these bruises?'

'Sorry, I can't help you. It was just an accident.'

'I don't believe you.'

'Suit yourself.'

'So this is your idea of being helpful to the police?'

Cook remained silent.

'I suggest you think about it, then,' said Jago. 'I'd appreciate your assistance. Now, one more question. Did Terry Watson tell you about taking some time off work not long before he was killed?'

'Not as I recall, no, but then I hadn't seen him for a while. We work different areas, see. You'd better ask Mr Ashdon about that – he'd know all about any time off.'

'It was Mr Ashdon who told us. What I want to know is whether Terry Watson told you.'

'No, he didn't, but if Bill says he took some time off he must've done.'

'It's also been suggested that Mr Watson was robbed. Do you know about that?'

'No, I don't. You'd best ask Mr Ashdon about that too.'

'We may do just that, Mr Cook. Now, for the last time, who attacked you? If you won't help me with this, it could happen again, and I don't want that.'

'Fred?' said Dolly, but Cook merely shook his head and looked down. 'Well,' she continued, 'will that be all, Inspector?'

'For now.'

'Right, then,' said Dolly. 'I'll just see the policemen out, Fred. No need for you to get up.'

She led them down the hall and out of the front door onto the street.

'I'm afraid your husband wasn't as helpful as you'd led me to believe, Mrs Cook,' said Jago.

'I know – I'm sorry. He always tries to help you lads when he can, only not about his cousin's business – that's family, see, and it wouldn't be right, would it?'

'I see.'

'He told me about your little meeting down at the Duke of Clarence – I don't suppose you found him very helpful there, either. I hope you didn't think he was being awkward, but, well, it just got him a bit scared when these two coppers he didn't know turned up and started grilling him right where everyone could see him. In his line of work that can be bad for business, see.'

'Do you think there may be a connection between that and whatever happened to him on his way home just now?'

'I haven't a clue, but you never know, do you?'

'Can you get anything out of him, Mrs Cook?'

'I'm sorry, I don't think I can. Fred doesn't always tell me when he's in a spot of trouble – I reckon he likes to think he's protecting me, but I can look after myself. You have to down this street, I can tell you. It's got a bit of a reputation – you know, one or two slightly dodgy neighbours. I think they like it here because the houses are built at the top of the railway wall, you see, so if you need to get away a bit smartish you can just slip out the back of the house and climb down the wall, then at the bottom there's a little footpath that goes all the way to the river. Very handy for getting away from anyone who's after you, if you know what I mean – one bloke keeps a rope handy and gets down with that. Fred told me about that trick.'

'Handy for bobby-dodging, you mean?' said Jago, surmising that the Hugh Street rope trick might be as useful for evading the constabulary as it would for fleeing any other danger.

'Ah, well, that'd be saying, wouldn't it?'

'I suppose it would. But perhaps there's something you

can say – do you have any idea who might've given your husband those bruises?'

'No, I don't, and if I did I couldn't go behind Fred's back and tell you.'

'I understand that, Mrs Cook,' he replied, resigned to prising no further information out of her. 'Thank you for trying to help.'

She glanced up and down the street. 'I'll say goodbye, then, gentlemen.' She lowered her voice. 'Word to the wise in the meantime, though. If you're ever down Effingham Street way, near the old Thames Bank Wharf, and you find yourselves in need of a cuppa, there's a cafe there run by a fellow called Alf Stubb. A very interesting man, he is – I'm sure you'd find it an education having a chat with him.'

As she turned away to go back into the house, she paused for a moment and gave them what Jago could only have described as a knowing look.

CHAPTER TWENTY-FIVE

Jago had not slept well. It wasn't just trying to get a good sleep in a strange bed, it was trying to get any sleep at all on a bunk in the basement of a police station while anti-aircraft guns fired barrage after barrage at enemy bombers hidden in the dark sky above. But as the noise provoked memories of nights under bombardment in a cold, wet trench in France, he'd reminded himself he'd seen far worse. At least his temporary billet here was dry.

He grabbed a quick breakfast in the station canteen, where he was interrupted by a constable.

'Excuse me, sir, but we've had a phone call for you. The lady left a message.'

Jago's instant but unspoken response was that the lady in question might be Dorothy calling about her job. He was still wondering at the alarm in his reaction when the constable continued.

'It was a Mrs Edgworth, sir. She said you knew her, and

she asked if you could call on her today. She said she'd be at home all day.'

'Did she say what it was about?'

'No, sir, but she sounded upset. Shall I call her back, sir? She left a number.'

'Er, yes, that would be helpful. Tell her DC Cradock and I will try to drop by later this morning.'

'Very good, sir.'

As the constable departed, Jago's sense of relief that it wasn't a distressing message from Dorothy was followed swiftly by a kind of detached curiosity about why he'd included Cradock's name in his answer to Sally Edgworth. It was as if he'd felt some instinctive need for a chaperone.

He dismissed this distraction from his mind and drove from Rochester Row to Ambrosden Avenue to pick up Cradock.

'Good morning, Peter,' he said when his colleague had got into the car. 'I trust you slept well and had a hearty breakfast?'

'Yes, thanks, guv'nor. Well, not the sleep – it was a bit noisy last night, wasn't it? But breakfast was nice – fried egg, two rashers of bacon and four slices of toast. That should keep the wolf from the door.'

'Yes, for an hour or two at least, I should think.'

Jago started up the engine and headed west down Francis Street towards Vauxhall Bridge Road.

'So what's on the menu for today, sir?' said Cradock.

'Well, I want to see if we can catch Mrs Trubshaw at home this morning while her husband's at work in his shop. I'd like to talk to her a bit more about him when he's not there to shut her up. But first I thought we might

206

take a quick look at that place Dolly Cook mentioned in Effingham Street.'

'Yes, that was odd. She was tipping us off, wasn't she?'

'I got that impression, yes. But tipping us off to what, that's the question. I think I'd like to keep a low profile this time, just observe, then decide whether we want to go back and talk to him.'

'I was thinking last night that it's a bit strange – Terry Watson gets roughed up by three men and then gets himself killed, and now, not even two days later, it looks like Fred Cook's been roughed up too. Quite a coincidence – could it be something to do with their work? I mean, it's a shady business, whatever Ashdon says.'

'It's possible, but there could be all sorts of other connections too – I mean, maybe Cook knows more than he's telling us about the murder, in which case whoever gave him that beating yesterday might've been warning him to keep his trap shut. The man's a police informant, after all, and that little matter might not be as confidential as he'd like. There's still a lot we don't know about Watson, too – that "treasure hunting" business sounded decidedly dodgy to me.'

'That reminds me, sir – I got a message from the Yard about those prints too. The ones I got in the shelter and in Watson's room are his, so no surprises there, but they also say they've checked his prints against the records and he's not on file, so no previous convictions.'

'That's useful to know. So he's either an upright citizen or a rogue who was never caught, or at least never charged or convicted.'

They drove on until they came to Effingham Street

207

and parked halfway along it. The street led down to the Thames, and above its terraced houses and shops they could see again the two tall chimneys of Battersea power station and a towering gas holder on the opposite side of the river. Looking at the chimneys and the white vapour that poured from them, Jago was reminded of the distinctively tall buildings he knew near the Royal Docks. Perhaps, like them, this vital generator of London's electrical power had been spared bombing because it offered an unmistakable riverside landmark for enemy bombers steering their way to strike at the railway lines, Victoria station and beyond – destroying the homes and lives of people who had the misfortune to live close by them.

'Do you reckon that's it, sir?' said Cradock, pointing to a small shopfront a little farther down on the other side of the road. It had the name 'Alf's cafe' painted above it.

'Well,' Jago replied, 'it's the only cafe in the street, and he's called Alf Stubb, so I'd say that's a reasonable assumption. I don't want him to know we're coppers, though, so try not to act like one, and watch what you say. Don't mention Watson or the Cooks or anyone else to do with the case, and try to observe what's going on without looking like you're snooping.'

'Yes, guv'nor – will do.'

Jago glanced down at the battered fedora in his hand and the disreputable old coat he was wearing and sighed. 'Fortunately for me, the way this war's already ruined my clothes I don't think I'll look very official.' He ran an eye over Cradock's appearance. 'And you're not looking too smart yourself, so I suppose you'll do. Come on, let's go.'

They crossed the road and entered the cafe. The air

inside was heavy with the smells of fried breakfast, overlaid with a thick layer of cigarette smoke. A harassed-looking girl in an apron was weaving her way between the tables, each hand holding aloft a plate of food with a cloth to protect her skin from the heat. She deposited the plates in front of two waiting customers and then hurried to a swing door at the back of the cafe and disappeared from view.

Judging by the number of customers, trade was brisk – most of them focused on downing a quick meal on their way to work or perhaps on their way home from a night shift, Jago guessed. The place wasn't full, but full enough, he hoped, to save two strangers from being too conspicuous. A bull-necked thirty-something man in a collarless white shirt that looked in need of a wash stood behind the counter with an air of presiding over the proceedings without being too busy himself. With the girl in the apron gone, no other staff were visible.

'Grab that table over there,' said Jago to Cradock, pointing to the side of the room. 'Then we can see who's coming and going and keep an eye on the bloke who seems to be in charge. I'll get you a drink. What do you want – tea or coffee?'

'Coffee, please,' said Cradock. He stopped himself adding 'sir' just in time, mindful of Jago's instruction to watch his words, and went off to secure the table.

Jago crossed the cafe to the counter and ordered their drinks, then rejoined Cradock. 'He's bringing them over in a minute,' he said.

They sat for a while, observing the array of customers around them. Some were locked in animated conversation with their tablemates, while others ate and drank alone, steeped in their own silence. Jago noticed a short, grim-faced man with a cap pulled down over his forehead and a large shopping bag in his hand who entered the cafe but didn't look for a table. Instead he went straight to the counter and spoke to the man behind it, who took him through a door behind him, apparently abandoning the drinks Jago had just ordered. Within what seemed like seconds, however, the two men reappeared and the visitor scuttled out of the cafe again with a noticeable grin on his face.

Jago followed the short man out with his eyes, then switched back to the other customers. He spotted the girl in the apron again, pushing her way through the swing door with more orders, her face now flushed as she tried to move quickly across the room. She stopped abruptly, though, when her path intersected with that of the man with no collar. He was ambling towards Jago and Cradock, carrying their drinks. Only when he'd passed did she resume her hurried route.

Jago watched the man as he approached. His face reminded him of one or two retired boxers he'd met over the years: it had a lumpy look to it that suggested too many unsuccessful bouts. The conspicuous scar running down the left side of his face was also perhaps an indication that not all of his fighting had been regulated by the Marquess of Queensberry's rules, although on the face of a civilian in Britain in 1940 it was most likely a shrapnel scar from the Great War. But, he reckoned swiftly, the man was too young to have fought in that war. His train of thought was interrupted by the arrival of their drinks.

'Here you are, gents,' said the man, placing the two mugs on the table. 'Sure that'll be all?'

'Yes, thanks – we haven't got long,' said Jago. 'Looks like you've got enough on your hands already today. Is it always as busy as this?'

'Up and down, you know. It'll ease off later.'

'Your waitress seems to be working hard.'

'Yeh, well, she's getting paid for it. She's got no cause to grumble. If she don't like it she can try her luck somewhere else.'

Jago wasn't sure how to respond to this, so he merely uttered a vague 'Hmm' and gave a non-committal nod of his head. 'So is this your own place?' he said.

'Yeh, that's right,' the man replied. 'Don't think I've seen you in here before, though. You from round here?'

'No,' said Jago. 'We're just passing through.'

'What sort of business are you in, then?'

'Legal stationery – we're calling on some solicitors.'

'Lawyers? Huh. Nothing but trouble, that lot – they'd barely give you the time of day if you met them on the street, but they'll take all your money as soon as they get the chance. Nothing but a bunch of overeducated pickpockets, that's what they are. I run two honest businesses and can barely make ends meet, but they drive around in big fancy cars and wouldn't be seen dead in a place like this.'

'Two businesses, eh? That must be a handful.'

'Yeh, well, a man in my position's got no choice, has he? Last few years things've got really tough, especially with all those foreigners coming over here and taking our jobs – if you're running a place like this you've got your work cut out just keeping your head above water. You've got to have more than one string to your bow, that's what I say.'

'I see what you mean, yes. So what's your other string?'

'Oh, nothing much. I just sell bric-a-brac on the side – you know, bits of this and that. If you're looking for a little present for the missus I might have just what you need – bargain prices too. If there's something particular you're thinking of, I've got a lot of contacts in the trade and I can ask around and probably find it for you.'

'I'll keep that in mind, then. Thanks.'

'My pleasure. Anyway, I can't stand around chatting – got to get back to work. But don't forget if you're looking for something, let me know and I'll find just what you want. Enjoy your drinks. Pay at the till on your way out.'

CHAPTER TWENTY-SIX

When they left the cafe Jago took a deep breath and began to walk slowly down the street in the direction of the river. Cradock followed him.

'I just need a bit of fresh air, Peter,' he said by way of explanation. 'Unlike most of our fellow citizens, I prefer the smell of it to cigarette smoke, and you could've cut it with a knife in that place.'

'You can say that again, sir. Worse than a London bus.'

'And I don't know about you, but I thought I could smell a rat too. We need to come back soon and find out a bit more about Mr Stubb and his business interests. What did you make of him?'

'Well, not the sort of bloke you'd want to complain to about your fried egg, was he? Very touchy – he sounded just like that bloke Trubshaw when he was going on about foreigners and his business.'

'Perhaps they read the same newspaper.'

'Hmm . . . He didn't look like much of a reader to me. More of a bruiser, I'd say – not sure I'd like to bump into him in the blackout.'

'Or even in broad daylight. I could imagine him not being best pleased to be crossed. Not exactly mother's little ray of sunshine, was he? I got the impression if he ever smiled his face would crack.'

Cradock nodded. 'Still, he must've done something to cheer up that bloke who came in with the shopping bag – when he came out he looked like a cat with nine tails.'

'Two, Peter.'

'Sir?'

'Two tails – a happy cat has two tails, not nine. It's lives they have nine of, but perhaps you're thinking of a cat-o'-nine-tails – that nasty thing they flog you with when you're sentenced to penal servitude and fifteen strokes of the cat.'

Cradock's face suggested he was no longer sure what he was thinking of.

'But don't worry about it,' Jago continued. 'I'm sure happy cats don't mind how many tails they've got.'

'Right. Yes, sir.'

His need for fresh air satisfied, Jago turned round and began to walk back to the car. 'Come along,' he said. 'I don't want us to miss the exotic Mrs Trubshaw.'

They got into the car and drove eastwards along Lupus Street until they came to Cornwall Street, a quiet Regency-style turning on their right that led to a modern seven-storey block of flats at the far end. They knocked at the door of house number 10. It was opened by Deirdre Trubshaw, as stylishly dressed as she'd been the previous day.

'How delightful to see you again, gentlemen,' she said. 'I did so much enjoy meeting you both yesterday. Do come in, please.'

She ushered them into the house and then bustled ahead of them into the living room, plumping up the cushions on the sofa and arranging them neatly for her guests.

'Do take a seat. May I get you a coffee?'

'No, thank you. We've just had a drink, actually.'

'Very well – just let me know if you change your mind. Now, to what do I owe the pleasure of this visit?'

'It's just one or two things we'd like to ask you, Mrs Trubshaw. We're still trying to build up a picture of what kind of man Mr Watson was. Your husband gave us his impressions when we were with you in the shop, but we didn't hear yours.'

'Yes, well, he was talking about politics, and when Cecil gets onto that subject I don't get involved. It only annoys him. All I get from him is Mosley this, aliens that, hurrah for the Blackshirts – that's why we moved here, you know.'

'Really?'

'Yes, three years ago, when Sir Oswald Mosley moved into Dolphin Square – that's the flats you can see at the bottom of the street. He had an apartment in Hood House, where your colleagues arrested him in May this year and carted him off to prison, but back in 1937 people like my husband were convinced he'd be running the country by now. Cecil wanted to move here so we'd be right on his doorstep, and you'll have seen we couldn't be much closer. He volunteered to drive Mosley around, for nothing – he thought it was his way of serving the country, the silly old fool. I think it was Mosley who took him for a ride.'

'So Mr Trubshaw was a member of the British Union of Fascists?'

'Oh, yes, the good old BUF. You know, I think my husband even fancied himself as a leader of the people. I've never actually seen him striking poses like Mussolini in front of the wardrobe mirror, but it wouldn't surprise me if he did. Really, though, apart from anything else he just hasn't got the name for it, has he? I mean, if you call yourself Adolf Hitler even your name sounds angry and aggressive – but Cecil Trubshaw? You sound like a bank manager. It must be bad enough being lumbered with a name like Sir Oswald – no wonder his followers always just call him Mosley. But can you imagine the crowds shouting "Hail Trubshaw!" like they did for him? Doesn't sound like a twentieth-century man of action out to conquer the world, does it?'

Jago judged it prudent not to be drawn into answering this question.

'If you ask my opinion,' she continued, 'the trouble with my husband and his friends is they used to think they were dashing young heroes who were going to save the nation, but now if they had a scrap of humility I think they'd realise they're just a bunch of middle-aged men who are rapidly going to seed. Quite frankly, most of them have turned into bores with nothing better to do than chew over their old politics that no sensible person wants to know about any more. I don't know what Terry Watson would've been like when he got older, but I must say he was a refreshing change from my husband in one respect at least.'

'And may I ask what that was?'

'Yes. Where Cecil's concerned I think I've always played

second fiddle to his politics and his precious Mosley, but Terry took an interest in other people – he took an interest in me. The first time I met him was at one of the cycling club's social gatherings at the Drill Hall in Regency Street, just by that police training place of yours at Peel House. I sometimes think clubs like the Pimlico Wheelers are more about meeting members of the opposite sex than they are about cycling, you know. I was only there in my capacity as the chairman's wife, of course, so perhaps I should've expected to be invisible, but Terry came over to talk to me, which was charming.'

'How did he strike you?'

'Well, charming, as I said, full of life, and he was interesting, too.'

'And his views?'

'Definitely on the left – Cecil was right about that. But then again, he'd probably say Attila the Hun was a leftist. Terry's outlook on life was generally more humane.'

'What do you mean by that?'

'What, humane? Well, I suppose it's just that he seemed gentler than a lot of my husband's friends. He didn't seem to hate people.'

'You liked him?'

She closed her eyes and smiled briefly, as if remembering Watson. 'I did. You see, Cecil and his friends have had their day but either can't or won't see it. Maybe it's because my husband's considerably older than I am, but I have to say I find them insufferable. I feel closer to the younger generation – the young men of today have so much more attractive . . . what's the word? Yes – values, that's it. Much more attractive values.'

CHAPTER TWENTY-SEVEN

'I think I got you out of there just in time, Peter,' said Jago once Deirdre Trubshaw had closed the front door behind them and they were safely out of earshot. 'She was like a tiger waiting to pounce, and I rather fancy she would've devoured you first, what with you being such a fine specimen of the younger man.'

'Kind of you to say so, guv'nor. And thanks for rescuing me – I wasn't quite sure what she meant when she was talking about young men's values at the end.'

'Neither was I, Peter, but I thought it was best to leave before your values were put to the test. Now, then, it's not far from here to Mrs Edgworth's house, so we'd better call in as she asked and see what's been bothering her.'

When they got to the house in Ponsonby Place and rang the bell, barely seconds elapsed before Sally Edgworth flung open the front door and hurried them in.

'Oh, thank you for coming, Inspector,' she gasped. 'I've been so worried.'

'Well, let's sit down, and you can tell us all about it.'

'Yes, of course.' She pushed the living room door open, and as soon as they were seated she continued.

'It's about Mr Silver – your friend, Mr Cradock. Have you seen him yet?'

'Yes,' Cradock replied. 'We dropped in at the shop yesterday morning and saw him and Mrs Silver.'

'Did they tell you about Eliza?'

'Yes – that was a surprise to me. I haven't kept in touch with them, you see.'

'Was she all right?'

'We didn't actually meet her – they said she was at school.'

'Good.' She turned to Jago. 'Now, Inspector, the reason why I asked you to call was because of Mr and Mrs Silver and their shop. It was yesterday, you see. I was walking home from my work at the British Legion office in Eccleston Square and was hoping to buy an evening paper from Mr Silver on the way. There was no one around and it was quiet on the street, but as I was approaching the shop something peculiar happened. The light was fading, but I could see up ahead what looked like Mr Silver standing outside on the pavement talking to two other men. I was too far away to hear what they were talking about, of course, but he suddenly turned round and went back into the shop, and that's when it happened.'

'Yes?'

'I saw one of the men bring his arm back and then let it fly forward, as if he were throwing something, and immediately there was a crashing sound of broken glass. I thought he must have thrown something like a brick through the shop window.'

'What time was this?'

'Well, I finished work at five o'clock, tidied my desk and put my coat on to walk home, so it must have been about ten past five, maybe a quarter past. I'm afraid I didn't have the presence of mind to check my watch at the time.'

'Thank you. What happened next?'

'Not surprisingly, perhaps, the two men didn't hang around – they ran away. I was rather worried, because they were running straight towards me, but I was right by an archway between two houses that leads to the mews behind, so I slipped in there and peeped out. I thought I might see Mr Silver in pursuit, but there was no one coming after them, so they didn't seem worried at all – they slowed down and were laughing. I shrank back into the archway so they wouldn't spot me, but I could see them as they passed by the end. They were just strolling along as though nothing had happened.'

'Did you get a good look at them?'

'Just a glimpse.'

'Did you recognise either of them?'

'No, not at all.'

'Can you describe either of them?'

'Not in any detail, I'm afraid. They both looked fairly young – well, in their thirties, maybe – and quite heavily built, and they weren't smartly dressed. More like workmen, I suppose. I don't remember anything unusual about the first one, but when the one nearer me walked past I fancied I saw a long thin scar on his cheek. I couldn't swear to it, though – the light was fading, as I said.'

'Which side of his face was that?'

'Well, they were walking from my right to my left, so it would have been his left cheek.'

'Anything else?'

'Yes, he was wearing one of those pork-pie hats some of the young men have taken to wearing. It caught my eye because I think they look rather silly, especially on a heavily-built man.'

'Thank you – that's very helpful.'

'Not at all – I only hope what I've said will help you to find out who did this horrible thing.'

'Don't you worry about that, Mrs Edgworth. We'll do whatever we can. Did you speak to Mr Silver after this incident?'

'Yes, of course – I felt I had to.'

'Did he say whether anything had been stolen?'

'You mean a smash-and-grab raid? No – he said nothing had been stolen.'

'Do you know if he's reported it to the police?'

'I don't – I told him he should, but he seemed uncertain whether to bother. That's why I thought I should tell you. It's not right that anyone should damage such a nice man's property, but what's been worrying me is that it might not have been a robbery at all. I mean, it's just like Germany, isn't it? I can't help thinking about what happened there – Kristallnacht they called it, didn't they, when the Nazis broke all the windows in the Jewish shops? I said that man I saw was a hooligan, but I keep thinking it must be because Mr Silver's Jewish. I hate that kind of thing, and I'm very concerned about poor young Eliza. How can she go out like anyone else when there are thugs like that on the streets? We must protect her, Inspector.'

Her voice broke, and he thought she was going to burst into tears. Instead, she calmed herself, but she looked up at him with pleading, melting eyes that made him feel a little uneasy.

'Don't you worry, Mrs Edgworth,' he said. 'We'll go and have a word with Mr Silver and see what we can do.'

'Oh, thank you, Inspector. I knew I could rely on you.'

'Just doing my job, Mrs Edgworth. Now, is there anything else you wanted to tell us, or is that all?'

'That's all I needed to tell you, but I think Alice wants to have a word with you, too. Would you excuse me while I fetch her? I think she's in the kitchen.'

Sally left the room and returned with Alice Mason. 'Here she is, Inspector. Now Alice, you take your time. I'll stay here with you.'

'Yes. No hurry, Miss Mason,' said Jago. 'What do you want to tell us?'

Alice composed herself and looked him in the eye. 'It's about that question you asked me on Monday when you came here for tea,' she said. 'About the young men in the park. The thing is, I wasn't entirely straight with you. There was a young man who bought two white poppies.'

'I see. Well, thank you for telling me, Miss Mason. What day was this? You said you were in the park on Saturday and Sunday.'

'It was Saturday.'

'Could you describe him for me?'

'Yes. He was about thirty, not too tall, fair hair, blue eyes – pretty much like you said on Monday, really.'

'Indeed. And did he have a bike with him?'

'Yes, he did.'

'Is there anything else you can tell me?'

'Yes – I can tell you his name. He's called Terry Watson.'

'Ah, right. So you knew him?'

'Yes.'

'Why didn't you mention this before?'

Sally Edgworth leaned forward and touched him gently on the sleeve. 'This isn't easy for Alice, Mr Jago, as I think you'll understand if you let her tell you the story in her own time.'

'Of course.'

'Go on then, Alice,' said Sally. 'Tell the inspector.'

Alice took a deep breath and steadied herself before continuing. 'I think Sally's told you about the emergency home, hasn't she?'

'Yes, she has.'

'Well, the reason why I was in that home is because a man . . . took advantage of me. I met Terry at a dance a couple of years ago. He was really nice – good-looking and very charming, but—'

She broke off and looked away to Sally, who said nothing but nodded encouragingly to her.

Alice turned back to Jago but this time with her head down, staring into her lap. 'The thing is, I started seeing him. It was good, but then one day I found out . . . I was . . .' Her voice faltered. 'I-I couldn't believe it.'

'You can tell me, Miss Mason,' Jago reassured her.

She raised her head and looked him in the eye defiantly. 'I found out I was expecting a baby. There – you probably think I'm a stupid kid, and you're probably right. I didn't know what to do, what to think. I told myself it wasn't real. I didn't want it to be true, but I knew it was, and then I got angry.'

'And the father?'

Alice gave a short and bitter laugh. 'Yes, it was Terry Watson. I told him I was going to have a baby and it was his child, but he just laughed and told me to get rid of it. But I could never do that. It wouldn't be right – the baby hadn't done anything wrong, had it? I told Terry I never wanted to see him again, and he said OK, if that's the way you want it, and just walked away.'

'So what did you do?'

'I had to tell my mum and dad, but Mum just cried, and my dad said all sorts of things about me that he shouldn't have and threw me out. I had to find somewhere to live, so I stayed with a girlfriend, but that didn't work out. That's when the people at the home took me in – they were kind to me. And that's how I got to know Sally – she's been really good, too.'

She smiled at Sally, who raised her hand a little in a gesture of modesty.

'And the baby?' Jago continued.

'It was a boy,' Alice replied, 'born just over a year ago. I left the father's name bit of the birth certificate blank and I gave him up for adoption – I knew I wouldn't be able to give him a good life on my own, and there are lots of couples who can't have children who'd be able to give him all the love and opportunities he needs. I don't know where he is now, and I don't even know his name, but I know it's for the best.'

She sat up straight, a slight movement of her shoulders

giving the impression that she was shaking off the memory.

'So what happened in the park on Saturday?'

'Well, I was standing there with my poppies when suddenly there he was, pushing his bike along on the path. He just came up to me and said hello, all charm and smiles as if nothing had happened. He had the nerve to ask me if I'd got rid of the baby, so I said what business is that of yours? I mean, he'd just cut and run, hadn't he, the selfish swine. "You're a pig," I said, "and I hate you." He said, "OK, but let me buy a poppy." He asked me why they were white instead of red, so I told him it was about having peace instead of war.'

'And what did he say?'

'He just laughed at me again, and then he said, "Some of you girls are so naive." "Some of what girls?" I said. "Oh, just girls," he said, and he laughed again. I swore at him and told him to clear off. He said, "All right, but I'll take a poppy." Then it seemed like he changed his mind. He said, "Actually, I think I'll have two." "No skin off my nose," I said. "You can have as many as you like as long as you pay for them." So he took two and put some money in the tin – enough coppers to make it rattle, but he made sure I couldn't see how much, so it was probably twopence in farthings. Then he gave me a sly sort of wink and a smile that made it look like he was still laughing at me inside, and just walked off as if he hadn't a care in the world.'

'Did he tell you why he bought those two poppies?'

'No, but then people don't have to, do they? To tell you the truth, when he put that money in the tin it felt like he was mocking me – giving me some loose change that wasn't for me anyway, when he wasn't going to lift a finger to help

225

me with a baby. I meant what I said to him, you know – he is a pig.'

'And that was the last time you saw him?'

'Yes. Why?'

'There's no easy way to say this, Miss Mason, but I'm afraid Mr Watson is dead.'

Her eyes widened in a look of disbelief. 'Dead? But why didn't you say? I had no idea he . . . What happened?'

'He was found dead in suspicious circumstances, and we're treating it as a case of suspected murder.'

'Murder? That's awful. Do you know who did it?'

'Our investigations are still in progress. Can you think of anyone who might've had reason to want him dead?'

She stared at him as if she hadn't understood what he was saying. 'Reason to want him dead?' she said. 'Look, if he treated everyone else the way he treated me, I'd say there might be a queue. There was a time when I trusted him, Inspector, thought the best of him – back then I wouldn't have thought he had an enemy in the world, but that's because I didn't know what he was really like. I do now, but he cleared out of my life a long time ago, and I don't know anything about what he might've been up to since then. He might well've cheated one person too many, but no, I can't think of anyone in particular who'd want to kill him.'

'And you, Miss Mason – you've just said you told him you hated him. Did you hate him enough to want him dead?'

'What? Me?' she said in a tone of shocked incredulity. 'How can you say such a thing? Of course I didn't. That was just talk – yes, I was angry, and yes, I thought he'd behaved like a swine. When I said that, it was how I felt – I did hate him. But want him dead? Never, Inspector – I'm not that kind of person. And what would be the point? Like I said, he was out of my life, and I've been getting myself back on an even keel. I'm going to have a very good life without him, so why would I want to risk my whole future by killing him?'

She pulled out a handkerchief and wiped her eyes. Jago waited silently for her to regain her composure.

'I'm sorry, Inspector,' she said. 'It's not nice to be accused of murder.'

'No one's accused you, Miss Mason.'

'Well, that's what it sounded like to me. I swear to you, I don't know anything about it.' She folded the handkerchief carefully and put it back in her pocket, taking deep and slow breaths. 'Look, I'm sorry I flew off the handle,' she said, now calm. 'I think it was just the shock of hearing you say he'd been murdered. I don't think any man deserves that, no matter what he's done – not even Terry Watson.' She paused. 'When did it happen?'

'His body was found on Monday morning.'

She shook her head slowly. 'I still can't believe it. Gone – just like that. You never know what's waiting round the corner, do you?' She fell into a thoughtful silence.

'We'll be going now, Miss Mason,' said Jago. 'If we need to talk to you again we'll be in touch.'

He rose from his chair and turned to Sally. 'Thank you, Mrs Edgworth. We'll leave Miss Mason in your care – I expect she'll appreciate your support after this.'

'Yes, of course,' she replied.

'And Miss Mason,' he continued, 'there's just one other

thing I need to ask before we go. It's just a formality, you understand, but could you tell me where you were from Sunday night to Monday morning?'

Alice looked as though she was about to answer, but Sally spoke first.

'Alice was here with me, Inspector. We listened to the nine o'clock news on the wireless on Sunday evening and then went to bed – we have a coal cellar that we use for a shelter, and I made it quite comfy when the war started, so we usually sleep in there when the air raids are on. Alice was on duty at the hospital the next morning and I had a busy day ahead too, so we both thought an early night would be a good idea, especially with all the noise we get when the bombers come over. We were there together all night.'

'Is that correct, Miss Mason?' said Jago.

'Yes, it was just like Sally says.'

'Very well. And what time did you get up on Monday morning?'

'Seven o'clock.'

'And you, Mrs Edgworth.'

'The same – seven o'clock.'

'And what time did you leave for work?'

'About twenty to nine – I believe I mentioned it's about ten minutes' walk from here to the British Legion offices.'

'You did, yes. And you, Miss Mason, what time did you leave for work?'

'I don't remember, really. Probably about ten past eight, maybe twenty past. My shift doesn't start till nine, but I usually get there well before that – Sally says it makes a good impression, and besides, they're very strict at the hospital, and I don't want to get the sack for being late.'

'Thank you both.'

'Oh, and Inspector,' Alice continued, 'what I said about the baby and that – you won't tell anyone what I said, will you? Only I'm trying to make a new start, make my own life instead of letting other people decide who I am and what I should do. I don't want all that ruined. Please keep it under your hat, for my sake – and for my baby's.'

'I can't promise to do that, Miss Mason,' said Jago. 'I'll respect your privacy, unless doing so would obstruct the course of justice – in that case, I'm afraid the process of law has to take precedence. But I will do my best to be discreet.'

'Thank you,' she replied.

'Yes, Inspector,' Sally added, leaning forward with imploring eyes, 'please do whatever you can to protect Alice from any unpleasantness. And thank you for being so understanding. You're very kind, and that means a lot to me.'

CHAPTER TWENTY-EIGHT

'That Mrs Edgworth,' said Cradock as they returned to the car. 'Did you see the way she looked at you, sir? Like she was a damsel in distress and you were the knight she hoped was going to rescue her. That's what they call making eyes at you, isn't it?'

'Nonsense,' said Jago. 'She was very concerned about young Eliza's welfare, not to mention Miss Mason's, and she'd been through a distressing experience herself. It's quite natural for her to look to us for help.'

He had to admit to himself, however, that she had been eyeing him in a rather unsettling manner – just a little more friendly than was appropriate, he thought. Perhaps his instinctive feeling of being in need of a chaperone hadn't been too wide of the mark after all.

'Righto, guv'nor,' said Cradock. 'Whatever you say.'

They settled into the front seats of the Riley, and Jago changed the subject.

'I'm more concerned about your friend Benny Silver,' he said, pushing the starter button. 'I told Mrs Edgworth we'd have a word with him, so I think we'll pop into the shop and see what's what.'

'Thanks, sir,' said Cradock as they pulled away. 'Oh, and by the way, when you told Alice Mason you'd be discreet, what did you mean?'

'I meant I won't go around blabbing to everyone that she was in the family way and then asking them whether they knew. That poor kid's had enough trouble in her life without me adding to it.'

'That's true enough. It sounds like that Terry Watson wasn't such a charming bloke as people thought.'

'It depends what you mean by charming. The men with charm are often the ones most likely to get away with that kind of thing. If what Miss Mason says is true, that is.'

'You mean she was having us on?'

'No, I don't. She may be telling us the truth, but equally she may not be – there's no corroboration. In the end it's her word against his – and he's dead.'

'So now he can't defend himself, right?'

'Exactly. In which case it might be convenient for her to blame it on him.'

'But what would she stand to gain from that? She can't get paternity order payments from a dead man.'

'No, but there could be other reasons for her wanting to identify him as the father and not someone else. I'm not saying there are, but we should keep an open mind, that's all.'

Cradock thought for a while. 'So she could be trying to throw us off the scent, couldn't she? Maybe the father's

231

someone else and she wants to protect him, so she blames it all on Watson, who's dead and can't answer back.'

'It's a theory, but what evidence do you have for it?'

'Er, none.'

'Precisely. Besides, Alice has an alibi.'

'Yes, sir, but it was a bit funny the way Mrs Edgworth stepped in and told us what it was before Alice could get her mouth open.'

'She seems very protective towards young Alice, doesn't she?'

'Yes, but it was all very convenient, wasn't it? Both there together all night while Watson was being murdered?'

'Perfectly plausible, I'd say.'

'Yes, but Alice could've slipped out during the night and killed him, couldn't she? She might've done that and asked Sally to cover up for her in case we came nosing around. She wouldn't necessarily have told Sally she was out murdering someone – although if she didn't tell her, Sally might be putting two and two together now that she's heard our little conversation with Alice.'

Cradock paused to gather his thoughts. 'They could've been in it together all along, of course,' he continued. 'You know – they both slipped out in the night and killed him, then came back home together. That alibi means the two of them can cover for each other. Maybe that's why Mrs Edgworth jumped in before Alice could speak – she's smarter than Alice, so she made sure we heard the version that'd stand up. What do you think, sir?'

'I think anything's possible in theory, but we need to see what evidence we can turn up. Mrs Edgworth's told us she's been trying to support Alice, but what we don't know is how far that support might go. It's something for us to think about.'

Jago noticed Cradock's brow furrowing as if he were beginning to muse more deeply on the possibilities. 'But I think that will do for now, Peter,' he said before Cradock could get started. 'It's time to turn our thoughts to Benny Silver.'

CHAPTER TWENTY-NINE

The front window of Silver's shop had already been boarded up when they arrived. The sign hanging in the door still announced that it was open, however, and when they went in they saw he had a customer. A postwoman in a spotless blue uniform with a steel helmet and a capacious postbag slung over her shoulder was buying a packet of cigarettes at the counter, behind which stood both Benny Silver and his wife. Jago and Cradock hung back to one side, studying the newspapers, until she'd gone.

Miriam Silver came over to greet them. 'Hello, Peter,' she said, 'and good morning to you, too, Inspector. Can I get you anything?'

'No, thank you,' said Jago. 'We've just called in to check something with you.'

'Benny,' she called, 'look who's here.'

Silver glanced up and acknowledged their presence with a nod of his head. 'Good morning, gentlemen.' He slid out from behind the counter and joined them. 'Is this an official visit?'

'Yes, it is,' said Jago. 'We understand you had a spot of trouble here yesterday evening.'

'Trouble?'

'Yes. I believe someone smashed your shop window.'

'Ah, yes. How did you know?'

'Someone saw the incident and reported it. Did you report it yourself?'

'Er, no, I didn't.'

'Why not?'

'To be honest, I couldn't see the point. You know what it's like these days – half the schools have been requisitioned, and thousands of children are just running wild. I've heard of young kids going into public air-raid shelters when they're empty and smashing all the light bulbs with sticks just because they like the sound it makes. It beggars belief, doesn't it? We've only just got electric lights in some of those shelters, and now they're going round destroying them. I don't understand – you do something good to help everyone, and some kids just spit in your face. I can't imagine Eliza ever behaving like that – she thinks she's lucky to be alive. Her school's running two shifts to cope with the numbers, so she can only go in the mornings, but she knows where she'd be now if she'd stayed in Vienna and she's thankful for what she's got. Not all kids think like that, though, do they?'

'So you're convinced it was children who broke your window.'

'Yes. I'm sure it was just kids with nothing better to do with their time – little hooligans. I didn't see them, and they'd have been off before I even got out the door.'

'I don't think this was a case of juvenile delinquency, Mr Silver. We've had a report from a passer-by who saw two men throw something through your window. Are you sure you didn't see them?'

'I didn't see anyone throwing anything – I was in here when it happened. I found half a house brick lying on the floor.'

'According to our witness, you were talking with the two men in question before the incident occurred.'

'Well, I was talking to a couple of men, yes. They were just passing and asked for directions, so I told them and then came in.'

'Did you know either of them?'

'No – just a couple of strangers.'

'I see. Now, I'm sorry to mention a sensitive subject, Mr Silver, but when we were here yesterday you were telling us about those terrible things that happened in Vienna the year before last.'

'You mean Kristallnacht?'

'Yes. Do you think your window may've been smashed for the same reason? You're saying it was kids, but you didn't actually see them, did you?'

'No, I didn't. That thought about Kristallnacht obviously occurred to me and Miriam, but I didn't want to jump to conclusions and call the police in. I'm concerned about Eliza, you see, after what she's been through, and I'm worried that if she hears us talking about things like that it'll be very frightening for her.'

'My husband's right, Inspector,' said Miriam. 'We're not naive – we know there's plenty of people in this country who don't like people like us. Let me tell you what happened to me only a couple of weeks ago. I was caught out in an air raid in Gillingham Street up near Victoria station, so I took cover in the public shelter under the London Transport building, where the big new bus station is. There was a woman in there, old enough to know better, who started shouting and swearing and saying "This shelter's full of dirty Jewish women and prostitutes." The shelter marshal called a policeman, and he threw her out and took her to the police station. A few days later I saw in the local paper that she'd been fined fifteen shillings for causing a disturbance – but not for insulting Jewish women. I know we're at war with the Nazis now, but there's still some hateful people living right on our doorstep. So I hope you'll understand if we say the most important thing for us is to keep Eliza safe and happy so she can forget about the things that've happened to her family, not bring it all right into her new home here for no good reason.'

They were interrupted by the sound of a door opening at the back of the shop.

A young man came in, carrying a broom. 'I've finished doing the storeroom, Dad,' he began, then stopped when he saw the visitors.

Cradock stared at him. 'Daniel?' he said.

'That's right.'

'Daniel,' said Miriam, 'do you recognise our visitor? This is Peter Cradock – he used to come to our house when you were a little boy. He's a policeman now.'

'Ah,' said Daniel, examining Cradock's face more carefully and smiling, 'I remember you – you sometimes used to bring me some chocolate. How nice to see you.'

'You, too,' Cradock replied. 'I wasn't sure whether it was you, though. Looks like you're shaving now.'

'Oh, yes,' said Miriam, 'he's almost a man. Would you believe he's in the Home Guard?'

'Really?'

'It's true,' said Daniel. 'The government said you can join when you're seventeen, so I did. As soon as my birthday came round I went straight down the police station to register. In a year's time I'll be called up, so I thought I'd get some training in before then.'

'Keen to get into the war, then, are you?' said Jago.

'I am, yes. If you know anything about my family, you'll understand why I want to get out there and kill a few Nazis.'

'He doesn't know what war's really like,' his father sighed. 'I didn't before I was sent to the front, but now I do, and I don't want him to have to learn what I did.'

'Oh, come on, Dad, we can't just let them get away with it. What's going to happen to you and Mum and me and Eliza if they win? We've got to stand up to them and give them a taste of their own medicine, only bigger.'

'I know, Daniel, I know.'

The shop door opened and a young girl came in, carrying a bag. From the way Silver's face broke into a happy smile Jago guessed it must be Eliza. The appearance of a similar smile on Miriam's face suggested he was right.

'Hi, sis!' said Daniel, lunging forward to meet her hug. 'How was school? Have they run out of things to teach you yet?'

She giggled, but stopped when she saw the two strangers and drew back a little.

'Don't worry, Eliza,' said Benny. 'These are policemen.'
Eliza's face clouded.

'It's OK,' he reassured her. 'They're friends of ours.'

She nodded and gave them a polite smile.

'Mr Jago,' said Silver, 'if you don't mind, I think perhaps we'd better conclude our little discussion now that Eliza's home. She'll be wanting to tell us all about what she's been doing at school this morning, and . . . well, I'm sure you understand what I mean.'

'Certainly, Mr Silver,' Jago replied. 'We'll leave you to catch up – but if you remember anything else about those other visitors you had yesterday, please get in touch.'

'Of course,' said Silver.

Jago and Cradock left the shop. As Jago closed the door behind him he looked back and saw the family standing together, father and son each with a protective arm around Eliza's shoulders and Miriam holding the young girl's school bag close to her chest.

CHAPTER THIRTY

When Jago and Cradock had gone, Eliza recounted the highlights of her morning at school and went upstairs to start her homework. To the relief of the rest of her family she didn't ask why there had been two men from the police in the shop when she'd got home – especially the kind who wore ordinary clothes so you couldn't tell they were police until they arrested you.

Benny Silver and his wife and son went back to work in an awkward silence: Daniel opening a carton of Wills' Gold Flake cigarettes and replenishing the shelf behind the counter, his parents topping up the cash float in the till with bank bags of silver and coppers.

'Why didn't you tell them, Dad?' said Daniel as he turned back to the counter. Benny shut the drawer.

'Tell who what?'

'Why didn't you tell Peter and that other policeman what really happened to the window?'

'I don't know what you mean. I answered their questions, didn't I?'

'Yes, but you didn't tell them everything.'

'It's called discretion, Daniel. It's not always good to say everything you know – it can get you into trouble.'

'Trouble with the police, or with someone else?'

'With anyone.'

'But you can't just take these things lying down. We've talked about this before, Dad. It's not right.'

'It's easy to say things are right or wrong, but I've been around long enough to find out it's not always as simple as that. Doing something because you think it's right can end up hurting people.'

'Your father's right, Daniel,' said Miriam. 'You learn these things as you get older.'

'But if you know someone else is doing something that's wrong, surely it's not right to just stand by and let them do it. Isn't that why we're in this war? We've stood by for years and let Hitler do what he wants, and where's it got us? He's just laughed in our faces and carried on killing people. He got stronger because we did nothing, and now it's going to take everything we've got to beat him.'

'Perhaps you're right,' said Benny, 'but that's not something one man can do on his own. I don't want trouble for me or your mother, or for you and Eliza. I know this must sound weak to a boy of your age, but sometimes we have to come to terms with the fact that we can't do everything.'

'Maybe you can't do anything, but the police can – that's what they're for, isn't it? So, why don't you tell them? You know who it was, and so do I.'

'I don't want to make a fuss – once you tell them something, even if you trust them, you don't know who else's ears it might reach. When I was a soldier in the war we learnt not to stand up straight in a trench unless the sides were higher than we were. If your head showed above the trench, like as not a German sniper would spot you and take a pot shot, and you'd be dead. The only way to be safe was to keep your head down. I've never forgotten that, and you'd do well to remember it yourself, whether you end up in the army or not.'

'I see. So keep your head down and your mouth shut – that's the answer, is it?'

Miriam put a finger to her lips to shush him. 'Daniel, dear, please don't shout – I don't want Eliza to hear this.'

'I'm sorry, Mum, the last thing I want is for her to get frightened, but she's the reason why we've got to do something. She's escaped from one nightmare in Austria by the skin of her teeth, and we don't want her to end up in another one here, do we?'

'Of course we don't, dear, but we mustn't do anything rash.'

'You mean we should just put up with it and hope it goes away? You wouldn't do that if there was a tiger in the house, would you?'

'No, but I wouldn't go poking it with a stick, either. It doesn't pay to stir up trouble.'

'Oh, this is impossible,' said Daniel. 'Do I have to tell the police myself?'

The door creaked behind him, and Eliza came into the shop.

'Is everything all right?' she said. 'It sounded like you

were arguing.' She looked at each of them in turn.

Miriam was the first to speak. 'No, dear,' she said. 'We were just talking about something, but it's nothing to worry about. How are you getting on with your homework?'

'All right, I think, but I've got some history to do, and I still find all those English kings and queens confusing. We're doing the Wars of the Roses, but I can't work out who are the goodies and who are the baddies.'

'I'm not sure I can either, dear, but let's go upstairs and see if I can give you a hand.'

Miriam put an arm round Eliza and steered her towards the door, casting an admonitory glance over the girl's head towards the two men of her family.

'Right, son,' said Benny, 'I think we'd best get on with our work.'

'All right, Dad. But tell me you'll think about it.'

'Yes, Daniel, I'll think about it.'

CHAPTER THIRTY-ONE

'I'm still trying to piece all this together, you know, Peter,' said Jago as they sat in the car in Rampayne Street, 'and I'm still wondering whether any of it fits. We've got three men who've all been attacked in one way or another. Watson was set upon and robbed by three men, and a week or so later he's murdered. Fred Cook won't admit it, but it looks like he's been beaten up too. Now there's Benny Silver – not physically assaulted, as far as we know, but he's had his shop window smashed.'

'You're looking for some kind of connection, sir?'

'I am, and the obvious one's between Terry Watson and Fred Cook – both working for the same man, our friend Bill Ashdon. He hasn't really told us anything yet, apart from claiming Watson asked for some time off, so if it's true that Watson was robbed, I think it's time we pushed Mr Ashdon a bit harder. I want to know whether anyone's trying to put pressure on him for some reason by having a go at his employees. If it's true that the men who attacked Watson gave him a message for Ashdon, it would certainly look that way.'

'Shall we go and ask him then?'

'Yes, I think we will.'

Jago started up the car and they headed north towards Ashdon's office.

'If these attacks are connected,' said Cradock, 'any ideas on what might be behind them?'

'Well, if anything violent happens and it's something to do with horse racing and bookies, my first guess would normally be gangsters and protection rackets.'

'Could that be why Benny's window got smashed, do you think? A protection racket, I mean. That'd be a potential connection, wouldn't it?'

'Could be, yes.'

'There certainly seems to be something a bit fishy going on with Benny. I mean I don't like to say this about an old friend, but I don't think he was telling the truth back there in the shop.'

'In general, or in particular?'

'I don't know. It was just the way he was so sure it was kids who'd smashed his window, and he never mentioned those two blokes Mrs Edgworth saw him with until you told him there was a witness who'd seen him talking to them.'

'Yes, but he didn't claim he'd actually seen children doing it, and he didn't deny those men had done it either – all he said was that he hadn't seen anyone throwing anything, which strictly speaking was correct. At least it's correct if what Sally Edgworth told us was true, about him going back into the shop before the men threw the brick.'

'You think she was lying?'

'Not necessarily, but everyone's capable of lying if they have to. Besides, fading light can play tricks on you, just as much as memory.'

'I suppose so, yes.' Cradock paused as a new thought occurred to him. 'Talking of bricks, sir, there was a pair of them in Watson's saddlebag, wasn't there? Do you think there could be some connection there too?'

'What, between him and this window incident of Benny's? Well, there's a lot of bricks lying around these days and more than one way of using them, but there's no necessary link, is there?'

'No, but I'm just wondering – Watson might well've been using them for his bike training, but maybe he was putting them through windows too. You said as much yourself, sir.'

'Indeed I did.'

'And talking of connections, that scar Mrs Edgworth mentioned – were you thinking what I was thinking?'

'You mean Alf Stubb, I presume.'

'That's right – the way she described it, it sounded like the one he's got.'

'It did, although having a scar on your face isn't that unusual. And besides, she said she couldn't swear to it, so she wouldn't exactly be a star witness in court. But even so, I want to have a word with Stubb about that window.'

'Do you think we might be able to get Benny into the witness box? If it really is some kind of protection gang, I mean – it'd be horrible if it turned out people like that had their claws in him.'

'The trouble is someone who's got his whole life tied up in a little shop isn't likely to go telling the police who's putting the squeeze on him – those gangsters make it very clear to their victims what'll happen to them if they do. No, if someone's in that position he'll reckon it's safer to pay up and keep quiet rather than have his shop burnt down.'

'Maybe he'll tell me, though, sir. Benny and I are friends, after all, and I'm sure he trusts me.'

'All right, then, maybe we'll go back and see him later, but I don't expect to get much out of him. I want to see Ashdon first, and then Stubb.'

'Would it be worth finding out whether Ashdon's ever heard of Benny while we're there?'

'Yes, I think it would.'

Jago drove to Ashdon's office, where they found the bookmaker in. This time he recognised them through the window and unlocked the door without requiring them to identify themselves.

'Hello,' he said, letting them in, 'you're back soon. Am I to expect daily visits? Only I'm a busy man, you know.'

'We shan't take much of your time, Mr Ashdon,' said Jago. 'It's just that when we saw you yesterday you said Mr Watson had asked for some time off, but since then we've been told he was attacked and robbed of his bag, and now it seems Mr Cook's been beaten up too. You told me you look after your employees, but you don't seem to have looked after Mr Watson very well, or even your own cousin.'

'Be fair, Inspector – look, in my line of business, reputation's everything. My punters need to know they can rely on me. They've got to be sure that if they pick a winner I won't welsh on them, and their stakes aren't going to be nicked on their way here. If people start to think you're unreliable they'll take their money elsewhere, so I didn't want it to get around that one of my runners had been robbed.'

'And in my line of business, obstructing the course of public justice is a serious matter too.'

'Yes, well, my mistake, perhaps. But when you came here yesterday you didn't ask me anything about Terry being roughed up, so I thought it'd be better not to go into too much detail – that's why I said he'd just asked for some time off. It wasn't a big deal.'

'Not a big deal? Your man had been attacked and robbed.'

'Well, yes, but I didn't lose anything – the only thing they took was his clock bag.'

'But isn't that the one thing you wouldn't want stolen? It's got all the money in it.'

'No, that's it, you see. He delivered all the money and slips for the New Cambridgeshire Stakes and then went off again – there were three more races due that afternoon – and that's when he was attacked, so the bag they stole was empty.'

'I see. So now you're admitting you didn't keep the bag, and Mr Watson was attacked and robbed after all?'

'Well, that's what he told me, yes.'

'And did you believe him?'

'I wasn't sure – I mean, you'll understand if I say there wasn't much evidence. He looked a bit knocked about, but that could've been anything, and he didn't have the bag, but that doesn't necessarily mean someone had stolen it. He could've just made up a story for some reason. I'm not saying he did, of course, but I was keeping an open mind, so I told him to lie low for a while – I didn't want him to get roughed up again if it was true, and if he was up to something it wouldn't do any harm to keep him away from my cash for a while. You have to think about these things when you're running a business, you know.'

'I'm sure you do. So it wasn't just a case of Mr Watson asking you for some time off.'

'No.'

'Did he tell you who'd attacked him?'

'No, I'm afraid not. He said he didn't recognise any of them – they were wearing masks.'

'And do you happen to know who they were?'

'Of course not – how would I?'

'Did he say anything about them giving him a message for you?'

'For me? Certainly not.'

Jago paused for a moment. 'Before we go, Mr Ashdon. I'm just wondering – do you happen to know a man called Benny Silver?'

'Silver? No, never heard of him. Should I?'

'Not necessarily. How about a man called Alf Stubb?'

'No, sorry, can't help you there either. Is that everything?'

'Yes – apart from one simple but important question. To the best of my knowledge Mr Cook wasn't robbed, and all Mr Watson lost was an empty bag. So if stealing money wasn't the reason, why would anyone want to beat up two of your runners?'

'I don't know – it doesn't make sense to me.'

'Really? Could someone perhaps have intended it as a warning for you?'

'I don't know what you mean.'

'But it's an obvious possibility, isn't it? You told us yourself yesterday that in your line of business it's a question of the survival of the fittest. You do what you can to survive, so maybe someone else is trying to do the same at your expense. I'm thinking about gangsters who run protection rackets and like to boost their income by persuading people like you to part with some of theirs. It's not unusual in your line of work, is it? Is someone trying to lean on you?'

'Don't you worry, Inspector. No one leans on me, and if they try – well, just leave it to me. I can handle it myself.'

'I hope you're not thinking about taking the law into your own hands, Mr Ashdon.'

'Of course not, no – but like I said, you don't need to worry about me.'

'Well, in that case you'd better make sure you don't do anything to give me cause to worry. Do I make myself clear?'

'I understand what you're saying, Mr Jago. Let's leave it at that, shall we?'

Jago's smile was cold. 'We'll be in touch, Mr Ashdon. Goodbye.'

CHAPTER THIRTY-TWO

A quick glance round the cafe in Effingham Street as they entered suggested to Jago that whatever profits it made must come from its breakfast clientele. Compared with the packed and bustling establishment they'd seen yesterday morning, today's early afternoon equivalent seemed almost deserted. The waitress, who'd been run off her feet then, was now leaning against the wall behind the counter, looking bored. With only a few tables occupied, mainly by women chatting quietly over a cup of tea, Jago surmised that she probably wasn't needed. No chance of hiding in the crowd today, then.

Alf Stubb was standing by the till with a cloth in his hand and looked up as the door closed. His face was less than welcoming, and Jago thought it prudent to choose a table near the door. Perhaps it was the lack of customers, or maybe for some other reason, but today there was no need for him to go to the counter and order: Stubb came straight over to them as soon as they sat down. 'Afternoon, gents,' he said, giving the table a cursory wipe with his cloth. 'What can I get for you?'

'A tea and a coffee, please,' said Jago.

Stubb held his head back slightly and looked down his nose at them. 'You were in here yesterday, weren't you? Something to do with solicitors?'

'It was to do with the law, yes. Actually, we're police officers.'

'Oh, really? We don't get a lot of coppers in here. So what is it – business or pleasure?'

'Business. You're Mr Stubb, I presume?'

'That's right. And you?'

'I'm Detective Inspector Jago and this is Detective Constable Cradock.'

'Right, well, if it's business you'd best come out the back. We'll get your drinks on the way.'

They followed him to the counter, where he beckoned the waitress over.

'A tea and a coffee for these two gentlemen, Eunice, and a black coffee for me. Bring them through to the office, then mind the shop for a few minutes.'

Taking Jago and Cradock behind the counter, Stubb opened the door through which they'd seen the man with the shopping bag disappearing the previous day. It led down a short passageway to a second door. Stubb opened this too, waving them into a room that he announced as his office. The decrepit furnishings and overall unkempt appearance of the place suggested that the patron of this establishment wasn't exactly the Joe Lyons of southern Pimlico.

'Sit yourselves down,' said Stubb, motioning to a grubby sofa. 'I'll see your warrant cards, too, if you don't mind. Can't be too careful these days – there's a lot of crooks about.' He inspected their cards and took his seat behind a battered wooden desk. 'Right, so what's this all about?'

'We're here because of an incident that took place yesterday evening, Mr Stubb. Someone put a brick through a shopkeeper's window.'

'Oh, yeah? And where was this, then?'

'Rampayne Street.'

'So what's it got to do with me?'

'The description we've been given of one of the men throwing the brick matches yours.'

'This shopkeeper reported it to you, did he?'

'No. This was a witness.'

There was a light knock at the door and the waitress came in, carrying an aluminium tray with two cheap glass sugar bowls, three teaspoons and three mugs of tea and coffee. She distributed these to the men and left without a word.

'So,' Jago continued, stirring sugar into his tea, 'can you tell me where you were between five and five-thirty yesterday?'

'Yes, I can, and it wasn't Rampayne Street, I can tell you that for a fact. I think I told you yesterday about having a few extra strings to your bow, didn't I? Well, I do odd jobs here and there, evenings and weekends mainly, and as it happened I popped out about five o'clock yesterday to see a bloke who wanted a bit of painting done – just to tell him how much it'd set him back, you see. Ask Eunice out there – she'll be able to confirm what time I went out.'

'The fact that she may be able to confirm when you left the cafe isn't an account of your whereabouts, Mr Stubb – I want to know where you were at the time in question.'

'Oh, yeah, of course. You're quick, aren't you?'

'Between five and five-thirty, Mr Stubb.'

'All right, keep your hair on. I was up in Lupus Street – this bloke's got a shop, see, very respectable local trader, he is. I do some odd jobs for him now and then.'

Jago sipped his tea. It was neither hot nor a good brew, so he swilled down half of it and left the rest.

'What's his name, please?' he said, finding nowhere to put his mug and setting it down on the floor beside the sofa instead. He glanced at Cradock, whose expression suggested his coffee was not the finest he'd tasted either.

'It's Trubshaw,' Stubb replied.

'Mr Cecil Trubshaw?'

'That's the one – you know him?'

'We've met.'

'Right, well I was with him, in his shop. Number 69, Lupus Street.'

'What time did you arrive?'

'We'd arranged that I'd see him at five o'clock, so I got there just before that. It's only about five or six minutes' walk from here.'

'And when did you leave?'

'About half past.'

'And Mr Trubshaw will be able to vouch for that?'

'I can't see why not.'

'So you weren't involved in any way with this incident I've described?'

'What, smashing shop windows? I thought that was

Hitler's job these days – you should see how many his air force boys have smashed round here of late. I wouldn't have thought one more or less was worth making a fuss about.' He began to laugh at his own wit but stopped when it drew no response from Jago. 'Anyway, if you think I've got anything to do with it, you're mistaken. It's nothing to do with me.'

'Very well. By the way, Mr Stubb, I couldn't help noticing that scar on your face. How did you get it?'

'What, this?' Stubb rubbed the scar with his left hand. 'Oh, I just got into a fight.'

'Do you often get into fights?'

'No, no, that was years ago. I was just a kid then – I'm a respectable businessman now.'

'I see. Well, that will be all for now.'

'Righto – just let me know if I can be of any more help.'

'We will.'

Jago got up from the sofa, followed by Cradock, and opened the office door to leave. As Stubb came out from behind his desk, Jago paused in the doorway and turned to face him.

'Actually, there is one small thing you could help us with, Mr Stubb.'

'Yeah?'

'I noticed something on the floor over there and wondered whether we could take a look at it.'

Stubb looked puzzled.

'The rucksack, Mr Stubb, behind your chair.'

'Oh, right.' Stubb picked it up and handed it to Jago, who took the leather strap he'd found in Watson's room out of his pocket and matched it to the tear on one of the rucksack's pouches.

'That's interesting,' he said. 'I seem to have the strap that's missing from your rucksack.'

'Oh, no, it's not mine, Inspector – nothing to do with me.'

'Whose is it, then?'

'Er, it belongs to one of my customers. If I recall correctly, he brought some little bits of stuff in for me to buy. I didn't have time to look at it then, so he said he'd leave it with me and come back for it later. Funny thing is, he never came back.'

'What was his name?'

Stubb screwed up his face as if concentrating. 'Sorry, mate. Can't remember his name – he was a new one.'

'His address?'

'No – no idea. I don't need to know where my customers live, see, so I don't usually ask.'

'Well, I'm going to take this away with me.'

'Be my guest. It's empty now, anyway – I had a buyer, so I sold the stuff on.'

'And what exactly was the "stuff" your nameless customer brought in?'

'Odd little bits and pieces – I deal in bric-a-brac, like I said, so it's all sorts of things. None of it's worth much, so with a bagful like that I just have a quick look in case there's anything valuable, then sell it as a job lot – unless someone's asked me to keep an eye out for something in particular, and then of course I pick it out and save it for them.'

'And in this case?'

'Nothing special, no.'

'Can you describe the man who brought this rucksack in?'

'No. He was just an ordinary bloke, I think. Nothing distinctive about him that'd catch your eye and stick in your mind. Why – are you looking for him?'

'I'd just like to know who he was.'

'Well, I'm sorry I can't be of more help. But if you see him, tell him when he comes back I'll give him his money.'

'Thank you, Mr Stubb. We'll see ourselves out.' Jago reached into his trouser pocket and took out a sixpence, which he laid on a small table beside the door. 'That's for our drinks, Mr Stubb. Goodbye.'

CHAPTER THIRTY-THREE

'Looks like we've got a connection between Terry Watson and Alf Stubb, then, doesn't it, sir?' said Cradock as Jago stowed the grey canvas rucksack on the back seat of the Riley. 'Stubb made out he didn't know Watson, but that rucksack says he did. And that business of Watson and his so-called "treasure hunting" – you were right when you said it was really about looking for stuff in the blackout and pinching it, weren't you? And Watson was flogging it to Stubb.'

'But not quite, perhaps, Peter,' Jago replied, getting behind the steering wheel. 'There's no doubt the strap we found in Watson's room came off that rucksack, but the fact that we found it here in Stubb's shop doesn't necessarily mean it was Watson who brought it here, nor that he stole the items – and the rucksack's empty, so we've only got Stubb's word for what was in it. We need a bit more evidence before we can be sure of anything.'

'And what about that brick through Benny Silver's window? I mean, Stubb's a shifty-looking character, isn't he? And with that scar of his, I still reckon it's got to be him.'

'I share your suspicion, Peter, but I'm not so sure about why he'd do it. You could be right and it's to do with some kind of protection racket, but it could be that Sally Edgworth's right and it's because Benny's Jewish. Or it could be something – or someone – quite different.'

'Interesting coincidence that his alibi was being with Trubshaw, though, wasn't it?'

'It certainly was. Maybe it's just that Pimlico's a small world, but we'll need to go and test that alibi with Mr Trubshaw.'

'Don't you think we should try to get some more out of Benny first, though, sir? You said we'd go back and ask him whether his window getting smashed was anything to do with a protection racket, didn't you?'

'I did, yes, and after that little conversation with Stubb I think we should do so sooner rather than later. I'd regard Benny Silver's evidence as more reliable than anything Stubb came up with, alibi or no alibi.'

'Me too, sir. Funny how it's the shady characters like Stubb who can always pull an alibi out of the hat for exactly the right time, isn't it?'

'Yes, and if I'm any judge of Stubb, he's the sort of man who has ways of persuading someone to provide him with an alibi whenever he needs it. We'll check his story with Trubshaw, but we'll see your friend Benny Silver first – it seems to me he's got a lot more to lose in this situation than our local cycling club chairman. We need to push him and find out whether he knows Stubb. I think he's frightened, but we've got to give him the chance to help us. Let's go.'

They returned to the Silvers' shop, where they found Benny, Miriam and Daniel all at work. A customer was leaving as they went in, and there were no others in the shop, so Jago got straight to the point while the coast was clear.

'Good afternoon, Mr and Mrs Silver, Daniel. Sorry to disturb you again so soon, but there's a couple more things we need to ask you about.'

'That's fine,' said Silver. 'As you can see, business is a bit slow this afternoon. What do you want to know?'

'Well, I've been thinking about that incident with your window again. You see the thing is, in my experience, when a shopkeeper has a brick put through his window there can be quite a range of possible reasons. If it's a jeweller's window, it's usually going to be a smash-and-grab raid, but if it's a newsagent and confectioner's shop like yours, that tends not to happen so much. Sometimes a smashed window could mean a rival thinks he can profit from driving the competition out of business. And as we've already discussed, in Germany and Austria it was because of the unpleasant views some people held about the shopkeeper's background, so I can't rule out that being the case here. But there's another common cause, and that's what I wanted to ask you about – I'm talking about gangsters who want to cause a bit of damage as a warning, to put the frighteners on the shopkeeper so they can extort money from him. It's what they call a protection racket, and I'd be particularly interested to know whether that's what's happening to you.'

'The simple answer's no,' said Silver. 'I haven't had

anyone like that round here.'

Jago glanced at Miriam's face, then at Daniel's, but their expressions betrayed no sign of dissent or concern.

'I'm sure I don't need to tell you,' he continued, 'there are gangs like that operating in London, and possibly in this area. People like the Mullery Gang, or the Maldini Brothers. Have you heard of them?'

'No,' Silver repeated. 'I've heard of that kind of criminal, of course, but not those ones in particular.'

'Well, let me tell you, in my line of work their names are as familiar to us as the *Daily Mirror* and the *Sunday Times* must be to you. But perhaps we could try another name on you. Peter?'

He motioned to Cradock to step in with a question.

'Yes, Benny,' said Cradock, 'there's a name we've come across, and it'd be really helpful if you could tell us whether you've heard of him – just as a favour for an old friend, like.'

'OK,' Silver replied. 'What's his name?'

'He's called Alf Stubb. Does it ring any bells?'

'No. Should it?'

'Not necessarily, of course. But the thing is, he matches the description our witness gave us of one of the men running away from your shop after the window was smashed. That means we're wondering whether it was him that did it, so it'd help us a lot if you were able to say.'

'I'm sorry, Peter, but I can't.'

'Look, Benny, I can understand you not wanting to say who it was, but you must know that whoever it was, if you don't stand up to him he won't just go away and leave you in peace. He'll want more and more, until he's bled you dry and you're no further use to him. And if no one stops him it'll be worse for every other business in the neighbourhood.'

'Yes, I know what you mean, Peter, but I don't know him. Besides, these people you're talking about, these gangs – supposing it was this man Stubb you're talking about and he's working for one of them, what difference would it make if anyone accused him? If he was sent to prison, wouldn't whoever's running the gang just carry on and recruit someone else to do their dirty work? And supposing those gangsters had bought someone in the police, too. If they had a police officer in their pocket and he told them everything you and your colleagues had on them, what hope would there be for the poor shopkeepers who'd stood up to them and informed on them? Those gangsters would make short shrift of them, wouldn't they? Your witnesses would probably be found dead in the river.'

Jago could see nothing was going to persuade Silver, and he knew even he couldn't guarantee that the things Silver was predicting wouldn't happen.

'Right, well, thank you again, Mr Silver,' he said. 'I can only ask that you think very carefully about what Peter and I have said. And if you get any more trouble, please contact the police – there are things we can do to help and protect you. But if you choose not to, you'd better keep a close watch on your property – and your family.'

CHAPTER THIRTY-FOUR

Jago glanced back into the shop through its closed door as they left. He could see Miriam Silver talking to her husband by the counter, gesturing with her hands in a way that suggested their discussion was animated, but he knew he would gain nothing from going back and interrupting them.

'Sorry, guv'nor,' said Cradock. 'I thought they might trust me enough to confide in me, but they obviously didn't.'

'It's not your fault, Peter. You tried your best, but I'm not sure they trust anyone except themselves at the moment, and I can't say I blame them. We can ask them to help us, but we're not the ones who have to live with the consequences. Besides, we've still got a murder on our hands, and we need to talk to Fred and Dolly Cook, so let's go and see if they're at home.'

They got into the car, and Jago put the ignition key in the lock.

'So what are we trying to get out of them?' said Cradock.

'Well, let's see,' Jago replied, leaving the ignition key unturned. 'After what Dolly said about Watson being popular with the girls, and then that story Alice Mason told us about him, I'd like to know whether they can shed any more light on his love life. I'm also thinking about that message Dennis Bateman mentioned – the one he said Terry Watson was given for Ashdon by the men who attacked him.'

'Yes, and now Ashdon says Watson never breathed a word of it.'

'Exactly. I can think of reasons why Bill Ashdon might not want us to know about a threatening message like that, but equally he might be telling the truth – in which case, did Bateman get it wrong? He said Watson told him about the message, but that doesn't mean Watson himself actually passed it on to Ashdon. At the moment we've only got Bateman's word for it that whoever attacked Terry Watson gave it to him.'

'Yes,' said Cradock, pausing to think. 'But did you notice that other thing Ashdon said?'

'What was that?'

'When we were talking to him just now – he said when he saw Watson after that attack, he told him to lie low for a while. Now, we already knew that, because it's what Bateman told us, but we hadn't mentioned it to Ashdon – he told us off his own bat, didn't he? That means Bateman was right about what he said Watson had told him – so maybe he was right about the message too.'

'Very good, Peter – well done.'

'Thanks, guv'nor.'

'We've still got a problem, though – even if Bateman's a reliable witness, as that suggests, what he's told us is only hearsay. If that attack on Watson really was something to do with gangsters and it was the same people who roughed up Fred Cook, I'd like to know whether Fred got a message for Ashdon too. Let's see what Mr and Mrs Cook have got to say for themselves – if they're so keen to assist the police, perhaps he won't be as tight-lipped as he was last time we spoke to him.'

Jago turned the key to start the car. They drove northwards in the direction of Victoria station until they reached the Cooks' home in Hugh Street. A ring at the bell brought Fred Cook to the door.

'Sorry to disturb you, Mr Cook,' said Jago. 'We'd just like to come in for a quick chat, if we may.'

'That's all right – we're not planning to go out. Come in.'

Cook opened the door wider and let them in. Unlike their previous visit, this time the wireless was off, and their footsteps sounded heavily on bare floorboards as they made their way to the kitchen, where he announced their arrival to his wife.

'Oh, hello, Mr Jago,' said Dolly, wiping her hands on her apron. 'And Mr Cradock, wasn't it? Can I get you a cup of tea?'

'That's very kind of you,' Jago replied, 'but no, thank you. We've just popped in to see if you can help us with one or two things.'

'What can we do for you, then?'

'I'd like to ask about something you mentioned when we were here yesterday, Mrs Cook. I asked you about

Terry Watson, and you said you thought he was popular with the girls.'

'Yes, I remember – this was before you got home, Fred.'

'So I've been wondering,' Jago continued. 'Do you know whether he had a particular girlfriend?'

'No, I don't recall him mentioning one. Mind you, I never really thought of him as the settling down sort – you know what I mean? Although some men change their minds when they get a bit older, don't they? Did he ever say anything to you, Fred?'

'Not about that, no,' said Cook.

'Does either of you know whether he'd ever had any particularly close relationship with a woman, or any trouble in that area?' Jago asked.

'What, you mean trouble for him, or trouble for the girl?' said Dolly.

'Just any relationship problems.'

'I wouldn't know,' said Cook. 'He certainly never discussed anything like that with me – but then I was just someone he knew, not some kind of Dutch uncle. You should ask Dennis Bateman about that – he was mates with Terry, more than I was. He lives in Peabody Avenue, you know. It's just round the corner from here – turn right out of the front door, left at the end of the street, and it's on your right.'

'Thanks. I've got his address.'

'Good. But as for Terry, I agree with Dolly – he didn't strike me as the marrying sort.'

'Thank you, that's helpful.'

'Is that all, then?'

'Not quite, Mr Cook. You'll recall that when we were

here yesterday, you were covered in bruises but you said you'd just walked into a lamp-post. But judging by your wife's reaction at the time, I'd say she was a bit sceptical about that. So now you've had time to think about it, I'll ask you again. Was it just a lamp-post that gave you those bruises?'

Dolly snorted again, just as she had when her husband had offered this explanation the previous day. 'Three lamp-posts, more like,' she said.

'Ah,' said Jago, 'do I take that to mean you were set upon by three assailants, Mr Cook?'

Cook shifted his feet awkwardly. 'Look, I told you I can handle it myself. It's nothing for you to worry about.'

'I dare say, but if three toughs set about an upstanding member of the community like yourself, I can't help but worry about it.'

Cook said nothing and avoided Jago's eyes.

'Now, there's something I'd like to ask you about those three gentlemen. Did they give you a message?'

'A message?'

'Yes – a message for your cousin, Mr Ashdon, perhaps.'

'No.'

'Are you sure, Mr Cook?'

'I'm sure. No one gave me a message for anyone.'

'Very well. But if you find you suddenly recall such a message, you'll let me know, won't you?'

'Of course he will, Inspector,' Dolly broke in. 'I told you, didn't I? Fred likes to give the police a helping hand when he can.'

'Indeed you did, Mrs Cook,' Jago replied. 'And speaking of helping hands, you might be interested to know that since we last saw you, Detective Constable Cradock and I have been talking to Mr Stubb.'

Cook shot an enquiring glance at his wife.

'Don't worry, dear,' she said. 'I just happened to mention his name, that's all.'

'That's correct, Mr Cook,' said Jago. 'Mrs Cook didn't betray any confidences. But having met the man, I'd be interested to know anything more you can tell me about him.'

'What's there to say?' said Cook. 'He's nothing, a nobody.'

'I see, but I'm wondering whether there might be more to him than meets the eye.'

'Less, more like,' said Dolly dismissively.

'I got the impression that he might be a man with, let's say, some bad habits.'

Dolly gave a derisive laugh. 'You wouldn't be far off the mark there, Inspector. He's a thug and a bully who'll do anything for the right price. He thinks he's a big shot, but he isn't – he's got ideas above his station.'

'Mr Cook?'

'Look, Inspector,' Cook replied, 'let's get this straight – I know who he is, but I haven't seen him do anything and I haven't heard him say anything, so I'm not a witness, and neither is Dolly. He's just a young bloke who's got muscles but hasn't been overly blessed with brains. It's like bacon – you know, he's only got the basic ration, just about enough to get by on, but not enough for a proper meal.'

'That sounds like a good description for a man who runs a cafe, Mr Cook, but when we were there I began to wonder about some of his other business interests.'

'What do you mean?'

'Well, for one thing, he mentioned he has a sideline in buying and selling bric-a-brac, and that reminded me of something else your wife mentioned yesterday. You remember, Mrs Cook? You said Terry Watson used to like scavenging for what he called "treasure", like those people who go mudlarking on the Thames foreshore. I'm wondering now whether that might've involved removing items from bomb-damaged properties that didn't belong to him. Do you know anything about that?'

'No,' said Dolly. 'He never mentioned anything like that to me. Why would you think that?'

'Well, it's just that I thought that might be how Mr Stubb came by some of his bric-a-brac. Especially as we found a rucksack belonging to Mr Watson on his premises.'

'Right, I see. Perhaps it was, then.'

'Can you add anything, Mr Cook?'

'No, but I have heard Alf Stubb has a bit of a reputation as a dealer in second-hand goods. I can't say more than that.'

'I understand, thank you,' Jago replied. 'So, Mrs Cook, is that why you suggested I pay Mr Stubb a visit yesterday?'

'No, no, I didn't know Terry was mixed up in anything like that.'

'I'm not certain he was either, and he's not here to defend himself, so I'm just wondering and trying not to jump to conclusions.'

'I hope he wasn't. No, I only mentioned Alf Stubb because of what happened to Fred.'

'That's enough, Dolly,' Cook interrupted her. 'You mustn't interfere – just leave it to me.'

'But you can't just keep taking that treatment, love – it's not right. If you don't do something about it, I will.' She turned to Jago. 'Look, Inspector, it's like I said. That Stubb's just a bully and a thug, and if someone takes him off the street it'll do us all a favour. Just don't ask me to give evidence against him – I don't think that would end well.'

'So, Mr Cook,' said Jago, 'was Alf Stubb involved in the incident that got you all those bruises?'

Cook shrugged his shoulders.

Jago fixed him with an intense stare. 'Yes, or no?'

'I don't know. I didn't see, did I?'

'Do you know of any reason why he might have some connection to it?'

'No, I don't.'

'Let me ask you something else, then. Are you aware of anyone trying to muscle in on your cousin's business? Offering him protection, for example?'

'No – that'd be Bill's business, not mine. It's nothing to do with me. That's all I've got to say, Inspector – I don't know anything.'

'So you've said, but I'm concerned about you, Mr Cook. You need to watch your step – you know as well as I do there are people who'd chiv you without so much as the blink of an eye if they thought it'd send the right message to your boss.'

'No one's ever taken a knife to me, Inspector. I haven't got any enemies.'

'Perhaps not, but that doesn't mean your cousin hasn't got any, does it? I wouldn't be surprised if there were plenty of people round these parts who'd like a slice of his money – and who'd take a slice out of you to get it. You're his only family, aren't you?'

'Yes, I am. But that's no reason for me to be scared – like I told you, he's always looked after me. I appreciate your concern, Mr Jago, but that's all I've got to say.'

'All right, Mr Cook. But be careful – there are some unpleasant characters out there, and next time it might be more than a lamp-post you walk into.'

'Thanks. Are we done, then?'

'For now, Mr Cook. For now.'

CHAPTER THIRTY-FIVE

The steady chuff-chuff of a locomotive pulling a train out of Victoria station echoed from the railway track behind the houses in Hugh Street as Jago and Cradock returned to the car. Damage inflicted by the air raids was wont to play havoc with the railway companies' timetables these days, so there was no knowing whether this particular train was on schedule or not, but there was something reassuringly familiar about the sound of a steam engine that made Jago feel that not every vestige of peacetime had yet been swept away. The country was being bombed day and night, but commuters still seemed determined to get to and from work by hook or by crook.

'I'm thinking of maybe taking Fred Cook's advice,' he said, 'and popping in to see Bateman, if he's at home. We can find out if he knew anything about Terry Watson's love life.'

'Good idea, sir. Shall we walk? Cook said it's only five

minutes, and I could do with stretching my legs.'

'Yes, me too.'

Jago locked the car and they set off on foot. Experience had taught Jago that 'just round the corner' was an elastic term, and he usually took such guidance with a pinch of salt, but in Cook's case it proved to be accurate, and they were there within minutes.

Peabody Avenue was a wide, straight line stretching into the distance, its length marked off by the squat, flat-roofed shapes of communal surface air-raid shelters. Knowing the frailty of these brick-and-concrete death traps, Jago hoped their visit wouldn't entail taking refuge in one.

More substantial-looking blocks of flats lined the street on both sides, four-storeys to their left, five to their right. On closer inspection Jago noticed that over each block's central entrance there was a large wrought-iron letter: 'A' and 'B' at the beginning of the eastern side, with 'N' and 'O' opposite them on the western side. It wasn't difficult to guess that Bateman's flat in Y Block would be at the far end, so they headed briskly down the avenue.

From the outside there were no signs of life in the flats, but when they reached Y Block and climbed the bare concrete stairs to Flat 3 they found Bateman at home.

'Well, this is a surprise,' he said when he opened the door. 'You should've said you were coming – I'd have tidied up for you. But come in.' He squeezed himself against the wall so they could get past him into the small, spartan living room. 'Please excuse the mess – I got off early today, so I suppose I ought to be using the time sweeping and dusting, but you could probably see for yourselves when you came to the park that things are busy at work, and

273

these days when I get home all I want to do is sit down and recover. By the time I've made myself something quick to eat, likely as not the sirens'll start off and it'll be down into one of those shelters in the street for the rest of the night. Not that that's an excuse, mind. This flat's only two rooms, with a shared scullery on the landing, so I ought to be able to keep up with the housework. Anyway, make yourselves comfortable.'

He moved the newspaper that was spread open on the sofa so that they could sit down and pulled up a wooden chair for himself.

'Thank you,' said Jago as he sat, the loose spring he could feel in the sofa beneath him suggesting that 'comfortable' was another elastic term. 'There's just a couple of things I'd like to check with you.'

'Certainly. Can I get you something to drink? I can offer you a bottle of Mackeson, but that's about all, I'm afraid.'

'No, thanks.'

'So what do you want to know?'

'Well, first of all, you mentioned that you work in the park at the weekends, so were you there last Saturday?'

'Aye, I was.'

'I just wondered whether you happened to notice anyone selling poppies that day?'

'Well, I expect there would've been, but I think they usually stand over by the gates so they can catch people on their way in and out. There wasn't anyone there when I came in, but then perhaps they don't start as early as I do – they're usually well-dressed ladies who don't look like they have to work. Maybe there was someone there later, but you can't see from where the allotments are.'

'Did you see anyone else that you knew?'

'No. I do sometimes see people from the club there, but not last Saturday.'

'Is that the cycling club?'

'Aye. Cycling used to be all the rage there in the old days, apparently. It wasn't allowed in the royal parks, like Hyde Park and Regent's Park, but our one in Battersea was run by London County Council, and they said you could, so there used to be thousands of people out on their bikes there. It's still a popular place for cycling now – it's flat, you see, and the paths are smooth, and if you go all the way round it's about six miles, with plenty of nice things to see on the way. You should try it.'

'I can see the attraction. Did you and Mr Watson ever cycle there?'

'Oh, aye – it's very handy, you see, just across the bridge.'

'But you didn't see him there on Saturday.'

'No. Like I said, I didn't see anyone I knew.'

'Thank you. There was something else you mentioned when we spoke to you before about Mr Watson – you said he could be a bit of a loner. Is that right?'

'Yes – he liked his own company. But I don't mean he was shy. He was quite confident, really, a strong sort of man in his way. What I call a "speak as I find" type of fellow, not too bothered about minding his p's and q's. I suppose I just meant he didn't seem to need other people.'

'You also said he didn't get on well with all the rules in that camp you were in. So would you describe him as a rebel?'

'Aye, I suppose he was, after a fashion. I mean, he didn't have much time for what you might call social conventions, and he didn't think much of bigwigs and bosses either. He liked to get his own way and he didn't care what other people might think. That's probably why he didn't want to end up in the army, now I come to think of it – too many rules and regulations, and too many people telling you what to do.'

'Since we last spoke to you, someone's told us he was popular with the girls. Was that your impression too?'

'Well, I said he wasn't shy, didn't I? I can't say what the girls made of him, but I dare say he'd have been confident enough to think they were all keen on him.'

'Was he closely involved with any young woman in particular?'

'No, not to my knowledge – if he was, he never told me about it.'

'It's been suggested to us that there was someone – and that he got her into trouble.'

'What?' Bateman looked horrified. 'Is that true?'

'It's been suggested.'

'If it is, the man was a swine.'

'He hadn't confided in you, then.'

'No. He never breathed a word of such a thing. I can't believe it. Who is this girl?'

'I'm sure you'll understand if I say I can't divulge the young lady's identity.'

'Of course. It's just such a shock.'

'I'm sorry, Mr Bateman. May I ask you one other thing?'

'Go ahead.'

'Thank you. Do you remember ever seeing Mr Watson with a grey canvas rucksack?'

'I do. He used it a lot, for carrying things around.'

'What kind of things?'

'Oh, I don't know – his shopping if he was using his bike, his sandwiches, that sort of thing. All the usual stuff you might need to carry on a bike. Why do you ask?'

'Because it was missing from his room at Mrs Baker's house, and now we've found it in a place that suggests it might've been used in some illegal activity.'

'Really? What activity? Where?'

'We suspect Mr Watson may've been involved in the removal of items of value from buildings damaged by the bombing. Do you know anything about that?'

'No, I don't – sorry.'

'That's all right. Oh, and by the way, did Mr Watson ever mention a man called Stubb?'

'No, I don't recall hearing that name. Was it a mate of his?'

'I'm not sure, but thank you anyway.'

Jago got up from the sofa, relieved to escape the attentions of its rogue spring. 'Very well, Mr Bateman, we'll be on our way now,' he said. 'Thank you again for your help.'

'My pleasure,' Bateman replied.

He showed them out of the door, and they went down the staircase to the street.

'Well,' said Jago as they began to walk back to Hugh Street, 'I'm not sure we got much for our time there.'

'No, sir, he didn't seem to know as much as I was expecting him to. But then, if your mate's a loner, perhaps it's not surprising if there's a lot you don't know about him.'

'You're right. No one's really been able to lift the lid on Terry Watson's private life for us, have they? Even Bateman said Watson never breathed a word about getting a girl into trouble, and they were quite pally. Which reminds me – when we saw Alice Mason, she said she couldn't think of anyone in particular who might've wanted Watson dead, but she also thought there could've been plenty, because of the kind of man he was. Now, if it's true that he got her into trouble and left her in the lurch, we know what she means by that – and that was the end of their relationship. But I'm just wondering whether she was close enough to him before it ended to have picked up information that might be useful to us.'

'Things he might've let slip that he wouldn't have told anyone else, you mean?'

'Yes, simple things like people he might've crossed or had a row with, or who maybe had something against him. It's just a possibility, but I think we should have another word with her. But not now – I want to have another go at Ashdon first, and Stubb too, and then it'll be time to call it a day.'

'Very good, sir. I'm certainly ready to pack up for the day.'

'And what plans do you have for this evening?'

'I haven't made any, really.'

'Pining for Emily, perhaps?'

Cradock laughed. 'Not much privacy for pining in a section house, is there? No – more likely I'll be having a game of billiards with some of the lads at Ambrosden Avenue, and maybe a beer. They've got a billiards room there, so it's a chance for a little spot of social life, even if it's only with some other coppers. And you, sir? Any plans?'

'Yes. I'm going to see the doctor, actually.'

'Not sickening for something, are you, sir?'

'No, no – Dr Gibson's invited me round for a drink, so I'm going to pay him a little social visit and pick his brains while I'm there – he's got a flat in Knightsbridge near the hospital, apparently.'

'A bit posher than West Ham, then?'

'I expect so, Peter, but don't worry – I don't always speak as I find, and I'll definitely be minding my p's and q's.'

CHAPTER THIRTY-SIX

Jago unlocked the Riley and he and Cradock got in. He sat in silence for a few moments before speaking.

'I've been thinking about Alf Stubb,' he said. 'If you're right about that rucksack, Peter, and it really was Terry Watson who brought it to the cafe, it means there's definitely a link between Stubb and Watson. And then if I'm right, and Watson and Cook were both roughed up because some protection gangsters wanted to put pressure on Bill Ashdon, it's not beyond the realms of imagination to reckon Stubb might've been involved – he certainly fits the bill for that kind of work. That might explain why Fred Cook denies all knowledge of anything like that going on – he won't want to go looking for another dose of trouble by sticking his neck out, and Ashdon might've told him to keep his mouth shut anyway if he's got some gangsters on his tail.'

'In which case it's interesting that Ashdon says he

doesn't know Stubb. He was a bit evasive when you asked him about protection rackets too, wasn't he?'

'Yes, as you'd expect when he says he can handle anything like that himself – he doesn't want us anywhere near it.'

'So do we ask him again?' said Cradock.

'Yes, Peter, we do. But there's something else – maybe this whole thing's not what we think.'

'How do you mean, sir?'

'Well, we've been reckoning maybe Ashdon and Silver are both being leant on by some protection gang, and Stubb's working for whoever's doing that. So he was beating up Watson and Cook to intimidate Ashdon, and smashing Silver's window to do the same to him . . . But supposing the boot's on the other foot.'

'You mean if it's Ashdon running the protection racket himself?'

'Why not? The first time we met him he talked about moving into property, didn't he? What if it's Ashdon who's got his eyes on Silver's shop and wants to force him to sell up?'

'But why would Ashdon get his own men beaten up? I mean, one of them's his cousin. And why would he get someone to give Watson a threatening message for himself?'

'No idea, but then again, we still don't know whether that message ever existed – Ashdon says it didn't, and it's quite possible that Watson made the whole thing up, or even Bateman for that matter. But it would make a good decoy, wouldn't it? It makes Ashdon look like the victim, not the perpetrator.'

'Yes, but would he murder Watson? That'd be a bit extreme, wouldn't it?'

'Murder's always extreme, Peter. But I agree – I can imagine Ashdon arranging to have Watson beaten up a bit to create the right impression, but I can't see any reason why he'd need to murder him.'

'So either way, we need to see Ashdon again, right?'

'Yes. If we're going to make sense of whatever he's involved in we need to go straight to the horse's mouth – and if anyone knows about horses, it's him.'

It was a short drive to Wilton Road, and within minutes they were climbing the stairs to Ashdon's office for the second time that day. But this time there was something different about the place: an acrid smell assailed them all the way up, one that over many weeks of bombing had become an all-too-familiar part of London life. It was the smell of burnt wood. They got to the top and saw where it was coming from: the door to Ashdon's office was badly scorched.

Jago knocked, and Ashdon unlocked it.

'What do you want now?' the bookmaker snapped as he opened the damaged door. The relaxed and confident demeanour of their previous visits had gone. 'I'm busy.'

'So I see,' said Jago. 'What happened here?'

'Don't ask me. As far as I can see, some toe rag must've thought they could put the wind up me by setting fire to my door.'

'I'd appreciate it if you could spare us just a few minutes, Mr Ashdon.'

'All right, then. I suppose you might as well come in now you're here.'

Ashdon let them in, and Jago noticed that this time he

didn't lock the door behind them: perhaps the presence of two Metropolitan Police officers made him feel safe enough from thievery. They followed him into the office: apart from a few smoke stains on the walls and ceiling round the doorway, it looked undamaged. They sat down.

'That sounds a very unpleasant experience,' Jago continued. 'It must've been a shock.'

'No, it was nothing, really. It takes more than that to get me rattled. I was just having a quick bite to eat here at my desk earlier on when I heard footsteps outside the door, but no one knocked. I had it locked as usual, so I thought nothing of it, but then next thing I knew there was a whooshing sound on the other side of the door, and smoke coming under it. I rushed over, unlocked the door and pulled it open, and it was on fire.'

'Did you see anyone?'

'Of course not – whoever it was had made themselves scarce. I was more worried about the fire spreading, but I keep an extinguisher in here, so I just banged that on the floor and sprayed it all over the flames and put it out. Lucky I was here, or the whole place would've gone up in smoke.'

'So it was an arson attack.'

'Yes.'

'Who did it? Some punter who didn't like the odds you'd given them for the twelve o'clock at Newmarket? Or was it perhaps someone connected with that protection racket I asked you about earlier today? You seemed a bit coy about it then.'

'All right,' Ashdon sneered. 'So what? Yes, if you must know, it's some lowlife trying to muscle in on my business, but don't you worry – I'll take care of it, and I don't need your help. In my profession we're used to solving our own problems. It's not good for business to have your name dragged through the courts – it can dent the clients' confidence, you see.'

'And did this lowlife give Terry Watson a message for you?'

'Yes, he did – it was like you said, it was private, for me.'

'What did the message say?'

'It was "Tell Ashdon we're waiting to hear from him, and we're not waiting much longer."'

'What did you make of that?'

'Nothing – I mean, anyone can say something like that. It's not the sort of thing I take any notice of, and in any case, like I said, for all I knew Terry could've made the whole thing up.'

'And what about your cousin Fred? I've been wondering whether whoever gave him all those bruises gave him a message for you too.'

'Is that what he's told you?'

'No, he says no one gave him a message for anyone.'

'Ah, that's Fred all over – loyal to the end.'

'So was there a message?'

'Yes. It was "Don't mess us about, or we'll mess you about." They told Fred to tell me, and he did. I thought it sounded a bit amateurish, to be honest – the sort of thing kids might say if they'd been watching Chicago gangster movies. But don't be harsh on Fred for not telling you. He's loyal, yes, but you can see for yourself he's not a young man any more. He'd be too scared to shop people like that, and he wouldn't be running down to the police station to make a statement – the most you might get would be a vague hint that couldn't be traced back to him. I know he likes to keep well in with your boys, but he's not going to put his life at risk, is he?'

'This message didn't bother you, then.'

'No. These people aren't worth the time of day. I ignored it.'

Jago walked over to the door and opened it to examine the charred outer surface. 'And presumably this was the result. You were lucky to get out alive – does this make you think you should've taken the warnings more seriously?'

'Yeah, maybe. I'll take it as seriously as I need to – I'll get the door fixed, and I'll see to any other fixing that needs doing too.'

'So who was behind it? You must've given it some thought. The Maldini brothers, perhaps? They've never liked competition in your line of business, have they? But I should think they're still locked up in the Isle of Man – I don't think the government made an exception for gangsters when they decided to round up all the Italians and intern them over there, did they? Do they still have representatives operating in London on their behalf, keeping the business ticking over until they get back? Or is it someone else taking advantage of their absence to expand their own business interests?'

'You think I know? And if I did, do you think I'd tell you?'

'You're not listening, are you?'

'Of course I am, but I can look after myself.'

'I'm sure you can, Mr Ashdon. I'm more concerned about your cousin Fred. Can he take care of himself? He's collected quite a few bruises this week, and you weren't there to take care of him then, were you?'

'No, I wasn't, but I'll make sure he's all right, don't you worry. Now, is that all?'

'Not quite, Mr Ashdon. I asked you earlier today whether you knew a man called Stubb, and you said no. Would you like to change your mind about that?'

'No, I wouldn't. I don't know him.'

'And Mr Silver?'

'No. I told you – I've never heard of him. Why do you keep asking?'

'Because I've been wondering whether you might've decided to diversify your business interests by acquiring a property of his – and using some rather ugly methods to persuade him to sell up.'

'What? That's ridiculous. I'm an honest bookie, not a gangster. I think you'd better go now.'

'We'll be on our way in a moment, but before we go, can you tell me what time it was when this fire incident happened?'

'Oh, no you don't. Don't you start thinking you're going to investigate this. It's my business, and I'll take care of it.'

'Very well, but if you change your mind, I'd like to hear from you.'

'All right, Inspector, but don't stay in specially. Now, like I said, I'm a busy man, so if you don't mind, I'll bid you good day.'

'Good day, Mr Ashdon.'

CHAPTER THIRTY-SEVEN

'He's a cool customer, isn't he?' said Cradock when they were back out on the street. 'Nearly gets burnt to death in his office, but he just puts the fire out and carries on working as if nothing had happened.'

'He likes to give the impression he's a respectable businessman,' Jago replied, 'but he's in a rough business, and I suspect that sort of thing's all part of the job. I don't think you get very far as a bookie if you're not thick-skinned.'

'Well, he's certainly no shrinking violet – but at least he's finally admitted he's having trouble from some kind of protection racket. Do you still think that could be a decoy, though?'

'I'm not sure. I'm mainly interested in finding out who this lowlife is that he claims is trying to muscle in on his business. The man who sprang to mind when he said that was Stubb, but Ashdon's still denying he knows him, and I'd expect him to do that whether

Stubb was working for him or against him.'

'Well, like you said, sir, Stubb certainly fits the bill. Fred Cook's admitted he was set about by three toughs, and you couldn't look more like a tough than Alf Stubb.'

'Yes, but has he got the brains to run a protection racket? Cook didn't seem to think so, did he?'

'No, and Mrs Cook said he's a thug and a bully who'd do anything for the right price, so maybe he's just doing the dirty work for someone else.'

'You could be right. Either way, it doesn't look as though we'd ever get the Cooks to give evidence against him, and Ashdon seems determined to take the law into his own hands, so I think it's time we put some pressure on Stubb – and this time we'll skip the tea and coffee.'

It took ten minutes to drive to Stubb's cafe, and this time, as soon as Jago and Cradock walked in, the owner took them straight into his office.

'What is it now?' he said. 'Haven't you two got anything better to do?'

'There's something else I want to ask you about, Mr Stubb.'

'Oh yeah? What's that, then?'

'It's about a few things you've been getting up to recently. There's been a number of incidents, and I think they're connected with you.'

'I don't know what you're talking about.'

'I'm talking about that brick through the shopkeeper's window. That's the kind of thing I associate with protection rackets – intimidating local businesses so they'll pay you to leave them alone. Is that what you're involved in?'

'What, me? You're kidding me, aren't you? I'm just a simple man who runs a cafe and tries to live a quiet life. I mind my own business, Inspector – I work hard all day and every day, trying to get by and hoping I won't get blown to kingdom come.'

'And what about your evenings, Mr Stubb?'

'Well, I might go down the pub for a pint or two before the air raids start, but otherwise I'm here – it's not a nine till five job, you know, running a place like this. Not even nine till six.'

'But you managed to slip out at about five on Tuesday, didn't you?'

'You still going on about that? I told you what that was about. You ask Mr Trubshaw – he'll tell you.'

'We're going to, Mr Stubb, don't you worry.'

'You've got it in for me, haven't you? Look, I'm just an ordinary bloke – I don't get mixed up in stuff like that.'

'I'd like to think that's true – in my experience, when what you call ordinary blokes try their hand at the protection business, it doesn't end well. You should be careful you don't tread on anyone's toes – there are professionals out there who'd make mincemeat out of you. Or perhaps you're already on their payroll – I've been told you're a thug for hire, and I'm beginning to believe it. Who are you working for?'

'I'm not working for anyone – I'm a self-employed small trader, aren't I? An honest businessman making an honest living.'

'When I hear a man describe himself as an honest businessman, Mr Stubb, I always wonder why he's so keen to make me think he is. We were talking about having those extra strings to your bow before, weren't we? Do they include beating people up for money, or is that something you do strictly on your own initiative? Or what about setting fire to people's premises to underline the attractions of your business proposition?'

'Setting fire to people's premises? What's that all about?'

'Don't you know?'

'Of course not. I wouldn't be asking you if I did, would I?'

'A local bookmaker's had his door torched.'

'Well don't look at me.'

Jago gave him a sceptical look. 'I'm sure you know that bookmakers are often the target of protection gangs,' he said, 'just like shopkeepers are. I believe someone's trying to muscle in on that bookmaker's business, and I want to know if it's you.'

'First you say I'm putting bricks through a shop window that I know nothing about, and now you're saying I've set some bookie's door on fire.'

'So you deny it?'

'Of course I do. Who says I've done all this?'

'You'll understand I'm not prepared to tell you that at this stage. I should emphasise that no one's shopped you, but that's usually the case in the protection business, isn't it? You make sure they're too scared to talk to the police. I've been looking into a few incidents, and it hasn't escaped my attention that yours is the one name the victims swear they've never heard of, and I'm drawing my own conclusions.'

'Well, that's not surprising, is it? It's because none of that's got anything to do with me. You're barking up the wrong tree, Inspector – you're wasting your time.'

'We'll see about that. There's also the matter of your little bric-a-brac business. You remember – that rucksack?'

'Look, I told you before, it belongs to some bloke who left it here, but I don't know his name.'

'Yes, but we do, Mr Stubb. It belongs to a Mr Terry Watson, or to be more precise, it used to belong to him. Do you remember him now?'

'Terry Watson? No, it doesn't ring a bell, sorry. But actually, now you come to mention it, I think maybe he said his name was Wilson, or something like that, but I didn't really take it in. What does he look like?'

'Medium height, fair hair, about thirty.'

'Well, I said he was ordinary looking, didn't I? So that'd fit, but I could've had a hundred blokes through here looking like that.'

'Did he have a bike?'

'Yes, he did. I remember him asking if he could bring it in off the street, so I let him wheel it through. It was quite a smart one, drop handlebars and all that. Do you think he could've given me a false name?'

'I don't think my skill at suspecting false names would be any greater than yours, Mr Stubb.'

'Yeah, right. You reckon it was your Terry Watson, then? What's he done to get you so interested in him?'

'We're interested in Mr Watson because he's been murdered.'

Stubb seemed taken aback by Jago's words. 'What? Blimey. I'm sorry, Inspector – I had no idea. Why did that happen?'

'That's what we're investigating, Mr Stubb. And what's

more, we have reason to believe the items you received from him were stolen.'

'Stolen? Well, listen, Inspector, I took them off that lad in good faith. I'm a respectable cafe proprietor just trying to make a living so I don't have to go on the dole and sponge off the government. If you're telling me now he'd nicked that stuff . . . well, that's news to me. He told me it all came from his old grandma – she had a house full of knick-knacks and trinkets and was fed up with dusting them, and said she'd rather turn them into some cash before Hitler came over and bombed them to pieces, so she'd asked him to get rid of them for her.'

'When did he bring the rucksack to you?'

'It was about this time last week – Thursday, I think. So did he steal all that stuff from her, then, and tell me a pack of lies?'

'No, Mr Stubb, I don't think he stole them from his grandma. We've reason to believe he acquired those goods by looting.'

'What? So he was a criminal, then. Well, in that case I'm glad I stopped doing business with him.'

'You did?'

'Er, yes – it's all coming back to me now. He tried to pull a trick on me, see. The next day – that'll be last Friday – he came back. It was after I'd closed up for the day. I told him I hadn't had time to look at his stuff yet, but he said it wasn't about that – he'd got something else he wanted me to look at, for a quick sale. It was a silver cigarette case, quite nice, so I offered him a few bob for it, but he said he wanted a few quid instead. I said don't be stupid – I've offered you a fair price and you won't get a penny more out of me, my lad. Then blow me down if he didn't say, "I'll get the police on you then." He said he'd shop me to your lot – anonymous, like – tell them I was a fence, receiving stolen goods and all that.'

'I see. This bric-a-brac business of yours must be quite a profitable little sideline for you. I believe the current rate offered by fences is ten per cent of the item's actual value, isn't it?'

'Don't be daft – just because he threatened to report me doesn't mean I'm a fence. He was just chancing his arm. Anyway, I knew he wasn't going to do that. I had his bag of stuff, didn't I, so I could always just toddle over to Gerald Road nick and tell them he'd tried to flog me some stolen goods. I could say I'd taken them off him without giving him any money and was bringing them round so they could be restored to their rightful owners – and reporting him at the same time. I told him not to push his luck with me – I wasn't born yesterday. "Sling your hook," I said, and I kicked him out. I put the wind up that little twerp, and I reckon that's why he never came back for that old rucksack of his.'

'He wasn't in a position to come back for it, though, was he?'

'Of course, yeah – murdered, you say. Poor blighter. I reckon he must've pushed his luck a bit too far with someone else then, eh? Don't look at me, though – I don't do murdering.'

CHAPTER THIRTY-EIGHT

Dr Gibson's flat was a striking contrast to the one Jago had visited earlier that day in Peabody Avenue. After dropping Cradock off at the section house for his evening of beer and billiards, he'd driven straight to the address in Knightsbridge that Gibson had given him and found an imposing red-brick mansion block looming above him in the moonlight. Here, unlike Bateman's residence, there was a commissionaire on duty in the entrance lobby and a choice between carpeted stairs and a lift to get to Gibson's floor. And not surprisingly, when he reached the door of the pathologist's flat there was no sign of a shared scullery on the landing.

He buzzed the doorbell, and Gibson welcomed him in. The first thing Jago noticed was the flat's cosy warmth: the heavy cast-iron radiator by the wall in the hallway looked of similar age to the building and suggested the Victorian architect had considerably specified central heating. Gibson took his coat and hat and led him through to the living room. Like Bateman's, the flat appeared to be small, but judging by what Jago could see, it was tastefully furnished and had more than two rooms. It was perhaps a modest home for a man in Gibson's professional position, but nevertheless the kind of place a gardener on Battersea Council wages could only dream of.

'I'm glad you could make it,' said Gibson, waving him to an armchair. 'I expect you've had a busy day.'

'No more than yours, I'm sure, Dr Gibson,' Jago replied, relaxing into the chair's ample upholstery.

'Quite possibly – but please, none of that Dr Gibson here. My name's Thomas, and my friends call me Tom, so please do the same.'

'Of course, and mine's John.'

'Good. Now, let me get you something to drink, John. If you like whisky, I've got some Glenlivet pure malt that I'd be delighted to share.'

'Thanks – that'd suit me fine.'

'I don't know about you, but I'm finding Scotch a bit hard to get hold of these days. I can't quite make sense of it, though. We've got the government cutting production by two-thirds because the farmers need the cereals to feed their animals, but telling us there'll be no shortage because there's enough in stock to keep us going for years – but then they admit there is a shortage.'

'I thought they'd said that's only because we're buying too much.'

'Well, I suppose that's one way of looking at a shortage, but you can't blame people for feeling in need of an extra nip or two when they're being bombed every night, can you?'

'No, it's probably what keeps a lot of people going. Don't ask me to explain, though – I suppose it all makes sense to the politicians, but not to me.'

Gibson crossed the room to a cabinet from which he produced the Glenlivet and two glasses.

'Anyway,' he said, pulling the cork stopper from the bottle, 'let's have some of this while it's still here.' He poured two generous measures and handed one to Jago. 'Cheers.'

'Cheers,' Jago replied. He sipped the whisky and found it very acceptable.

'Before I forget,' Gibson added, settling into another armchair, 'as I believe I mentioned to you on Monday, we have a very substantial basement under this building, so if we get an air raid this evening while you're here, all we have to do is go downstairs and we'll be able to shelter there quite comfortably.'

'Thanks. That sounds a more attractive proposition than the surface shelters I saw this afternoon in Peabody Avenue.' Jago surveyed the room appreciatively. 'You seem to have all the comforts here – it's a nice flat, and a very respectable area to live in.'

Gibson laughed. 'It certainly looks respectable, but I'm sure I don't need to tell a detective to be wary of judging by appearances. There are plenty of wealthy people in Knightsbridge, but you don't necessarily know how they made their money, do you? And some of the most respectable aristocrats are living on wealth they've inherited from crooked ancestors. I'm lucky to have a reasonably paid job and simple tastes, and I don't have a wife and children to support – are you a family man, by the way?'

'No, I've never married.'

'In the same boat as me, then. It may not be the boat either of us would have chosen, but there it is. Anyway, with no dependants I can manage perfectly well without any inherited wealth – unlike some of my fellow residents, I can say with a clear conscience that every penny I have is money I've earnt through my own honest labour.'

'I find you not guilty, then. But with Hyde Park over the road and Buckingham Palace just round the corner . . . Well, if you saw where I live and work over in West Ham, you'd realise this is a different world.'

'I can't deny that. I haven't always lived here, but I like it because it's handy for getting to work, and I love being so close to Hyde Park. We've got anti-aircraft guns in there now, of course, which make it a rather noisy place when the bombers come over, but the rest of the time it's like an oasis of tranquillity. Ever since I've been at St George's I've found it a very peaceful place to stroll after a busy day shut up inside a laboratory or a post-mortem room, and these days it's quite therapeutic to be somewhere quiet and green in the middle of a war. Although I know there's no escaping it – the war, I mean. Even the park hasn't gone unscathed.'

'Bombed, you mean?'

'Well, it's had a few bombs, yes – some people say it's because the planes aim at the bottom of the searchlight beams, but I don't know whether that's true. But no, it's the railings I'm thinking of. There was a nice stretch of them inside the park, between Hyde Park Corner and Stanhope Gate in Park Lane, but it seems the Minister of Supply decided they were non-essential. Next thing I knew they'd been pulled down and carted off for scrap. Accepted as a gift by the Iron and Steel Control, apparently, no doubt on behalf of a grateful nation. I can only assume they're now part of a tank or a ship at the service of King and Empire, but I'm worried this could be the thin end of the wedge. We could end up with no railings left anywhere.'

'Do you think they had to persuade the King? It's a royal park, after all, so presumably that means they belong to him. It may even have been his own idea – you know, doing his bit.'

'I suppose so, yes.'

'Still, I met a woman with a little house in Pimlico just the day before yesterday and she said she thought her railings may've been spared for safety reasons, and I've heard about places where the local residents've kicked up a fuss and managed to stop theirs being cut down, so perhaps you should've had a word with some of your respectable and influential neighbours. Leaving aside the question of how they may've come by their money, there's probably a few who can have words in ears at extremely high levels.'

'Unfortunately, having a flat here doesn't qualify me to move in those circles. I am a respectable doctor, of course, but there are degrees of respectability, and you don't need to walk five minutes from here to find the full spectrum. In fact, talk of railings reminds me of a very strange case that my predecessor at St George's told me about a few years ago. But look, before I start telling you stories, how about something to eat? This is a serviced flat, so I've only got to phone down to the kitchen and they'll rustle something up for us.'

'That's very kind of you – but just a snack would be fine, thanks.'

'Well, they do a delicious Welsh rarebit – I can recommend it. I had some last night, served with what they said was a salad, although it turned out to be grated raw carrot and shredded cabbage leaves. But as they say, there's a war on.'

'I'd like that very much, thank you.'

Gibson stepped out into the hallway and phoned his order down. 'It'll be up in a few minutes,' he said, taking his seat again. 'So, where was I?'

'You were about to tell me about a very strange case.'

'Ah, yes, the railings. Well, you see, there was a man who had an apartment here in Knightsbridge, like this one perhaps. He was an educated fellow, and presumably not without means, but he was found dead – impaled on the railings in Hyde Park, and with practically no clothes on. The coroner's verdict was accidental death – he was known as an eccentric character, apparently, and people said he used to go running in the park at night, possibly naked. They decided there must've been something wrong with his mind – they thought maybe he was hallucinating and slipped while he was climbing over the railings. There was no way of proving it, though, so who knows?'

'I suppose a post-mortem can't tell you whether a man was having hallucinations when he died, can it?'

'No – which tells you something about the limits of pathology. I can find out a lot about possible causes of death by cutting up someone's body, but I can't cut up their mind. A post-mortem couldn't tell me what a man who ran naked round the park at midnight was thinking, or why – I'd need to know what he might have experienced in life.

Was he of an age to fight in the war, for example? If he was, and there's any mention of hallucinations, I'd immediately think of shell shock.'

'Yes, those poor men – I saw enough of that to last me a lifetime.'

'You were in the war, then?'

'I was. France – infantry.'

'At the front?'

'Yes. And you?'

'I was there, but not fighting – I was a medic. Not that that stopped us getting shelled and blown up like everyone else, mind. I qualified just before it started, and I was sent out to France as a temporary lieutenant in 1915. They put me to work in dressing stations in dugouts and bunkers at the front line, and you know what those were like – so many wounded that men died before we could treat them. Then later I was in casualty clearing stations further back. It was hell, wasn't it?'

'Yes.'

They both fell silent, then Gibson spoke.

'The war changed me, you know – I guess it changed all of us, for better or worse. But what I realised at the front is that life's the most astonishing thing in the universe, and God gives each one of us just one life, and yet how easily we squander it – and worst of all, how readily we squander other men's lives. I think that's why I hate war and I hate murder – and that's why I do the work I do.'

Jago gazed silently into his glass, watching the liquid swirl gently as the faces of wasted lives drifted through his mind.

'A toast,' said Gibson quietly, raising his glass. 'To those we lost.'

Jago looked up and raised his own. 'To those we lost.'

They both took a sip of whisky, each deep in his own thoughts. Jago had nothing to add, but he knew that words were unnecessary. They had both been there.

Their silence was broken by a buzz at the door signalling the arrival of supper. A man in a white jacket brought their snacks on a tray, deposited them on the small dining table on the other side of the living room, and left.

Gibson invited Jago to take a seat at the table, then sat down opposite him. 'For what we are about to receive, may the Lord make us truly thankful. Amen,' he said.

'Yes, er, amen,' Jago replied.

'Sorry, it's a habit of mine. After the food we had to survive on at the front, I've been truly thankful ever since for everything I eat – no matter how bad it is, it's always better than that.'

They ate their supper without further conversation, then returned to their armchairs and whiskies. Jago was still lost in his thoughts. Drinking to those he'd lost had pierced him with the thought that perhaps Dorothy would soon be added to their number. Not that she would die, but that her job would take her to the other end of the world, from one war zone into another, with no guarantee that he'd ever see her again. She might have reached her decision already and if not it would surely be soon. He wondered whether he should have said more, even asked her not to go. She'd said he was a rock and an anchor, and that she needed someone like that – but she hadn't actually said she needed him, and he supposed that was why he hadn't said he needed her. If he'd been a praying sort of man like his host, he knew what he'd be praying for, but he wasn't. Still, he knew how to hope, and he knew what he was hoping.

'So,' said Gibson, interrupting his silent reflection, 'how's your investigation going?'

'My investigation? Oh, going round in circles, I think. It's rather like what you said about the limits of pathology – in my line of work, it's all about trying to piece together what happened, but the best witness, the one who could tell you exactly what happened, is the poor fellow who's dead. I think we're making progress, though.'

'I understand you're working for Detective Superintendent Hardacre.'

'Yes. You know him?'

'It has fallen to me to work with him on a few occasions. Not the most patient of men, in my experience. One of your colleagues once told me that his men call him "Old Harry" behind his back, which doesn't say much for his style of leadership. Hardly complimentary to equate him with the devil himself, is it?'

'Well, he does seem to have a particular way of going about things. I expect they mean it affectionately.'

'You're too charitable,' Gibson laughed. 'Not what I expect in a policeman.'

'I try hard to be. I'm told he's got a good record for nicking villains, though.'

'Which is also what it's all about, I suppose. I trust you'll soon be nicking your own villain.'

'Thank you. Actually, forgive me for bringing up a professional question when you're off duty, but there's a small point you may be able to help me with – something I wasn't aware of when I last saw you, after the post-mortem. Could I possibly tax your brain for a moment?'

'Feel free. I suspect any pathologist who works with the police soon forgets what the concept of "off duty" means anyway. What is it you've discovered?'

'It's not so much a discovery, just something somebody mentioned. The dead man's landlady told us he wasn't keen on being conscripted, but one of his friends said he hadn't been expecting to get through his call-up medical and had said something about diabetes. Was there anything in the post-mortem to suggest he was diabetic?'

'No, I didn't find any signs of diabetes, nor of any other underlying health problems that could have contributed to his death. If he was diabetic, of course, he might have been wearing one of those special identity discs – the idea is they wear it round their neck, so then if they're found injured in an air raid it'll tell the doctor they need to be given insulin. He wasn't wearing one of those, but I'm not sure whether they've all been issued yet.'

'I see. Is it possible to fake diabetes?'

'Are you thinking your Mr Watson might have had ideas of doing that in order to fail his medical and avoid conscription?'

'It did cross my mind. I remember hearing about a case towards the end of the last war when a man tried to pass himself off as unfit for military service by bribing someone to inject a sugar cane solution into his bladder. He reckoned that'd give him symptoms of diabetes. He didn't get away with it, but I wondered if there was some way of doing it today.'

'I don't think so. You could try the same trick, of course, but the doctors who conduct those medicals aren't wet behind the ears. If they thought a conscript was swinging the lead they'd probably keep him back for a bit and then do a second test, by which time any glucose would be diluted and might be out of his system, so he wouldn't get the result he wanted. I think these days if someone wants to dodge the call-up by faking a health problem he's more likely to try obtaining a forged medical certificate or finding some way to persuade a less scrupulous member of my profession to provide a false one. Is it important?'

'Not now that he's dead, of course, no – it's just part of understanding what kind of character he was.' Jago glanced at his watch. 'Time's getting on,' he said, 'and I expect we've both got a busy day tomorrow, so I think I'd better be on my way. But I just want to say I've had a very enjoyable evening, so thank you.' He drained the last drop of whisky from his glass and put it down. 'And thank you for a very agreeable drink.'

'One for the road?'

'No, thank you, one's enough for me.'

'I'll get your coat and hat, then. And thank you, too, for a very pleasant evening. I hope you'll get your case wrapped up soon, but if I can be of any more help, just call me.'

Gibson left the room and returned with the coat and hat. Jago put them on and said goodbye, then took the stairs down to the lobby for the sake of a little exercise and walked out onto the chilly street and got into his car. He'd taken his leave of Gibson somewhat later than he'd planned, but as he made his way back to Rochester Row he appreciated having spent the evening with a man who'd lived through some of the same horrors as himself. Sometimes it was good not to have to explain.

CHAPTER THIRTY-NINE

The next morning a mist had crept in from the river, not heavy enough to be anything like a proper fog, but enough to give a hazy look to the streets and buildings as Jago drove towards Vauxhall Bridge Road with Cradock beside him. He was not a man to let the weather affect his mood: he'd worked out long ago that anyone living in the British Isles who did so would surely be in for a dismal life. But it did remind him of the wave of uncertainty that had swept over him the previous evening at Gibson's place when he found himself thinking about Dorothy and the possibility of her new job. 'Live for the day': that's what people were saying now that a year or more of war had clouded everyone's tomorrows with uncertainty, but he'd realised it didn't work. He couldn't push the future out of his mind when the fork in the road ahead was looming so abruptly: one way with her, the other without her.

The question of which direction that future would take,

however, was beyond his control. The choice was out of his hands. Like a man turning his wireless dial from Hilversum to the Home Service, he forcibly switched his thoughts onto a different track.

'So how was your evening at the section house, Peter?'

'Not so bad, sir – the lads there are quite a friendly bunch. How was yours?'

'More relaxing than yours, possibly – we just chatted over a glass of pure malt.'

'Nice work if you can get it, eh? A nice contrast to Alf Stubb, I should think. What do you reckon, guv'nor? Is he lying? It wasn't very convincing, what he said last night, was it?'

'I'm inclined not to believe a word that man says. And that reminds me – we haven't checked his alibi for the window-smashing business at Benny Silver's shop yet, have we? I think we should get down to Trubshaw Cycles straight away and do that. Let's go.'

They parked in Lupus Street about twenty yards away from the shop, and as they walked towards it, Jago noticed a woman in a green coat and beret coming out of the door. She appeared to be rummaging for something in her handbag as she approached, her head down, and was quite close when she looked up and saw them. She stopped abruptly and seemed a little flustered.

'Good morning, Mrs Edgworth,' said Jago.

'Yes, er, good morning, Inspector. You made me jump – I wasn't expecting to see you.'

'Very sorry. We're on our way to see Mr Trubshaw, and it looks as though you've just been doing the same.'

'Yes, that's right.' She calmed herself. 'A little British Legion business to attend to. I had a couple of cheques for Mr Trubshaw to sign. The bank requires two signatures for any cheque drawn on the branch committee's account, so since I'm the treasurer and he's one of the other authorised signatories, I prepare the cheques and we both sign them.'

Her explanation for her presence there struck Jago as more detailed than the circumstances required, and there was a formality in her tone that he hadn't expected. Unlike their previous meeting, it gave him the impression that she was distancing herself from him.

'Is everything all right with you, Mrs Edgworth?' he asked.

'Yes, I'm fine, thank you.'

'Good. And how's Miss Mason?'

'She's as well as can be expected.'

'I hope you don't mean she's poorly. The thing is, I've been thinking I'd like another chat with her.'

'A chat about what?'

'About Mr Watson. She may be able to help us with our enquiries into his murder.'

'I don't think that would be wise, Inspector.'

He noticed that she hadn't smiled since their conversation began. 'Why do you say that?'

'Because I've been thinking too. When I invited you to my house to meet her, I thought it would be helpful to you. Perhaps it was, but it wasn't for Miss Mason. It seems to have had a bad effect on her, and I now regret introducing her to you. Raking over those difficult experiences she had as a result of meeting Mr Watson has dragged her down into a sort of melancholy that I think has severely set back her recovery. I can't allow you to talk to her.'

'With respect, Mrs Edgworth, you told me yourself she's twenty-one, so it's for her to decide who she speaks to.'

'Alice may be of age, Inspector, but she needs protecting, and I'm her protector. I don't expect you to understand, but this wasn't just some romance with an unfortunate ending – that man's behaviour was unforgivable. He treated her despicably, and for you to interrogate her further about it would only rub salt in her wounds. So the answer is no, Inspector – I won't let you do that.'

She seemed on the brink of tears. She brushed past him and continued on her way without another word.

'Well,' said Cradock, 'she's changed her tune, hasn't she? I'd say she's gone off you, guv'nor.'

'Don't be facetious,' Jago replied. 'Something's certainly touched a nerve, and I'm wondering what. I can understand Alice Mason having second thoughts about confiding in us the way she did – it's a very personal matter, after all. But it does seem a rather sudden change in Mrs Edgworth's manner. Maybe there's something she knows that she's not telling us.'

'Or maybe she's discovered something Alice knows, and it's something she doesn't want us to find out.'

'Indeed. I think perhaps we should find an opportunity to speak to Alice on her own again – at the laundry, perhaps, when she's on duty. Mrs Edgworth won't like us going behind her back, but it could be important. Right now, though, we need to go and see a man about an alibi.'

Jago glanced back down the street to make sure Sally Edgworth hadn't changed her mind and was returning to speak to him, but she had already crossed the road and was some distance away. He pushed open the shop's door and went in, followed by Cradock. Inside they found Mrs Trubshaw holding a ladies' bike while her husband, bent over the front end, tightened the wheel nut.

'Puncture repair,' said Trubshaw, straightening up with a hand pressed against his lower back. 'Proper cyclists repair their own, but we have a number of customers who either aren't inclined to do so or don't know how. Lamentable, but I suppose it's good for business. Anyway, welcome back, gentlemen. Can we help you?'

'Yes, I'm hoping you can. There's something I need to check with you.'

'With both of us?' said Deirdre.

'Yes, if you don't mind.'

'No, I don't mind at all – a little distraction's always welcome.'

'Fire away, Detective Inspector,' said Trubshaw, wiping his hands on a cloth.

'Thank you,' Jago replied. 'Now, first of all, Mr Trubshaw, do you know a man called Stubb – Mr Alf Stubb?'

'Well, er, yes, I do. Why do you ask?'

'Was he here on Tuesday evening?'

'Yes, he was, as a matter of fact.'

'And what time was that?

'Well, now, it was certainly before closing time – we close at six – but I'm afraid I can't recall exactly what time it was.'

'Can you say approximately when?'

'I'd guess it was sometime between five and six – not later than six, but possibly a little before five. I'm sorry I can't be more precise.'

'Were you here, Mrs Trubshaw?'

'No, Inspector, I'm very sorry, but I wasn't – if it's the time my husband says, I'd already gone home to get the tea on. You'll just have to rely on what he says.'

'Thank you. Mr Trubshaw, can you tell me why he was here?'

'It was to talk about possibly doing some painting for me – we have a ceiling that needs a fresh coat of distemper.'

'And may I ask how you come to know Mr Stubb?'

'We, er, met through a shared interest in local politics.'

'Would that be the BUF?'

'Yes, it would – how did you know?'

Deirdre caught Jago's eye with what he took to be a warning look, then turned her head to stare out of the window.

'Someone mentioned it to us,' said Jago. 'So, Mr Trubshaw, speaking of local politics, when we spoke to you on Tuesday you said small shopkeepers are suffering because what you called "alien financiers" in control of the chain stores are driving them out of business. But there are small traders that some people regard as aliens too – Jewish shopkeepers, for example. Am I right?'

'Inspector, we all have our different views on politics, and this is, as you say, a political question, but it's also a matter of simple fact. I know that Sir Oswald Mosley's out of favour these days with the powers that be, but I must say that to his credit he's always been a great champion of the small shopkeeper and he campaigned to protect people like me who are struggling in the face of unfair competition. He could see the threat from the chain stores, but he also knew, as I do, that even our small shops don't all operate on an equal footing – the laws, for example, that give certain alien religious groups unfair exemptions from the Sunday trading regulations because they have a different Sabbath. I want to see my business grow, to show it's not just aliens and immigrants who can succeed – that's not an unreasonable ambition, is it? I'm not saying we should discriminate against such people. I'm merely saying that we shouldn't allow certain groups an unfair advantage in trade. If you want my view, it's simply this – I want to make our high street British again. British shops selling British goods for British people.'

'Thank you. Do you happen to know a small shopkeeper called Silver?'

'No, I don't believe I do.'

'As a shopkeeper yourself, are you aware of any protection rackets operating in this area?'

'No, I can't say I am.'

'Have you ever heard anything to suggest Mr Stubb might be involved in activity of that nature?'

'No – on the contrary, actually.'

'What do you mean?'

'Well, we had a conversation a while ago, and he mentioned in passing that he'd once had some sort of threat against his cafe – people saying they'd break into it or wreck it if he didn't pay them some money. He said he'd sent them packing, although he didn't say how. Anyway, he said I ought to watch out, and if I had any trouble like that I should let him know, because he had friends who could do the same for me – send them packing, that is.'

'Have you ever taken him up on the offer?'

'No – I've had no need to, fortunately. No one's ever tried that sort of trick on me, but I have to say I've found it quite reassuring to know I could count on some extra muscle should the need arise. I mean, we can't have gangs of thugs taking over, can we?'

'No, indeed.'

'Mind you, I've just heard something that's rather put that reassurance in question.'

'Yes? What was that?'

'Well, apparently Stubb seems to have been the victim of some kind of assault himself this morning, at his home.'

'Really? How do you know that?'

'A mutual acquaintance found him. He mentioned it to me.'

'Was this a BUF acquaintance?'

'It was, as it happens, yes. He said he happened to be near Stubb's place and decided to drop in and say hello, but found him in a bit of a state. He thought he might need to get Stubb to a doctor, but the local bobby was passing on his beat and took over.'

'So where's Mr Stubb now?'

'I don't know. I say, do you think that could be something to do with a protection racket? I mean, Stubb did say he'd been threatened. Perhaps he hadn't been as successful in sending them packing as he'd thought. Could that be it?'

'I don't know, Mr Trubshaw, but thank you for letting me know.'

He glanced at Deirdre to check her reaction to the news of Stubb being attacked, but she seemed unmoved.

'Will that be all, Inspector?' said Trubshaw. 'It's just that I'm rather busy this morning.'

'Yes, that's all for now, thank you. We'll be on our way.'

Deirdre nudged back the end of her sleeve to look at her wristwatch. 'Oh, my goodness,' she said. 'Look at the time. I must get down to the post office or I'll miss the post.' She moved quickly to the counter and scooped up a handful of envelopes. 'Do you have your car here, Inspector? I wonder if you could possibly give me a lift.'

'By all means,' Jago replied.

She grabbed her coat and hat and led Jago and Cradock briskly to the door.

'Back in a tick, dear,' she said over her shoulder to her husband as she sailed out into the street.

Jago opened the car's front passenger door for her while Cradock pulled the rear door open and clambered into the back seat.

'It's just down there, after the third turning on the left,' she said, getting in. 'Now, is there anything else you'd like to know? I'm not as busy as my husband, you see.'

'There is, actually,' said Jago as he started the engine and set off. 'Are you acquainted with Mr Stubb yourself?'

'I suppose I am, really. I mean, I can't say I know him well, but I've met him a few times – through my husband, you understand.'

'What kind of man would you say he is?'

'Mr Stubb, or my husband?'

'Mr Stubb.'

She gave an apologetic laugh. 'Of course, silly me. To be honest, I'd say not the most pleasant man I've ever come across. I don't have a daughter, Mr Jago, but if I did, he's not the kind of man I'd want her to bring home. He seems a very rough type. And as you so astutely guessed, he's one of my husband's old BUF pals – I told you Cecil was a member, didn't I?'

'You did.'

'Well, I say a pal, but I'm not sure that's what Cecil would call him. Can you see the post office, by the way? It's just up there on the left. Neither friend nor equal, that's what I expect Cecil would say. If there's one thing my husband takes more seriously than his politics, it's his social standing. I think he rather resents the fact that he has to make his living as a shopkeeper – it's somewhat beneath his dignity. He likes to imagine himself as a leader of men, a general with an army, whereas my impression of Stubb has always been that he's more of a natural follower, a mere foot soldier in the ranks of the Blackshirt cause. Not that Cecil has ever been anything like a general. You know that stuff he spouted about being proud to serve his country? Well, for the record I should note that he wasn't a front-line hero or a brave infantry officer. He was in the army, yes, but he wasn't charging machine guns with a sabre – he was a corporal in the Pay Corps, stationed at Woolwich.'

Jago had more to ask, but they had arrived at the post office. He pulled in to the kerb and stopped the car.

'Hang on here if there's anything else you want to know,' said Mrs Trubshaw as she got out with her clutch of envelopes. 'I shan't be long.'

She disappeared into the post office and a few minutes later came out again, having disposed of the envelopes within, and rejoined Jago and Cradock in the car.

'Now, where was I?' she said, settling back into the car seat.

'The Pay Corps,' said Jago. 'But do I need to get you

back to the shop now?'

'There's no hurry, Inspector. I caught the post and I can walk back. So yes, the Pay Corps. Probably not the stuff of which military legends are made, but as one, perhaps, who knows him as well as any, I would imagine he fulfilled his duties diligently.'

'Quite. And what about the BUF – what was your husband's role in that?'

'He was very active in their branch here in Pimlico, but of course all that stopped when the BUF was banned in May. Fortunately he wasn't senior enough to be interned by the government, but he was always hankering after a higher rank – I suppose it's the desire for power. I gather about six hundred members are still being detained, so I think he should be thankful he hadn't risen high enough to be noticed. Anyway, that's how he knows Stubb – I think Stubb was in the little section or whatever they call it that he was in charge of, so I suppose Cecil was at least a leader in that respect. Not that being a leader of men has ever resulted in any apparent reward or distinction for him. He spends too much time thinking about politics and not enough on his business.'

'Has Mr Trubshaw experienced financial difficulties?'

'Well, you don't exactly make a fortune running a bicycle shop, do you? And there have been times when things were so bad I've been expecting the bailiffs to come in, and for me and Cecil to find ourselves out on the street. As for politics – well, some people like Churchill seem to do all right out of it and stroll around with top hats and cigars, but my husband's definitely backed the wrong horse in that race, hasn't he? He still thinks he's going to be a raging success one day. I've told him before, if you're so keen on having the world at your feet looking up to you, you'd better start making some money. But does he listen? I tell you, it would try the patience of a saint. But we've got to be cheerful, haven't we? That's what the government tells us, so that's what I do – always look for the silver lining.'

'And do you find it?'

She looked at him with a coy expression. 'Oh, I have my moments, Inspector.'

Jago had the feeling that she was trying to twist him round her finger, so he resisted the temptation to follow her down this line of discussion.

'I'd like to ask you about Terry Watson,' he continued. 'When we last spoke, you said you found the values of the younger generation more attractive than your husband's. Can you tell me what it was about Mr Watson's values that attracted you?'

'Well, he wasn't always going on about wars and fighting, for one thing. And there was something unpretentious about him, as if he wasn't trying to be anything more than he was – which is a kind of integrity, I suppose. I'm afraid I don't see the same in my husband and his friends.'

'Was that why you liked him?'

'Terry, you mean? I suppose so, yes. But there was more than that. He had . . . how can I put it? More energy, more . . . vigour.' Her face broke into a broad smile, as if in some fond remembrance. 'Ah, yes, a delightful boy in so many ways.'

'Pardon me for asking a rather personal question, Mrs Trubshaw, but are you suggesting there was some kind of connection between you and Mr Watson?'

She gave him a sideways glance with a dreamy expression and raised her eyebrows in a manner which he thought rather exaggerated. 'Oh, Detective Inspector, what exactly are you suggesting?' Without pausing for him to reply, she continued. 'I don't think that's the sort of question a strange man should ask a lady, even if he's a policeman – but I suppose since you are a policeman I'd better deny it, lest you get the wrong impression of me. I'm a married woman after all. In any case, I fancy some quite different creature had caught his eye. He was altogether too sweet on that girl.'

'Girl, Mrs Trubshaw? Who do you mean?'

'Why, his landlady's daughter, of course.'

'Jenny Baker?'

'That's the one. Not that we've met, of course. I only know her by what Terry told me about her – the charming, innocent young Jenny, compared with whom I find I'm just another middle-aged woman. The old, old story. If it's not the girl next door they fall for, it's always the landlady's daughter – such a banal cliché, don't you think? But the mother doesn't always take kindly to the idea, does she? I told Terry to watch out. Don't get on the wrong side of her mum, I said, or she's likely to skin you alive.' She stopped short. 'Oh – that sounds bad, doesn't it? I didn't mean it like that. It's just that mothers can be a bit protective, let alone fathers. Mind you, I don't know what sort of fellow her father is.'

'I understand Mrs Baker lost her husband in January.'

'Oh, sorry – I'm always putting my foot in it. Whatever I said to Terry, all I meant was be careful not to cross your landlady, because you're just the lodger, and you don't want her to heave you out onto the street, do you? Anyway, perhaps Terry and Jenny had a rosy future ahead of them – but we'll never know now, will we? If we women could tell which men will make good husbands, we'd be spared a lot of pain and grief in our lives. Which reminds me, I'd better be getting back to the shop. Is there anything else you want to know?'

'No, I don't think so. You've been most helpful.'

'I'll be off then,' said Deirdre, turning to face him. 'But before I go, Inspector, I hope you won't mention anything of what I said about Terry – Mr Watson, that is – to my husband. He's the sort of man who could easily take it upon himself to interpret an innocent friendship as philandering. And – well, he can be a little intemperate at times.'

Before Jago could answer she had opened the door. She flashed him a final brief smile and then got out of the car and shut it behind her. Deirdre turned away with a dismissive wave of her hand and strode back down the street in the direction of the shop and her husband.

CHAPTER FORTY

'Well, that's certainly something no one else has told us, isn't it?' said Cradock, following Deirdre Trubshaw with his eyes as she disappeared down the street. 'Quite a revelation.'

'Which particular revelation are you thinking of?'

'Terry Watson having his eyes on Jenny Baker, of course.'

'Yes. Mrs Trubshaw seems rather fond of making dramatic revelations, though, doesn't she? It's like rabbits out of a hat. I wonder how much of it's for effect.'

'You mean she might be making it up?'

'Not necessarily, but she strikes me as the kind of woman who feels perhaps there's a bit of spice lacking in her life, and this might be her way of adding some.'

'It does sound as though she and Watson were friendly, though, and it seems like he confided in her.'

'Undoubtedly friendly, Peter, and that makes me wonder why she mentioned a connection between Watson and Miss

Baker to us. Was Jenny Baker as friendly with Watson as Deirdre Trubshaw was? And if so, could there be a bit of jealousy at play? I think we need to hear the other side of the story.'

'You mean Jenny Baker's?'

'I do, Peter. And meanwhile, what did you make of Stubb's alibi for that window business?'

'What Trubshaw said, you mean? I'd say it was pretty useless. You asked Stubb where he was between five and five-thirty, and he said he was with Trubshaw, but then Trubshaw says he can't recall exactly what time it was, and he can only guess it was sometime between five and six. If he said that in court it'd be thrown out.'

'Yes, it wasn't entirely convincing, was it? It's the kind of thing you hear when a crook's told someone to come up with an alibi for him. You know how it is – the witness is too scared to refuse but knows if he commits perjury he could end up in jail himself.'

'Or in this case, maybe not scared, but keeping his options open so he can drop Stubb in it if he wants to?'

'Maybe, but either way it means Stubb hasn't got a cast-iron alibi for the attack on Benny Silver's shop, and after what Deirdre Trubshaw's just told us about his old BUF links with her husband I'm beginning to wonder whether painting's not the only odd job he's been doing for Trubshaw recently.'

'I see what you mean, sir. Interesting that someone seems to have had a go at Stubb himself too, isn't it?'

'Yes – a case of the biter bit, perhaps. If Alf Stubb's the thug we've been led to believe he is, maybe he's run up against someone who's given him a taste of his own medicine. I'd like to know more, if we can find someone who'll tell us – I doubt whether Stubb will. First, though, I want to follow up on this business of Watson and Jenny Baker – I'll be interested to see what she's got to say.'

They found Jenny on duty at the telephone exchange, and as before, she joined them in the entrance lobby.

'So,' she said, 'are you here to talk about Terry again?'

'Yes, that's right, Miss Baker,' said Jago. 'I'm sorry to take you away from your work, but this won't take long.'

'That's all right. My supervisor knows it's something official, and to be honest, a little extra break from the switchboard's always nice – we're on the go non-stop most days. Not that I'm complaining, of course – it's not like my mum's job. That's what I call real work. But how's your investigation going? Have you found out who did it yet?'

'Not yet, no, but we're making progress. How is your mother, by the way?'

'Not so bad. I think what happened to Terry . . . well, I think it knocked her sideways for a bit, but she's a fighter, you know. Stronger than me – I don't know how she does it. I mean, she's working six days a week in that new job of hers, so she only gets the one day off, on Sundays, and then she spends all night at the rest centre looking after other people. She's a saint, you know. And it may be voluntary but it's not just a few hours – it's a full twelve-hour shift, eight in the evening till eight in the morning, with just one break in the middle, and you can't exactly pop out for a nice bite to eat in the local cafe at one o'clock in the morning, can you?'

'Is that a fixed time? For her break, I mean.'

'I believe so. Why?'

'Oh, nothing. I just wondered. I suppose she'd have to take a sandwich with her, then.'

'Yes, although since she's a volunteer and she's making the things all night, I think they let her have one of the rest centre sandwiches and take it out somewhere quiet for her break.'

'Yes, of course.'

'Anyway, I assume you didn't come here to talk about sandwiches. How can I help you?'

'I want to ask about you and Mr Watson. The last time we spoke to you I asked you what was the nature of your relationship with him, and you said he was the lodger and nothing more. We've been talking to one or two people since then, though, people who knew Mr Watson, and one of them said – and I'm quoting the expression they used – they said he was sweet on you.'

'Who said that?'

'I'm afraid I can't tell you that, Miss Baker, but I'd like to know if it's true.'

She cast her eyes about the room as if looking for a way out, then drew herself up with a sniff. 'Well, what if he was? What's it got to do with anyone else?'

'I've no wish to intrude unnecessarily on your privacy, Miss Baker, but I'm sure you understand that in a case like this we do have to ask some personal questions. So, just to get this straight, you're saying he did have some kind of romantic attachment to you, yes?'

'Yes,' she said in a reluctant tone. 'I suppose he did. But a girl can't help that, can she?'

Jago chose to treat this as a rhetorical question and

continued. 'That accounts for his feelings, but what about yours? How serious was this relationship?'

She pouted, as though the question was of little importance to her and not one she'd thought about. 'Not very. At least, not on my part it wasn't. He seemed nice enough, and it made a change to have a man paying some attention. The operators at the exchange are nearly all women, so the chances of meeting a boy there who'll ask you out are very limited.'

'Did Terry Watson ask you out?'

'Yes, he did. Just once or twice. Here, you won't tell my mum, will you?'

'Why don't you want me to tell her?'

'I'm sorry, Inspector. It's just that I don't think she knows, and I'm not sure she approved of Terry where I was concerned. Mind you, I suppose it doesn't matter whether you tell her or not now, does it? It's all water under the bridge now he's dead. Look, Mr Jago, Terry was a charmer, to be sure, but it wasn't like he was the man for me for life. I couldn't see myself marrying him, but he was all right to be with, and there's not a lot to do of an evening these days, is there? Anyway, strictly speaking we didn't actually go out together, but we did spend the odd evening together in the house – but only when Mum was out at work.'

'You told us that on Sunday evening your mother left the house at about ten to eight, then you and Mr Watson washed the dishes, and then he went out, didn't you?'

'Yes, that's right.'

'Can anyone else corroborate that?'

'Of course not. Once my mum had gone there was only me and Terry in the house.'

'And you had no visitors to the house that evening?'

'No. What are you getting at?'

'We only have your word for it that Mr Watson went out – he might very well have stayed in the house with you for the rest of the evening. Did he?'

'No! I've told you he went out, and that's the truth.'

'And you still don't recall him telling you where he was going?'

'No, I don't.'

'Was he in the habit of going out during the blackout, when other people take shelter? Some people would regard that as foolhardy.'

'Maybe they would. You wouldn't catch me doing it, but Terry was braver than me. Sometimes he'd say he had business to attend to in the evenings and it couldn't wait. He didn't seem to mind going out in the air raids – he said if you're caught out in a raid when you're on a bike, the thing you have to do is fling yourself off and land flat on the ground whenever you hear an explosion. Someone told him that's what they used to do in the Spanish Civil War, and it meant you were fifty per cent safer, so he'd taught himself to do it. He said sometimes you couldn't put business off, even if there was a raid.'

'Did he say what that business was?'

'No, he only ever said one evening he had to go out and pick some things up, but I don't know what he was referring to. I said he shouldn't go out in the air raids, but he said he had to. Some people might say that was foolhardy, but I think it was brave.'

'Does your mother know about these business activities of his?'

'I don't think so – she's never said she did, anyway. And I've never told her anything about me and Terry, because I think she'd worry. She can be a bit protective, you know – I suppose I'm all she's got now, since Dad died.'

'Ah, yes, your mother told us he'd passed away. My condolences.'

'Thank you, but it's OK. The truth is, Inspector, my dad was not a nice man. He liked being mine host at the pub, playing the part – you know, the genial landlord, everyone's friend, always ready with a smile and a joke, but I saw another side to him. I told you that pub was a rough place, but he was rough too, a real bully. He had a vile temper on him. When I was a kid I felt like I was constantly walking on eggshells because he was so unpredictable – you never knew when he might turn on you. It was the same for my mum. That's what I meant when I was saying how I like the way everything's so calm and under control at the telephone exchange. He couldn't control himself, you see.'

'So you don't grieve his passing?'

'Well, obviously he was still my dad, for all that, but I can't say the world's a poorer place without him. When I heard he was dead I was more surprised than anything else. You just don't expect that kind of thing. Bombs, yes, but not that.'

'Not what?'

'I mean something as simple as that – being knocked over in the blackout. But it's happened to a lot of people, from what I've heard.'

'I'm so sorry – I didn't know how he'd died. What happened?'

'I'm not entirely sure. I mean I wasn't there myself to

325

see, but the policeman who turned up on the doorstep and broke the news to us said he reckoned it was a bike – he said there was a man who said he'd seen what happened, but he didn't want to give his name or address and slipped away pretty quickly. Perhaps he didn't want his wife finding out where he'd been – I don't know. Anyway, the witness said it was a bike, but he couldn't see who was riding it. I don't suppose anyone could be much of a witness in the blackout – but apparently he saw someone go past quite close, and the bike had no lights on. And that's illegal, isn't it? I thought you were supposed to have dimmed lights on.'

Jago nodded, and she continued.

'Then this witness said he heard a little bell tinkling, like one of those bicycle bells, then a sort of clattering noise. That must've been the bike hitting Dad, because it seems next thing there he was, lying dead in the road. Banged his head on the cobble stones, they reckoned. Just another accident in the blackout, but Dad was in the wrong place at the wrong time.'

'I'm sorry to hear that.'

'Thanks. I suppose I should be missing him terribly and grieving for him, but somehow this war doesn't give you much time for that, does it?'

She paused and stretched her mouth into a wide smile, but he could see no trace of a smile in her eyes.

CHAPTER FORTY-ONE

The mist had cleared by the time the two detectives emerged from the telephone exchange, but the autumn sky was still overcast. A painful grinding noise came from the gearbox of an elderly taxicab making its way along Greencoat Place, causing a pigeon that was pecking at crumbs on the pavement to flutter up onto a window ledge.

'So,' said Jago, 'Nancy's husband was knocked over and killed by a cyclist. That's interesting, isn't it?'

'Yes. Could be a coincidence, though, couldn't it? A lot of people are getting killed in road accidents because of the blackout. It's probably like Jenny Baker said – wrong place, wrong time.'

'It might be a coincidence, and it might not, but I'd like to find out more about it, and I think Nancy Baker's the one to ask – she's never mentioned how he died, has she?'

'We've never asked her, sir.'

'That's right – so now we should. She never breathed a

word about anything going on between her daughter and Watson either, but I'd like to know whether she knew about it, and if she did, why she never saw fit to tell us.'

'Jenny didn't think her mum knew, did she? And she didn't want you to tell her either.'

'Yes, and I didn't make her any promises – I think I'm going to have to disappoint her on that. We're going round to knock on Mrs Baker's door – and if she's still sleeping off her night shift, we'll just have to wake her up.'

When they arrived at the house in Tachbrook Street and duly knocked, there was no response. Jago waited, studying the door's peeling paintwork, and was just about to give up and turn away when it creaked open to reveal Nancy Baker, tired but awake and dressed for the day.

'Ah, good morning,' she said. 'I'm sorry to keep you waiting. I was just on my way out the back door when I heard you knock – I've got Dennis here pulling up some carrots for me and tidying the vegetable patch, and I was just taking him a drink. Anyway, do come in.'

She let them into the house, and they followed her to the living room and sat down.

'I'm relieved to see you're up and about, Mrs Baker,' said Jago. 'I was afraid we might disturb you while you were still sleeping off your night shift.'

'Don't worry – no harm done. I'd usually be asleep now, but if Dennis is kind enough to come and do my vegetables on his day off I feel obliged to stay up until he's finished. I'll have my sleep later on. Can I get you anything?'

'No, thank you. I'd just like to check a couple of things with you.'

'Oh, yes? What's that?'

'It was something you said when we spoke to you before. I asked you whether Mr Watson had any lady friends, and you said you didn't know of any.'

'Yes,' she replied cautiously. 'So what?'

'Well, it's just that since then it's been suggested to us that he was sweet on your daughter Jenny, and she's just confirmed that he was. Did you know that?'

'Well, since you're asking, I did. Is that a crime?'

'No, but why didn't you tell me when I asked you? Was it a secret?'

'No, it wasn't a secret – what I mean is, she'd never said it was. She just never told me anything about it, so I thought she probably reckoned I didn't know. But anyway, she's old enough to choose her own friends now – she doesn't need my permission.'

'So if she didn't tell you, how did you find out?'

'I suppose you could put it down to a mother's instinct, or feminine intuition, Inspector, or maybe it's just that I've been around long enough to know how men's minds work. I hardly ever saw the two of them together, but call it what you like, I could just tell – it was like I could smell it in the air. It was the same last Sunday – we had tea together, and I just caught him looking at her. Jenny suddenly came over all shy, and she isn't a shy girl. I could tell.'

'Your daughter said she wasn't sure whether you approved of Mr Watson.'

'Well, the way I see things, that's neither here nor there. You could say it's none of my business, but if you must know, I quite took to him at first – or at least maybe I did just feel sorry for him after all. But either way, when all's said and done I just didn't think he was a particularly good prospect for Jenny.'

'Why did you think that?'

'I suppose I reckon when a young man doesn't say what his job is and can only afford to rent a room in a house like mine he isn't necessarily the best choice for a girl like Jenny. But these things often come to an end by themselves, don't they? And in this case they certainly did. I reckon she'll have forgotten him in a month and then she'll find someone who's a much better catch.'

'Do you have someone in mind?'

'No, I don't, Inspector. I just hope she finds herself a man who's honest.'

'What do you mean by that?'

'Oh, I don't know. I couldn't put my finger on it, but just recently I started thinking there was something a bit shifty about that Terry. He was getting too cagey for my liking – you know, secretive, coming and going at all times of the day and night. I used to wonder what he was up to.'

'And did you find out?'

'No, but when a man sneaks out in the blackout these days and he hasn't got some kind of fancy armband or tin helmet on, you can't help asking yourself whether whatever he's getting up to is strictly legal.'

'Do you have any evidence for that?'

'No, it's just the impression I got. That's all I can tell you, really. Anything else you wanted to know?'

'Yes, there is, actually. It's something else your daughter mentioned to us.'

'Yes?'

'You told us your husband had died at the beginning of

the year, but you didn't say how he'd died.'

'Didn't I? Well, I'm sorry, but I don't recall you asking and I must've thought it wasn't relevant. So what's Jenny told you?'

'She said he was knocked down in the blackout by a bike. Is that correct, Mrs Baker?'

'Yes, it is.'

'Is there anything else you'd like to tell us?'

'I don't know – what more is there to say? It was just an accident.'

'Are you sure it was?'

'Of course. What else could it be? You're not suggesting someone ran him down deliberately, are you?'

'It has to be a possibility. Did Mr Baker have any enemies?'

'Enemies? No – he ran a pub. You're everyone's mate if you run a pub.'

'Not necessarily in my experience, Mrs Baker. Can you think of anyone who might've wanted to be rid of him?'

'No, I can't. Why would anyone want to do that? He rubbed along all right with everyone.'

'That's not what your daughter says.'

'What? Jenny? What's she been saying?'

'She says her father was a bully with a vile temper.'

'The little madam. She's no right to say that, Inspector. All right, he had his moments – he flared up occasionally, but he couldn't help it. He'd had a hard life, and things were very tough when he was a kid. So yes, Percy could be harsh at times, but it wasn't his fault. He went through things in the war that he couldn't talk about, and I think they marked him for life. When he came back he wasn't the same man

I'd married – he never really managed to adjust back to peacetime, and it all got even worse when this new war started. I was his wife, though, and I made allowances for him, but Jenny never could – I think she wanted everything to be perfect, but he couldn't be something he wasn't, not even for her. I think that's why she likes that job of hers – it's all a bit more calm and peaceful than what she grew up with at home, but I'm afraid if she's not careful she's going to end up too la-di-da for her own good. You can't expect other people to be perfect all the time, can you? And I don't think you should judge them if they're not – but that's not the way she is.'

'It may be that you've been very generous to your husband with your understanding and compassion, Mrs Baker, but there's a lot of women in your position who'd have wanted to be free of a man like that, especially if they were pushed to the limit. That means I have to consider the possibility that someone did exactly what you're saying they shouldn't do.'

'What do you mean?'

'I mean the possibility that someone did judge him – and found him guilty. And that could mean it wasn't an accident.'

'You're not suggesting that I . . . You must be mad. I don't even know how to ride a bike.'

'In that case, do you know who was riding that bike?'

'No, I don't know – they never caught him. It could've been anyone.'

'Was it Terry Watson?'

She seemed to recoil in disbelief.

'Terry? Of course not – that'd be absurd. Do you think

I'd take a man in as my lodger if he'd killed my husband?'

Jago said nothing.

'Oh, I see – you think he was my fancy man and we plotted together to do my Percy in? Don't be ridiculous. I'm sorry, Inspector, but I think you've been reading too many racy novels. Are you finished now?'

'No. I have one more question for you. I understand that when you're on duty at the rest centre overnight you have a break at one o'clock in the morning. Is that correct?'

'Yes, it is,' she replied cautiously. 'So what?'

'And that was the time of your break on the night Terry Watson was killed?'

'Yes.'

'How long was your break?'

'About half an hour.'

'And what did you do?'

'I had a sandwich – they let me take one for myself – and I went outside.'

'For the whole half hour?'

'Yes. I just sat outside in the night air with a cup of tea and a sandwich, and looked up at the stars for a bit, trying not to think about all those people in the rest centre who'd been bombed out of their homes.'

'Was anyone with you?'

'No. I'm busy with people all night, so I like to be on my own for my break, get a bit of peace and quiet.'

'Did you go back to your house during your break?'

'No!' She raised her voice. 'Are you insinuating that I went back and killed Terry? How could you say such a thing?'

'I didn't say that, Mrs Baker, but I do need to establish

your movements during that night.'

'Well, I'll tell you straight, then – I slaved away in that rest centre for five hours, helping those poor people with their crying children, then I popped out for a bit of a break, then I went back in and slaved away for the rest of the night. Will that do?'

'Yes, that will do for now, thank you.'

'I should think so too. Saying I killed Terry? That's so cruel. I help people, I don't kill them.'

She pulled a handkerchief from her sleeve and began crying into it.

CHAPTER FORTY-TWO

The door to the living room swung open and Dennis Bateman looked in anxiously, first at Nancy and then at Jago.

'Are you all right, Nancy?' he said. 'I was just bringing my mug back into the house and I thought I could hear shouting, so I thought I'd better check.'

She gave no reply, but calmed herself as he crossed the room to where she was sitting and knelt before her.

'Have you been crying?' he asked.

'Yes, I have.' She wiped her eyes with the handkerchief and pointed at Jago. 'He's been trying to make out it was Terry who knocked my poor Percy off his bike in the blackout and it was because Percy'd been knocking me about and Terry and I were lovers and I wanted him done in. And then he's saying I killed Terry – that I came home from the rest centre in the middle of the night and murdered him. But it's not true – it's all lies.'

'That's not exactly what I said, Mrs Baker,' said Jago.

'Maybe not in so many words, but that's what it sounded like to me. Help me, Dennis – tell him – he's got it all wrong.'

'Don't worry, Nancy,' said Bateman. 'We can sort this out – leave it to me.'

He perched beside her on the arm of her chair and said nothing as she slipped her hand into his and gripped it. His face took on a thoughtful expression as he turned towards Jago. 'I think you should leave her alone, Inspector,' he said. 'I'm sure she's telling you the truth.'

'About what? Her husband's death, or Mr Watson's?'

'About both.'

'So are you saying you know what actually happened to Mr Baker?'

'No, I'm not – I wasn't there, but I'm telling you it's got nothing to do with Nancy. No one saw what happened to Percy, so no one knows, but there's no reason on earth why she'd ever want to get rid of him and lose her home and her business in the process. Unless it's true that she was carrying on with Terry, but that's ridiculous – she didn't even know Terry when Percy was killed.'

'You're sure about that, are you?'

'Of course I am – I'd have known. Terry was my friend. I don't have many friends, but he and I were pals, right from when we were in that camp together, and that was very important to me. It's why I moved down here, and it's why I helped him get a job when he needed one. Then when he had nowhere to live I fixed up for him to rent a room from Nancy. I probably knew him better than anyone else.'

'Friends talk to each other, don't they? So did he ever tell you who was riding the bike that knocked Mr Baker down, if it wasn't him?'

'No, of course not – he didn't know anything about it.'

'And what about his private life? Was he in the habit of confiding in you about personal matters – affairs of the heart, for example?'

Nancy let out a sudden sob.

'Now look what you've done,' said Bateman. 'You're upsetting her.' He slipped his hand out of hers and put his arm round her shoulder to comfort her.

'It's all right, Dennis,' she said quietly. 'I'm just tired – it's too much for me. You carry on.'

'OK,' said Bateman. 'So, Inspector, if you want to know whether Terry used to confide in me about personal stuff, the answer's no, he didn't. I told you before, he was a private sort of bloke, kept himself to himself, so he didn't talk about things like that. Not usually, anyway – it was just sometimes his tongue ran away with him when he'd had a pint or two over the odds.'

'Did he ever let slip anything concerning Mrs Baker?'

'No, he didn't. Look, I've told you, there was nothing going on between them. I knew it wasn't Nancy he was interested in, because it was someone else.'

'Really? And who was this person?'

'It was a girl – a girl he'd got involved with. I was shocked when I found out – it was like a bolt from the blue. I just couldn't believe it.'

'But when we spoke to you yesterday afternoon in your flat we asked you if he was closely involved with any young woman in particular, and you said no.'

'Well, that wasn't quite right, was it? I actually said he

never told me, and that was true . . . up to a point. He'd never let on about it – not until Sunday night.'

'And why was it a shock?'

'Because like I said, I knew Terry, I knew what kind of man he was. I may've been his friend, but I wasn't blind, and I knew what he was like with women. He treated them badly. Love them and leave them, that's what he used to say, and he'd laugh. I didn't think it was funny, but I never said – he would've just laughed at me too. But this time it wasn't just any girl. I didn't know the others he'd been caught up with, but this one I did – I cared for her. And when he told me—' He bit his lip, as if to control his feelings. 'Well, I don't know how to say it . . . she was just the sweetest girl I've ever met.'

'And this girl – was it Alice?'

Bateman's face changed. He jerked his head up and stared at Jago blankly. 'Alice?' he said. 'Who's Alice? I don't know anyone called Alice.'

'Are you sure?'

'Of course I am.'

'I'm sorry – I was thinking of another young lady we've met.'

'Not someone else who got involved with Terry?'

'I'm afraid I can't say.'

'I don't believe it – I'm beginning to think there wasn't a shred of decency in that man's body. If that's how he was carrying on he deserved everything he got.'

'Mr Bateman, can you tell me who this girl is that you've been talking about?'

'Aye, I'm talking about Jenny – Nancy's daughter. He said he'd been seeing her, but in secret, like. He'd never mentioned it to me, even though we were supposed to be pals.'

'Do you mean you thought he was under some sort of obligation to tell you?'

'No, not in the normal way he wasn't, but this was different. You see, I—' He broke off and turned his eyes to the ceiling, running his hand through his hair, then switched his gaze back to Jago. 'The thing is, when Terry was looking for somewhere to live back at the beginning of the year and I sent him round here to see Nancy, I told him what a good landlady she'd be, very considerate and all that, and he asked if there was anyone else living in the house. I said only her daughter, but then I said some nice things about Jenny – too many, I think. I'd known her for years, you see. I'm sorry, Nancy.'

'It's not your fault, Dennis,' said Nancy. 'And what you've said about Terry and Jenny – it's not a surprise to me.'

'You mean you knew about it? They told you, and you didn't tell me?'

'No, neither of them told me – I just read the signs and put two and two together. I suspected there was something, but I didn't know whether it was serious or not. Jenny never said anything about it, and Terry certainly didn't give anything away.'

'So, Mr Bateman,' Jago resumed, 'you were saying you'd known Miss Baker for years.'

'That's right – ever since I started going to Percy and Nancy's pub.'

'And you liked her?'

'I did. I suppose I'd always been fond of her, but I'm not

the sort of man who knows his way around when it comes to girls. If I'd had a bit more of Terry's confidence I'd have asked her out myself, but I never quite knew how to do it – we're not all Casanovas, not where I come from.'

'But still, you had affectionate feelings for her?'

'More than affectionate. Inside myself I knew I . . . well, I knew I loved her. But somehow it never came out – I've never told her. Pathetic, isn't it?'

'So your friend became your rival?'

'That's right.' A note of bitterness came into Bateman's voice. 'I think she just fell for him. Terry used to say all's fair in love and war, and he was right, wasn't he? It's every man for himself. I think he could see I was soft about her, and he wanted to beat me. That was Terry all over. He couldn't help being competitive – it was in his blood. That's what made him a better racer than me.'

'So what happened on Sunday night?'

'Well, we'd been out during the air raid – Terry had this habit of going out in the blackout and, er . . . looking for stuff.'

'You mean looting.'

Bateman shrugged his shoulders and sighed. 'What can I say?'

'You can say what really happened. Yesterday we told you we suspected him of taking things from bomb sites and you said you knew nothing about it.'

'I know, and I'm sorry. I didn't want you to think I was mixed up in that sort of thing, because I wasn't.'

'But you admit you were out with him in that air raid on Sunday night.'

'Aye, but it was just that once, and I didn't really want

to go. I wasn't as bold as him, and I didn't think it was right anyway, but he talked me into it. Terry reckoned it wasn't looting – he said he was just keeping an eye out for interesting stuff. He said if we didn't pick it up someone else would. No one was going to miss a little bit of this or that if they'd lost their whole house, and they might be dead anyway, so if we could get a few bob for it, why not?'

'Did he have that grey rucksack with him?'

'No, he didn't. He said he was looking for a few things small enough to go in his coat pockets, so he wouldn't look conspicuous.'

'We noticed there were a couple of bricks in his saddlebag – did they have anything to do with this?'

'I'm not sure. He used to put them in his bag for training, but I think . . . well, I think maybe sometimes he went a bit further – like when he saw something useful and it was on the other side of a window that hadn't been broken by the bombs. But I never saw him do that, mind.'

'So what happened on Sunday evening? And before you answer that question, I must caution you that you are not obliged to say anything, but anything you say may be given in evidence. Do you understand?'

'I do.'

'Please continue, then.'

'Well, we had a look round a few places, but I don't think Terry saw anything that took his fancy. Then he said he was having some trouble with the gears slipping on his bike and wanted me to help him adjust them. I said yes, of course – I was still his pal, or so I thought – so we went back to Terry's Anderson shelter, where he kept his bike, and got to work on it.'

'And you had a drink?'

'Aye. He had some whisky – he said he'd found it somewhere. So anyway, we had a drop or two of that, and then we got to talking about politics. I should've known better than to let Terry get onto that subject, but I just said something about Chamberlain dying. I said how I thought he was a bit of a drip, dithering all the time and waving bits of paper round in the air as if he'd saved the world when what we really needed was a strong leader who'd make Hitler think twice about starting any trouble, and of course that set Terry off. He was anti-war, see, and said it was politicians like Chamberlain who'd got us into this mess, and now he'd popped off so he'd never have to get us out of it. I think he was just trying to annoy me. I've never been as good at politics as he was, so I couldn't be bothered to argue about it. I got my cigarettes out instead and offered him one. He took one, and I asked him for a light. He pulled a box of matches out of his pocket and I saw something fall out, so I picked it up.'

'It was a white poppy?'

'Aye, as a matter of fact it was.'

'You didn't mention this when I asked you about white poppies.'

Bateman gave him a sullen look. 'Aye, but you only asked me if I'd ever seen him wearing one, and I said I hadn't – and that was true.'

'So what happened when you picked it up?'

'I asked him why it was white, and he said something like it was the key to peace. Then he sort of smiled to himself and said that wasn't the only thing it was the key to either. I asked him what he was talking about and he just smirked – like I was an idiot. He used to do that, you know – make out I was stupid. He always knew how to get my goat.'

'You were angry?'

'More annoyed than angry, but he wouldn't drop it. He just laughed – to himself, like it was some sort of private joke. He said "The key to Jenny, of course – what did you think?" He said she didn't approve of the war, so he'd told her he was against it too, and then he'd bought two white poppies to prove it. He was going to give one to her the next day – Armistice Day – and tell her it was one for her and one for him, as a token, like.'

'And what did you say to him?'

'I said he had no right, and I made a grab for it. I threw it on the floor and stamped on it. But he just picked it up, cool as a cucumber, brushed some of the dirt off and said "I suppose this'll have to be my one, then, and I'll keep the nice clean one for Jenny." He put it back in his pocket, and then he gave me another one of his smug little smiles and said "Actually, Dennis, I have every right in the world."'

Bateman paused, as if uncertain whether to continue.

'And?' said Jago.

'I said something like "What do you mean by that?" and he said of course he had every right, what with her being his girl and all.'

'That must've been hard for you to take.'

'You bet it was. I mean, how could a lovely girl like Jenny fall for someone like him? I tried to act like it was all the same to me, but then he started going on about how he reckoned he'd have his way with her soon. He said "She's not the Mona Lisa, is she? But she's a woman, and I

343

think her resistance is weakening – I think we're looking at another notch on the bedpost, Dennis, my boy."'

He broke off and stared at Jago as if pleading for understanding.

'I couldn't bear it,' he continued, choking on his words. 'Jenny's beautiful – she's like a flower, and I had to protect her. I shouted at him. He'd always treated me like a doormat, and I'd put up with it because I thought we were mates. But now – now I kept thinking that's my Jenny you're talking about, my lovely Jenny – you're not fit to kiss the ground she walks on. I couldn't find words to say what I was feeling. I had this picture of him and her in my mind, and I couldn't get rid of it. He'd stolen her – stolen the most precious thing in the world from me.'

'So you hit him?'

'I did. I threw a punch at him, and then another. I hit him again and again. There was this sort of rage inside me that just came from nowhere. He tried to get out, but I pushed him back. That's when I saw the emergency spanner hanging on the wall, so I grabbed it and lashed out at him. I caught the side of his head with it once, maybe twice, and he went down, just like that. He stopped moving, and I thought . . . well, I just panicked and ran away. I never meant to do that to him.'

'You knew he was dead?'

Bateman nodded. 'I knew. I killed him, Inspector – but I swear it was only because I loved Jenny.'

CHAPTER FORTY-THREE

Bateman sat meekly in the car as they drove him to Gerald Road police station. Jago had seen plenty of men fighting to resist arrest in his time and had half-expected a fresh outburst of the rage that the gardener claimed had overtaken him in the Anderson shelter, but there was no sign of it. In contrast to Nancy Baker, who had burst into angry tears and indignant protest when Jago arrested her friend, he was subdued and seemed resigned to whatever his fate might be, barely uttering a word on their short journey.

At the station he was charged and taken away to a cell. Jago requested the use of a telephone and told Cradock to stay where he was while he went to use it. He made two calls. The first was to Scotland Yard, to report to Hardacre that they had a man behind bars on a charge of murder. The second was a private matter and not for Cradock's ears.

'Right, Peter,' he said when he returned, 'Mr Hardacre wants to see us in his office at Scotland Yard at half past three.' He turned to the uniformed officer who presided over the front counter. 'Sergeant, do you think you could get one of your men to rustle up a quick cup of tea for us before we go?'

'Of course, sir.' The desk sergeant collared a passing constable and dispatched him to fulfil this request. 'Anything else, sir?'

'Yes, there is, actually. Is there anything in your occurrence book about a man called Stubb being roughed up in Effingham Street this morning?'

'I believe there is, sir. If you'll just bear with me for a moment.' He fetched the book and turned the pages. 'Here we are. Report by the beat constable – says he was alerted by a man who said Mr Alfred Stubb was in a bad way in his flat and the door was open, but then left without giving his own name. Our constable saw he had some bruises, but Stubb said it was nothing, he'd just slipped and fallen over.'

'Do you know this man Stubb?'

'I've heard of him. He runs a cafe down there – in Effingham Street, like you said. Alf's Cafe, it's called. I don't know him, though – he's fairly new round these parts, I believe. Why, have you got something on him?'

'I may do.'

'Right, well, let us know if you need a hand, sir.'

'Thank you, Sergeant, I will.'

The constable returned with a cup of tea for Jago and Cradock and took them to a small but vacant cupboard of a room where they could drink it in private.

'What about this Stubb business then, sir?' said Cradock

as they sat down. 'Him getting roughed up, I mean – it doesn't look like that's connected with Terry Watson's murder, does it?'

'Not now we've heard what Bateman's had to say, no,' Jago replied.

'So what do you think happened? Someone seems to have had it in for him – something to do with this protection racket, do you think?'

'I'm positive it is, but the problem is getting enough evidence to bring a case against him. Ashdon's admitted that he's been targeted by a protection operation but said he doesn't know Stubb, but given how confident he seems to be about fixing this sort of problem by himself, I could easily believe he'd arranged this to frighten him off. Proving it, though – that's a different matter.'

'You don't think Stubb's working for Ashdon, then?'

'I'm more inclined to believe Stubb's trying to set up his own little racket. He's a thug and a bully, but he's not what you might call part of the intellectual elite, so if he's got ideas above his station like Dolly Cook said, maybe he fancied himself as a protection gangster getting rich quick and now he's regretting it. It certainly sounds as though he's trodden on someone's toes.'

'And the fencing?'

'I'm certain that's what he was doing with Terry Watson's bag of stuff, but again, it's a question of evidence. We can't prove Watson looted the goods, because he's dead and we don't know what was in the rucksack. Stubb's never going to tell us who he sold the stuff on to, and we're never going to be able to trace the original owners if we've no idea what it was they might've owned. All we can say is we think

Stubb's definitely a wide boy and almost certainly a crook, but we've no evidence.'

'And Benny's window? Are we any clearer on whether it was a protection thing or an anti-Jewish thing?'

'From what we know about Stubb now, maybe it was both. I reckon he saw your friend Benny as an easy target – smashing a window like that was an obvious way to put the wind up a Jewish shopkeeper, and also a way of inducing him to cough up money. With his BUF past it might also just've been a matter of personal malice.'

'Which is where Trubshaw comes in. You said you wondered whether Stubb might've done some other odd jobs for him apart from a spot of painting – did you mean maybe it was Trubshaw who got him to put that brick through Benny's window?'

'Yes, that's what I was thinking – but if he did, I'd guess it would've been for political reasons. I can't see Trubshaw running a protection racket – judging by what he said about Stubb so kindly offering to protect him against gangsters, he didn't even seem to realise he was probably the next mug in Stubb's sights.'

'We're not likely to get anything out of Trubshaw by way of evidence against Stubb, then, I suppose.'

'No, I think you're probably right. Silver's too scared to speak, Ashdon reckons he's strong enough to fix any problems by himself so won't get involved, Cook's too loyal for his own good, and as for Trubshaw, it seems to me that with him and Stubb having the same politics he's too blind to see the man's actually a threat to his own property and business.'

'So we've got no case against him because no one's willing to speak up.'

'That's often the way it is with gangsters, though, isn't it? People either can't speak up because they're afraid, or won't because they think they're safe and no one'll touch them. It's how Hitler got where he is today, and he's not the only one in the world. Thugs and bullies, Peter, that's all it is – with a few fancy uniforms thrown in.'

'So we're going to give up?'

'Not necessarily. Stubb still hasn't got a convincing alibi for the time of the attack on Benny Silver's shop. He had both the opportunity and the motive, and if the means was a brick, that's not too difficult to find lying around these days. I'm not sure he's bright enough to wriggle his way out of everything that's pointing in his direction, so I'm keeping an open mind on whether to interview him under caution and see where we get. I don't want him to get off scot-free.'

'I'm glad to hear that, sir. I feel like I've let Benny down – I should've been able to help him and I didn't. And now that we've got Bateman locked up, I suppose we'll be going home and I won't see him again. Do you think we could drop in on him and the family on our way to Scotland Yard, so I can say goodbye?'

'I don't see why not, as long as we're not late for our appointment with Detective Superintendent Hardacre. I suspect it wouldn't be good to keep him waiting. And I can understand why you've got a soft spot for the Silvers – they strike me as a decent sort of couple, and it's not their fault if they're too scared to tell us what they know. I'll come in and say goodbye too. I'm just hoping that going there doesn't mean we bump into Mrs Edgworth as well, though.'

'You mean after what she said outside the bike shop this morning, sir?'

'Yes, a bit odd, wasn't it? Suddenly all cold and defensive like that.'

'Did we say something to offend her?'

'Not that I can think of, but the way she was trying to warn us off talking to Alice Mason was beginning to make me think Watson's murder was a case of the jilted lover's revenge.'

'Me too, sir. Alice had more than enough reason to do it after the way Watson treated her.'

'Well, it looks like we were wrong about her, doesn't it? I'm glad we didn't go straight down to that laundry and upset her even more.'

'Yes, sir. But even so, I don't think we're going to be invited to tea with Mrs Edgworth again, are we?'

'No, Peter, but perhaps we should be thankful for small mercies.'

CHAPTER FORTY-FOUR

When they arrived at the Silvers' shop they discovered the entrance door was locked shut.

'Of course,' said Jago. 'I should've checked – today must be early closing day round here. Let's see if there's anyone in.'

He banged hard on the door, and eventually Benny Silver came from somewhere within the shop and opened it. Recognising his two visitors, he welcomed them in and locked the door again behind them.

'I'm sorry to disturb you on your afternoon off, Mr Silver,' said Jago. 'And you too, Mrs Silver,' he added, seeing her and Daniel across the shop.

'Don't worry about that, Inspector,' said Silver. 'Early closing day doesn't usually mean an afternoon with no work – just an afternoon with no customers. What can I do for you?'

'We've come to say goodbye, Benny,' said Cradock. 'It

looks as though we've tied up our investigation here, so now it's finished we'll probably be going. I just wanted to say how lovely it's been to see you again, especially seeing Daniel now he's all grown up, and meeting Eliza, too. And thank you again for being such good friends to me when I was here for my training. I'm sorry you've had all this trouble with the window and everything. I wish we could've done more to help you with that.'

Silver shrugged sympathetically. 'That's life,' he said. 'What can you do?'

'Yes,' said Jago. 'What can you do? We'll be leaving soon, Mr Silver, and I wanted to say goodbye too. But I don't like to leave unfinished business, so let's not beat about the bush. We know it was Alf Stubb who smashed your window, and you know it too – we want to do something about it, so will you please drop this pretence?'

'Ah,' said Silver. He looked cautiously at his wife, and she nodded to him. 'Very well, Mr Jago. I have to apologise to you. I'm very sorry – I should have told you before, and I should have told you the truth. I do know Stubb, and it was him who broke the window. But the thing is . . . well, he was asking for money.'

'For protection?'

'That's right. At first, from the way he talked I thought he was offering a service to protect me from people who want to cause trouble for Jews and go around doing things like smashing their windows – and worse. I said no, I don't need that sort of protection – I have no trouble here. But then he turned nasty. He said if I didn't accept his generous offer, I certainly would have trouble, and plenty of it.'

352

'So it turned out he wanted you to pay him money to protect you from himself?'

'That's right.'

'Did he tell you who he was working for?'

'No. From the way he spoke, I got the impression he was just working for himself – I think he'd got the idea he could build a little empire round here by throwing his weight around and intimidating people. He certainly talked as though he was the local big shot.'

'And he'd be building this empire at your expense?'

'Yes, at mine and other people's, no doubt. He threatened me, and I was foolish. At first I gave him a little money, because I hoped that would keep him away, but I think it only encouraged him to demand more. If I'd been a young man and stronger than I am now I'd have knocked him down on the spot, but I'm not. I just hoped he'd go and pick on someone else instead, but I can see now that was stupid of me. A week or so ago he said he was a businessman and was interested in "acquiring" my shop. I knew what that meant. He came on Tuesday with one of his stooges and . . . well, you know what happened to our window.'

'Thank you, Mr Silver. I really appreciate you confirming that – I know it's not an easy thing to do when you're dealing with violent people like that. Between you and me, I suspect he's going to be facing a few awkward questions soon that might result in him being put away for a while. I can't guarantee that he'll be locked up, of course, but I fancy at the very least he'll be looking over his shoulder from now on. In fact, maybe he already is – it seems someone's taken some action to frighten him off.'

'I see – that sounds like an interesting development.'

Silver glanced across the room to his son. 'Daniel, you remember what we were talking about?'

'Yes,' said Daniel. He turned to Jago and looked him in the eye. 'Mr Jago, the thing is, when you came here yesterday and talked about protection rackets I didn't say anything because I knew my dad wasn't going to admit knowing Stubb, so there was no point – and I didn't want to embarrass him in front of you. But since then he and I have been talking about all that business with the window getting smashed, and there's something I probably ought to tell you, just so you get the whole picture straight, if you know what I mean.'

Jago wasn't entirely sure he did know what the lad meant, but nodded encouragingly. 'Do go on.'

'Well, you see, I'd said some things to my dad that I shouldn't have, and I've said sorry to him now for that because I knew he was only trying to keep us all safe. That's why he told you some things that weren't entirely true, but I know he hated lying to you. He and I both knew who threw that brick, but he couldn't tell you, and I knew I couldn't tell you if he didn't. We've talked it over now, though – Dad said he'd have no rest until he told you the truth, so I'm going to tell you the truth too.'

'About Alf Stubb?'

'Yes. He was the one who smashed our window on Tuesday evening, like my dad said, but the truth is he did something far worse than that – he threatened to hurt Eliza. He's not a businessman – he's just a thug, no better than those Nazis we're fighting. You know what they've done to the Jews in Germany. They've done it in Austria and wherever else they've ended up, and they'll do the same here if we let them. I'm not going to stand by and let anyone harm Eliza, no matter who they are or what they try to do to me. My dad may not be young and strong any more, but I am, and I decided to do something about Stubb.'

'Tell me more.'

'I followed him once after he'd been here – they train us in that kind of thing in the Home Guard, you know – and I found out where he lived. Then I got a couple of my pals together, lads who feel the same way as I do about characters like Stubb, and we made a little plan.'

'To do what?'

'Simple – to beat the living daylights out of him and teach him a lesson he wouldn't forget.'

'You attacked him?'

'No. I wanted to, but I changed my mind – that would've made us just as bad as him, so I thought of something better. We waited for him when he got home last night and, er, invited ourselves in with him. He wasn't too keen to entertain us, but there were three of us and we made it clear to him that he was going to do as he was told.'

'Which was?'

'To take early retirement.'

'And how did he take to that?'

'He tried to act tough and threw a punch at me, but I dodged it, and he slipped and fell over. Hurt himself, I think. We laughed at him – told him he was finished. We basically put the wind up him good and proper – told him if he tried to get up we'd put him down again until he'd learnt his lesson.'

'I see.'

'I'm not going to apologise for what we did, Mr Jago.

You can punish me if you like, but I won't care – he threatened my mum and dad and Eliza, and I couldn't let him get away with it. We warned him off, and I think we did a public service.'

'You don't think he'll come back?'

'Come back where? He doesn't know who we are.'

'You're sure of that?'

'Well, I wasn't going to say I'm Mr and Mrs Silver's son from Rampayne Street, was I? No – we all wore balaclava helmets so he couldn't see our faces, and we didn't use any names.' He gave Jago a conspiratorial grin. 'Well, except one, that is.'

'What do you mean?'

'It was one that you'd given us, actually. When you were here talking to my dad yesterday afternoon you mentioned a couple of those protection gangs – the Mullery Gang and the Maldini Brothers. I thought the second lot sounded more intimidating – you know, more like Italian Mafia gangsters – so when he was on the floor we grabbed him and shook him about a bit to show him who was in charge. Then while we were holding him I just whispered something in his ear. I said Mr Maldini wasn't very happy to hear that Stubb was trying to muscle in on his business interests in this area, and I said he'd asked us to pass this message on to him. Stubb didn't say anything, but I think I heard a sort of whimpering sound.'

'I see,' said Jago thoughtfully. 'So what state was he in when you left him?'

'Nothing broken, if that's what you mean – except perhaps a bit of his arrogance. He likes to play the gangster, but he's just a bully.'

'Do you intend to do this again?'

'No – like I said, I think he's learnt his lesson.'

Jago pursed his lips and nodded his head slowly.

'So,' said Daniel, 'are you going to arrest me? I don't mind – it'll be worth it if I've got that man off my dad's back.'

'No, I'm not going to arrest you.'

'Really?'

'Really. Luckily for you, the law says a policeman can only arrest you for assault if he's present when it happens, and I wasn't. If Stubb wants to pursue the matter, it'll be up to him as the aggrieved party to go to the magistrates and take out a summons against you. But from what I know of Mr Stubb, I suspect he'll not be too keen to bring himself to the attention of the magistrates.'

'Oh, thank you. I am sorry – and the same goes for you too, Peter – but I couldn't let him come marching in here and ruin our lives just because he thought he could get away with it, could I? People like him reckon if they can scare you enough you'll keep your mouth shut and take whatever they want to do to you, but I think we've got to stand up to them, otherwise we're finished.' He paused and looked to his left. 'I expect my mum'll be pleased if I'm not hauled up before the magistrate, though.'

Jago glanced at Miriam, whose expression had changed from anxiety to one of relief and motherly pride. 'I'm sure she will, Daniel, but I'll give you just one bit of advice. Save all that strength and initiative for when you're called up – then you can put it to better use.'

'I will, Inspector.'

'Good. I shall look forward to hearing from your mother

and father that you've managed to keep out of trouble from now on. Stay on the right side of the law, OK?'

'OK,' Daniel smiled.

'And before you go, Inspector,' said Benny, 'there's something I need to say, too. When Daniel told me what he and his friends had done it made me think the whole thing over. I was trying to protect my family, and it felt like it was me on my own against the whole world with no one to help me. I thought there was only one way to do it, but I was wrong, and I'm sorry. I know I can't send all the bullies in the world packing, but I can stand up to one, so I've changed my mind – I'll give evidence against Stubb, any time you and Peter want.' He turned to Cradock. 'It's like you said, Peter – a favour for an old friend.'

CHAPTER FORTY-FIVE

Jago smiled to himself as he and Cradock drove north along Millbank towards the Houses of Parliament, with Westminster on their left and the Thames to their right. He'd been right to suspect someone had given Stubb a taste of his own medicine, but there was a kind of poetic justice in the discovery that it was Benny Silver's own son and a couple of other young lads who'd decided to take the would-be gangster down a peg or two. It made for an entertaining story, but perhaps not one he would tell Detective Superintendent Hardacre. Not until he'd got the measure of the man, anyway, and perhaps even then he'd keep it strictly for his own amusement.

When they reached Parliament Street, he drove through Scotland Yard's western entrance at Derby Gate and parked. The two detectives showed their warrant cards to the man on the desk at the back hall entrance and were admitted, and as they waited for the concertina-gate lift to take them up to Hardacre's office, Cradock took in their surroundings.

Jago could tell from his face that he wasn't impressed. 'Your first time here?' he asked.

'Yes, sir. It's not as smart as I was expecting – I mean, it all looks very grand on the outside, but this is a bit of a let-down, isn't it?'

Jago couldn't disagree. In contrast to the building's elegant Gothic exterior, with its distinctive bands of red brick and stone, their immediate surroundings on the inside were decidedly austere. Up to about shoulder height the walls were of dark-green tiles or possibly glazed bricks – he couldn't tell which by looking, but either way they reminded him of hospitals, schools and public lavatories, none of which he'd ever had any desire to work in. Above this height they were finished in a dull cream paint that looked as though it had been in urgent need of a new coat for some years – too long for their degraded condition to be blamed, as so many things conveniently were these days, on the war.

The same style continued in the long, dingy and windowless corridor that led to Hardacre's office. By the time they were admitted to the detective superintendent's modest accommodation, Jago was almost beginning to feel sorry for him. Any faint sparks of pity were soon dampened, however, by their brusque welcome.

'Right,' said Hardacre, 'come in, sit down, tell me what you've got.' Jago and Cradock sat facing him while he finished reading a sheet of paper, signed it and dropped it into the out-tray on his desk. 'So this man, Watson – who was he, and what happened to him?'

'He was a bookie's runner, sir,' said Jago, 'killed by a

couple of blows to the head in his Anderson shelter.'

'I see. Usual riff-raff, then. I nicked a good few of them in my younger days – slackers and layabouts who'd never done an honest day's work in their lives, most of them. Anyway, you say you've charged someone?'

'Yes, sir. His name's Bateman. He's a gardener and was a friend of the deceased. It seems he was in love with a girl and discovered Watson was making up to her, so they ended up in a fight and Watson was killed.'

'Two men fighting over a woman, eh? The same old story. Young fellow, is he? The bloke you've locked up, I mean.'

'Thirty-five, sir.'

'Old enough to know better, then. People don't seem to know what self-discipline is these days – the world's gone to pot.'

'Yes, sir. From what we've learnt about the two men, though, I'd say Bateman had more self-discipline than the man he killed – Watson had got a girl into trouble and abandoned her.'

'Another old story. Was this the girl they were fighting over?'

'No, sir, it was a different young woman. Bateman seems to have had a crush on her, but he says Watson had designs on her and that's what they were fighting over.'

'This Bateman's admitted to killing him, has he?'

'Yes, sir. He came quietly.'

'Good. That should simplify things. Anything else I need to know?'

'Well, sir, in view of what you were saying the other day about looting, you might be interested to know that it seems to be something the murdered man was involved in.'

'Good. That's one more taken out of action, then – and permanently. Did you get any leads to others, any connections?'

'Not to other looters, sir, but there are one or two interesting connections. We've come across a man called Alf Stubb who runs a cafe down in the rough end of Pimlico, and I suspect he was fencing the stuff Watson was pinching. Unfortunately, with the thief being dead and no trace of the stuff he was stealing, I don't think we've got enough evidence to charge him.'

'That's no use to me, then, is it?'

'No. Sorry, sir. But we might be able to nail him for something else. It seems he fancied himself as a gangster and was trying to set up a protection racket – he's been leaning on a bookie and at least one local shopkeeper. He's a nasty piece of work, but it looks like we've got someone willing to give evidence against him.'

'Hmm, that sounds better. Has he been arrested?'

'Not yet, sir. I'll leave that to the local boys at Gerald Road. In the meantime it seems he's had a run-in with someone who's found his behaviour anti-social and decided to teach him a lesson about law and order – had what you might call a private word with him and advised him to mend his ways, so hopefully that'll dampen his enthusiasm a bit.'

'Good for them. Nothing illegal, though, I trust.'

'Nothing for us to get involved in, sir.'

Jago smiled to himself: Daniel Silver should probably be safe from retribution from the higher echelons of the Metropolitan Police.

'We may only be able to get a conviction for malicious damage to a shopkeeper's window,' he continued, 'but that could still land him in prison for a month, and by the time he gets out I wouldn't be surprised if he'd had second thoughts about building a protection empire.'

'That's not bad. What about these other interesting connections?'

'Well, sir, there's the bookie I mentioned – name's Bill Ashdon. He's the one Watson was working for, and someone set fire to his office door.'

'I see – so this Ashdon's the one who sorted out your man Stubb, right?'

'No, sir. Ashdon's still saying he doesn't know Stubb, and he doesn't strike me as the kind of man who's likely to help us, and of course Stubb swears it wasn't him. But like I said, I think a conviction and a month in jail might give him some food for thought, and after that – well, I suspect he may decide to sell his cafe and move on to pastures new.'

'Good. Right, I don't need to know anything more about that – the local lads can keep an eye on them. Any questions?'

'Well, speaking of the local lads, sir, how is Sergeant Wilks getting on?'

'Not too well, from what I've heard – I believe he's now permanently off sick. The doctor's calling it "nervous stress" – says it's on account of Wilks being caught over at West End Central when that landmine hit it. But like I said, I call it shell shock. I suppose when a man gets blown up it doesn't matter whether he's at the front in France or on the street in London – some men can take it, some men can't. I think for Wilks it just pushed him over the edge, and he can't cope.'

'I'm very sorry to hear that, sir. I hope he gets better soon.'

'Yes, well, we'll have to see about that. All I know is it leaves us another man down – but don't you worry, no one's going to park you at Gerald Road for the rest of the war. The chief constable says he's no intention of letting the grass grow under your feet, so you'll be staying with me at the Yard and deployed wherever we need an extra pair of hands.'

'And me, sir?' Cradock enquired tentatively.

'I told you before, Constable, your job is carrying his bag, so that's what you do, and you go where he goes. Understood? One day if you're lucky you might make it to sergeant, and then you can carry it around for an extra quid a week.'

'Yes, sir. Thank you, sir.' Cradock retreated into silence.

'Will that be all, sir?' said Jago.

'Yes, that'll do for now. You've got a man charged and locked up, so that's not bad – now you need to make sure you get a conviction. Then we'll see whether this was just beginner's luck or not. In the meantime, you make sure you keep on your toes – all right?'

'Yes, sir,' said Jago.

'Right – off you go, then.'

Jago and Cradock left the office and took the stairs back down to the ground floor.

'He didn't exactly say well done, did he, sir?' said Cradock.

'No, he didn't,' Jago replied. 'Nor thank you, for that matter. But I suspect in his heart he's still a sergeant in the infantry, and some of them never let those words pass their lips. You'll get used to it. Anyway, you can leave him to me – all you need to worry about is what I think of your work.'

'Yes, sir. So, er, how was it? My work, I mean.'

'Your work, Peter? I think I'd put it a bit more positively than the superintendent did – I'd say it was definitely not bad.'

Cradock caught his eye to check whether Jago was being serious. 'That's very kind of you, sir,' he laughed.

'Well, what more can I say? Thank you, Peter – and well done.'

CHAPTER FORTY-SIX

By the time they emerged from the building, Jago's mind was already setting Superintendent Hardacre to one side and turning to his plans for what remained of the day. When he'd asked for the use of a telephone at Gerald Road police station, the reason why he'd wanted to make the second call out of reach of Cradock's ears was because it was to the Savoy hotel, and its purpose was to arrange to meet Dorothy. Reckoning that Hardacre would be unlikely to detain them for as much as an hour, he'd invited her to join him for afternoon tea at a place about halfway between the Savoy and Scotland Yard.

'Well, Peter,' he said as they stood by the car, 'I think that just about concludes our business for today. You and I both deserve an evening off, and since we've probably seen enough of each other over the last few days, I propose we go our separate ways. Would you like a lift back to Ambrosden Avenue, or would you rather stroll around the sights of Westminster for a bit and make your own way back?'

'I think I'd like to walk back, sir, thank you very much. It can't be more than a mile, and the pubs'll be open soon, so I fancy finding a nice cosy hostelry somewhere and having a beer. But what will you be doing?'

'Oh, I'm going to meet up with a friend for a cup of tea.'

'I see, sir. Would that be Miss, er . . . ?'

'Never you mind, Peter. You just go and enjoy yourself, and I'll see you in the morning.'

'Thank you, sir – and I hope you, er, enjoy yourself too.'

Jago shooed him away and watched until he'd disappeared from view through the gateway towards Parliament Street. He consulted his watch and found he had plenty of time for a gentle walk to the rendezvous he'd arranged with Dorothy, a little cafe near Charing Cross Station, so decided to leave the car where it was.

He set off in the opposite direction to Cradock, under the granite archway that linked the north and south buildings of New Scotland Yard and through the grand wrought-iron gates from its private roadway onto the Embankment. He walked slowly along the road beside the Thames, preparing himself for their meeting. The one thought on his mind was whether she'd reached a decision about the new job: he'd asked her to tell him when she did, but he'd heard nothing. Perhaps she was saving it until she could tell him face to face, or perhaps she was still undecided. Either way, he knew he mustn't rush her as soon as they met: he'd be patient and self-controlled.

He saw a young couple approaching on the other side of the road. They were arm in arm, walking even more slowly

367

than he was, the woman resting her head against the man's shoulder. To Jago they seemed immersed in each other, sufficient for one another, and oblivious to his presence and their surroundings. The sight of their closeness brought a tender sadness to him as he counted the years through which he'd not truly cherished anyone or anything. He'd learnt in war that everything and everyone could be taken from him in an instant, that no happiness was for ever, but now he yearned deeply for that not to be true. It felt as though in some illogical way he wanted to apologise to himself and be given another chance.

He was still absorbed in these thoughts when he arrived at the cafe, and was pleased to see that he'd got there before Dorothy. By the time she joined him he'd calmed himself.

Jago hung up her coat for her and they sat at the table for two that he'd secured in a relatively secluded corner. The cafe was less than half full, but he was relieved to find there was enough conversation going on in the background for their own not to be at great risk of being overheard. He ordered afternoon tea, and they exchanged pleasantries about the day until the waitress brought them a selection of small sandwiches, a variety of equally small cakes and a pot of tea.

'So,' he said, pouring the tea, 'are you all finished with Chamberlain now? He was buried yesterday, wasn't he?'

'Yes, in Westminster Abbey – although strictly speaking he wasn't buried, he was cremated, and they interred his ashes there. I wrote it up for the paper yesterday afternoon. The thing I thought was interesting was that the government had kept the time and date of the funeral secret because of the risk of an attack by the Luftwaffe – that's the kind of detail that brings the situation alive for our readers. But then again, looking at it from here it's not surprising – two of the pall-bearers were Churchill and Attlee, so if word had got out and there was an attack they would all have had to run for shelter in the crypt.'

'Yes,' Jago laughed, 'that wouldn't have looked very good, would it? All the great and the good having to scuttle for shelter. German propaganda would've had a field day.'

'Sure – Dr Goebbels would be rubbing his hands. But fortunately for Mr Churchill, Mr Attlee and myself, there was no attack. And how about you – are you finished with your case too? Last time I saw you, at Rita's, I don't think you got much of a chance to tell me how it was going. Something about a body in an Anderson shelter, wasn't it?'

'That's right. You might say it was a case of rivals in love – two men had a fight over a woman, and one hit the other on the head with a spanner.'

'What we'd call a wrench, right?'

'If you say so.'

'And it killed him?'

'Yes. It was a sad story, really. It seems the man who did it was pretty much in love with the girl but too shy to tell her, and then a friend of his who was quite the opposite started to work his charm on her. It ended up with the two men coming to blows and . . . well, one of them died.'

'That is sad, yes. I guess if the first guy had followed his heart it might never have happened.'

'Maybe, but unfortunately in my job I have to deal with what did happen. We've arrested the man and charged him, and now it's up to the magistrate to decide whether to commit him for trial.'

Jago paused to take a sandwich from the cake stand positioned between them on the table. The menu hadn't specified the contents, so he prised it open as discreetly as he could.

'What's in it?' said Dorothy.

'It appears to be cream cheese and grated carrot,' he replied. 'Not a combination I think I've had before, but you know what they say.'

'There's a war on?'

'Precisely.'

Dorothy smiled and took one for herself. 'Hmm, not bad, though,' she said after her first bite. 'I've eaten a lot worse.'

'I can assure you I have too.'

He thought of what Gibson had said the previous evening about the food at the front in the last war. Jago's own memories were still vivid: bully beef and dog biscuits too hard to break if you were lucky, or nothing for days on end if the supply lines were shelled. Like Gibson, it seemed, he'd been permanently affected by the experience: ever since he was demobbed he'd cleared his plate every day and been grateful.

'You're sure you've got the right man, then?' said Dorothy. 'The murderer, I mean.'

'Oh, yes,' Jago replied. 'And he's confessed. It was strange, really – up till then, he'd seemed quite a decent fellow, the sort that wouldn't hurt a fly. The other man was more of an unsavoury character, a crook. But now one's dead, and the other may be facing the hangman's noose. They say we're all equal in death, don't they?'

'They do, and it's true – especially in days like these.'

'That's what I was thinking when I saw that body in the shelter. It reminded me of men I knew in the war, the ones who didn't make it home – one minute they were there, next minute they were gone, and it made no difference whether they were crooks or saints, they all ended up just as dead in the end.'

'The rain falls on the just and the unjust.'

'That's in the Bible, isn't it?'

'Yes.'

'Well, it seems to me it's not just the rain – it's bombs and shells too. Death doesn't discriminate, whether it's on the front line in France or in someone's back yard in London. Bad men die, and good men die just the same.'

'But the good men are the ones we remember, aren't they? No one cries over the bad ones. And maybe it's losing the good ones that makes us want something better for the future.'

'I'd like to think so. I've been talking to some poppy sellers this week as part of the investigation, and I know a lot of those men we wear our poppies for thought that's what they were doing – fighting the war to end all wars, to make the world a better place. And the ones that survived were told they'd won it, but looking back now it seems like the Armistice was just that – a pause in hostilities – and now we've picked up again where we left off. If this was making a new world, we haven't made a very good job of it.'

'There's a lot of people in my country who think we made a mess at the end of the last war, especially with the League of Nations. It was President Wilson's big idea, the way to guarantee peace, but we never joined it because we thought it'd get us tangled up in foreign wars. Back then we reckoned we had two big oceans to protect us, so we could get on with our life and leave the rest of the world to its own devices. A lot of Americans still think the same way.'

'Would it really have made any difference if you'd joined? The League of Nations may've been a noble idea, but it couldn't stop Hitler.'

'That's right, but he picked off his victims one by one – Austria, Czechoslovakia, Poland, and that was just the start. If he'd been facing a League of fifty nations with the USA at the heart of it he might not have gotten away with that, and the world wouldn't be in the mess it is today.'

'Maybe, yes, but we'll never know, will we? I suspect that with a man like Hitler, there was never going to be a way out, not for the League of Nations, not for Chamberlain. We may not've wanted a war, but we've got one and now we've got to win it.'

'As your own Archbishop of Canterbury himself said.'

'Really? When did he say that?'

'Back in September. He broadcast a speech to America on the NBC wireless network – we reported it in our paper. He said what you're facing in those Nazis is a really evil thing, so you have to fight it – you're holding the fort for the whole world. It was just a week before you had the first big air raids here – and since then I hear he's been bombed out of his own home at Lambeth Palace.'

'I trust he forgave them.'

'I don't think he's revealed that, but he has spoken out against the people who say you should repay the air raids in kind. He's said if you start competing with Germany's air raids you might fail – and if you succeed in out-bombing them it'll bring irrevocable dishonour to your cause.'

'Not much of a choice, then.'

'No, and somehow I can't see your Mr Churchill just standing by while London gets reduced to rubble. But isn't that how wars get so bad? Once you start trading blows, it can only get worse and worse.'

'So Chamberlain was right after all?'

'No. Trying to keep out of the war didn't help the Dutch or the Belgians or Norway in the end, did it? I just think we shouldn't repeat the mistakes we made after the last war. We need to find a better way of fixing things when a war finishes, and America needs to be part of it. It's just like when two people fall out – you can either go on hating each other for the rest of your lives, or you find a way to forgive and make it up.' Dorothy took a half-slice of fruit cake from the stand and began to eat it. 'I'm sorry, John,' she smiled, 'when I get onto politics I get a bit carried away sometimes.'

'No need to apologise – I find it very interesting to hear how things look from the other side of the ocean. But as far as making up's concerned, I just don't think the Versailles conference could ever just've been about forgiving each other for four years' total war and promising to be pals in the future.'

'Of course not, but there has to be some way of reconciling the two sides that've been at war. Isn't that what you British police do when you find two kids having a fight – break it up and get them to shake hands?'

'Occasionally, perhaps, but when you've got two countries at each other's throats it's a bit different.'

'Same principle, though?'

'Maybe.'

Jago fell silent. He found it difficult to imagine such an outcome, but he also remembered the stories he'd heard of Christmas truces at the front in the Great War, when men on both sides came out of their trenches to swap cigars and play football in no-man's land. After Christmas they resumed firing and became enemies again, but for two days they'd been friends. So perhaps it was possible – but he also knew that it was Christmas 1914, when the war was young, and when he got to the front in 1916 he never saw anything like it himself.

'Maybe Rita was right,' he said. 'We should all just be nice and get along with each other.'

'She's got a point,' said Dorothy. 'It's either that or go on hating each other. In the long run, if you want peace you have to find a way of being reconciled.'

'What about things that are unforgivable, though?'

'What do you mean?'

'I mean like what I did to that German, the one I told you about – he's dead, so how can he and I be reconciled? It just doesn't work. He'll never be able to forgive me, and I don't think anyone could, because what I did was wrong – I took his life. Not even God could forgive me – and if he turned up here this moment and offered to, I'd say no, you can't.'

There was another silence between them.

Finally, Jago spoke again. 'Look, I'm sorry, Dorothy, I didn't mean to get all serious with you. It's just that these thoughts go running round in the back of my mind sometimes, and there's no one to share them with.'

'That's what friends are for.'

'Exactly, and I'm beginning to realise friends are something I'm short of – friends I can talk to like this, I mean.'

'Like this?'

'About things that matter, what I think, how I am inside. You make me feel I can say those sort of things to you. You listen and you understand.'

'That's part of my job. After all, I'm a journalist – the *Boston Post* pays me to understand.'

He smiled. 'Yes, but that's not all you are, though – or is it?'

'No,' she replied. 'I'm a journalist and I love my work, but that's definitely not all I am. But then I don't believe a police detective is all you are either.'

Jago felt suddenly vulnerable. To agree with her would risk exposing uncertain hopes and dreams of which he'd spoken to no one, but to deny her claim would be to stifle them. He hesitated, and when she broke the silence it was as if she'd read his mind.

'Forgive me,' she said. 'You don't have to answer that – I'm not looking for a confession. Let's just say I have a suspicion that I'm right, but I'm still gathering evidence.'

The smile with which he responded to her was as much one of relief as of amusement: she'd let him off the hook.

'Thank you,' he said. 'I'm sorry – I suspect that after all these years as a detective I've learnt too much about how to cover my tracks.'

Dorothy glanced at the clock on the wall. 'I'd better be making tracks myself pretty soon. It's getting late.'

Jago checked his wristwatch. 'Ah, yes, of course.

I'll walk you back to your hotel.' He adjusted his jacket cuff back over the watch and cleared his throat. 'So,' he continued in as casual a tone as he could manage, 'before we go, how about this new job of yours? Have you made your decision?'

'Yes,' she replied. 'I have.'

'And?'

'It's not been easy, I can tell you. It's been keeping me awake at night, just thinking about it. Going to China is a wonderful opportunity, and covering another major war – well, it would be a significant feather in my cap.'

'Yes, of course, I can see that.'

'It'd be great for my career, another huge story in a different part of the world, but . . .'

'But?'

'Well, the thing is, I'm not so sure I want to quit London. The story's huge here too, and with Roosevelt back in the White House it could become crucial for America. There's so much to write about, and people back home appreciate it. The situation here is a clear make or break, too – will Britain stand or fall? I don't think they have quite the same interest in Chinese politics, even though it's a big war in their own back yard that they might get sucked into one day. And besides . . .'

'Yes?'

She looked up at him. 'Well, I'm happy here.'

She said no more, and he didn't dare ask her why she was happy here. Instead, he just nodded his head like a judge weighing up a ruling.

'That's an important consideration,' he said. 'Sometimes being happy is worth more than taking a step up in your career. So . . . ?'

She paused before replying. 'So . . . I'm thinking I'm going to stay.'

Jago was unable to stop a broad grin spreading across his face. He struggled to find the right words to say. 'I'm so pleased,' he said, feeling immediately that this must have sounded very lame.

Dorothy cocked her head slightly to one side and looked him in the eye. 'Oh?' she said. 'And why's that?'

Jago found he couldn't meet her gaze and think of an answer at the same time, so he focused instead on the sleeve of his jacket and brushed off an imaginary piece of fluff.

'Because I think it's a good decision,' he replied awkwardly, then forced himself to look at her. 'It's your choice, of course,' he continued, 'but the thing is, you see . . . well, I think I – that is, I think we need you here.'

Dorothy's expression softened as she responded with a gentle smile. 'Thank you,' she said, 'I think it's a good decision too.'

ACKNOWLEDGEMENTS

One of the challenges in writing historical fiction is sorting the myths from the realities, the truth from the propaganda, and of course for people who were living at the time in question that was part of their everyday reality. As I write the Blitz Detective stories, I sometimes come across things that are true and yet so extraordinary that I fear my readers will think I made them up.

In this book, for example, the idea that in 1939 the British government would decide that a bookmaker who paid his runner's court fine for breaking the law on loitering could claim the sum as a tax-deductible expense: surely too absurd to be true? Fortunately, it was so absurd that a member of parliament questioned it in the House of Commons, and no less a person than the Chancellor of the Exchequer confirmed that it was correct. If you don't believe me, you can read it for yourself in Hansard, the official record of parliamentary proceedings.

Like many other treasures, Hansard is now accessible via the Internet, which has opened the door to so much knowledge for all of us. Unfortunately, of course, the Internet is also a haven for no end of inaccuracy, both accidental and intentional. The Pimlico Murder includes a reference to that much-maligned second world war foodstuff, powdered egg. My story's set in 1940, and if you consult the Internet you'll find that this was not introduced to the UK until 1942. So before you write me off as a dunce, I hasten to note that powdered egg was actually on sale in Britain not just in 1940 but in 1939, and even in 1918.

As it happens, in this story Sally Edgworth could find neither eggs nor egg powder for her cake at the grocer's shop, so she had to make an eggless sponge. I'd like to say a special thank you to my wife, Margaret, who went the extra mile to help my research by offering to bake me a sponge without an egg. As a result, I can vouch for the fact that when Jago said 'It's delicious,' he was right.

There are other points in this book where my research took me down some fascinating rabbit-holes of history, but of course I'm very capable of getting something wrong. So if you think I have, or you're just curious to know whether a particular detail is true, please drop me a line.

As always, I've appreciated beyond measure the support and encouragement I've received from my family and friends while writing this book. Thanks are also due to Dr Juulia Ahvensalmi, archivist at St George's, University of London, for her resourceful assistance in recreating St George's Hospital in its Hyde Park Corner days, to Dr David Love and Dr Roland Guy for their wise guidance on some of the medical aspects of Jago's latest case, to Rudy

Mitchell and Roy Ingleton for theirs on American English and 1940s policing respectively, and to John Dowell for his on Gerald Road police station and the old New Scotland Yard. I'm grateful for all this input, and any errors in what I've written will of course be due to my interpretation and creative application of the advice I've received, not to the competence of that advice.

And lastly, thanks to Pimlico residents Matthew Edwards, Paula Bransfield, Paul Winter and his neighbour Ray, who so kindly shared their time, knowledge and memories of the area and its history with me: without you I would never have learnt how to dodge the local police in the old days or seen the inside of an original Pimlico coal cellar.

MIKE HOLLOW was born in West Ham, on the eastern edge of London, and grew up in Romford, Essex. He studied Russian and French at the University of Cambridge and then worked for the BBC and later Tearfund. In 2002 he went freelance as a copywriter, journalist, editor and translator, but now gives all his time to writing the Blitz Detective books.

blitzdetective.com   @MikeHollowBlitz